ALSO BY ERIC BROWN

Novels
Xenopath
Necropath
Cosmopath
Kéthani
Helix
New York Dreams
New York Blues
New York Nights
Penumbra
Engineman
Meridian Days

Novellas
Starship Fall
Starship Summer
Revenge
The Extraordinary Voyage of Jules Verne
Approaching Omega
A Writer's Life

Collections
Threshold Shift
The Fall of Tartarus
Deep Future
Parallax View (with Keith Brooke)
Blue Shifting
The Time-Lapsed Man

As Editor
The Mammoth Book of New Jules Verne Adventures
(with Mike Ashley)

First published 2010 by Solaris
an imprint of Rebellion Publishing Ltd,
Riverside House, Osney Mead,
Oxford, OX2 0ES, UK

www.solarisbooks.com

ISBN: 978 1 907519 15 4

10 9 8 7 6 5 4 3 2 1

A CIP catalogue record for this book is available from the
British Library.

Designed & typeset by Rebellion Publishing

Printed in the US

ERIC BROWN
GUARDIANS OF THE PHOENIX

SOLARIS

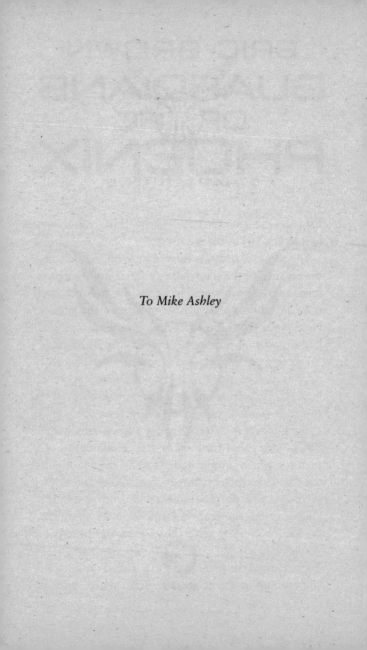

To Mike Ashley

CHAPTER ONE

PAUL WAS CLIMBING the tower to the lizard traps when he saw the girl in the red dress.

The sun rose over the eastern horizon, silhouetting the remains of the shattered city. Later in the day the metal of the tower would be impossible to touch, and if he did so he'd leave a layer of skin on the girders. He'd made that mistake once, a long time ago, and had suffered for days with pain and then infection.

He climbed the cross-pieces and curving spars with practised ease, reaching above his head, gripping girders and hauling himself higher and higher above the desert lapping at the foot of the tower. It was as if the builders had seen into the future, anticipated Paul's daily quest for food and incorporated design features which would make scaling the mammoth tower all the easier. Flanges, giant bolts and cross-pieces seemed purpose built hand- and foot-holds, allowing Paul to scale the tower to its shattered, buckled mid-point with the ease of the lizards he was seeking.

He reached the first cross-piece, rolled onto it, and squinted up to the horizontal girder where he'd set the traps. He saw that a dozen of them had sprung, and smiled with relief.

At sunset every day for years he'd baited the traps high on the tower. In the early days he'd used flies, insects and even small pieces of lizard meat as bait. Nowadays he didn't come across many flies or insects, and lizard meat itself was too valuable to use. On Elise's suggestion he'd started using pieces of his own dung, sceptical at first that the lizards, stupid though they were, would be attracted to the hard, dry pellets. But they had been as desperate for sustenance as he was, and from that day on he'd set the traps with his own waste, cheered by the circular efficiency of the ploy.

He grabbed the arcing girder overhead and climbed. When he reached the next cross-spar he paused again, sitting with his legs dangling. Long ago he'd taken Elise's words to heart and imposed order and regimen on his days. He did things at a certain time because that was the best time to do them. Efficiency gained results. An ordered day not only meant survival, but imposed purpose on the long hours of the long days that stretched into the future. Elise had seen many people go mad from lack of purpose. Without routine, she'd told him, without strict adherence to small, daily duties, a mind could dwell on the future, on what might be – and that way led to despair and finally madness.

Every day at this point Paul paused in his climb to catch his breath and take in the city sprawling beneath him. Or rather what was left of the city.

Over the years he'd watched the slow encroachment

of the sand. From street level it was almost impossible to discern. He'd noticed, little by little, a thicker patina of dust on everything, then a fine coating of sand – then drifts that created beautifully geometric curves at the intersecting angles of streets and buildings. The accretion of the fine yellow sand was so gradual as to be almost unnoticeable, like the slow progress of the fiery sun as it climbed up the sky. But from up here he could monitor the street by street creep of the desert, note the slow sinking of the shorter buildings into the sea of sand. Now only the tall apartments and office blocks, and some of the cities' older monuments, showed above the parabolic sweeps and curves of the dry wasteland.

The monuments, for their part, had suffered too: they might have stood for centuries, proud and regal signifiers of grand events of a culture long dead, but the past decade had done what previous centuries had failed to do. The features of statesmen and soldiers, their proud staring faces, their pens and swords, had been sand-blasted and reduced to anonymous nubs and stumps.

When Elise had been mobile, and the sand had allowed better progress through the streets and by-ways, she had taken him on a tour of the city's monuments, describing the once great men and their contribution to civilisation. Paul had listened diligently, but did not admit to her that the history lessons meant nothing to him.

He saw the city now, but was looking for more. He was searching for movement, other than that of the wind-swept veils of sand that drifted across the open spaces: he sought the scurrying of animals, the flight of birds. He rarely saw animals these days. A year ago he'd spotted a dark shape skulking through the ruins, and that night set a trap of lizard meat for the beast, reckoning the sacrifice of a small animal for one ten times its size well worth making. The following morning he returned to the trap to find the animal snared, and he'd been overcome by elation at the thought of the food it would provide for two or three days. He'd slit its throat and carried the body proudly back to the basement he shared with Elise. She'd smiled as he dropped it before her, and she reached out and stroked its sable pelt. "Do you know what it is, Paul?"

He didn't recognise the animal from the many books he studied with Elise. "No."

"Once upon a time they roamed wild in packs of hundreds," she said. "And before that they were man's best friend. It's a dog."

The animal was thin, but its meat had been the best Paul had tasted in years.

The dog had been the last big animal he'd seen. As for birds, he hadn't spotted a bird for months, even though from time to time he set traps higher up the tower, in hope.

So he scanned the city for animals, for movement and for tracks made during the night. He'd long ago stopped looking for, and hoping to see, fellow human beings. Elise had counselled him to be on the lookout, for according to her, human beings were the most dangerous animal of all. He'd last seen a man – well, three men – perhaps ten years ago, in the year which, according to Elise, he reached thirteen. They had passed through the city on foot, armed with guns, and he and Elise had watched them from behind the cover of a wall with fear and breathless apprehension. The three had stayed for a week – Paul had crept silently through the city, monitoring them without being seen – until they'd fought among themselves. One man had been killed immediately, stabbed through the chest. The remaining pair had stripped him of clothes, taken a bottle of water, and retreated to a basement not far from where Paul and Elise lived. A few days later he'd heard screams and the sound of scuffling, and when he went to investigate only one man remained, a wild, long-haired maniac who ranted and raved and cut slices of flesh from the man he'd killed and ate them raw. He'd survived a month, ignorant of how to scavenge for water and food in the city, and then set off raving into the desert. Paul had found his corpse a few days later, blistered black by the sun and gnawed by predators. He'd set traps around the body, using the flesh of the man himself as bait, and captured a dozen lizards and a couple of skinny rodents, but had balked at returning to the basement with slices of human meat for fear of Elise's rage.

He looked up at the lizard traps, and began climbing again.

OVER THE YEARS, Paul had noticed the increase in the lizard population. They'd moved into the city with the sand, inhabiting the ruined streets and boulevards where people had once swarmed, sitting on vertical walls in sunlight like the emblems of a new age. They had proved to be Paul and Elise's salvation.

They had grown a little food in the old days, before the earth turned to sand and water became too precious a commodity to waste on puny plants. Not long after the last crop of spinach failed, Paul noticed more and more lizards sunning themselves on the tumbledown walls and scurrying through the sand drifts, and he'd set about building more traps. There was little eating on the lizards, but three or four provided a decent meal for one person.

Lately, though, their numbers had diminished – or his traps had proved less effective. Perhaps the creatures were becoming tired of their fare of dung, their tiny reptilian minds revolting at the thought of second-hand cannibalism. More likely, he knew, the system that had kept the lizards alive – and therefore kept himself and Elise alive – was breaking down. There were fewer and fewer insects for the lizards to eat.

He reached the cross-girder where he'd set the dozen traps. All but two of them had sprung. Elise would be proud of him when he returned with a belt full of lizard meat.

He was moving along the girder to the first trap when he heard the sound.

His senses were finely tuned to change. He noticed differences in the fall of light, and so was able to tell the time of day; scents came to him, faint and from a distance, and he was able to detect the presence of animals. The sounds of the dying city were unvarying. He knew the keening of the wind through skeletal buildings; the fall and crash of dislodged masonry; the rare skitter of animals.

The sound of the wind was ever present, the other sounds less so. And when a cry rose in opposition to the wind, the sound was like a piercing alarm that stopped him in his tracks with fear and an anticipatory thrill.

The scream ripped through the air, high and harsh and thrillingly human.

He squatted and scanned the area around the tower. The ruins of the city began a couple of hundred metres away, laved by the sand. He stared in the direction of the scream, but saw nothing.

The cry came again, followed by a deeper, masculine shout. He stared at a row of buildings, perhaps five hundred metres from his vantage point. The sand level had risen above the line of the buildings' first floor windows, abbreviating the height of the *maisons* and giving the street scene a surreal, truncated aspect.

A girl or young woman was struggling through the sand between the buildings, a tiny figure at this distance, stumbling and falling as she headed towards an open, second floor window.

A red dress. The woman was clothed. He registered the fact with something like amazement. If she were dressed, then she must have come from a colony somewhere. Paul himself went naked; Elise, too, though she had protested and railed at the disintegration of her last shreds of clothing.

Then his thoughts were wiped by the arrival of the three men giving chase. They appeared one by one from behind the tottering masonry across the boulevard, opposite the window the girl was now scrambling through. They saw her, shouted something and gave chase.

The girl had vanished, hugging the interior walls to keep from sight of the men.

Paul returned his attention to her pursuers. They were dressed in ragged shorts, their torsos slung with cross-bandoleers holding items indistinguishable at this distance. Either weapons, Paul thought, or scavenged food – biltongs of meat, perhaps. The men were brown, burned by long exposure to the sun. One was bald and other two wore their hair in long, dreadlocked comet-tails.

They reached the building, climbed through the window and continued their pursuit.

He could hear Elise's voice in his head, telling him to leave well alone and return to the basement. He ignored it. He quickly emptied the traps, strung the lizards on the cord around his waist and, their dry skins chaffing his thighs and buttocks, retraced the route of his climb and jumped the last three metres to the sand.

As a sop to Elise's imaginary warnings, he would follow with extreme caution. Humans meant food, after all.

As he ran through the sand surrounding the tower, heading for the boulevard, he wondered if that was all he was seeking: the possibility of acquiring – stealing – food... or whether his hopes aspired to greater things.

He dreamed, even now, of finding a colony – or rather a colony finding him and Elise. A sizeable, travelling community of human beings not gone the way of most and reverted to savagery, but retaining the vestiges of civilisation: law and order. He had told Elise of his dreams, and he knew she'd restrained herself from telling him what she thought: that it was a hopeless dream, that no colonies existed out there any more, just lone humans living like animals.

He came to the shattered wall rising from the sands, and slowed down. He moved along the line of the wall, sinking to his knees in the drifted sand, until he came to a V-shaped rent in the masonry and peered through. The rest of the building was an empty shell, and he could see through to the boulevard beyond.

Evidently the girl had crossed this boulevard and sought to escape in the terrace of buildings to the right. He caught a glimpse of the last man as he disappeared around a distant corner.

Paul pulled himself through the rent and headed for the far buildings. He would go around the ruins to the lee-side of the buildings, where the drifts might not be so deep, and follow the four.

The dead lizards danced against his legs, telling him to take what he had, go back to Elise and cook the meat and eat well for a day. He was endangering not only himself in this brainless pursuit, but also Elise.

Only then did he wonder if the thought of food, the possibility of finding a human colony, was all that drove him on.

If he could save the girl from the men...

He heard the cries of the pursuers again, and gave chase himself.

He had lived in the city for all his life, knew every street and alley, every shell of a building and half-buried monument. Elise had told him that, in the old days, the city had been divided into districts, and that each district, or *arrondisement*, had had a name. She'd even attempted to teach him the names of the various areas, before realising that he had no use for names: names were for a long gone, civilised time, she'd told him.

The city's appearance changed, of course, with the shifting sands and the crumbling buildings, but he ranged the city every day, took notice of the changes, remembered the new lie of streets altered by deepened sand or fallen walls. He was alert for the dangers of falling bricks and flying glass, ever on the lookout for stores of foodstuffs revealed by the crumbling of bricks, the subsidence of buried ceilings. He'd once, unbelievably, put his foot through a slate roof concealed by sand and tumbled into a room where he'd found himself, dazed, staring at a man or woman whose skeleton still clutched, in a possessive claw against its arched ribs, a rotting sack containing half a dozen tin cans.

He'd taken the cans back to the basement, hardly daring to hope that their contents might still be edible, and revealed them to Elise with the flourish of a magician. With shaking fingers he'd managed to open the cans with his knife, overwhelmed by the aroma of fish, then beans and then peaches. He'd wept as he ate that banquet with Elise, as much out of joy of hunger relieved as at the loss of a world where such delicacies had been commonplace.

He still had the cans' labels, bearing the likeness of their contents, pinned to the wall above his bunk.

Now he passed the place where he'd fallen through the roof, and suddenly wondered if the girl knew where she was heading. Not far from here, up ahead, was the basement from which every second day Paul drew two precious litres of water. He had no idea what the building had been, but Elise suspected a pumping station. At any rate, years ago the long since extinct colony had dug a deep well in the bowels of the building and drawn water from the depths. It still provided meagre buckets of warm, brackish water, which he had to boil to make safe.

But there was no way, he told himself, that the girl or the men might know about the well. Unless, of course, they had stumbled upon it accidentally. The thought filled him with dread.

He heard a sound up ahead. The men were gasping for breath, panting hard. The sun was up now, burning flesh not covered, superheating the air and making it almost unbreathable. Under normal circumstances, Paul would be back at the basement by now, cooking the lizards. At sunset he would venture out again, setting the lizard traps and trekking to the well for water. He knew the dangers of being caught out in the sun. Elise would demand to know the reason for his late return.

He caught a glimpse of movement ahead, a flash of brown flesh as the last man vanished through a gaping window. They were a hundred metres from him, in a building across the street from where the well was situated. He knew the place, and knew that there was only one way in and out of it. So... they had tracked the girl to this dead end... or perhaps this was the building they were using as a base. He had considered using the very same room, relocating from their present basement, but had ruled it out because the room did not afford the luxury of a second exit in the event of an emergency.

The girl cried out again. He suspected that the men had cornered her, and for the first time he wondered at the reason she had attempted to flee from them. For that matter, how had they arrived at the city? He had heard no sound of engines, and was it possible that they had trekked through the desert to the city, in this merciless heat? Perhaps, he told himself, they had travelled by night... It was impossible that they had lived in the city for long, or he would have discovered them in his rovings. So, how had they arrived, and why?

The chances of their having come from a larger, thriving colony, he told himself, were low – or else why had they chosen this benighted city? They were loners, stragglers – and those types were the ones to avoid at all costs, or so Elise was always warning him.

The girl's scream rang out again – and then was abruptly cut off.

The silence that followed seemed, oddly, as loud as the screams themselves.

Paul edged down the sand-filled boulevard, concealing himself in window recesses and piles of scattered bricks as he moved towards the building.

He crossed the boulevard and entered the building next to the pumping station. The room was filled with sand to the level of the sill, and he moved across to a hole in the wall. He paused, looking down at the confusion of pipes and gauges that filled the neighbouring room. So far as he could tell, no one had entered the room since his last visit: the plank which he'd slanted across the window to his right, leading to the boulevard, was still in place, and the sand around the hole in the floor seemed undisturbed.

He dropped into the room, hurried to the window overlooking the boulevard, and crouched, concealing himself behind the diagonal plank.

From here he could see into the room opposite. The open window there afforded him a partial view of the room. He could see five men, moving about in the shadows, and the orange glow of flames. They had built a fire, obviously to cook something. There was no sign of the girl.

He wondered how many of them there were altogether. He had seen three men following the girl, but there were at least five men in there, and there might be more. Caution told him to leave now and return to the basement, but something stopped him. He would try to work out first if the men could be trusted.

He could learn nothing more from this vantage point.

He moved back to the hole in the interior wall and climbed through, then exited through the window and crept across the boulevard to the row of buildings opposite. Here he climbed through another window and crossed to a flight of steps up to the third floor.

Last year, when considering whether to move from the basement, he'd investigated this area thoroughly. He'd checked out room after room, assessing its suitability, and found each one wanting in turn. Some were too open to the elements, others too dilapidated.

He moved through the third storey rooms until he arrived directly above where the strangers had made their camp. Silently he crept across the fragmented floorboards and knelt beside a gap in the floor. A hole in the plaster of the ceiling allowed him an aerial view of the room and the people in it.

He carefully lowered himself onto his stomach, lay his cheek on the floor, and peered through.

He was aware of the thudding of his heart, and it had nothing to do with the danger of being seen. He would soon have a close view of the girl, the first young girl he would have seen for over ten years. Back in his area of the basement he had hoarded magazines showing women in various degrees of nakedness; some were fashion models displaying the ridiculous luxury of fine clothing, and others were models displaying nothing but themselves.

The first things he noticed, simultaneously, were the heady aroma of cooking meat and the girl's red dress, discarded and thrown in a heap on a pile of bricks. Heart thumping, he looked around for the naked girl, and his mouth filled with saliva at the scent of the meat.

He couldn't see the girl, but he could make out the men – six of them – sitting around the room and tearing at what might have been meat on the bone. Then he saw what was cooking in the fire.

Retching, he rolled away from the hole and clamped his mouth shut in order to allay the cry that swelled in his throat. He had his answer, now, as to the trustworthiness of the strangers.

Gathering his thoughts, he pushed himself into a crouch and paused, considering what to do next.

Seconds later he retraced his steps along the row of buildings, the load of his fear lightening with every step that took him further from the strangers. He moved faster when he judged he was too far away to be heard, quit the terrace and came out on an area of sand behind the buildings, momentarily blinded by the dazzling light of the sun.

He stopped, brought up short by what he saw there.

Now he knew how the strangers had come to the city.

A squat truck sat in the lee of the building, a small, battered half-tracked vehicle covered with ancient solar panels. He wondered why it had stopped there, and why the men were camping in the ruined building. Then he worked it out: they had used the building as place to build a big fire because they could not have cooked what they wanted to cook inside the truck itself.

He listened, and could detect no sounds from within the vehicle. He moved around it cautiously, stepped closer and peered in through a side window. He made out a shadowy jumble of possessions, clothing and canisters of what might have been water.

The sunlight was burning his exposed skin. He

moved to the truck's door, reached out and tried the handle experimentally: it was hot, but not unbearably so. He snatched at the handle and the door opened. Clearly the men had assumed the city to be deserted. He slipped inside, the interior of the truck stifling. His eyes adjusting, he peered around.

He found it hard to imagine what it might be like to be in this room when the truck was moving. How would you walk around as the vehicle sped through the streets? He wondered if the strangers experienced sickness when the truck was in motion.

He saw two big five litre canisters of water. Tempted though he was to take them, he decided not to. He didn't want to alert the strangers to his presence, at this stage. He opened a metal trunk, and smiled at what lay inside. This was their larder, their food supply. Stacked cans, strips of dried meat, other things shrink-wrapped in silver foil.

He looked around the room. A mattress lay in the middle of the floor, marked with a dozen dark stains, some of which looked like blood. He turned away, tears stinging his eyes. He knew now what he had to do.

He went through the truck in search of weapons, but found none. That made sense. Any working weapons would be carried and used by the men. He closed the lid of the metal food trunk, vowing to come back later and take it all, then quit the truck and hurried across the sand-drifted square.

He dodged through the ruins of the city, attempting to keep to the shadows, away from the merciless burn of the sun. Ten minutes later he came to the tumbledown terrace of buildings beneath which he and Elise made their home.

He climbed through a window and crossed the shadowed room, exiting through a hole in the rear wall. Buildings on four sides surrounded a courtyard, the high walls over the years preventing the build up of sand. He crossed the courtyard and hurried down a short flight of steps, at the bottom of which was a wooden door. He opened it and slipped through.

At the far end of the room, a high window allowed in a bright column of light, illuminating a room choked with the possessions of a long life.

He stepped quietly across a carpet Elise had informed him was Persian, moving around elegant brown furniture she claimed was even older than herself. Antiques, she called them, from the reign of Louis XIV. A line of paintings crammed the walls. Old masters, Elise had told him: originals.

He unstrung the lizards from the thong around his waist and dropped them in the cooking pot.

On a mattress below the window, Elise turned to him. "Paul?" It was barely a whisper. "You're late..." She pointed a frail hand towards the far wall, indicating the line to which the sun had climbed. She had marked it with a series of horizontal lines, so that the shadows gave an approximation of the time, if only until a couple of hours before midday.

"I can't stay, Elise. I've got to go back out."

"What have you found?"

"Food." He knew that would placate her. She worried for his safety, or perhaps for her own safety if anything were to happen to him.

"Food? A supply? Where?"

He moved across the room and reached over his mattress to the shelf where he kept his crossbow. In the early days he had never ventured out without it, wary of wild animals and even wilder humans; nowadays he found it an encumbrance on his daily rounds.

"Paul?" Elise called.

He crossed the room and knelt before her mattress. She reached out and grasped his hand. He smiled, stroking her cheek. Her skin was papery, soft, and warm. She was in her mid-eighties, at the end of a long life which had seen the fall of civilisation. Her proud claim, which she had regaled continuously in the early days, was that she had survived.

She lay naked under a thin cotton sheet, able only to raise herself a couple of times a day, with Paul's help, in order use the chamber pot she claimed had belonged to the last King of France. Her night-dress had worn to threads and fallen from her bones many years ago.

"Tell me," she said, gripping his hand and staring at the crossbow.

"Strangers. Over by the pumping station."

She looked into his eyes, her expression pleading. "Don't kill, Paul. We can survive without killing. We're doing alright, aren't we?"

He hesitated. "I won't kill. I just want to make sure... make sure they don't find the water supply."

He leaned forward, laid his lips on the ineffably soft tissue of her cheek, and kissed her.

"Paul..."

"I'll be fine."

"Take care!" She wouldn't let go of his hand. "Come back to me."

He prised his fingers from her grip and stood up. "I'll be back soon." He moved to the far wall and scored a line in the plaster half a metre above the leading edge of the sunlight. "A couple of hours. No later, okay?"

"Don't kill!" she said again, as he moved from the basement and eased the door shut behind him.

HE CAME TO the square where the strangers had left their truck.

It sat like an oversized beetle, coruscating in the sunlight. He guessed they wouldn't be back until sunset; until then they would take the opportunity to sleep, after having gorged themselves. He gripped the crossbow and hurried across the square, stepping into the shadowy interior of the building and climbing the steps to the third floor.

Two minutes later he crept towards the gap in the floorboards, knelt and peered through. The six strangers sat around the fire, picking through the girl's bones – sated, he guessed, but greedily searching for choice morsels – and chatting and laughing among themselves.

They were well armed. Rifles and pistols lay discarded around them. He wondered how proficient they were with the weapons.

Perhaps he should just return to Elise, and wait for them to go on their way. Who was he to avenge the murder of the girl?

Because he knew that that was why he was lingering here. The thought of all the food, the weapons to be had, was secondary to the idea of punishing the men for their barbarism. No doubt Elise, who hailed from a more complex age, would argue with him over the morality of his intentions, but to him it was cut and dried. The strangers had committed a crime more terrible than any other, and therefore they must suffer the consequences.

Their leader – at least, the man to whom all the others deferred – was a big, bald European, perhaps German, who laughed a lot and spat gobbets of greased saliva into the dying embers. He was drinking something from a flask, and Paul guessed, from the man's extravagant gestures and loud utterances, that it was alcoholic. He recalled that Elise had once found a bottle of vodka in the ruins. She had guarded the bottle jealously, allowing him none, and sometimes after an hour or two of drinking she had been loud and angry, and then tearful.

The other men sniggered and grinned at what he said, and occasionally their leader allowed one of them a quick nip from his flask.

They're like wild animals, Paul thought. No better.

The German reached into the ashes with a stick, prodding something. A skull rolled, its black eye-sockets gazing up at the ceiling. The man said something in English, and Paul could just make out the sense of his words.

"What you think?"

Someone grunted.

The German said, "Should we have kept her alive?"

An emaciated Arab grinned. "What for?"

At this, the German bellowed a laugh. "What for? Listen to you, you ball-less bastard!" He grunted a laugh. "Thing is, when we were fucking her – I could only think about her meat. And now we've had her meat..." his leer took in his men, ensuring that all eyes were on him, "now all I want to do is fuck her!"

A chorus of laughs greeted this. Someone said, "You think they'll find us? I mean..." the man gestured towards the ribcage sitting among the ashes, "I mean, Edvard'll be pretty sore."

The German laughed. "Let him. And Dan'll be even sorer when he finds out what we got."

Paul shifted silently, easing his prone position on the floorboards.

After a long silence below, someone said, "You think we'll find it?"

"Why the fuck you think I took the map, you moron?"

In a more commanding voice, an African sitting next to the German reached out a big hand and said, "Let me see."

Hans unslung a bag from around his shoulders, opened it and withdrew a wad of folded paper. He cleared an area in the sand before him and spread the paper. He, the African and one or two others leaned over the map.

Paul pressed his eye to the gap, attempting to see what was drawn on the paper. He made out lines that might be streets, blocks that might denote buildings, but from this far away he was unable to recognise the area of the city they might represent.

Hans was saying, "...comb the city, block by block. When we recognise a building, the shape of a street, a square... then we'll know we've found it."

The African said, "And then the hard work begins."

Hans shook his head. "There's six of us. How heavy is sand? We'll have a way dug within a week."

The African stabbed the paper with a big forefinger. "You sure it's here?"

When he lifted his finger, Paul made out a red circle drawn within a block of shade.

"Dan was pretty damned sure the circle marked the store-room," Hans said. "And Dan might be a bastard, but he's pretty smart up here."

"Of course," the African said, "the store might've been emptied years ago."

The German just stared at him.

The Arab, Achmed, pointed at the map with a diffident finger. "What you think's down there, Hans?" His eyes gleamed.

The German shrugged. "Stores, was all Dan said. Government supplies, for emergencies. So... food rations, tinned and dried. Water. Maybe weapons." He paused, staring into space. "I know this, we find the store and it's all still there, we're set for life, okay?"

The African muttered something.

Achmed chuckled, "Sure, Hans..."

The others laughed at the thought of being set for life.

Paul rolled away from the gap in the floorboards and lay on his back, his heart dancing. He had to think about this. Assess what he'd found out and change his plans accordingly.

If what they were claiming was true, then there was a big food store hidden somewhere beneath the city. If they found it, then Paul guessed they'd make the city their home for quite some time.

And he didn't like the thought of that.

Voices sounded from below. He applied his eye to the gap again.

"You and Dan, you were close, once, right?" Achmed said.

Hans thought about that. "Depends on what you mean about close, yeah? I saved his life, once. So he trusted me. Big mistake, Achmed. If you learn only one thing, learn it good. In this world, trust no-one, okay?"

Achmed made some ingratiating reply. The African stood up, moved from the group, and stretched out on the floor by the back wall.

Others took his lead, cleared spaces on the floor, lay down and tried to sleep.

Paul watched Hans tip the flask to his mouth again and again, smiling between swallows. He picked up the map, folded it and returned it to his shoulder bag.

He didn't loop the bag around his shoulder, however. He merely lodged it beneath his bald head and lay on his back, staring up at the ceiling. For a terrible second, Paul thought the giant was staring directly at him. Then Hans closed his eyes, and Paul let out a long breath.

He wondered how long he should give them before they were all asleep – and then he wondered whether he would have the courage, or foolhardiness, to enter the room.

He would give them a couple of hours, then look in again and see if they were sleeping. He was tired himself, but dared not fall asleep up here. Elise said he snored, and he didn't want to give himself away so stupidly.

He moved to the next room, silently, dropped to the darkened second storey and curled in the cooling sand. In minutes, despite the excitement of the situation racing through his mind, he was asleep.

He dreamed of the girl in the red dress, and in his dreams she was beautiful. She resembled one of the models in the magazines, and he knew with heart-pounding certainty that she was about to reveal herself to him. She faced him, smiling, and reached up to unfasten her dress. It dropped from her body, and she looked so young, her body unlined and so unlike Elise's, her breasts...

Oh, Christ... He reached out for her.

He came awake suddenly, angered at being denied the touch of her flesh, and then swamped by the reality of what had happened to the smiling girl.

He looked down at his crotch. His cock was slung across his thigh, slack now that it had shed its load of semen.

He dashed tears from his cheeks and clutched his crossbow. If he could secure one of the stranger's rifles, then he stood a chance of killing them in their sleep.

Hans, he thought... He would like to wake up Hans so that the bastard would face his death in the full knowledge of what was happening to him.

He stood and padded up the stairs to the third

floor, then passed into the room above where the strangers were gathered.

He knelt and peered through the gap.

All was silent below. The men were stilled in sleep, not a movement among them. Hans lay on his side, his head lodged on the material of the shoulder bag.

He watched for a further five minutes, then made his move. He crept down to the boulevard, into the searing heat of the sun, approached the open window and peered through.

Hans was in the middle of the room, snoring. The others lay beyond him, their backs to the window.

Paul eased himself over the low sill and felt cool sand beneath his bare feet. He breathed in through his nose, taking shallow breaths, and exhaled silently through his mouth. Taking exaggerated steps, he crossed to where Hans was sleeping and eased himself into a crouch beside the man's gross head.

He knew that it was going to be impossible to ease the bag from beneath the sleeping man. Another ploy was called for. He steeled himself, planning his movements after grabbing the bag. He would dive from the window and sprint across the boulevard to the terrace opposite. Once through one of the many open windows, he was confident he'd be able to lose himself before Hans and his men had time to give chase.

It was the only way he could secure the map.

He would be giving away the fact that the city was occupied, but he was confident that he could keep himself undetected. The alternative, if he failed to get the map, was to have the barbarians resident in his city for who knew how long.

Very well. He would do it.

He reached out...

He felt a hand on his neck, paralysing him. "Hans!" Achmed cried.

Hans surged awake, along with the others. The German rolled over, crouched and faced Paul, his expression ugly with incipient violence. He nodded, once.

And before Paul could fully comprehend the futility of his situation, a blow to the back of his head tumbled him into oblivion.

Chapter Two

Built into the mountainside in the middle of the twenty-first century, the castle had all the outward appearances of being a thousand years old. It projected from the cliff-face as if half-buried there, presenting its implacable foursquare façade to the plain below. Two vast, square towers parenthesised crenellated battlements, beneath which was the arched gateway and portcullis.

From this vantage point in the central massif, vast swathes of desert could be seen stretching to the horizon. As Samara stood before the gateway, waiting for the rest of the hunting party to join her, she gazed to the west where the sun was going down on another blistering day. Now was the only time to hunt, in the all-too-brief interim between the start of sunset and the creeping darkness; not that she could really grace what they were about to do with the grand title of a hunt: a hunt was what she had enjoyed as a child, when there had still been wild boar and dogs to chase through the dying forests. In thirty years the desert had encroached and the wildlife all but died out, apart from lizards and what they would soon be capturing in their nets: bats. The colony was reduced to subsisting off lizard and bat stew now, accompanied by moulds and lichen scraped from the walls of the subterranean caves deep within the mountain.

As ever, the hunting party was tardy in joining her at the appointed hour. Selected from the rapidly diminishing ranks of the fully fit, the able young men and women resented not only this twice weekly trip out to the bat caverns, but balked at Samara's leadership. Long gone were the times of comparative plenty when her father could lead the colony with lenience and a liberal hand: her father was on his death-bed now, and times were hard. Samara had assumed leadership and instituted radical and unpopular regimes: a cut in rations for everyone, for starters, and a loosening of the ban on mechanisation. Her father might have been a rabid anti-scientist, but the fact was that certain mechanical tools, carefully employed, would be a benefit to the continued survival of the colony. Samara knew and understood her father's – and his ageing council's – loathing of science and technology, but she reasoned that the proper use of approved machines, trucks and rifles, hydroponics systems and water pumps, need not be the first step on the slippery slope towards the kind of materialist, mechanised society responsible for the present state of the world.

For the past year, little by little, she had argued her corner, gained concessions from the council, and instituted the use of certain approved devices, always for the good of the colony. In time, she thought, the colony might come to recognise that they had her to thank for their continued survival. In the meantime she could bear the burden of their dissatisfaction.

A dozen men and women moved across the courtyard, carrying the rolled net over their shoulders. They looked tired and laggardly, having just woken from a day's sleep. Increasingly the colony had taken to sleeping during the heat of the day and going about their business at night.

Giovanni smiled at her, an expression halfway between genuine pleasure to see her and timid servility. He had known her for six months, ever since she had selected him to help in the hunt, and he still had no idea how to conduct himself in her company. He moved between garrulous agreement with her every suggestion and a maddening fascination with her breasts. The fact was that he feared her, and the thought pleased her. She had promoted him to act as her deputy on their hunting expeditions, and she knew she had his loyalty.

She had watched her father, and learned from him how to manage those beneath her.

"You've made it, at last," she said to him. "And why only twelve?"

He almost flinched. "Silvio and Gregor are down with the ills, Samara."

"And the rest of you are late on account of visiting them in the hospital?"

He had no idea whether to laugh at her quip or deny the charge, so he shrugged obsequiously and slid a gaze to her chest.

She turned, denying him the pleasure, and led

the way from the gate. They moved along the front of the castle's looming façade, skirting the lapping desert, and headed towards the tumbled base of the mountain a kilometre distant.

Sunsets always reminded her of her childhood. This one was huge and bloody, as if the sun itself were haemorrhaging and leaking its vitality onto the land. The chance, she thought, would be a fine thing. At the age of six she had told her father that although she thought the sun was beautiful, she didn't like it because of what it was doing to the earth: drying up the land and killing all the animals and all the people. He had smiled his gentle, tolerant smile and hauled her onto his lap and explained, for the first time, what had really caused the breakdown of civilisation.

Scientists, he had told her, had brought about the destruction of the world. In a greedy bid to use all the world's resources, to create countless machines and so make easier the lot of the rich, scientists had unleashed pollutants into the air, noxious chemicals which had killed the atmosphere and allowed increased heat and sunlight to burn away the world's water. That was why they were living as they were now, scrabbling like animals in the ruins of civilisation in a bid to scrape a living.

"My father," he had told her, "was a scientist, and I will never forgive him the fact."

From that day on, the sun had reminded her of her father. The sun was huge and powerful; it could give life, but it could also take life away; it was, also, ever-present.

As a girl she had always thought that her father would be ever-present, and only recently had he shown that he too was as vulnerable to the ills of the flesh as lesser mortals.

Like the sun, his life was setting; unlike the sun, his going down was in no way beautiful... and there would be no rising from the darkness to which he was destined. As she led the way along the rocky path high above the desert, she turned her head away from her followers in case they noted her tears.

Giovanni caught up with her and hopped alongside. "Samara?"

"Giovanni?" She kept her eyes on the treacherous path.

"I thought you'd like to know what people have been saying, Samara."

"And what is that?" She tried to keep amusement from her tone, but she found his tactics, puppy-like and ingratiating, a source of humour.

"They're sick of bat," he said, and it sounded so comical that she had to laugh now.

"Well, so am I, Giovanni. I'm heart sick of the foul-tasting, bony air-borne rats. But tell, me, they're not blaming me or my father for their diet, are they?"

He was quick to counter the suggestion. "No, no! Of course not... It's just that, well, people think that we should hunt further afield. Ten years ago there were pigs a little north of here, so I'm told, and rats in the ruins at Aubenas."

She slowed her pace and stared at him, and he coloured and looked away. "Giovanni, years ago I went hunting to the north, and let me tell you that

I didn't see one animal, apart from lizards. And Aubenas is flooded in sand – show me a rat surviving there and I'll eat it raw."

"I'm just reporting what people are saying, Samara."

"Then tell them to come and spout their stupidity to me personally, will you, instead of talking behind my back?"

His head bobbed. "Yes, Samara."

She sighed and said, "I'll have a word with the chefs later, Giovanni. See if they can come up with a variation on *chauve-souris plate du jour*, okay?"

He beamed in gratitude and pointed ahead, as if their arrival at the mouth of the cavern was his doing and he expected praise.

Samara's party was late, so they had to work fast. "You know what to do, and we've around ten minutes to spare, so I suggest you get a move on. Giovanni, you're in charge."

He needed no further telling, but strode about issuing superfluous instructions to those already well versed in the skills of draping nets. Samara stood in the light of the dying sun and watched six men and women swarm up the cliff-face, carrying the rolled net on their shoulders. They moved like insects, their ascent swift and sure, and edged along the ledge above the cave mouth. Next they attached the top edge of the net to metal loops stapled into the rock and, on Giovanni's shouted command, dropped the net. Samara watched it unfurl and fall with loud, fast susurrus, and instantly the yawning maw of the cavern was covered with a fine charcoal gauze.

The six remaining men and women on the ground crouched like sprinters, gripping the bottom edge of the net with their backs to the cave, and waited.

Samara moved to the net and pulled the material aside, turning sideways and slipping through the gap. She trod a familiar path into the cave's cool, welcoming shade. There was a rocky feature to the left, shaped like a chair, which she had discovered when she was ten and where she had come to sit to watch the nightly exodus of the bats. Three years ago, recalling the swarming bats and recognising the need for protein in the colonist's diets, she had suggested to her father that he institute the bat hunt. Now she took her cool seat, sat back and awaited the twilight show.

Before her, the net covered the arch of the cave mouth like a grey film, dense enough to capture the animals, but fine enough not to register on the creatures' sensitive natural sonar.

She never failed to feel a thrill of anticipation as the light dimmed and the high, almost inaudible chirruping of the bats at her back sounded like the tuning up of an orchestra. What was about to happen, she thought, could be likened to a symphony, but one more visual than auditory.

She braced herself for the rush, knowing from long experience that it was imminent, and seconds later it happened. The high squeal crescendoed and the papery flutter of a thousand wings filled the air, and suddenly she felt the cool down-draught of the creatures' flight as they swooped in a great black shoal from the cave and flew into the waiting net.

Samara hugged herself and laughed, ignoring the high, pungent reek of bat bodies and excrement and concentrating on the sight before her as the net bellied with its flapping cargo of a thousand bats.

She heard the cry from outside as Giovanni instructed the men and women above the cave mouth to let loose the net. What should have happened, what had happened a hundred times before, was simple: instantly the weighted top edge of the net should have fallen, as the lower edge was pulled back into the cave by the hunters below, resulting in a tubular mass of struggling, writhing bats – food that would last the colonists almost a week.

But this time the operation did not run as expected. For some reason, a woman perching high above the cave failed to release her net in time with the others; she was seconds late, and in struggling to unsnag her section, she pitched forward and fell to the rock below, dragging the net with her.

She hit the rock with a sickening crunch that Samara would hear in her nightmares for weeks to come.

After a frozen second, the hunting party left the struggling haul of bats and hurried across to their fallen colleague.

Samara relinquished her throne and joined them.

The woman had landed head first, and the debris of her split skull was dashed across the rock alongside splashes of bat guano. Samara closed her eyes. The woman had been young and fit, of child-bearing age, someone they could ill-afford to lose in a stupid accident like this.

"Hanna..." Giovanni knelt beside the body, holding the woman's hand, his eyes averted from the mess.

The reaction of the hunters varied from ghoulish fascination at the grisly remains to numbed shock at the loss of a friend. Some turned away, moaning; others retched.

Samara indicated the pulsating net, from which individual bats were escaping.

"Okay, there's nothing we can do for her. Let's get the net back to the castle. Giovanni, Eve, take the body. The rest of you..."

The hunters pulled squares of sacking from their shorts and loin-clothes and slung them over their shoulders, then hoisted the bulging net and carried it like a felled log. The bats were still active and writhing, frantic to escape, and the sacking protected the hunters from the creatures' vicious teeth and claws.

Samara watched Giovanni and Eve as they debated the best way to transport the corpse back to the castle, or rather the least messy way. In the end they elected to take the body by its ankles and shoulders; as they lifted, the remains of the woman's head fell back, spilling still more pulverised grey matter.

She slung her own patch of sacking over her shoulder and inserted herself into the line of bearers, fighting to subdue the struggling mass of animals that seemed to move as one, like some great, muscled snake. The stench of excrement and urine expelled in fear was overwhelming, and she fought to keep her last, meagre meal where it belonged.

The sun was down now, and the path along the edge of the cliff bottom was even more hazardous. They moved slowly, aware that one mis-step could send them tumbling down the ravine to the desert twenty metres below. Samara wondered what the hunters feared the most: the likely injuries such a fall would incur, or the punishment she would mete out to someone endangering the loss of the precious cargo.

An hour later they arrived at the gateway to the castle. She squirmed from beneath the still bucking net and instructed the hunters to proceed straight to the kitchen. She waited in the half-light provided by the flickering torches set in sconces on either side of the timber gate, and waited for Giovanni and Eve to catch up. They arrived five minutes later, sweating and panting with their load.

Samara gestured Giovanni to join her. They lay the body reverently on the cobbles and Eve straightened up, a hand massaging the small of her back. Giovanni hurried across to where Samara stood staring out across the star-lit desert.

"Samara?"

"Take the body to the cool room."

He stared at her. "Not the morgue?"

"You heard what I said."

"But her family? Samara, she had a mother and a sister –"

"Go to them now and tell them that Hanna had an accident while collecting moss in the cavern. Say she fell into a chasm, and that we attempted to retrieve her but the chasm was too deep and we were unable to reach her. Understood?"

Wide-eyed with apprehension, the boy nodded. "Yes, Samara."

"And I am sure that I can rely on you not to breathe a word of this to anyone?"

Giovanni nodded. "But Samara, the others, they saw..."

"Tell them that if they contradict my story, then they're on half rations for a month, understood?"

The boy bobbed his head. "But... I don't understand, Samara. The cool room – ?"

"Is next to the kitchen, Giovanni." She smiled at him. "Why look so shocked? You said earlier that people were sick of bat meat."

His startled expression slid to one of grinning complicity as he nodded and hurried back to Eve and the corpse.

Samara strode into the castle and made her way through the labyrinth of interior corridors to the hospital situated in the walls overlooking the desert.

Once a week she made her rounds of the infirmary, checking on the progress of those colonists whose absence was most missed in the smooth running of the castle. Work was hard in the colony, and she suspected some of feigning injury and illness in order to benefit from hospital rest and the increased rations doled out to the sick.

Her rounds were intended to root out malingerers, and to monitor the state of the seriously ill.

Both malingerers and terminal cases, the colony could well do without.

* * *

THE CASTLE WAS built by rich survivalists back in the twenty-first century as a fortress against the storms to come; its outward appearance of a mediaeval fortification was not continued in its modern, functional interior. Samara suspected that it had once been as plush as the five star hotels she'd seen advertised in old magazines, although now the wear and tear of almost a century had knocked the smooth edges from the palatial rooms and corridors. The interior of the castle had a rough, lived-in feel, and the lack of electric lighting – prohibited by her father, though she had overseen the scavenging and repair of solar arrays which would one day make electricity within the castle a reality – hid the state of the threadbare carpets and ramshackle furniture. Along the corridors through which she now passed, infrequent candles provided scant illumination. The same was true of the hospital ward itself, though more candles burned here to allow doctors and their attendants to work in the relative cool of the night-time hours.

Dr Mortenson was as old as her father, in his early seventies, and one of the few people in a position of authority not to be cowed by Samara's familial eminence. The doctor had watched her grow up, had often been on hand to look after the infant Samara when her father had been too busy to attend to her demands.

He was grey and weary, and carried his years like a physical load.

He looked up from his battered desk as she entered. "Another week? How the time passes! We should meet recreationally, Sam. I haven't lost to you at chess in months, if not years."

She placed a kiss on the old man's brow. "I'm busy, Mort. You wouldn't believe how busy, not that father appreciates..." She looked at him. "Have you seen him recently?"

"I drop by every other day."

"And?"

"Do you want the truth?"

"Have I ever asked for anything else?"

He smiled to himself. "Very well. He's very ill. I'd have him in here, but you know what he'd say to that."

Samara nodded. "But you can treat him?"

"I can use what little medicine I have. I make sure he isn't in pain."

She looked into the old man's grey eyes. "How long?"

Dr Mortenson considered, before replying, "Perhaps a week."

To herself, Samara said, "That soon..." She had known he would one day die, of course, but it had always been an abstract notion.

"Transition will be smooth, Samara. I'm on your side, and a majority of others on the council, too. We know things have been hard lately, and can only get harder, but no one blames you."

She smiled. "That means a lot, you know?" She pushed herself away from the desk. "And the situation here...?"

The doctor joined her on her stroll along the line of beds. Most patients were unconscious or asleep.

Others lay groaning or staring silently at the ceiling. Orderlies passed among the sick, administering what little relief they could by means of medicine or verbal consolation.

"Three more with no hope of recuperation," he said, extending a hand to indicate the darkened room at the end of the ward. They passed inside. Samara made out three bed-ridden figures, two men in their middle years and a young woman.

"I've ceased medication, as instructed. Should I...?" He let the final words hang, unsaid.

She nodded. "I'll send someone up in the morning."

They left the room, where death seemed to hang in the air, and returned to the desk at the far end of the ward. "And can you discharge the pair I mentioned last week? They're essential workers – and we're short-staffed in the joinery."

"They'll be fit for work in a day or two, Samara."

She stepped forward and embraced him. "I'll see you next week, Mort."

"One thing," he said, a hand on her arm. "When I saw your father yesterday, he said he wanted to see you."

She pulled a contrite face. "I've been so busy... But I'll drop in later tonight, I promise."

She left the hospital, telling herself that she really should make the effort to see her father, and wondering what it was that was stopping her. She knew, of course: his censure, his irritable criticism at the changes she'd instituted – it was going against everything in which he believed, and his admonition of her, as if she were a little girl, diminished the self-belief she had built up in command over the past year.

She made her way to the kitchen, attempting to push thoughts of her father to the back of her mind.

The aroma of cooking meat assailed her long before she reached the kitchen. The scent, heavy and gamey, was far better than the taste would prove to be: they had long ago run out of herbs and spices, and while salt was in plentiful supply, it did little to add flavour to stringy bat meat and tasteless lichens. She supposed the unvaried menu was serving its purpose, however; keeping alive the hundred inhabitants of the castle, just.

Although the kitchen was fitted with what must have been all the latest appliances when built, there was something almost barbaric in the scene that met her eyes. Torches illuminated a dozen men and women toiling over half a dozen huge cauldrons cooking on open fires. A window at the far end of the kitchen provided a little ventilation, but even so the room was thick was acrid smoke. And – this was a touch that lent an air of absurdity to the proceedings – a number of bats had escaped and were flapping through the air, chased by kitchen hands.

Most of the bats were piled in a corner of the room, some struggling limply but most dead now after being battered into submission by the hunters. A production line had been set up on a long table. Handfuls of the creatures were tossed onto one end of the table where six men and women stood with knives and scrapers. The bats were de-winged and gutted and thrown into the cooking pots on the far side of the table. In the early days the bats' heads had been removed; now, with protein a priority, the heads remained in order to fill out the colonists' meagre rations.

Samara had instructed her own servants to remove the bones and skulls before they served her the nightly stew, but for everyone else the dish was served bones, skulls and all.

Ivan caught sight of her across the torch-lit room. His big ruddy face glowed in the heat, behind the silver flash of the blades he was sharpening against each other like a circus performer. "Samara!"

The blades, she saw, were too large to use on the tiny bodies of bats.

Ivan had appeared at the gates of the castle a year ago, ominously well-fed for a man who claimed to have trekked for days across the desert from the failed colony of Turin. He was a Russian, he was proud to claim. He said he came from a long line of Cossacks – Samara had had to look up the word in the castle's meagre library – and told her that he was an accomplished cook. She had smiled at that, and told him to work his magical accomplishments on the scant pickings the land around the castle had to offer.

"Samara," he called, gesturing with a flashing knife to the heaving mound of bats. "A poor haul. What happened?"

She joined him. "We had an accident. One of the hunters fell. A lot of bats escaped."

His eyes gleamed. "Fell?"

Samara nodded. "She's in the cool room – and a

message from Doctor Mortenson; there'll be two more to collect in the morning."

"Just two?" He appeared disappointed.

Samara flashed him a look. "What do you want me to do, start a cull? Institute the death penalty for thieving?" She eyed his ample girth and told herself that Ivan would be the first to the gallows if she did that.

"Samara, how do you expect me to feed a hundred people on a few bats and the occasional corpse?"

She shook her head. "What can I do? The bat numbers are falling, but what do you expect when we take them in their hundreds every week?"

He went back to sharpening the long knives against each other. "You know what I'd do," he said casually.

She nodded. She had considered his suggestion, but the thought of the danger in which she would be putting her people had made her hesitate.

"I don't know..." She was not averse to the idea, but perhaps what was preventing her agreement was what her father might have to say on the matter, if he found out. He tried to run the castle on old-fashioned liberal principles, without realising that they were living in times when such principles were a luxury.

"Come with me..."

She followed him across the room to a smaller version of the kitchen, at the back of which was the cool room. Samara peered into the shadowy recess. The hunter's corpse hung upside down, jugular opened to release the last of her blood. Beside it hung the butchered remains of another colonist, this one from the hospital.

Samara stepped back, gagging, and looked away.

Ivan gestured with a knife. "That's the extent of the meat, Samara." He gestured across the room to an earthenware pot. "Lichen and moss. That's our stock of food. If the bat stocks get any lower..."

His piggy eyes peered out at her.

Samara nodded. "I can't suggest it to my father. We'll have to do it without his knowledge. If he found out..."

"And how would he find out?"

Samara smiled humourlessly. "He finds out about everything that happens, in time."

Ivan gestured. "Forgive me, but word has it that time is one thing he does not have a lot of."

"In that case perhaps it'd be wise to wait until my father is no longer around."

Ivan considered her words, and nodded. "There are two colonies within striking distance. I know the layout of the Turin community inside out. It's badly defended, just fifty men, women and children. The last thing they'd expect is a raid."

"And food stocks?"

"Not a lot, but perhaps enough for three months. They grew their own hydroponic wheat last year. They have surpluses of dried meat – rat and lizard."

"Lizard? I'd rather eat my own boots."

Smiling, the fat chef looked down at her bare feet.

She said, "A figure of speech, Ivan." She paused, then said, "Doctor Mortenson told me that my father has perhaps a week to live. We'll discuss the matter further then, okay?"

Ivan nodded. "Excellent, Samara."

As she left the kitchen and made her way to the residential tower, she wondered how she might get Ivan's latest suggestion past the ruling council. She coloured at the thought of Doctor Mortenson's likely reaction to her scheme. He would be more than disappointed in her, and would tell her so. Perhaps there might be some way of going about the raids without informing the ruling council?

SHE HURRIED ALONG the corridor to her room, and paused before the door to her father's chamber.

After brief consideration, she knocked on the huge timber double-door.

Her father's maid, a shrivelled, grey women in her fifties, opened the door and stood back to allow Samara in. "How is he, Gretchen?"

"Frail, but eating... Dr Mortenson comes every day with drugs..." Samara could see the resentment in the woman's eyes, that an old and dying man should receive such precious medication. As far as Samara was concerned, her father's leadership over the decades had earned him the right of preferential treatment.

"I'd like to see him."

"I'll go and ask..." Gretchen bobbed her head and moved to the door at the far end of the room, opened it a crack and slipped inside.

Her father used – or rather *had* used – this outer room as a study. Books and papers littered desks, chairs and the floor; old maps and charts adorned the walls, along with posters and paintings showing landscape scenes of how the world had once looked.

Samara stared at the soaring, snow-capped mountains, green meadows, forested plains; it was so unimaginable to her, so alien, that it no longer even represented an ideal of beauty, even though she had seen her father weep at the images.

The door opened and Gretchen emerged. "Your father is awake. He would like to see you."

"Thank you, Gretchen." She entered her father's bedroom and shut the door behind her, her heart beating fast.

The old man sat up in bed, something regal in his demeanour despite his thatch of greying hair and sunken, lined face. He was huge – the biggest man Samara had ever seen – and to see him reduced by illness like this reminded her of a wild animal, caught in a trap.

And like a trapped animal, he resented the state in which he found himself and was prone to lash out.

Samara approached the bed timidly.

He patted the counterpane on his bed. Despite the heat, he wore a night-shirt and lay under thick blankets. "Sit down." It was less a request than an order.

Samara perched on the bed, wanting to take her father's hand but at the same time wary of his reaction. He rarely showed physical affection to her, and often repulsed her own attempts at contact. She didn't want that, now.

He peered at her. "Who are you seeing these days?" he snapped the question, surprising her.

"Father..." She found his enquiries into her personal life annoying. "There's been no one since..."

"Him!" he said, unable to bring himself to say the name. "I was glad when he left the castle."

"You've never stopped telling me."

"I haven't?" He looked at her, confused.

Was his mind failing him, she wondered, along with his body?

"I've been asking Mortenson to fetch you. I know you're busy, but..."

"Well, I'm here now," she said.

"I have things to tell you."

She closed her eyes, expecting the blast of his criticism. She wondered what she might be doing wrong this time.

He looked around the room, as if gathering his thoughts. She followed his gaze. His bedroom was filled with an incongruous medley of junk gleaned over a long life-time: old metal toys – cars and rockets – along with stuffed bears and children's books. There was even a suit of armour, standing to awry attention in one corner.

"Samara... more and more you remind me of your mother."

"And that's what you had to tell me?" She was unable to keep the impatience from her voice, discomfited by the mention of the woman she had never known. Her mother had died giving birth to her, and from time to time the fact unleashed a tirade of grief from her father.

She had often wondered if this was responsible for her father's distance towards her over the years, his ambivalence, even his cruelty.

"What I wanted to tell you, Samara, is that the colony is failing, dying."

His words surprised her. "Dying?"

"Five years ago the population here was... what? Do you know that?"

"Two hundred, a little less."

"Correct. And now?" His rheumy eyes regarded her.

She shrugged. "A little over a hundred."

"And what does that suggest?"

"But we're stable, now. People die, but babies are born..."

"Sam, lack of proper nutrition accounts for the deaths. People are dying young, much younger than they should be."

She wanted to say that that might not be the case had he allowed mechanisation years ago, solar arrays and hydroponics. When you're gone, she wanted to cry, then things will be different, and the colony will prosper.

She said, "What are you suggesting?"

He looked at her, something like doubt, or even confusion, in his grey and watery eyes. "We need more food, supplies. Nutrition..." he faltered.

She was of a mind to tell him then about the notion of a raiding party – that was one way of garnering supplies, she'd tell him. But she knew that would be a mistake.

"Father...?" she said.

He came to life again, as if from a far away reverie.

"Fetch me that..." He pointed a long, wavering finger across the room.

She slipped from the bed and padded across the worn carpet. "This, the bear?"

"No! Next to it. That thing..."

"This?" She picked up the metal rocket-ship.

He nodded. "Here..."

She returned to the bed and handed him the lightweight, garishly painted metal rocket. "What about it?"

"This..." he said, staring at its sleek lines as if for the first time.

"It's a rocket-ship." She took it from his loose fingers, turning it over in his hands and reading something printed on one flaring fin. "Made in Taiwan," she said, wondering where that place was. Or had been.

She passed it back to her father. "What do you want to tell me?" she asked.

He looked up, smiled at her, and shook his head. "I... I still don't know if the time is right. For so long I've ruled here, but now that things are failing..."

She shook her head, impatient with his ramblings.

She heard the discreet clearing of a throat over by the door. "I think your father is growing tired, Samara," Gretchen said.

"I'll go," she said to her father, but her eyes were distant as she stood and moved from the bed. She passed from the room, and Gretchen said, "He's easily confused, Samara. Some days he's as bright as water, but others..."

"I'll stop by tomorrow, Gretchen."

"Of course," the maid said, and Samara could tell from her tone that she doubted the promise.

She returned to her own room and asked a servant to fetch her a meal, then moved to the window, opened it and gazed out. A hot desert breeze lapped her face. The sand was an expanse of darkness, the stars above a field of a million brilliant lights.

She thought about her father, and what she would do when he died.

Minutes later the servant returned with a tray bearing a bowl of stew and a mug of watered wine from her father's cellar.

She sat on the window seat, stared out across the desert and brought the spoon to her mouth.

She tasted the stew and looked down at the chunks of meat emerging from the thick gravy, and wondered if Ivan had prepared the dish especially for her.

CHAPTER THREE

"THIS ISN'T A decision I've taken lightly," Dan said. "I've been going over the options all night. It's important we move now. The longer I remain here... well, the greater the chance that the bastards get there before us."

Klausner said, "Always assuming the store wasn't raided years ago."

Dan bit back his impatience. "That's a given. We can't just sit here and assume there's nothing there. If we uncover it, then... think of what that'll mean."

The other man nodded, and was silent.

It was an hour before dawn, Dan's favourite time of day. It was the coolest hour, before the sun came up and scorched the already blistered landscape. He liked to rise an hour or two before dawn and walk around the perimeter of the colony, ostensibly checking the defences but in reality day-dreaming, attempting to imagine a better future. He would miss the familiar routine.

The two men stood on the highest point on the ramparts of the ancient castle, staring out over what had been, until a decade ago, the Baltic sea. Now the land fell away in a great, desiccated scoop, fissured by zigzag cracks, like the photographic negatives of lightning bolts, where the last of the sea had drained away. At their backs was the nub of the castle, the ruins which had been the colony's home for the last fifty years. Patchworked into the ancient grey stone were brighter panels of plastic walls, newer bricks scavenged from the dead city, and the incongruous rectangles of a dozen bright, white uPVC doors.

A year ago, the castle was home to three hundred, before the cholera epidemic that claimed the lives of over a hundred men, women and children. Others had left, in fear of being struck down. Perhaps a hundred and fifty people remained now, and the fact compounded Dan's guilt.

Klausner said, "You made a copy of the map?"

Dan turned to him, surprised at the question. "Of course."

His deputy nodded. "Good." He paused, then went on, "I don't have to tell you to be careful. Hans is..."

"Hans is an animal."

Klausner smiled. "I'm glad you realise that, now."

"Look, I admit I was wrong. You knew, so did Kath. I should have listened to you at the time."

"This isn't about who was right or wrong, Dan. We've all made mistakes. But... I want you to be very careful when you get there. I want to see you back here, whether you manage to unearth the stores or not."

Dan nodded, unable to bring himself to look his deputy in the eye.

He had another map, one which he hadn't told Klausner about.

After a long silence, Klausner said, "Does Edvard know they've taken Lisa?"

Dan shook his head. "I haven't told him. The condition he's in... I thought it was the last thing he'd want to know right now."

"But you're taking him with you?"

"Look at it from my point of view. He stays here, gets over his fever and finds that the bastards have got his daughter. He'd want to be with us. Wouldn't you, in his position?"

Reluctantly, it seemed to Dan, Klausner nodded. "You're right, of course."

Dan looked away.

"Do you think she's safe with them?" Klausner asked.

"Christ knows. I know she had a thing going with Hans... But that was a while back. They hadn't been together for months. And Hans resented that."

"You think she didn't go willingly?"

Dan shook his head. "I honestly think she was forced, kicking and screaming. She loves her father. She'd have said something to him if she'd decided to leave voluntarily."

"Even though she knew how much Edvard detested Hans?"

Dan nodded. "Even so. She was – is – an honest kid."

"I just hope you can find her, Dan, bring her back."

Dan glanced at Klausner. The man was fifty, Dan's age – but looked twenty years older. Cholera had sapped his strength, his spirit. Before the outbreak, the colony could make-believe they had a future.

Dan felt warmth on his back and turned. The first filaments of the sunrise were showing to the east, burning orange. Within an hour the sun would be up, a huge magnesium-white ball sapping the life of everything it surveyed.

"We'd better be on our way."

"The truck ready?"

Dan nodded and moved to the worn steps that led down to the castle courtyard. His tracked truck, angular with its tegument of solar panels, stood on the cobbles before the high timber gate. Behind it was the long trailer carrying the all-important paraphernalia of the drilling rig, the bits and tools and even a failing computer.

He hurried across the courtyard to one of the uPVC doors and yanked it open, then moved down a short corridor to the room he shared with Kath.

She was embracing Renata, the young woman Kath had worked with in the repair rooms for years. Their closeness was entirely understandable: Renata had lost her mother at the age of fifteen, ten years ago, and he and Kath had never had children. There were times when Dan didn't know whether that had been a blessing or a curse. He knew full well what Kath thought, of course.

"Dan," Renata said, embracing him. She was tearful. "We'll miss you, all of us."

He felt uneasy in the girl's bear hug.

He took Kath's hand and led her out to the courtyard and the waiting truck.

A small crowd had gathered. Dan tried not to label the gathering pathetic, but that was the word that immediately sprang to mind. Thirty or forty bedraggled souls, dressed in rags, thin and malnourished. Christ, but a year ago they'd have been proud and confident.

Klausner was standing beside the cab. He held out a hand and took Dan's hand in a strong grip. "Take care, Dan. See you soon."

Dan looked him in the eye and said, "We'll be back."

Kath was saying her farewells to friends. Dan waited until she was finished, then climbed into the truck, moved through the living area and climbed over piled supplies to the cab. He slid into the driving seat and gripped the wheel, comforted by the familiarity of the cab's solid fixtures and fittings.

Every month he'd set off in the truck for a day or two, searching for likely sources of water and drilling with the rig in the trailer. These days away from the castle he had looked upon as a break from the exigencies of helping to run a colony that faced new dilemmas every day.

There was a large part of him now that looked upon this latest mission as nothing more than an escape.

He heard Kath climb aboard and slam the hatch shut. She appeared in the entrance to the cab. "I'll just go and see how Edvard is."

He nodded and started the engine. They'd loaded Edvard into the truck earlier and settled him in his berth in the rear of the truck. He was still feverish and hallucinating, but he was on the mend. Three days ago he'd come down with fever, and at first Dan had assumed the worst – cholera.

Edvard, one of the colony's three doctors, had put Dan right during a lucid spell. He had malaria, first contracted more than thirty years ago; he said he would ride out the fever and with luck would be well again within a week.

Then, yesterday, Hans had left the colony along with Edvard's daughter Lisa, and Dan had elected not to tell the doctor.

The great timber gate swung open, and with a last wave at Klausner and the others, he steered the truck through the grey archway and down the cobbles towards the cracked tarmac that once, many years ago, had been the ring-road around the city of Copenhagen.

THE SANDS HAD not yet reached this far north.

On his drilling trips south, Dan had entered the northern fringes of the new sandy region. While he feared the slow encroachment of the sands, he had to admit that visually at least the sand-covered landscape was a feature of stark and austere beauty. Contrasted with the blitzed landscape of Copenhagen and its environs – a nightmare of tumbled ruins, abbreviated roads and dead parks and gardens – the desert seemed natural, an obvious consequence of a world without water. The drifting sand, its vast, gentle sweeps of khaki valleys, ridges and escarpments, had inundated all traces of civilisation and seemed to wipe clean the collective mistakes of humankind's sorry past.

There was something redemptive and purifying about the vast landscape of dunes, he thought, and he looked forward to leaving the apocalyptic city

landscape behind him and hitting the stark simplicity
of the sand-shaped world.

At the same time, he knew what the encroaching
sands would bring; not only an end of the old world,
the old order, but an end to any hope that the future
might grant an approximation of the life they had
led in the past. The old times were gone, and only
uncertainty lay ahead.

THE TRUCK RATTLED over the broken highway, passing
an enfilade of concrete stumps that had once been
lamp-posts. The posts had long since been cut down
and used for building materials, the components of
the lamps used and reused in countless small machines
pressed into the service of the colony. Beyond the
highway, empty housing projects stretched away for
as far as the eye could see. There had been a time,
years ago, when nature had taken over the cities,
greened the angular man-made surfaces with natural
mantles, proving abundant foodstuffs for surviving
humans and animals alike. Or so Dan had been told.
He had been born around this time, and recalled
only his mother's stories of plentiful greenery and
roaming wild animals.

Now, the brutal shapes of the urban landscape
seemed nightmarish without the accompanying fields
and trees to alleviate the visual monotony of grey and
black, the hard right-angles of empty buildings.

He turned onto the coast road, or what once had
been the coast road, and headed south. To his right
was the grey regolith of the old sea bed, fissured and

cracked, and dotted here and there with the tipped carcasses of boats. To his left, the countryside was beginning to resemble the grey sea, illimitable and lifeless, marked only by ancient farm buildings, themselves resembling larger boats, becalmed; even the country roads and lanes had been blurred away by the denatured soil. Soon they were travelling over a surface as bare as a lunar landscape, a great plume of dust rising in their wake.

Kath eased herself into the cab beside him. He looked across at her, smiling. "How is he?"

"Asleep, but sweating like hell. At this rate he'll use his water ration in a day." She laid her head back against the rest and closed her eyes. "How are you?"

"I'm okay."

Eyes still closed, she said, "You sure?"

"I'm fine."

He looked across at her. She was in her mid-fifties, and he thought her still beautiful. He'd often reflected on how his appreciation of her beauty had endured over the years. He had a photo somewhere of Kath in her late twenties – which she refused to allow him to display because, she said, it reminded her of how much she had aged. But the fact was that in her lined face, her grey hair, her still-bright blue eyes – shaded though they were with the blight of experience – Dan detected a timeless, elemental beauty that had nothing to do with comparisons to her past appearance. She was beautiful to him, and always would be.

He turned his attention to the land beyond the windscreen, and wished he could say the same about the ageing world without.

He had no idea how much time might have passed before Kath asked, "You think they'll be okay without us for a while?"

He wondered, for a second, if she had somehow worked out his intentions. But that was impossible. "They'll be fine. They've done okay before now."

"But then," she pointed out, "we were away for a day or two at most. It's going to be a little longer this time, isn't it?"

She looked at him.

He shrugged. "Of course."

"How long?"

He hated lying to her. "What...? Ten days minimum, a couple of weeks." He hesitated, then went on, "They have water enough for a month, maybe more. And they have the mobile rig."

"I just hope the cholera doesn't come back. And what if some other disease takes hold? What if Renata...?"

"Kath, they have Doc Symmons." He gripped the wheel and concentrated on driving.

They had left the shattered outskirts of Copenhagen in their wake and were barrelling through what had been farmland. He tried to imagine a fertile landscape, white farmhouses dotting green pastures, but all he saw was the monotonous plain as grey as iron filings stretching to the twilight horizon.

"How long will it take us to reach...?"

"I reckon two days, if we don't stop."

She nodded. "I'm frightened, Dan."

He considered lying and telling her that everything would be fine, but she'd see through him. "I know. So am I."

She had insisted on accompanying him when he told her his plans last night, as he'd known she would. Ordinarily, he would have made sure she'd stayed behind, but not this time.

She said, "I've been doing nothing but going over and over what might happen when we get there."

He shrugged. "We'll be careful, take no risks –"

"Dan, there's half a dozen of them! I wouldn't trust one of the bastards, and as for Hans..."

"I know, I know." Another aspect of his guilt was the danger he would soon be putting her in. He twisted his grip on the wheel and stared ahead.

For the next ten minutes he wondered when might be the best time to tell her.

She interrupted his thoughts with, "I'd feel a lot better about Lisa if I thought she went along with them voluntarily."

"Yes... so would I."

Just over a day ago he'd awoken in the early hours, roused by something that might have been an engine. He'd convinced himself otherwise, however, and slipped back to sleep. But on waking early and setting off on his rounds of the castle walls, he'd discovered that the second working half-track was missing – along with Hans, five other men, and Lisa. There was no sign of a struggle in her room, but that wasn't to say she had gone with them of her own free will.

An hour later, nagged by an awful suspicion, he'd hurried to the filing cabinet in the cellar of the castle, where he'd stashed the map, and found the cabinet prised open and the map gone.

He'd experienced contradictory emotions, then.

Anger at the theft, and fear for Lisa's safety, of course... But he'd meant to leave the colony and head south anyway, and this was the perfect opportunity to do so with an ostensibly legitimate reason.

He had a sudden flash of Hans's gross bullet head then, his squashed nose and curled, sneering lips...

"Dan... tell me the truth, mmm?"

Her words shocked him. "What?"

"You've given up hope of finding her, bringing her back. You said we might not even come across them."

He was relieved that she'd not detected his deceit. "Christ... when I said we might not come across them —"

"You were only trying to make me feel better? Well, thanks a lot, Dan. We've been together over thirty years and you come out with a line like that."

He felt himself colour. "I'm sorry." Barely a whisper.

"You know what, Dan?" she said after a while.

"What?"

"I really want to find Hans and the others and shoot them dead one by one and watch them die in agony."

He was about to express his surprise, but she went on, "For what they've done, who they are. For taking Lisa, stealing provisions... I never liked Hans and his crawling sycophants, but I want to see them dead, now."

"It might even come to that, Kath."

She smiled at him. "We're well armed, Dan."

He nodded. And so were Hans and the others. Food and water wasn't all they'd taken from stores.

He reckoned they were about fifty kilometres from Copenhagen; this was as far as he'd ranged on his excursions in search of water. A few kays back they'd left the last vestiges of civilisation behind: the road was gone, lost beneath fine drifts of dead soil, and no houses, or even the shells of dwellings, showed in the desolate landscape. He was navigating by dint of the truck's compass, and would be doing so all the way to Paris.

"You haven't told Edvard yet?" Kath asked a long time later.

"About Lisa? Of course not."

"When do you intend to?"

"Soon. When his fever breaks and he's stopped hallucinating."

"Break it to him gently, okay? Say she might have elected to go with them. I don't want him thinking they dragged her off..."

He nodded. "I'll play it by ear, okay?"

An hour later Kath brought him a bottle of tepid water, a ration of dried meat and a bowl of greens grown in the colony's scant hydroponics station – though to call the lashed together greenhouse on the castle's tower a hydroponics station was taking a liberty with the facts. The meat was tough and almost tasteless, and the greens – some kind of spinach – salty and bitter, but if he were to tell the truth he'd long ago ceased to appreciate food as a culinary experience: it kept him alive, and that was all he asked.

Kath took over the wheel while he ate, and when he finished he said he'd go and see how Edvard was. "I'll take him some water."

He climbed from the cab and walked drunkenly through the living area, clutching for hand-holds as the half-track swayed back and forth. He took a bottle of water from the rack and moved along the short corridor which gave onto two small berths.

The sliding door was open. Dan hung onto the door-frame, staring in at Edvard.

The old doctor was propped up in his bunk, smiling his thin-lipped smile at Dan. He was the nearest Dan had ever come to seeing a living skeleton. The waste-band of his shorts hung across his shrivelled belly, supported by prominent pelvic flanges, and his ribcage was a lesson in osteo-anatomy.

"You look better."

"I'm through the worst." He tapped a small bottle of pills in his lap. "Physician, heal thyself."

"Water?"

"Could kill for it."

Dan sat on the edge of the bunk and passed the bottle. With a shaking hand, Edvard opened the bottle and tipped it to his lips. His prominent Adam's apple bobbed like a fishing float.

"So... we're on our way. How did you break it to everyone?"

A week ago, when he'd come to a decision about heading south, the only person he'd taken into his confidence had been Ed: he wanted to know if the doctor would accompany them, whether he thought it a risk worth taking. He had known Klausner and the others would veto his plan, but Ed was more far-sighted.

Dan gestured. "I haven't. I mean, I didn't have to..."

Ed's yellowed eyes regarded him suspiciously.

"You're not making sense."

"Hans and his mob took the other half-track and some provisions. They stole the map – the Paris map."

Ed raised a long, brown finger as thin as a cigarillo. "Don't tell me. You told Klausner you had to go after him, get to the cache before Hans?"

"You know me pretty well, Ed."

"I've been watching you for twenty years, Mr Sagar. Of course I know you." His eyes twinkled. "And you haven't told Kath yet, have you?"

Dan looked up, more than surprised. "How do you know?"

"You wouldn't, because Kath would be against the idea. She's essentially conservative, Dan. Against any risk taking. You know that. So you've... what's the expression...? Kept mum. I don't blame you. The thing is, when do you intend to break it to her?"

Dan shook his head. "I don't know. Oh, at some point after we've got Paris out of the way."

"I'll back you up, tell her the truth: that we're doing it for the good of the colony. She knows you were finding less and less water every time you went out. It's time for radical action."

"I just hope she sees it that way, Ed. Christ, I wish I'd told her what I was thinking weeks ago."

Ed smiled. "You were fearful, subconsciously, that she'd talk you out of it."

Dan laughed and clapped Ed's scrawny shoulder. "And I thought you were a general practitioner, not a psychiatrist."

Ed shook his head. "I was neither, Dan. Never qualified, remember? Everything went pear-shaped a year before I was due to take my finals – we just got out there and did what we could."

That was almost sixty years ago. Ed had been in his early twenties then – and the rest of his life had been spent attempting to survive the fall of civilisation. Dan often thought it must have been far greater a hardship for people like Ed, who had tasted the luxuries of civilised life and could contrast that with the privations that followed.

Dan had never known civilisation before the fall, and though part of him regretted never having had the experience, another part of him had no regrets at all.

Ed said, "I take it Lisa's with us? I mentioned it to her, you know, before I fell ill. I told her to keep it to herself, of course."

Dan opened his mouth to say something.

Ed said, "What?" His expression seemed to collapse. "You don't mean she decided to stay back there?"

Dan shook his head. "Ed... you think I'd take you away without giving you the chance to say good-bye – ?"

Ed leaned forward. "Then what?"

"Ed, she went with Hans and the others."

Ed sat back, taking in Dan's words in silence. At last he said, "You mean they took her, don't you?"

Dan shrugged helplessly. "Look, I honestly don't know. There was no sign of a struggle in her room." He gestured uselessly. "Her bag was packed."

"Dan, credit me with a little intelligence. She wouldn't have left without saying goodbye."

"You were ill, delirious."

"Then she would have refused to go with them, period." He took a long swallow of water, then looked at Dan. "They took her, Dan. The bastards took her."

Dan nodded, then looked Ed in the eye. "We're on our way to Paris, Ed. We'll get her back, okay?"

"Are we armed?"

"Of course."

"Good. I'll take great delight in gunning the bastards down myself."

Dan smiled. "A bit earlier Kath said exactly the same thing."

"Always liked the woman's spirit, Dan. Now help me up, I need the toilet."

FIVE MINUTES LATER Dan returned to the cab. Kath smiled at him. "How did he take it?"

He shook his head. "You know Ed. He always puts a brave face on things, whatever happens."

"I'll go talk to him. I'll take some food."

She stopped the truck and clambered from the cab. Dan slipped into the driving seat, wiping sweat from his palms, then started the engine and eased the truck forward.

The sun was directly overhead and the temperature was in the high thirties. Despite the tinted windscreen, the glare was dazzling. The interior of the truck was sweltering, but it would be worse outside: hot enough to fry food on the truck's unshaded metal, should the need arise; hot enough to burn unprotected skin in minutes.

Three hours later, as they were heading south-west over the endlessly flat landscape of what once had been the Netherlands, Dan realised that the terrain had segued seamlessly from the lifeless gunpowder grey soil of the north to the just as lifeless ochre wastes of sand that now covered most of Europe. The going slowed as the half-track churned its way through banked drifts. Occasionally he found the remains of a highway heading south, its surface buried beneath sand and demarcated by parabolic stretches of lamp stanchions, something beautiful and tragic in the way they swept through the blighted landscape, good for nothing now other than guiding the half-track south towards Paris. Dan wondered if Hans had taken this very road; there was always the possibility, he knew, that their truck had failed to make it all the way. He half expected to come across it, stranded in this inhospitable terrain. It would certainly make things easier if that were so, if the confrontation were to take place here, out in the open. He possessed greater firepower than Hans, grenades as well as rifles. He was grateful that the grenades had been in a locked container: Hans and his mob had taken only rifles from the stores.

So far, in all his fifty years, he had managed never to take a human life, though he had lived through hard times and seen others around him driven to fight for their lives. He had seen killings and had even condoned them in the circumstances, the inevitable consequence of kill or be killed, but he had always looked back on the events with a profound gratitude that he had not been called upon to pull the trigger.

He considered the events of ten months ago...

The Copenhagen colony welcomed all comers, with the proviso that newcomers relinquished their weapons and abided by the rules of the colony, a set of dos and don'ts which attempted to retain some semblance of law and order in a lawless world. A year ago Hans, an African called Hamed, and a few others had arrived at the gates of the castle. They were starving and desperate after a long trek from a colony in the south of France. Hans, it transpired, was well versed with all things electric; they were willing to give up their weapons, agreed to abide by the rules, and were accepted into the colony. At the time Kath, Klausner and a couple of others in the ruling committee had expressed reservations about their moral suitability: Kath was a good judge of character, and something about Hans, especially, didn't ring true. Dan had had to set aside his own prejudices – he had to admit that Hans was arrogant and egotistical – but he was willing to give them a chance.

A couple of months later an armed gang raided the castle, entered the workshop where Dan had been repairing a solar array, and held him hostage: the gang, two men and a woman, had demanded supplies in return for Dan's release, and for a couple hours Dan had sweated while they negotiated terms with Klausner.

The gang had just one weapon, an old pistol, and Dan had serious doubts as to whether it was loaded; something about the woman's uncertainty as she pointed the weapon at Dan convinced him that the weapon was either a fake, unloaded, or possessed only one bullet. Close by him, on a shelf beside the window, was a rifle he'd repaired the day before, fully loaded. He had no doubt that he could reach the rifle and take out the woman in seconds... but what stopped him wasn't so much the thought that he might be endangering himself in the process, but that he would have on his conscience the death of someone who, after all, was merely fighting for survival.

Three hours into the siege, the door burst open and Hans came in firing. The woman and her two companions were dead within seconds, three careful, concerted bursts of fire ripping their torsos to shreds.

Dan's reaction shuttled between relief at his rescue and horror at the carnage. He had never seen violent death at such close quarters before, and the reality of men and women being torn to fragments, transformed from alive to dead in an eye-blink, he found profoundly shocking. Almost equally as shocking was the way Hans had strode into the room in the aftermath, turning over the lifeless meat with the toe of his boot and smiling at the efficacy of his marksmanship.

Numbed, Dan had taken the pistol from the woman's severed hand, opened the chamber, and stared at the four bullets lodged there.

He received another shock minutes later when Klausner entered the room and examined the corpses. He knew the woman, he said; ten years ago, when Klausner had been living in the Hamburg colony, the woman had cold-bloodedly killed a family of four – mother, father and two girls – for their store of food and water.

That day had marked a change in the relationship

between Dan and his saviour. He still felt a residual horror at what had happened, and revulsion at Hans's reaction in the aftermath, yet the fact was that in all probability Hans had saved his life. He and Dan had become closer, and Dan had even brought himself to trust the man. In retrospect, he could see that Hans had played on this to ingratiate himself, to work to gain Dan's trust and, through him, the trust of the ruling committee.

And now this.

So much for trust, he thought, as he drove on through the dazzling desert sand and looked ahead to the time of his confrontation with Hans.

"You're miles away."

Kath leaned between the seats, a hand on his shoulder.

He smiled. "Day-dreaming. How's Ed?"

"Sleeping, now. He's had a little food. I think he's through the worst."

"Did he say anything about Lisa?"

"Not a word, and I didn't mention her." She climbed into the cab and sat beside him.

He was thirsty, but he'd had more than half his daily ration of water so far, and wanted to save the rest to accompany his evening meal. He was also hungry, despite the meal a few hours ago, but then these days he was always hungry. That was his default state, along with everyone else in the colony. Month by month, he'd seen the rations cut as the hydroponics gave fewer and fewer returns and the hunting parties came back to the castle empty handed.

"You're quiet, Dan."

"Just thinking..." He paused, then said, "Trying to recall the last animal..."

Kath thought about it. "Last year. The hunters brought back a... what was it, a goat?" She snorted. "For all the meat on the thing."

He recalled the emaciated animal, slung over the back of the hunter. It had been added to a cauldron of broth to feed everyone in the castle, but the animal had hardly flavoured the meal.

"It's been at least five years since we had rats and mice."

He smiled at the recollection of the rodent kebabs he'd eaten then.

"And bugs, Dan. We don't even see many of them, these days."

Until a year ago they'd enjoyed a steady supply of locusts and similar, unidentified insects which, roasted and spiced, made delicious snacks.

He had no doubt that the resulting lack of protein in their diet, along with the failure of some of the legume crops, had made the colony susceptible to the illnesses that had gripped the castle this year.

He changed the subject. "We'll drive for a couple of hours, then how about a break? We'll eat, take a short sleep. We've made good progress so far. We'll set off again around midnight. Should make it to Paris by the end of the day."

Kath nodded. "Let's do that."

The rhythmic swaying of the half-track, and the monotony of the landscape, lulled Dan into a daze. He hallucinated images of long tables piled with food, and Kath, naked, walking towards him.

He shook himself and stared out at the desolation through the windscreen, then turned his attention towards Kath's intent profile as she stared ahead.

"Dan. Look."

He slowed the truck, and stared at where she was pointing. He stopped the truck. The sun was going down directly ahead, a spectacularly bloody, oblate sphere sinking slowly behind a line of dunes.

The view through the windscreen was uniformly ochre, tinged with the blood of the sunset, but ahead and to his left was a spread of colour that, for long seconds, his brain was unable to decode.

Kath said, "Bottles. Plastic bottles. Millions of them."

And with her words, his eyes resolved the illusive images. Light and indestructible, the bottles had floated around the oceans for decades, and then with the vanishing of the seas had blown about the parched land, chivvied by winds, before fetching up in the great drift before them.

"Let's take a look," Kath said.

Dan nodded and smiled, propelled by her infectious enthusiasm. They were no more than bottles, after all, the gross waste product of a sybaritic society, but he knew that to Kath they were things of accidental, surreal beauty – as visually arresting as a natural wonder.

He climbed from the cab, the heat of the late day sealing around him like a cloying blanket. Kath rounded the nose of the truck and together they walked the hundred metres to the foot of the drift. The bottles had caught in the bend of the highway, trapped before a great dune, and rose like so much polychromatic scree.

Laughing, Kath ran ahead and danced into the drift, scattering empty bottles and containers with a series of hollow, percussive rattles. She waded in until she was up to her midriff, then turned to him and held out her arms, an unlikely Venus in the shallows of an artificial sea.

He came to her and they embraced. He felt the softness of her breasts and belly beneath the threadbare fabric of her shirt.

She whispered, "Let's get back to the truck."

They left the plastic shallows hand in hand and entered the truck, hurrying through the lounge to their berth. Kath was already stripping off her shirt and shorts. He stopped in the doorway and watched her, and wondered if he would ever tire of the sight of her nakedness as she lay in the bed and reached out for him.

Afterwards they slept, waking hours later as moonlight slanted in through the circular window at the head of the bed. Dan held her to him, savouring the moment, kissing her lips as a prelude to rising and dressing again.

They ate quickly, and Kath looked in on Ed as Dan moved to the cab and gunned the engine into life. She rejoined him – reporting that Ed was still sleeping – and he steered the half-track back onto the moonlit highway and accelerated.

Through the night and the following day they drove non-stop, taking turns at the wheel, and by mid-afternoon they came at last to the sand-drifted outskirts of Paris itself.

* * *

DAN SAID, "DON'T CRY."

She sniffed. "Can't help it. Just look at it..."

He had brought the truck to a halt on a rise outside the city, and for a while they had sat in silence and looked down on the ruined metropolis. The sand had submerged many districts, but not entirely; the upper storeys of buildings showed above the golden sea, outlining streets and boulevards and hinting at the city's old magnificence. Nothing moved, other than drifts of sand that blew between the buildings.

Ed joined them, appearing between the seats and leaning forward like some ancient, weathered figurehead. "Gay Paree," he murmured. "I never thought I'd see it again."

Kath dashed tears from her eyes and looked at him. "You've been here before?"

"When I was... what? Twenty-five? Around then, anyway. It was still a great city, beautiful and optimistic." He shook his head, then asked quietly, "Do you think Lisa's somewhere down there?"

"We'll find her, Ed," Dan said, with what he hoped sounded like conviction.

"What happened to that?" Kath pointed at a distant, girdered tower, planted seemingly in the centre of the city like some inverted dart in the bulls-eye of a target. Its upper sections were mangled, leaning over at a precarious angle.

"Bombed by terrorists forty years ago," Ed told them. "Some religious fundamentalists, protesting at something. I can't recall. The tower was a symbol of

French greatness, and for 'French' read 'Western.' It had to go. They didn't bring it all down, but what they did was symbolic – France disintegrated as a nation not long after."

Kath said, "And the fundamentalists?"

"Oh, they'll be safe in their paradise, watching us," Ed said without humour.

They sat in silence, staring, until Kath said, "I wonder if anyone...?"

Dan shook his head. "I very much doubt it. The place is lifeless. How would anyone survive?"

"I don't see any sign of the truck," Ed said.

"It might be anywhere in there," Dan said. "I don't know if Hans thought we'd follow him, but he's no fool. He wouldn't take a chance. He's probably concealed the truck in the shell of an old building."

He pulled the map from under the seat, where he'd stowed it before setting off. It was a meticulously drawn copy, which he'd transferred to the precious sheet of pristine paper the day after he'd obtained the original.

He unfolded it carefully and lay it on the gear housing between the seats. In traditional fashion – perhaps in homage to some long forgotten boyhood day-dream – he had marked the position of the cache with a piratical cross. He tapped it.

"It's here, under what apparently was a bank. This street isn't named, but look there..." He indicated a street running parallel with the street where the cross was marked. "Rue Dauphine," he said. "And this one here's the rue Christine."

Ed smiled. "They might not be that hard to find."

Dan looked up. "No?"

"Paris street names were often positioned high on the buildings at intersections," he said. With a bony forefinger he indicated a junction between rue Dauphine and rue Christine. "If we're in luck..."

"It's a pity the tower isn't marked on the map," Kath said.

Dan shrugged. "But this cathedral is, see?" He indicated an ecclesiastical cross to the east of the marked cache.

They returned their attention to the view beyond the windscreen, searching for any sign of a building that might be the required cathedral.

Ed pointed. "How about that?"

Dan made out a long, humped construction, much of its tower crumbled, mired in a sargasso of sand.

"Let's go take a look," he said.

Ed said, "We'd better arm ourselves, just in case."

"Are you up for the search?" Kath said. "Wouldn't you be better staying in the truck?"

"I'm fine, for a malarial octogenarian with revenge fantasies. Are you going to stop me, Kath?"

"Go get the rifles," Dan said. "I'll try to get through to Copenhagen and tell them we've arrived."

He picked up the radio receiver and opened the channel to the castle.

He'd lashed up the first set over twenty years ago in Mont St Catherine, after finding disparate components in a rubbish dump outside the deserted city of Toulouse. Guided by a rat-gnawed do-it-yourself electronics manual, he'd managed to lash together a serviceable two-way set.

For days he'd ranged the wavelengths, tried every frequency, and took the lack of response as evidence that he'd failed somewhere in his manufacture of the radio receiver-transceiver. Then, just as he was about to despair, he'd heard a faint, scratchy voice replying to his plea, "Is there anyone out there?"

Almost inaudible – but filling Dan with the joy that another colony existed somewhere out there – he heard the momentous words, "This is Copenhagen calling. Please come in. I repeat, this is Copenhagen calling..."

Dan still recalled the thrill of that first contact as if it were just yesterday.

From then on he'd kept up daily contact with Copenhagen, exchanging everything from food recipes to advice on the repair of basic machinery with the Danish radio-operator, Jens Klausner. Little did he realise, at the time, that one day he would trek north and be part of the Copenhagen colony, and that Klausner himself would become a good friend.

Now a scratchy reply could be heard, faintly. "Dan... Klausner here."

"We're in Paris, Jens. Do you read?"

The reply was almost inaudible. "...made it. Well done. Any sign of...?"

"No, not yet. We're on the outskirts. I'll call again in a few hours."

A gale of static filled the cab. Dan kept the line open for a few minutes, then cut the connection.

"Nice to hear his voice," Kath murmured, "but it does make me realise how far from home we are."

Dan smiled at her, reassuringly. He started the engine and eased the half-track down the slope towards the first of the derelict buildings.

Ed returned with three rifles and passed two of them through into the cab. Kath took them and lodged the weapons against the dashboard. The sight of the oiled, black weapons gave Dan a flashback to Hans and the siege. One of them might have been the very same rifle Hans had used to kill the woman.

He rolled the half-track past the buildings, sunk up to their middles in the flowing desert. He scanned for any sign of Hans's truck, parked up in the shadows. There was no way the truck's tracks would show in the sand; no sooner had his own truck laid down its distinctive snakeskin patterning than the wind began to cover them with the shifting granules.

They moved through the quiet city and came at last to the remains of the cathedral, a gaping hole at the front of the building affording a view down the aisle to the nave and the crucifix hanging there at an angle.

Dan consulted the map. "If we take it that this is the cathedral," he said, "then the cache is within walking distance. How about we leave the truck here and go the rest of the way on foot?"

Dan eased the truck through the rubble and into the cathedral. The pews had been cleared long ago – gleaned by survivors for firewood, no doubt – and the body of the building was one vast, empty, echoing chamber.

Dan retrieved a flashlight from the glove compartment and clipped it onto the belt of his shorts. From the lounge he fetched half a dozen bottles of water, and from the weapons chest he took three grenades, stowing everything in a backpack. He climbed from the truck and stood with Ed and Kath, staring around the vast interior of the building.

To their right was a high circular window, which ages ago had held stained glass; shards of it still remained, catching the burning sunlight and sending slashes like ruby rapiers across the sand-covered floor tiles.

They turned their backs on the crucifix and walked from the cathedral, Dan leading the way and Kath taking Ed's arm and helping him over the rubble.

They set off west, into the face of the blazing sun. Sand had banked between the walls of the buildings, making the walk a painful slog. Ten minutes later they came to an intersection and, panting, Ed pointed. "What did I tell you?"

A faded blue street sign read: *rue St Michel*.

Dan smiled, allowing himself a scintilla of hope.

He led the way to the end of the street and turned right. The sun burned down, smiting his head in waves; they crossed the street and stepped into cool, dark shadows, the relief from the burning heat immediate.

At the end of the boulevard, Dan hunched down and opened the map.

He pointed. "That row of buildings... the third one along. That's the one."

He stood and checked his rifle, and the others did the same. With a sense of purpose, and not a little apprehension, he set off across the street, back into the sunlight, and approached the grand façade of the erstwhile bank.

The sand had drifted as far as the building's second floor windows, which had been smashed long ago. Dan paused at the foot of the slope, staring up at the blank openings, and then up and down the street. He listened, but the only sound was the constant soughing of the wind, the rasp of sand against stone.

Dan scanned the buildings opposite the old bank, with three high windows overlooking the street. They crossed the street and entered the shadows, then clambered into the building, located the staircase and climbed to the third floor. A broken metal chair lay on the floor, its minimalist design rendering it useless in its fractured state. Kath crossed to the chair, stood it up and tried to work out if it could be repaired. She flung it aside in frustration, then stopped as she saw a picture on the wall.

Dan had seen it too. It was the reproduction oil of a young, dark haired girl in a red dress.

Dan looked at Ed. The old man was staring at the painting.

Dan moved to a window, leaned out and looked up and down the street. He turned to Kath and Ed. "I'm going over to have a look..."

"What if the bastards turn up?" Ed said.

Dan shook his head. "I won't be long."

"I'm coming with you," Kath said.

Dan knew better than to argue with her. He looked at Ed. "You okay here alone?"

"I'll be fine. Just go, and hurry up."

Dan led the way down the stairs and out into the blistering sunlight. They crossed the street, then climbed the drift to the nearest window opening.

It was a relief to be inside again, out of the sun. They stood on bare floorboards, regaining their breath. Sand had seeped in here, covering the timber with its gritty residue, but Dan was glad to see that the building wasn't deep with the stuff.

He led the way across the room to where a staircase gave onto the ground floor. They descended carefully, step by step, aware that others might be just ahead of them.

They reached the ground floor. Sand filled the room to the height of their knees. Three doors led from this room; one, hanging from its hinges, had once opened onto the boulevard. Another gave access to a small neighbouring room. The third opened onto a staircase that led into the bowels of the building.

Dan exchanged a glance with Kath and knew what she was thinking: Could it be so easy?

He unclipped his flashlight, but left it off as he negotiated the first few steps in the half-light. He peered ahead, looking for the tell-tale sign of light down there – but all was gloom.

He switched on his flashlight and played it around, revealing a staircase that corkscrewed further into darkness. He set off down the stairs, moving circum-spectly, aware of Kath's breathing just behind him.

He counted every step as he went, unable to work out why he was doing so. Kath would mock him, calling him... what was it?... anally retentive – the buzzword of some long dead mind-guru. She was always mocking his intellect, hers being superior... though his response was always to ask where intellect had got the human race. Here, he thought now: scrabbling through the ruins in search of precious food supplies.

The spiral staircase unwound and deposited him at the end of a long corridor. There was only one direction in which to head, and he took it.

At one point he felt a touch on his elbow. Kath pointed down at the floor. A fine powdering of sand covered the concrete. He nodded to her: no one had passed this way for quite a while. Ergo, Hans had yet to get here.

According to Klein, the Frenchie from whom he'd obtained the map, the cache was located underground, stashed away in a bank vault by desperate government officials as citizens rampaged through the city, rioting and looting, raping and killing...

Klein had heard about the stash from the son of a bank official; he'd even seen the vault himself, many years ago, but had been unable to penetrate the steel door and the concrete walls protecting its contents.

Dan only hoped that, if they did find the vault intact, then the grenades would prove equal to the job of ripping it open.

The corridor turned at a right angle; his bobbing circle of light illuminated the dusty floor stretching before him, with doors on either side. He tried the first one. It was unlocked, but revealed nothing but a storeroom full of empty shelves. The next one was the same, and the one after that. The fourth door opened onto a waist-deep mess of paperwork.

He walked on, Kath at his side. Ahead, his light illuminated the door of a bank vault, the great wheel of its operating mechanism like the lock on the hatch of a submarine.

He paused, his heart thudding. He said. "This is it..." then realised it had come out as barely a croak and repeated himself.

He exchanged a glance with Kath.

She reached out and touched the wheel. To his surprise, and obviously Kath's – as she exclaimed and stood back – the door swung open ponderously.

He stepped forward and played his flashlight around the interior of the vault. The chamber was vast, and vacant. They passed inside, as if to check every corner for anything that might have been overlooked. The chamber was empty; even dust had not found its way inside.

He returned to the door and checked the mechanism. The great barred lock was discoloured, and the steel jamb of the doorframe was twisted, misshapen.

Kath murmured, "I thought it was too good to be true." She paused. "Let's get out of here. I'm getting spooked."

They hurried back the way they had come, walking fast. It would be just their luck if, after finding the cache empty, they should run right into Hans and his cohorts.

They climbed the spiral staircase to the ground floor, then took the staircase to the first floor room and emerged, blinking, into the dazzling light.

To their right, the rectangle of the window burned like a gold ingot with the late afternoon sun.

"And now?" Kath said as they paused before the opening.

He said, "We might not have found the cache, but at least we got here before Hans and company..." He let it hang.

He helped Kath over the window sill and down the sliding sand. He looked up, across the street. Framed in the central window, Ed peered out at them. Dan waved, then gave a thumb's down sign. They crossed the boulevard; as he was about to step over the sill into the building, he looked back. Their footprints showed as series of staggered dimples, but already the wind was working to cover the evidence of their passage.

Minutes later they were climbing the stairs to where Ed was waiting. He turned from the window. "Nothing?"

Dan told him what they'd found.

"I can't say I'm all that surprised," Ed said.

Dan nodded. "It was a long shot," he said. "I was still hopeful, though. Call me a fool."

He moved to the central window, leaned out and looked up and down the street.

The city was silent.

He opened his backpack, pulled out bottles of water and passed them round.

Cradling their weapons, they sat on the floor in the shadows and waited.

CHAPTER FOUR

ONE OF XIAN'S earliest memories was of her father leaving home for the very last time.

The year was 2025 and she was four years old. She lived in London, in one of the new towerpiles reserved for top government officials – or government high-ups, as her mother liked to joke. Xian thought the granting of such a wonderful place to live, with spectacular views of the capital city all around, was a reward for all her father's hard work. Only later, in her teens, did she learn that the towerpiles were like mediaeval castles, where politicians and civil servants lived for protection. Even then the world was breaking down little by little, and politicians were bearing the brunt of the citizens' collective anger.

At the time, though, as far as Xian was concerned, her childhood was idyllic and the towerpile a fairy-tale place to live.

Her best friend was Richard, a boy a year older than Xian, whose father worked in the foreign office. "Daddy was posted abroad last week," Richard once told her. "He's working in Tashkent now."

With the literal-mindedness of a child, Xian imagined Richard's father being packed up in a big box and posted off to a far away land with a strange name.

One day they were playing in the sand-pit at the foot of the towerpile. A grey metal barrier prevented her from seeing the surrounding city. She was slathered in factor one hundred sun cream, to which the sand adhered and made her itch.

Richard was an irrepressibly happy boy who wanted to do nothing but build high, improbable towers from building blocks, and was comically disappointed when gravity thwarted his efforts.

"What does your daddy do?" Richard asked her one day.

Xian thought about that. "He works for the government."

"Yes, but what exactly does he do?"

She pulled a face. "I think he's a scientist," she replied. "He studies the poles."

Richard squinted at her. "Like, telephone poles?" he asked innocently.

Xian laughed. "No, silly! He goes to the North Pole and does experiments and things."

He was part of a UN commission charged with calibrating the melting of the polar ice caps, though that was another fact she found out about only in her teens.

That night, she said a tearful goodbye to her father. He was taking a plane to the North Pole again, for the second time that year, and told her that he would be back in a few days.

Xian had cried herself to sleep, and dreamed of her father in the land of Inuits and polar bears.

Three days later, when she arrived home from school, two tall men in suits were talking to her mother in the lounge. Her mother had been crying, and gripped a shredded tissue in her right fist. One of the men saw Xian as she appeared in the doorway, and she would never forget the expression of compassion on his face as he regarded her.

That night, her mother told her that her father had died of a heart attack while working at an ice station at the North Pole.

Not long after that, she and her mother left the towerpile and moved into the country north of London. She didn't even have time to say goodbye to Richard.

Her mother managed a hydroponics farm, one of many created to provide food for the growing population, and Xian attended a tiny village school.

She loved the village, though she missed her father. She was surrounded by wildlife, rabbits and squirrels in the garden, and at night she was allowed to camp out on the lawn. She would lie with the tent-flap open and stare at the massed stars overhead, and dream of exploring distant planets in a rocketship.

To Xian, the future was still a place of limitless possibilities.

CHAPTER FIVE

SAMARA WAS IN the workshop when she received the summons from her father.

A day had passed since Ivan had again brought up the idea of a raid, and Samara knew that that would only be possible if they had suitable transport to carry a raiding party hundreds of kilometres across the desert to the Turin colony. To this end she had summoned a meeting of her engineers and technicians in the workshop adjacent to the garage where a couple of old transporters were kept.

They were a motley crew, she had to admit. Arno and Salif were in their fifties, but retained in their greying heads a knowledge of mechanics Samara had thought long lost. A couple of years ago, when she put out a discreet call among the colonists for people who had worked in the sciences, no one had volunteered themselves, perhaps for fear of retribution from her technology-hating father. Only as her father's hold on power in the castle waned, and Samara gained influence, had people with scientific knowledge come forth. Arno and Salif had worked on solar arrays and refrigeration in other colonies; Giovanni and a couple of other young men and women had volunteered themselves as eager and willing to learn.

For the past year, Samara had sent out scavenging parties to scour the old cities and towns, many subsumed by the desert, in search of machinery parts. Solar arrays had been easy to find, glittering like diamonds in the light of the sun; most were dysfunctional, but even these could be cannibalised to provide parts for working units. Sometimes they even came across arrays that needed no work at all. To date they had perhaps fifty large panels, which they would distribute around the battlements of the castle and on the carapace of the most reliable transporter.

Samara inspected the panels under repair. Arno was supervising Giovanni in the soldering of leads and circuit boards. Salif and a couple of youngsters were attaching functioning solar panels to the roof of the transporter.

Samara stared up at the work in progress. The stench of burning solder filled the air. "And the engine itself?"

Salif paused in his work and looked down at her. "We'll know more when the arrays are running. It seems to be in good repair, considering it hasn't been working for a couple of years."

If the raiding party came off, and the hydroponics garden improved its yield, then Samara foresaw a prosperous time ahead for the colony.

She was about to pay a visit to the repair-shop next door where another team was working on the hydroponics system, when a young man appeared at her side. "Samara, your father wishes to see you."

Such a forthright summons from her father was uncommon. She dismissed the messenger and wondered what her father wanted. She decided to visit the repair-shop later, and made her way across the central courtyard to the residential tower.

Gretchen met her at her father's door. "How is he today?" Samara asked.

"It's one of his better days, Samara. He's alert and lucid."

She hurried into the outer room and passed into her father's bedroom, closing the door behind her.

She was surprised to find that her father was not in bed. He was seated in a big armchair before the window, staring out across the desert at the setting sun. Another surprise: he was fully dressed in the casual trousers, white shirt and cravat he had made his uniform over the years.

He appeared massive, a king dominating the room in his throne.

"Pull up a chair," he ordered. "Here. Sit next to me."

Samara found a straight-backed chair and placed it next to her father's.

He gestured with a big hand, indicating the desert scene and the dying light. "It's beautiful, isn't it?"

Samara smiled. Had he brought her here to discuss the aesthetics of the sunset? "Very."

"Nature is deceptive, Samara. Or is it that our senses are deceptive?"

"Father?"

He gestured again. "Such beauty we perceive – the grandiloquent colours, its spread... It conjures happiness in the heart, joy even. That's what our senses perceive. But... our minds? Our minds appreciate that it's this very object, this fiery ball that is bringing death to the world."

He regarded her sadly, and Samara had to suppress her irritation. Had he brought her here to tell her what she already knew?

"Samara, why is it, do you think, that for so long I have counselled against the use of technology here in the castle?"

She sighed. "You mistrust it. You said it brought us to where we are today."

"And so it has. But there's another reason."

Ah... she thought: at last, close to the end, he is about to unburden himself of his past, his fraught relationship with his own father.

He said, "Thanks to what the old society, fuelled by the unrestrained quest for scientific understanding, has done to the world, we stand on the edge of extinction. One way out – a short term fix, as I see it – would be to harness technology... but there is a flaw in this thinking."

She stared at his lined face, his sad, watery eyes. "Which is?"

"Quite simply that to use technology to make easier our lot would require a manufacturing infrastructure we do not possess. There are few of us left – on the planet, never mind here in the colony – and we've lost the skills required, quite apart from the manpower, to mine resources, to produce the materials we would need to sustain whatever technologies we deemed useful." He shook his head. "Your instigation of the use of solar panels, electricity –"

She looked at him, shocked. "You know?"

"Do you take me for a fool? Of course I know." He waved this away. "As I was saying, the use of technology is all very well, but without the manufacturing base to back it up it's doomed to failure: systems will atrophy, parts will wear out and be impossible to replace. It might work very well in the short term, with the bits and pieces we can scavenge and repair, but entropy will win out in the end."

She marshalled a reply and kept her voice even. Even as she spoke, the small child within her quaked at her effrontery. "And so your answer is to give in, is it? To go on living as we have been for years, and eventually descend into barbarism, scraping an existence like animals?"

Something hardened in his regard of her. "No, of course not."

"Then I don't see an alternative. If you proscribe the use of technology –"

"Listen to me! I have an answer."

She shook her head wearily. "Go on."

"The surface of the planet is parched, water burned away. Life on the surface is doomed. But underground..."

She stared at him. This was evidence, if any were needed, that he had indeed parted company with his senses.

"Hear me out!" he snapped. "Many years ago, when I was young, my father worked for the European Space Agency. They had a top secret project – all the countries of Europe were in on it – a means of saving the planet from the inevitable catastrophe it faced." He looked across the room, his gaze falling on the old tin rocket from his childhood. "They developed a propulsion system, a means of taking a starship from earth by means of phasing it into a void that underlay this reality..."

She stared at him as he jabbered on, clearly out of his mind. At last she said, as gently as her irritation would allow, "First you said our salvation was underground, and then you go on about starships?"

He waved testily. "Listen to me. My father and the other scientists and technicians constructed a vast ship – underground, kilometres underground – in a great cavern, a cavity of concrete hives and chambers, with at its core the launching dock and the starship itself."

She smiled to herself. It sounded like the fantasy of a deranged mind. "I don't see..." she began, tired.

"My father left papers, plans." He gestured across the room, to a desk burdened with reams of yellow paper, old folders and print-outs. "They're in Spanish and Dutch, and incomplete. I've worked for years to try to make sense of them."

"What happened to the ship?" she asked, humouring him.

"My father told me, in my teens, that it had been damaged or destroyed – I can't recall which – by terrorists opposed to the salvation of a select few...

this was many years ago, just before the Breakdown and the wars. The scientists sealed the breach in the cavern, tried to save the project, but it proved impossible."

"And our only hope of survival...?"

He gestured to the papers. "I've been translating what my father left among his effects, piecing together facts. I know where the underground headquarters of the operation was situated, and I have the operating codes which would allow access to the buried chambers."

"And you're suggesting that we relocate, live underground?"

He turned his grizzled head and regarded her, as if trying to detect mockery. "Samara, according to the literature, the Agency stock-piled food supplies that would last as long as it took to get the ship launched, decades if need be. What I suggest... what I have been dreaming of for" – he waved – "for a long time, was that we could make an exploratory trip, locate the chamber, find the stores. Then we could begin the migration, with a view perhaps to relocating underground. We could dig ever deeper, locate hidden aquifers. There must be water in plenty far beneath the surface." He stared at her, his gaze hard. He reached out and gripped her arm, the gesture in no way affectionate. "Samara, one day the human race might not be dependant on the sun as a source of life. If we as a species were to become troglodyte, starting in the early days with the resources at our disposal in the chambers..."

He fell silent, the light of fanaticism in his eyes,

and Samara detached his fingers from her arm and massaged the reddened skin.

The idea of taking her people and living underground was sheer madness, she knew, but the idea of hoarded stores, reserves of food and presumably water in the sealed underground chambers... If she could locate the provisions, transport them back to the castle – or perhaps even establish a fortified colony...

She asked, "Where is the chamber?"

"It is situated in north Spain. Not far, relatively speaking, from here. The agency had its headquarters in Bilbao, and the chambers were located just outside the city on a coastal plain." He looked at her. "What do you think?"

She nodded. "It's... it's an interesting idea."

He waved towards his desk. "I've translated most of what I deemed relevant. Take the papers. Study them."

The thought of stores and provisions hoarded underground filled her chest with a tight sensation of excitement. "I'll do that."

"Despite your wayward ideas, Samara, you might make a leader yet." He paused, then went on, "You're so much like your mother. Have I told you that?"

"Often," she said. "I must go."

She stood, and he raised himself unsteadily to his feet and watched her. She had a sudden urge, or desire, to embrace him, but nothing in his stance was in the least encouraging.

She moved to the desk and took a pile of print-outs and folders.

"Good luck, Samara."

She paused by the door, and looked back at the big, stooped old man who for so long had loomed large in her thoughts. He sounded as if he were making his last farewell.

Samara hurried from the room.

SHE TOOK HER father's papers to the library in the eastern tower of the castle, opposite the residential quarters. There she lit two short, fat candles and pulled down an atlas from the crammed shelves. She sat at the bulky oak table her father had once told her was almost three hundred years old. As a child she had often retreated to the library and traced the scars and scores on the polished table-top, wondering at the people who had made these marks, people long dead and forgotten by history.

And now her father wanted her to lead her people to a new life... She wondered how she would be recalled by history, always supposing that there were people around in future to look back and record the events of long ago.

She opened the atlas, found France, and located the old town of Aubenas where the castle was situated. She gazed at the scattering of bigger and smaller dots and shaded areas that denoted villages, towns and cities, linked by the snaking lines of roads. It was hard to conceive that in each of these labelled dots had lived thousands and millions of people, going about their lives of plenty in ignorance of the future about to wipe them and their way of life from the face of the planet. She read the names of villages and towns, liking the way they sounded on her tongue, and wondered if she were the only human being on the planet at the moment pronouncing these place names.

All gone now.

She traced a long line across the bottom of the country and found the city of Bilbao on the northern coastline of Spain. The map showed roads straddling the mountain range known as the Pyrenees. That would have been the way to go, back then, but now there was an easier route to the Spanish city: across the desert as far as the dried up sea, and then south to the old coastline of Spain. She calculated that it would be a journey of around a thousand kilometres, and would take perhaps five days. Always assuming, of course, that Arno and Salif could get the transporter repaired and working.

She looked ahead, saw herself embarking on the perilous journey across the desert, and couldn't help feeling a frisson of excitement at the prospect. She wondered who she would take with her; people she trusted, of course, and who at the same time would have the skill and courage to defend the troupe from potential marauders.

She was getting ahead of herself.

She pulled her father's papers closer, opened the first folder and began reading.

There were pages and pages of technical details, reports from functionaries on the progress of certain mechanical procedures. The words meant nothing to Samara, and she skimmed.

She read through pages of reports on crew and technicians, physical and psychological profiles of scientists, technicians and pilots, all transcribed from the original Spanish in her father's neat, looped handwriting. These she found of more interest; at least she could understand what the words meant, and the personal details gave the plans a human dimension and at the same time brought home to her how vast and complex the project had been. She read that the starship would ferry five thousand colonists to the stars, and that three thousand ground-based technicians and scientists would be working on the project over a period of a decade. She wondered at the dashed hopes of the colonists as their dreams of life beneath other suns was doomed with the terrorists attacks on the base and the cumulative breakdown of society.

Then she came to the schematics of the base itself, and tried to make sense of the blueprints showing the various – six, so far as she could make out – levels. The subterranean base was indeed like a city, with marked dormitories, recreation areas including tennis courts and bowling alleys, pedestrian esplanades and factories. At the centre of the schematic was an area labelled as the embarkation berth, a vast well a kilometre deep, from which the starship would presumably phase into the void.

In her father's meticulous hand she read the locking codes to the vault hatches that gave access to each level, along with his precise instructions as to how to find the base in relation to the city. It was as if, she thought, he had known all along that he would not accompany whoever would make the final journey, but had laid down instructions for those who would.

There was no specific mention of supplies in his notes, but she supposed that they could be taken as a given: where thousands of humans lived in a community, there would be provisions for their day to day living.

She wondered if her father had considered the possibility that, upon the evacuation of the base following the terrorists' raid, the stores had been emptied.

She smiled to herself as, a little later, she read a note written by her father to the effect that, after the attack, the project base was sealed and the various government scientists and technicians, along with ancillary staff, moved to bases around Europe to work on the management of the ongoing civil crises that had stricken the continent. He had finished with: "I recall my father saying that stores and provisions were left in situ against the time when the ESA could return to Bilbao and renew work upon the project. Some hope!"

If the chambers were still intact and able to function, then perhaps they could serve as a base for a future colony. Already, life at the castle had become nocturnal, with more and more people choosing to sleep during the daylight hours. No one went out in the full light of the sun these days – unless they had a death wish – and scavenging and hunting parties were returning with less and less in the way of usable goods and foodstuffs. The heat of the day and the light of the sun were fast becoming inimical to human life, so perhaps her father's suggestion of a troglodyte existence underground was not as absurd as it seemed. If the colony could utilise solar arrays for power, and develop a sustainable hydroponics system, then trips to the surface would be minimal and life in the cool depths the way ahead for the human race.

Before any of that might be realised, of course, there was the simple matter of being able to make the trip from the castle, across the south of France to Bilbao.

There were more notes and papers to read, but she decided to save these for another day. She gathered up the papers, left the library and walked the long corridor to the residential tower. She locked the papers in her room, then descended and crossed the courtyard to the workshop.

Arno, Salif, Giovanni and the others were still working away in the glare of flaming torches, which gave the scene the appearance of an industrial hell. Salif was singing, something doleful in his native Arabic.

She moved to the adjacent garage and walked around the transporter, examining its chunky, segmented tracks and battered bodywork. It had been excoriated by countless sojourns beneath the merciless sun over the years before it came into the possession of the colony, and she wondered if it would be up to further punishment. A thousand miles through the desert was a long way, and the vehicle had last driven anywhere a couple of years ago, when it had arrived at the castle with refugees from the failed Florence commune.

As she watched, Salif and Giovanni carried a big solar array between them and hoisted it onto the roof of the transporter; a dozen others sat there, so that the vehicle was beginning to resemble an overgrown, jewelled beetle.

Giovanni grinned at her from his perch on the roof, and she favoured him with a smile. Maybe she would select Giovanni, with his unthinking devotion and his youthful physique, to accompany her on the trip to Spain.

She called up to Salif, "How soon before you can test the engine?"

He lifted the welding mask and peered down at her. "We'll have the panels in position and ready to test later tonight. After that, if they work... then perhaps we can check the engine."

She moved to the hatch of the transporter and climbed inside. The truck was long and low, the central section fitted out with shelves and storage units. The people who had arrived in the vehicle had told her father that the truck had belonged to a mineral exploration company, more than thirty years ago. It was a testament to its builders that it was still in working order.

A narrow corridor led to cramped berths to right and left and, at the very rear of the truck, a larger room with a shower unit in one corner. All it needed to make it a home away from home was a comfortable bed and a rug or two. She decided that this would be her room when the mission was finally underway.

She was stepping from the transporter when she noticed, across the workroom, the arrival of the same young man who hours earlier had come with the summons from her father. She was to look back, later, and reflect on the irony that the night had started and finished with her visiting her father.

She knew, as soon as the youth caught sight of her, that all was not well. Her stomach tightened. He hurried over. "Samara, it's your father... Dr Mortenson is with him..."

She hurried away with him, leaving Giovanni and Salif staring after her.

"What is it?"

"His maid found him and summoned the doctor."

She knew he couldn't be dead, not so soon after she had seen him. It would be another of his turns, his sick spells, and after a draft of something from Mort he would be on his feet again.

Yet, even as she told herself this, a small, treacherous voice was saying: not this time...

It took an age to traverse the courtyard and climb the stairs to her father's room, and on the way she saw the furnishings and fittings with a greater clarity. She noticed her father's favourite picture – a simple wooden chair in oils – and it appeared to leap out at her with its knobbly rusticity. And the carpet along the corridor leading to his chambers was worn by his constant pacing up and down.

She fought back the tears as she burst into his rooms.

The doors at the far end of his study were open, and through them Samara saw the hunched figure of Gretchen, weeping, and Dr Mortenson standing erect and solemn beside the figure of her father.

He was sitting up in bed, his head lax on banked pillows. Dr Mortenson hurried around the bed to her. "Samara, I'm sorry. By the time I arrived... there was nothing I could do."

She hardly heard his words. She sat on the bed, heavily. She saw that her father was clutching that ridiculous tin rocket-ship to his chest, and in his other hand he held a glass, whose powdery dregs were trickling onto the counterpane.

Hit by a dawning suspicion, she looked up. "No?"

Dr Mortenson lay a hand on her shoulder. "It was your father's wish, Samara. He was ill and dying, and he didn't want to linger. He would have felt no pain."

She was about to say that he could at least have said goodbye, and then smiled tearfully to herself as she realised that he had.

The wild animal, trapped, had finally released itself.

Apart from the grief, burning within her, she felt resentment and anger: she resented her father for not letting her show her affection, and hated him for never showing the same towards her. And now he was dead, and any rapprochement there might have been was impossible.

She removed the glass from his slack fingers and took them in her own. His hand was still warm. His eyes were closed, and his face appeared peaceful and at rest.

She wondered if he had died content, satisfied that he had told her about the base at Bilbao.

She stood suddenly. "We'll have the burial ceremony on the old rampart garden at sunset,

Mort. I want everyone in attendance." Her father had done away with funeral services years ago, as they had worked to lower the colony's morale. But this was different, after all. Her father had been not only their leader, but their saviour. She went on, "If you could say a few words..."

The doctor inclined his head. "Of course."

She managed to smile at Mort and Gretchen before she fled the room and hurried to her own chamber, where she flung herself across the bed and wept.

CHAPTER SIX

PAUL SLUMPED IN the corner of the room, his hands and feet tied painfully.

He kept his eyes shut, not wanting to alert the strangers to the fact he was awake. He supposed he should be grateful that they hadn't killed him immediately, but he wasn't looking forward to what they might do when they realised he was no longer unconscious.

His belly clenched with hunger pangs, and he realised it was a long time since he'd eaten. Then he thought of Elise. He'd said he'd be back in a couple of hours. She couldn't look after herself: she needed him to forage for food, to cook and feed her.

She'd be assuming the worst now, and the thought of the anguish she'd be going through, as she looked ahead into a bleak future, sickened him.

He opened his eyes a slit and peered around the room. Achmed and three others sat in the middle of the floor, around the remains of the fire and the girl's arched ribcage. Before the window was the red dress, its splash of colour the only beautiful thing in the room. There was no sign of Hans and the African.

Achmed had picked up Paul's crossbow and was turning it over, examining its sleek lines. Elise had told Paul that his father had made the bow. Paul treasured it, the only thing that linked him to his father; he didn't even have memories, as his father had died, according to Elise, shortly after his birth. Paul wanted to take the bow, smash its weighted butt into the Arab's sly, grinning face.

Only Achmed was facing Paul, and he seemed absorbed in his study of the weapon. He thought that if he could work loose the straps that bound his ankles, then even with his hands tied behind his back he stood a chance of diving through the window and fleeing, losing his pursuers in the intricacies of the city. Achmed and the others looked thin and weak to him, unable to sustain a prolonged chase. Of course, he had to untie his ankles first.

He rubbed his feet together, attempting to establish some play in the rope that bound his ankles. There was precious little, and the rubbing only served to burn the rope into his flesh.

Perhaps if he could free his hands...

Behind his back, he worked his hands back and forth. There was more give in the rope here, and for a second he felt a surge of hope.

Then Achmed looked up and snapped something in a rapid, glottal tongue to one of the others. He stood and aimed the crossbow at Paul. He'd taken the bolts from Paul's pouch and slotted one of them into the breach.

"I think that would be a mistake, my friend," Achmed said. "Hans would be very angry."

Paul opened his eyes fully and gazed at Achmed. All four men were looking at him now. He tried to keep his expression blank, not wanting to show his fear.

One of the men spoke to Achmed in his own language.

Achmed smiled. "Latif, he says Hans likes man as well as woman."

Paul tried to make his expression blank, uncomprehending. He didn't want to give the bastard the satisfaction of knowing he understood exactly what Latif meant.

The Oriental said, "You speak English, yes?"

Paul stared at the man, taking in his dull protuberant eyes, his moronic underslung jaw. There was something sadistic in his regard of Paul.

The Scandinavian spoke in French, "You understand me, yes? When Hans gets back, we'll decide: eat, or fuck?" He opened his mouth in a grin that revealed a set of rotting teeth.

Paul kept his expression rigidly neutral.

The Scandinavian said, in English, "Fuck first, then eat. Why not?"

The Oriental turned to the Scandinavian. All four spoke then in hushed, hurried tones, glancing at him from time to time. He detected that the mood among the men had changed, subtly, from one of sadistic fantasising to the understanding that there was nothing to stop them from turning theory into practice.

The Scandinavian slipped his hand down the front of his shorts and eased his erection into a more accommodating position.

The Oriental licked his lips, gazing over at Paul with something malign in his eyes. Then Achmed said, loud enough for Paul to make out, "But what would Hans say? You know he likes first dip."

Latif, said, "Fuck Hans!" He was unfastening the cord that tied his ragged trousers, and dropped them to reveal a huge, nodding cock. He smiled across at Paul, his expression all the more terrifying for its pantomime tenderness. He said, "Turn over," and accompanied the command with a gesture.

Paul attempted to push himself into a standing position. If the bastards came near him he'd go at them with his head...

From the corner of his eye, Paul saw something flash through the air. He heard a cry and Latif fell to the floor clutching his shoulder, a fist-sized brick on the floor beside him.

Hans climbed into the room, taking the sill in one stride, and stood looking around at his abject band. The African entered the room in his wake, taking in the scene with distaste.

Paul froze, attempting to make himself as small and as inconspicuous as possible.

The Scandinavian was attempting to stuff himself back into his shorts. Achmed danced around Hans, hands spread, pleading his innocence in ingratiating tones. Hans backhanded him out of his way, strode over to the squirming Latif and swung a vicious kick into the man's midriff. The Arab rolled away, moaning.

Hans stood over him and drew a pistol from his shorts. He looked back over his shoulder. "So this is what you bastards get up to when I'm gone?"

The Oriental said, "We were only..."

"They didn't mean to..." Achmed began, silenced by Hans's white hot glare.

"You were only going to fuck the Frenchie without asking my permission? I said guard him, not fuck him." He grinned. "Well, this is what happens to disobedient bastards who don't think..."

And he turned to the moaning Arab on the floor, aimed the gun at his head and pulled the trigger.

The body jumped once, and a shockingly powerful geyser of bright blood arched into the air and slashed across the far wall.

Somebody groaned. Achmed hugged himself, biting his lips, and turned away. The African stood tall, watching calmly, taking in the depravity of his cohorts with an air of what looked like superior contempt.

Paul could not tear his eyes away from the blood still pumping from the Arab's head. He considered what Hans had said and wondered how he might be of use to the German.

Hans slipped his pistol back into the band of his shorts and turned to the others, staring at them until one by one they turned away, cowed. Only the African remained staring at Hans, and this time it was Hans who turned away.

He moved across the room towards Paul and knelt before him. Paul tried not to flinch as the German's putrid body odour and bad breath washed over him.

He smiled at Paul. "You speak English?"

Paul looked blank.

"French?"

Achmed danced into sight. "We tried both, Hans."

Hans went on, in English, "You live in the city? You know the city?"

Paul played dumb.

The African said, "Tell him that if he speaks to us, agrees to help, then he can join us."

Hans, clearly piqued by the African's suggestion, stared at Paul. "Look, if you don't co-operate..." His eyes, eloquently, shuttled towards the corpse of the Arab in the corner of the room.

Paul held his tongue.

Hans stood and joined the African. They conferred in hushed tones. He pulled the map from his shoulder-bag, unfolded it and approached Paul again. He hunkered down and spread the map on the floor.

He tapped the centre of the map, and the red circle, with a meaty forefinger. "Do you recognise this area?" He paused. "Do you understand me?"

Paul tried to calculate the best response. He needed to buy himself time, give himself the opportunity to be untied, and take it from there.

He was about to nod that he understood when Hans yanked the pistol from his shorts and placed it against his temple. The circumference of its barrel was surprisingly cool against his skin.

The African shouted, "No!" He strode across to Hans. "Let me try..."

Reluctantly, Hans stood and moved away. The African knelt before Paul, who thought he detected something like sympathy in the man's dark brown eyes.

"Listen, pal," he said in French. "Listen to me... It's like this. We need to find things in the city – food and water, okay? You understand me? Now, you help us, and we'll feed you, okay?" He paused, then went on, "So do yourself a favour, hm? You recognise this area on the map?" He tapped the red circle and looked at Paul.

Paul turned his attention to the map. There was the cathedral, and rue Dauphine and rue Christine. The red circle marked a building about a kilometre from here.

He knew what he had to do.

He looked at the African and nodded. "Untie me and I'll show you where it is," he said in French.

The African smiled and looked up at Hans, who said, "Untie his feet, not his hands."

The African eased Paul to his feet, then cut the binds that chaffed his ankles.

Paul moved his feet, working the muscles. He tried not to smile. He was not free yet, but at least now freedom was a possibility.

Hans said to the Oriental, "Tie the rope around his hands and don't let go of it." He looked at Paul and said, "And don't even think about trying to get away." He tapped the pistol at his side and smiled.

The Oriental attached a length of rope to his bound wrists and led him across the room to the window. He eased himself over the sill, helped by the African.

They paused in the sand outside the building, the Oriental nervously clutching the rope as if Paul were a wild animal.

It was late afternoon, and the sun was easing itself down behind a line of buildings to the west. The heat of the day was abating. He thought of Elise, then tried to push images of her from his mind, along with his guilt.

"Okay," Hans said, "lead the way."

Paul turned towards the setting sun and set off through the sand.

HE LED THEM through the ruins of Paris, traversing the streets from one patch of shade to the next. He affected a limp, slowing their progress and, he hoped, buying himself some valuable time.

Even though the sun was dipping over the horizon, he guessed the temperature was still in the high thirties. He thought of the thermometer in the basement, which Elise had told him belonged to her grandmother. She would be fretting now, fearing him dead, crushed beneath fallen masonry or having fallen from the tower. He hoped she had not drained the bottle of water he had left beside her bed.

If he had not recognised the area on the map, he wondered, would they have killed him there and then, having first taken their pleasure? He would have been of little use to them – just like the girl.

Which made him realise that, once he had led them to the building, he would have served his purpose. He had little doubt that they would then butcher him.

He slowed the pace even further, grimacing with feigned pain and favouring his right leg. His captors said nothing, accommodating themselves to his slow progress. They shared a bottle of water amongst themselves, but pointedly refrained from offering him a swallow. Why, he thought, quench the thirst of a dead man?

He paused on the corner of the street, in a dense patch of shadow. Slowly, so as not to alarm his captors, he hunkered down, regaining his breath, and the others took the opportunity to rest with him.

Hans, he noticed, was constantly scanning the streets and buildings, as if wary of an ambush. This made Paul wonder if this group was not alone, was part of a larger band come to the city in a bid to uncover the stash of food and water.

What would their reaction be, he thought, when they discovered that the supplies had been taken from the building long ago? When Elise had been mobile, perhaps five years ago, they had explored the ruins together, Elise giving him a running commentary on the significant points of the once great city, and he recalled the place they were heading to now. Elise had called it a bank, and had to explain to him the meaning of the word and what it had represented. She had also told him that, years before his birth, the Paris colony had blown open the vault in the bank's cellar – hoping to discover a horde of provisions rumoured to have been placed there – only to find it empty.

He knew he had to make a run for freedom before they reached the old bank.

He glanced at the Oriental. The man was squatting on his haunches, his moronic expression sapped of anything but discomfort at the heat. His right hand gripped the rope, but not tightly. A good yank, Paul thought, would be all it'd take...

They were perhaps halfway to the bank now. Soon they would be passing a terrace of ancient apartments, the interior of which was a tumbledown warren where he judged that, even with his hands tied, he would quickly be able to lose his pursuers.

He told himself that soon he would be free.

In the meantime, he would bide his time and conserve his strength.

He looked around at the enclosing buildings, buried to their second floors by the all-consuming sand. He wondered what it would have been like to experience the streets before the arrival of the desert. They would have been deeper back then, the walls looming claustrophobically over the pedestrians, the shadows longer, and at night the streets would have been filled with artificial lights; crowds had thronged the streets at all times, and the roads would have been noisy with traffic. He had seen photographs of the bustling city centre in old books, and Elise had tried to explain how it had been, the noise and the constant activity, the surging crowds of thousands and thousands of citizens, each with only their own destinations in mind.

For so long it had been only Paul and Elise. His memories of other people, of the colony he had been born into, were so dim he hardly recalled them. He had fleeting impressions of perhaps a dozen people living in an underground system of basements, a dozen souls who, as the years progressed, had died or left, striking out north in search of fabled colonies, until only he and Elise remained. Or perhaps these memories were nothing of the sort, but instead the recollections of memories of Elise telling him how the colony had eroded over the years.

What he did know for sure was that this ruthless band of killers constituted the largest group of people he had come across in years.

"Okay," Hans barked. "That's long enough. Up." And he emphasised the order with a prod of his booted foot to Paul's thigh.

He stood and set off again, leading them around the corner into the last glare of the setting sun. They crossed the street and entered the shade. They were perhaps a couple of hundred metres from where Paul knew he had to make a run for it.

Something tightened in his stomach. He took deep breaths, calming his fear.

The African came alongside, glancing at him as he asked in French, "You live alone in the city?"

Paul saw no reason not to reply, though not with the truth. He nodded. "I live alone here, yes."

The African shook his head, as if in wonder. "How long? For how long have you lived alone?"

Paul shrugged. "Ten years."

"And what the hell do you find to eat in this hell hole?"

Paul glanced at him. "Lizards."

"Lizards?" The big man sounded surprised. "What else?"

"Nothing else. Only lizards. Once... years ago... I caught a dog."

"And water? You must have water?"

Paul shrugged again. "There is a little, deep down."

The African smiled, shaking his head. "That's amazing, you know that?"

Paul looked ahead. In a couple of minutes they would be passing the building where he would make a break for freedom.

He decided to keep the African talking; maybe, that way, he would have the element of surprise on his side when he took off.

He said, "And you? Where do you come from?"

The big man smiled. "Originally? A place called Nigeria, once upon a time. I've been heading north for twenty years. For a year we've been living in a colony in Copenhagen. In a castle. You know what one of those is?"

Paul nodded. "I've seen pictures in books, read about them."

"You can read?"

Paul looked at the big man's expression of surprise. "Of course."

They were approaching the terrace of ancient buildings. The first of the windows, dark shadows in the twilight gloom, beckoned to him, promising freedom.

The African said, "Hey, Hans, we've got ourselves a real survivor here, man. Listen up, how about we keep the boy with us? He could teach us a few things..."

"Yeah, like how to catch lizards." Hans's tone was scathing. "Listen, I got rid of Ali 'cos the bastard was a walking corpse, taking food and water. And you want us to keep the Frenchie?"

The African switched from French to English as he replied, "So... what you plan to do with the kid?" And he glanced at Paul as if to see if he'd understood.

He tried to keep his expression blank.

They were passing the first of the windows now.

From up ahead, Hans said, "What the fuck you think? He leads us to the stash, and then we're rid of him."

"Hans..." the African said, "I think that'd be a mistake. Like I said, he'd be useful."

Hans snorted. "Yah, useful like the girl, okay?"

Paul wanted to turn around and glance at the Oriental, to assess how alert he might be, but he knew that would be a mistake.

They passed another window, then another. Ten metres ahead, the terrace ended in a tumble of fallen masonry. He had to act within seconds.

The window after next... the room within was open at the back, a gaping hole giving access to a series of narrow passages, which led to a square. From there, if he reached it, he had the choice of half a dozen exits.

He passed the first window opening. He braced himself.

He slowed, exaggerating his limp. Perhaps a dozen paces, and closing... He tensed, willing the Oriental to have his mind on other things.

The opening approached. He would have to time his dive perfectly.

Here it was...

He yanked on the rope, heard the Oriental's startled yell and took off, leaping through the gap, rolling head over heels and coming upright in an instant. He was running in a zigzag dash through the rubble when he heard the curses and a gunshot.

He dodged, falling behind a pile of bricks and pushing himself to his feet. Without his hands free for balance, regaining his feet was almost impossible. He managed, somehow, and took off again, leaping through the jagged hole in the brickwork and turning left along a short corridor, then right. He allowed himself a quick sensation of hope. At least he was no longer in the line of sight of the bastards, though running with his hands tied like this was hell, and he wasn't making the progress he'd hoped for.

He heard sound of pursuit; cries and the scramble of feet on loose bricks.

Then: "Stop!" It was the African.

Paul turned right, found himself at the end of a long corridor, and felt despair.

The African's command came again. "Stop. I'll shoot, okay? One more step and I'll..."

He had no doubt that, even though the African had been the only one to show even the slightest humanity towards him so far, he would not hesitate to carry out his threat.

Paul came to a panting halt.

He heard footsteps behind him, then a strong hand gripped his upper arm and spun him around. He gazed up into the African's sweat-soaked face.

"Listen... I'm sorry, you know? I'll do my best, okay...?"

The others were close behind him. Paul saw Hans, looming. The German pushed past the African and

Paul felt something crack into his jaw. He cried out and fell to his knees.

Hans was striding away with the air of a man wanting to commit more violence but knowing that, this time, he had to restrain the impulse. Almost gently, the African pulled Paul to his feet and led him back through the shattered building and out into the street.

The Oriental was lying on the floor, blood leaking from his mouth. Hans barked, "Get up! And be thankful you didn't get a fucking bullet."

The others, Achmed and the Scandinavian, helped the Oriental to his feet.

The African gripped the rope tied to Paul's wrist. Paul felt a hand on his shoulder, urging him forward, and he led the way along the street towards the turning into the boulevard where the bank was situated.

They turned left. The boulevard ran east to west, and at the far end the bloated sphere of the sun sat as if lodged between the buildings, filling the street with its ruddy light. The scene, with the dark buildings, the golden pathway of sand leading towards the magnificent, bloody sun, was almost beautiful.

"This is it," Paul said, wishing he could free his hands in order to hold his throbbing jaw.

Hans pulled out his map and stared at it, then looked up and counted off the buildings. "There it is. Third one along." He spat on the ground. The gobbet hit stone and sizzled.

Paul wondered if this was where he would get the bullet – or would they save that until later?

Hans set off, leading the way, followed by the Oriental, the Arab and the Scandinavian. Paul trooped after them, the African in his wake.

He considered another attempt at running, but the buildings on either side were unfamiliar to him. He would stand even less of a chance if he tried to escape here.

They came to the gaping windows of the third building and stood beneath the great drift of sand that led up to the dark openings.

Paul found his voice and said, "Okay... I've brought you to the building. Now let me go."

Hans looked at him grinning. He glanced around his men and laughed: they joined in. "Hear that? He wants us to let him go!"

Hans approached him, pushed his fat face into Paul's and said, "You're going nowhere, kid."

Paul wished later he'd had the courage to spit in the bastard's face. Instead, all he could do was pull his face away and drop his gaze to the sand.

He saw a sudden movement to his left, then the startling sound of a voice, loud and clear in the stillness. "Don't move! Stay right there, all of you."

Paul turned, disbelieving.

He saw two men standing in the boulevard. They had emerged from a building and were directing weapons at Hans and the others. A third figure, above them in a window opening, called down, "You heard him. Stop where you are and drop your weapons."

Paul considered using this opportunity to begin running, but fear paralysed him. One of the figures stepped forward, and Paul saw that it was not a man but a woman, tanned and stocky and wearing faded khaki shorts and a threadbare shirt. She had short, iron-grey hair and startling blue eyes.

The man beside her was even shorter, broad and powerfully muscled and dressed in shorts and a holed green t-shirt. Something about the man, his clothing and lack of facial hair, told Paul that he was a part of an established colony.

The man said, "Drop your weapons or you're dead."

Paul glanced at Hans: the look on the German's face was a study in impotent rage. He seemed to be on the verge of acceding to the trio's demands when the Scandinavian beside Paul swung his weapon and began firing.

His shots were returned and the Scandinavian was dead in a second, his flesh shredded from his spine while his legs were still standing. Paul retched and reeled away, found himself shoulder-charging a brick wall as gunfire sounded all around him. He saw a window and dived through it. He lay still, panting, and hoped that no one had seen him in the confusion.

The fire-fight seemed to last an age. He wondered, then, if Elise could hear it. He was sure that, despite her deafness, she would.

Then, suddenly, all was shocking silence. After the deafening rattle of gunfire, the lack of sound was like sound itself, a dinning ring in his ears.

He lay on his face, his cheek pressed to the sand, his heartbeat loud. More than anything he wanted to climb to his knees, peer over the sill and see what had happened. He even made a move to do so, but found himself frozen in the act with the fear of showing his head in the opening.

Seconds later he heard the woman's voice. So she had survived, at least. "Where's the girl?" she hissed.

Paul struggled to his knees, trying to work his hands from the rope, but failing. He stood, leaned against the wall and peered out.

"I said, where's the girl!"

The woman stood above one of Hans's men – it was Achmed. He lay on his back, his left leg blown away and blood turning the sand black beneath the tattered stump. He stared up at the woman with a defiance he had never shown in life.

Paul took in the scene in the boulevard.

The Scandinavian's legs and spinal column lay in the middle of the road, grotesquely pointing the way towards the setting sun. The Oriental lay nearby, his torso a bloody mash but his arms and legs surreally intact.

There was no sign of Hans and the African. Paul wondered if they'd managed to get away.

There was no sign, either, of the stocky stranger; Paul looked up and down the street, but couldn't see his body.

The woman stepped forward, placed the barrel of her rifle to Achmed's forehead and said, very deliberately, "Tell me what you did with the girl, or you're dead."

Achmed said something that Paul couldn't make out. Then he realised that the Arab was laughing.

He looked at the woman, curious as to what her

reaction might be. He couldn't help notice the swell of her breasts beneath the material of her shirt, and the lines of her face. She was a lot younger than Elise. She was the first pretty woman he had seen, other than the woman in the red dress, for over a decade.

He experienced a sudden itch in his eyes, blinked, and felt tears roll down his cheeks.

Behind the woman, he made out movement. The figure in the upper window had left his vantage point and stepped out onto the street. The man was tall and thin, perilously thin, his bare arms and legs looking skeletal – and he was old. Even older, Paul, thought, than Elise. His long head was bald, with the parched skin drawn tight around the skull.

He walked slowly over to the woman and stopped, staring down at the Arab. "Where is Lisa, Achmed?" he asked in a soft, cultured voice.

So the two bands of strangers obviously knew each other.

Lisa... the girl in the red dress. They could only be talking about the young girl. Paul closed his eyes quickly, seeing again the vision of her fleeing her pursuers, followed involuntarily by the image of her skull in the embers.

The Arab reined in his manic laughter and stared up at the old man with fear in his eyes. "Fuck..." the Arab managed... "fuck you!"

The tall man said, reasonably, "Please tell me where she is, Achmed."

At this, the Arab resumed his mad laughter.

"Is she alive?" the woman asked, stabbing at Achmed's face with the barrel of her rifle.

The Arab yelped and tried to squirm away. The movement caused his shattered leg to shift in the sand, and the artery reopened; a neat parabola of blood looped through the air.

"We can treat you if you tell us," the woman said. "Do you want to live?"

She looked up, anxiously scanning the street east and west. Paul assumed she was looking for the third member of her party, the short, muscular man.

The oldster bent laboriously, folding himself into a squat beside the Arab. He reminded Paul, then, with the stark angularity of his arms and his long skull, of an insect – a locust.

"Is my daughter still alive, Achmed?"

The Arab was panting hard now as his life ebbed from him. "What the... what the fuck you think?"

Paul saw someone moving down the boulevard, silhouetted in the last light of the sun. The woman looked up. "Dan!" she said with obvious relief.

The stocky man took her in a quick embrace. "The bastards got away, Kath. They might be anywhere." He looked down at the Arab. "Any luck?"

The woman – Kath – shook her head.

Dan said, "What about the other one? They had a kid, tied up..."

At that moment, the old man looked up and saw Paul in the opening. Paul stared, unable to move. Dan stepped forward, raising his rifle. Kath said, "Dan, let me, okay?"

She gave her rifle to Dan and stepped forward, hands outstretched.

Paul stood where he was, frozen.

The woman approached and said in French, "We won't harm you. We know you weren't with Hans and the others. They captured you, right?"

The woman had a strange accent, harsh, grating. Oddly he wanted to trust her, but some deep-seated survival instinct was telling him to run.

He glanced around him. The back of the room was missing, giving onto a narrow, sand-filled alley. Paul took off.

The woman called. "Come back! We have food and water!"

Paul stumbled from the back of the building, almost falling over the piled bricks. "Please," the woman called, pleading, then, "We're in the cathedral, okay? We won't harm you. We have food and water."

Paul looked over his shoulder. The man called Dan was climbing through the window. Paul turned down the alley, running now, turned again and again, increasing his pace and heading in the direction of home, the basement. Five minutes later, breathing hard, he was confident he had lost his pursuers, if indeed they had come after him.

He slowed, orienting himself and cutting through the ruins of a monument-fringed square towards the basement. He stopped when he saw the ragged shards of glass projecting from an ancient window frame. Positioning himself with his back to the frame, he backed up until his wrists touched the old timbers. Carefully he located the glass, eased the knot of his binds upon the sharp edge of the glass and, laboriously, rubbed the rope back and forth until it frayed and finally snapped. He rubbed his abraded wrists and rolled his aching shoulders, then set off again.

Oddly, although he knew he should be feeling relief now at the fact of his survival, he felt nothing of the kind. He heard the woman's promise of food and water, recalled the look in her bright blue eyes; there had been kindness there, he was sure.

And the tall, thin old man... The girl in the red dress had been his daughter. The man carried his apprehension, his sadness, like a black cloak around his shoulders.

He found himself laughing, laughing madly like the Arab in his final moments, as he thought through the events of the day. For almost as long as he was able to recall, his days had resembled each other down to the last detail, a series of routines which had lasted for years and which he had known would last for years to come. Sleep, the scaling of the tower for lizard meat, the basement and a meal and Elise's stories... or lately her disconnected ramblings about the end of life on Earth and the beginning of new life on other stars... Every two days the fetching of water, and in the evening the setting of the traps, then sleep.

The odd thing was, why did he have the feeling now that, because of the events he had witnessed over the last few hours, his life of old was coming to an end? He had seen other people for the first time in years, had glimpsed another way of life – he had seen two beautiful women, women he had only dreamed about and seen in the pages of magazines – and, despite the comfort of his safe and established routine, he felt that a part of him, almost against his will, was being drawn away from the familiarity of his old life, lured by the promise of new experience, which both attracted and frightened him.

HE CAME TO the line of tenements beneath which was his home. He thought of Elise, and braced himself for her anger, her recriminations and then her tearful relief that he was still alive.

He would tell her everything he had seen, then prepare the lizards. Later he would ask her questions about the events of the day and Elise, in her wisdom, would construct a likely story about who the people were, where they had come from, and what they were seeking. He would ask her if he should make contact with the strangers.

He crossed the twilight street and hurried down the steps to the basement.

"Elise!" He scraped open the timber door and stepped into the room. The high window admitted the last, wine-red light of day. He made out the mattress beneath the window, and Elise's thin form upon it. He moved quietly around the room, gathering the candles Elise had made from the preciously-hoarded lizard fat. He stacked shards of dry wood in the hearth, then found his fire-maker – a simple device of wood and string, again of Elise's devising – and prepared to make a fire in order to cook the lizards.

Before doing so he moved to the mattress to check on Elise's water; her bottle was empty. He refilled it from the bucket he'd boiled that morning, and moved back to the mattress. The likelihood was that she'd been asleep for hours. If he ate without her, then she would only complain when she woke up.

She was lying on her side, her back to him. He reached out and touched her shoulder.

He stopped, his arm out, as if his fingertips had been frozen to her cold flesh.

He shook her. "Elise...?"

She rolled onto her back, with all the terrible, lifeless volition of an object – not a healthy, living human being. "Elise..." He fell to his knees and took her shoulders in his hands. Her eyes were open, staring up at him. He picked her up and shook her, shocked first by how light she was, then at his violence and how even this failed to rouse her.

Gently, he lay her back on the mattress and sat beside her, staring down at her lifeless face.

He reached out and touched her cheek, amazing himself yet again at how soft it was, and still warm.

He wept. He wondered if she'd heard the gunfire and assumed that he'd been shot... Had she died in despair, he wondered, at his failure to return?

Or perhaps she had gone gently, unaware of the fire fight, unaware even of his absence. The look on her face seemed serene, untroubled.

Suddenly he recalled her laughing, just yesterday, as in a lucid moment she had described finding him, rescuing him; she had been full of stories then about how she had raised him, and what a terror he'd been.

He looked around the room, at the crowded furniture and ornaments she had insisted on keeping, even though every one of them was useless. They seemed as much a part of her as the crucifix she wore around her neck.

He knew what he had to do now. She had told him, over and over, what to do when she died. She had insisted that he repeat her instructions, and made him promise that he would do as she bid. It had seemed such a crazy thing to be listening to, back then; it had seemed impossible to look ahead to a time when Elise would not be around, but to please her he had listened again and again with an air of abstraction.

And now she was dead and it struck him as crucially important that he carry out her wishes to the very last letter.

He picked her up, cradling her in both arms, strangely saddened by her lack of weight, and as he carried her across the room, through the door and up the stairs, he wondered where her life had gone. She had been so alive when he had left her this morning, so full of the person who was Elise Amelia Lacey, and now that was gone, had fled the insubstantial package of skin and bone, and it seemed to him that her corpse was not who she had been, and that the real Elise must be elsewhere.

He stepped into the twilight and moved around the building to the enclosed courtyard at the rear. Years ago, when they had moved to the basement, this had been a struggling garden, with grass and a few flowers and even a tree. They were all gone now, and the square was filled with sand, but this was where Elise had wanted to be laid to rest, so that she could watch the sun set, she said, and then gaze up at the stars as they came out one by one. She had told him she would look upon the distant suns and think about where humankind now dwelled, on planets of plenty in the light of kind suns.

Crazy old woman...

With his right foot he opened the lid of the box, which Elise had prepared years ago. It had half filled with sand over time, but that was okay; it acted as a bed on which to rest her. He lay her body down, pleased at how the limbs settled. He arranged her hands together on her stomach, and closed her eyes as she had instructed, then sat beside the open coffin and held her hand, gazing at her serene face, until the last of the sunlight ebbed from the air and her flesh grew cold.

He thought of the strangers, the men and the woman.

Later, he stirred himself, wiped the tears from his cheeks, said goodbye to Elise – even though he knew what lay before him was no longer the old woman – closed the lid of the box and retraced his steps back to the basement.

He lit a fire, not to cook by, but so that he could look upon the room. He gathered the lizards and strung them once again on the thong at his waist. He moved around the room, touching the polished surfaces of tables and chairs that had meant so much to Elise, wondering what object he might take so that he could look upon it and think of her.

Whatever happened, he knew, he could live here no longer.

Then he saw the bag; it was made from flowered fabric, and Elise had used it to carry her smaller possessions from their old dwelling to the basement; since then it had been unused, though Elise had often pulled it to her and caressed its embroidered material as if conjuring old memories.

He opened the bag and took down two books from the shelf beside the mattress, the medical directory they had found invaluable down the years, and a compendium of poetry which Elise had used to teach him to read. He pulled out another book, an encyclopaedia of nations. Elise had made a gift of it years ago, and he had spent hours poring over the pictures of the many countries and peoples represented. Once, the world had been so full...

But he could only take so much. He had to travel light. Sadly, he replaced the book on the shelf.

He moved to the box containing their scant medical supplies, a few old bottles and buckled tubes of antiseptic ointment. These he placed in the bag with the books.

He stood, shouldering the bag, and looked around the room.

The only other possession that belonged to him was his crossbow, and that was no longer here.

He moved from the room, looking back at the flickering shadows before climbing the stairs into the relative cool of night.

The moon was out, a phase from full, casting its silver light over the silent city.

He walked with purpose towards the tower, a skeletal shape in the moonlight. He set down his bag and climbed to the lizard traps. He had made a dozen in all, each one no larger than his fist, and now he gathered the wire cages together and strung them on a length of twine over his shoulder. He climbed back down, retrieved his bag, and set off again across the city.

He had often come out at night when the moon was high, climbed the tower and sat and stared over the utterly still, unmoving city, taking in its beauty, the only noise that of his breathing. And when he'd held his breath, the profundity of the silence, the total absence of any sound at all, struck him to his core and terrified him. Then he had resumed his breathing, and the noise had seemed like a furnace, filling him with the fact of his existence, assuring him that the city, the world, the universe with all its stars, was not dead.

He hurried through the city, keeping to the shadows and pausing to listen out for sounds of movement. The city was silent, but for the soughing wind. There was no sign of the strangers. He came at last to the boulevard on which was situated the pumping station, and across from it the room where...

He arrived at the building and stopped before the dark rectangle of the window. Lowering the traps and the bag, he left them in the sand and climbed through the opening. In the half-light within the room, patchily illuminated by the glow of the moon, he made out the charcoal blur of the old fire, and across the room the polished glint of his crossbow. He hurried across to it, picked it up and held the warm wood against his chest.

He rounded the remains of the fire towards the window and was about to step through when he saw the girl's red dress on the floor.

He thought of the old man, and his plea to the Arab to be told what had happened to his daughter. He picked up the dress and pressed the material to his face. Miraculously, he smelled the scent of the girl upon it, the musk of her sweat and something else, something sweet and heady.

He looked back to the fire, to the skull and the ribcage and the other bones.

It had seemed to matter to Elise, in a way he did not understand, that her remains be cared for in a certain way after her death; and now some intimation told him that the old man might share the same sentiments when it came to the disposal of his daughter's body.

He moved to the fire, knelt and pulled from the grey ashes the girl's skull and her ribcage; the individual ribs parted company with the spine on the way, and he gathered up all the bones he could find and placed them on the red dress. When he bundled up the bones and the skull, and knotted the dress, he was surprised at what small a package it made.

He returned to the boulevard, stowed the wrapped bones in his bag, retrieved the traps and set off south.

CHAPTER SEVEN

DAN AND KATH sat on top of a pile of rubble within the walls of the cathedral. From this vantage point he could see through the arched window, long since emptied of glass, across the ruins of the twilit city. The sun was going down, sending long, eerie shadows across the sand-drifts. The city was silent, as still as a graveyard. Not even the slightest wind stirred the sand.

Down below, within the cathedral, the truck squatted like a great beetle. Ed was sitting on a makeshift wooden stool, stirring a pot of stew on a fire made from shattered pews and desiccated kneeling-cushions.

For two hours after the abortive ambush, Dan and Kath had searched the streets around the cathedral for any sign of Hans and Hamed, Lisa or the strange wild boy.

In the fire-fight that had killed their colleagues, Hans and the African had managed to spirit themselves away, vanishing into the shattered buildings lining the boulevard. Dan had gone after them, confident of being able to track them down, but the city was vast and the deep, soft sand didn't retain tell-tale footprints for long.

He considered the abortive ambush.

When the bastard had opened fire, his automatic response had been to return the shots. Seconds later, three men had lain dead or dying. He knew he had killed one of their number: the corpse whose torso had been stripped from its spine. Ed had accounted for the other two.

Kath reached out and touched his hand. "Dan?"

He smiled. "Just thinking how we might have gone about things differently..."

She shrugged. "How?"

"Our intention was to find Lisa."

She squeezed his hand. "What else could we have done?"

"I don't know." He thought about it. "Kept quiet, followed them... Perhaps they might have led us to..."

"To Lisa? You think she's still alive?"

"There's always a chance. If we could've found their half-track..."

"Dan, Dan... we did the right thing. How did we know they'd open up like that? And we had to fight back, save ourselves."

He nodded. "It's still a hell of a shock to think I've killed someone."

"Come here..." she said, and when he edged towards her, she hugged him and kissed his cheek.

They sat in silence and watched as a near-full moon rose over the shattered city.

The presence of the boy had more than surprised Dan. More than fifteen years ago the Paris colony had given up its pretence of being able to continue in the city. He knew that, because a band of twenty survivors had headed north, with a few provisions, medicines, books and a failing half-track, and petitioned the ruling council at Copenhagen to be taken in. They had told of desperate times back in Paris: the desert was invading the city centre and water was running out; animals were scarce and their crops had failed for three seasons running. They said that they'd left behind just a few individuals, too old or too unwilling to leave the only life they had known.

He asked Kath, "The boy. Do you think he's a survivor from the old colony?"

"More than likely. Where else would he have come from?" She smiled. "The indomitability of the human spirit. I wonder what the hell he finds to eat in this place, let alone drink?"

"The very fact that he's alive..."

After a moment's reflection, Kath said, "I wonder what they wanted with him?"

"The same thing they wanted from Lisa."

Kath looked at him. "What do you mean?"

"Think about it. What are the three necessities of human survival? Sex, food and shelter – in whichever order you prefer. Well, the bastards had shelter, the truck..."

After a while, Kath said softly, "At least our intervention saved him from whatever they intended."

He nodded. "There is that." He stared down into the cathedral, watching the old man go about the slow process of cooking the evening meal.

"Dan, do you think Hans is still in the city?" Kath asked a while later. "We didn't hear the truck leaving –"

"How would we? The thing's almost silent. They could be miles from here by now."

Kath nodded, then said, "Has Ed said anything to you about Lisa?"

"Nothing. I think he'll suggest we search again in the morning."

Kath looked at him. "Wouldn't you, in the circumstances?"

"Yes, of course."

He took her hand in a fierce grip. Until just a few years ago he had lived in hope that he would be able to give Kath the child she so much desired. He had always been an optimist. While some in the colony had poured scorn on the idea of bringing children into the world, with scant resources and an uncertain future, there was another body of opinion which thought that only by perpetuating the species would humanity have any chance at all of regaining some measure of the old way of life; only by passing down hard-won knowledge and expertise could life go on... Dan and Kath subscribed to the latter theory, which made it a cruel irony that they had been unable to conceive a child of their own.

He wondered if his bad temper was in part due to the fact that he still hadn't told Kath what he wanted to do next: not head back to Copenhagen, but strike out south. Now would be a good time to broach the subject, following their failure to find provisions in the city. He would say that, rather than return north empty handed, they should at least head south in the hope of striking lucky.

He pulled Kath to her feet. "Come on. It looks like Ed's finished cooking. I'm hungry."

The scrambled down the hillock of rubble and approached the truck.

Ed looked up and smiled. "You must have been attracted by the wonderful bouquet."

"Well, we are in Paris," Kath laughed. "Wasn't this supposed to be the culinary capital of the world, or have I got it wrong?"

"Very true," Ed said. He gazed into the cooking pot. "Those *cordon bleu* chefs must be looking down in envy..."

Kath fetched bowls and spoons from the truck and Ed ladled out three huge helpings. "We need feeding up," Ed said. "It's been a tough day."

Dan took a mouthful of broth: there was a little meat in there, a few vegetables and... "Ed, how the hell did you do this?"

"It's flavoured with something I've never tasted before," Kath marvelled.

Ed smiled. "I took a wander around the ruins. You'd never guess what I found." He reached into his pocket and withdrew a handful of leaves.

"What is it?" Kath asked.

"Rosemary. I found a straggly bush, growing in the rocks."

"But there's no rain, no water," Dan said.

Ed shrugged. "A miracle," he laughed. Then, quietly, "A miracle."

Dan got up and fetched a map from the truck.

He spread it on the tiles of the cathedral floor, sat and stared at the representation of what had been France.

He looked up and asked Ed, "What now?"

Kath stopped eating and looked at the old man.

Ed considered, staring into the remains of his broth. He looked at Dan. "Perhaps we could remain here a while, search the city...?"

Dan nodded. "Very well, we'll do that. And then?" He looked across at Kath. She had resumed eating her broth, spooning in silence.

He prodded the map. "I've been giving this some thought..."

Kath looked up. "What? I thought we'd be heading straight back home?"

Home, Dan thought. She had called it home. He had not called anywhere home for a very long time. "The thing is..." he began. "Come here and look at the map."

Kath shuffled across and leaned against him. The top of the map ended in what had been Belgium. Dan placed his empty bowl north east of the map. "This represents the Copenhagen colony..."

Ed said, "Is that supposed to be symbolic, Dan? An empty bowl?"

Dan gave him a wry smile. He stabbed at Paris on the map. "We're here."

Kath glanced at him. "What are you driving at?"

"Here, to the west of Biarritz, in what was the Atlantic ocean, there's a deep trench. I reckon if we drill, then there's a possibility we'll strike water."

"A possibility?" She sounded sceptical.

Dan nodded. "We've never tried a deep trench," he said. "There was nothing like it in the Baltic. To me, it makes sense. It'd be a wasted opportunity if we were to turn tail and head back without..."

Ed said, "We're more than halfway there already, Kath. I think Dan's right. We should give it a go."

Dan looked up at him and nodded, acknowledging Ed's support.

"And if we strike water?" Kath said.

"If we do, then the sensible thing would be to relocate the colony," Dan argued. "The colony began in the castle back when communities needed defences from marauders. Those days are long gone."

Kath said, "Did you tell Klausner what you were thinking?" She smiled; did she suspect that he'd been hatching this idea for a while now?

He shook his head. "I thought it wise not to. Klausner founded the Copenhagen colony. He'd want to preserve what we've got."

Kath looked at him, then said softly, "You could have told me, Dan."

He hesitated. "Kath..."

"You knew I'd be opposed to it, so you didn't tell me."

He shrugged. "I'm sorry."

She hugged herself, withdrawing into the shell of her own thoughts. She gazed down at the map. "Okay... okay. I guess I'm outnumbered here, aren't I?" She paused then went on, "I see your point. You're probably right, we should give it a go. But I'm disappointed you didn't tell me, Dan."

Silently he put an arm around her shoulder, trying to draw her to him. She resisted, stiffly.

"If we do head south," she went on, "I want to make a small detour."

He looked at her, surprised. "To where?"

She placed a forefinger on the map, and Dan smiled. "Mont St Catherine," she said.

Ed peered down at the map. "It's not that far out of our way," he said. "But why there?"

Dan said, "There was a colony, a small one. What, twenty people? It's where we met."

Kath smiled. "My parents founded the place. It was home. When I was little... the place was green, with olive groves, fields of vegetables..."

"I arrived there thirty years ago, in my early twenties," Dan said. "I'd been working on a commune in Barcelona. Actual paid work, fixing vehicles, tractors... We saw the desert coming and a couple of us decided the time was right to head north. We were taken into the community by Kath's father... and one day I saw this blonde vision in the fields."

Kath had a far away look in her eyes. She whispered, "I'd like to go back there, Dan."

He paused, then said, "Fine, but it might be painful."

"I take it the colony's long gone?" Ed said.

"I presume so," Kath said. "We left a dozen men and women there... what, twenty years ago...? When we headed north."

"Twenty-one years now," Dan said. "Hell, that seems like a lifetime ago."

"My parents had died a couple of years before we left." She paused. "That's partly why I'd like to go back, visit where they're buried. "

Dan thought of returning to Mont St Catherine, and wondered whether it would be a terrible mistake. He retained an idyllic vision of the place in his mind's eye, a rustic paradise of trees and fields and relative prosperity, at least in the early years. The reality, now, would be very different.

Ed interrupted his thoughts, "What was that?"

Dan looked up, staring into the shadows where Ed was peering.

Kath said, standing, "I think we have a visitor."

DAN REACHED FOR his rifle, then halted the movement when he saw who was standing at the edge of the pool of light.

He joined Kath and they approached the boy.

He was naked but for some kind of scant kilt or dress – then Dan saw that it was not an item of clothing at all but a string of dead lizards tied around his waste. He carried a bulky bag, a crossbow and a jumble of wire, cage-like objects slung over his shoulder.

Kath addressed him in French. "Hello..."

The boy stood, staring at them uncertainly. Dan guessed he was in his early twenties, tall and lithe and well-muscled. His blonde hair was long, but his beard appeared to have been trimmed regularly. He saw no evidence of disease or malformation, and wondered how the boy had managed to scratch a living in such inhospitable surroundings.

Dan said, "We have food. Are you hungry?"

The boy nodded.

Kath reached out, coaxing the boy forward as if he were a wild animal. He moved further into the light, step by hesitant step; he was tanned a deep, burnished copper, and his body was striated by numerous healed scars, cicatrises which showed as silvery-white slashes against his tan.

Ed had already filled a bowl with broth. Now he offered it to the boy and nodded to a seat beside the truck.

The boy eased the bag from his shoulder and lay it on the ground, then did the same with the crossbow and the cages – traps, Dan guessed.

He took the bowl and nodded his thanks. Slowly, he sat down, glancing around at his benefactors.

They sat and faced him.

Dan said, still in French, "This is Kath, Ed, and I'm Dan. Good to meet you."

He nodded. "I am Paul." He took the spoon and lifted it, loaded, to his lips. He took a mouthful and smiled as he chewed. "This is very good. You found the rosemary?"

Ed smiled. "I wondered how it managed to grow so well here..."

"I water it every few days. I think it's the very last plant in the city."

Kath said, "Where do you get your water, Paul?"

"From the pumping station. That's what Elise called it."

"Elise?" Kath said.

The boy stopped eating. "I lived with Elise." He

stared at his food. "She looked after me, and then I looked after her."

"And now?" Dan asked.

"She's dead."

Kath said, "I'm sorry..." She waited, then went on, "Is there anyone else here?"

The boy paused long enough in his eating to shake his head. "We were the last ones. A long time ago... ten years or more... there were others. But they left."

Kath passed the boy a bottle of water. "How long have you been living alone here?"

The boy paused again, looking her in the eye. "Not long."

Kath looked at Dan, something pleading in her expression. He nodded and said, under his breath, "Of course."

"I don't know what your plans are, but if you'd like to join us...?" she said. "We have room in the truck, a bed, a little food and water. We're heading south, looking for water. We have a drilling rig, you see."

The boy nodded. "Thank you." He indicated the lizards at his waist, and then across at the traps. "I have lizards, and traps."

His manner, Dan thought, flitted between timidity and an almost brazen acceptance of his situation: which, he supposed, was to be expected with someone hardly socialised in the accepted sense. He had after all been brought up by this Elise, alone, with absolutely no other human contact for at least ten years. It was a credit to the woman that he appeared as civilised as he did.

For the first time since the boy's arrival, Ed spoke, "How did you find yourself captured by Hans and the others, Paul?"

The boy stopped eating, and in a soft voice he said, "I saw the girl. She was running from the men. I followed them. They came here in a truck, but had lit a fire in a building near the pumping station. I watched them." He faltered to a halt and dropped his gaze.

Ed said, "Paul, do you know what happened to the girl?"

Paul lifted his eyes and gazed levelly at Ed. "I'm sorry." His voice was almost inaudible. "By the time I came to where they were, she was dead. I... I heard a shot, a single shot. It would have been quick. I'm sorry."

Kath moved to where Ed was sitting, as immobile as a statue. She sat beside him and took his hand.

Ed gathered himself and said, "And where is she now?"

And Dan could see that Ed had tensed himself in preparation for the reply. Dan closed his eyes, almost wincing, as the boy said, "I have her... her remains."

Dan opened his eyes and watched as the boy stood and moved to his shoulder bag. He opened it and reached inside, pulling out a red bundle.

Only when the boy returned to the fire, and laid the bundle before Ed, did Dan recognise Lisa's red dress.

With trembling hands, Ed reached out and unfastened the loose knot. The material fell away to reveal a notched spine, several ribs, and a skull.

The boy went on, "I'm sorry. I took the bones from the ashes, a little while ago. Elise, she told me once that the burial of the dead is considered important."

Ed was weeping now, crying silent tears as Kath hugged him and murmured softly to him. "The bastards." Ed's curse was hardly audible. "The murdering bastards."

He pushed a thumb and forefinger up his cheeks, removing the tears. He looked at Paul. "Do you know who did this? Which one of them?"

The boy shook his head. "I was not there when the shot was fired. But I don't think it was the African... I think it was Hans. He was... he was the one who was in control. The others were frightened of him."

Kath leaned forward. "Do you know where Hans is now? He got away when the firing started, along with Hamed. Do you know where they went?"

"No," the boy shook his head, then said, "But I know where their truck was."

Ed looked up. "You do? Then..." He looked across at Dan.

Dan nodded. "Chances are they're long gone, but we could take a look."

Ed tied his daughter's remains in her red dress and carried the bundle into the truck. Dan and Kath busied themselves packing up the lights and stools, kicking out the fire and gathering up the bowls and spoons.

Dan watched as Paul moved across to a tumble of bricks. He knelt, reached out and teased a small, wiry plant from its precarious foothold in a crevice of sandy soil. He carried it back to the truck in cupped hands and presented it to Kath.

She smiled and fetched a small bowl.

Dan looked at the boy. "Ah... I think I'd better get you some clothes. Some shorts. We have spares in the truck."

Kath touched his arm. "You jealous?" she murmured, smiling.

Dan kissed her and gestured for Paul to enter the truck before them. He did so warily.

Dan found the boy a baggy pair of shorts and an old tee-shirt; Paul unfastened the thong of lizards at his waist and passed them to Kath. She hung them with the rest of the dried meat above the small wash-basin. She placed the rosemary plant in the basin and doused it with water.

Paul pulled on the shorts and shirt and looked down at them, frowning to himself.

Dan said, "Come with me," and climbed through the hatch into the cab. Paul followed, seating himself beside Dan. His movements were timid now, an animal in uncertain terrain.

When Dan started the engine and the truck throbbed into life, Paul grabbed the arm-rest and shot an alarmed look at Kath, who was leaning into the cab and smiling.

"It's okay," she said. "It'll make a bit of noise, but you've nothing to fear."

"I've only seen pictures of trucks and cars in books," Paul said, gazing around the cab at the lights and dials in silent wonder.

Dan backed the half-track from the shell of the cathedral, hanging from the cab and peering out at the mounded rubble. When they were safely out on the boulevard, he turned to Paul. "Okay, which way now?"

Paul peered through the windscreen, and pointed. "That way."

They rolled through the sandy streets, their way illuminated by the moonlight. It was an odd experience to be driving down city streets flanked by buildings. If Dan ignored the drifted sand, the empty window sockets on either side, he could almost believe the city was locked in a night-time slumber, that in the morning a million citizens would awake to resume their everyday life of work and play.

"Down there."

Dan slewed the half-track right, down a wide avenue, spraying sand in their wake, and then on Paul's instructions turned left. The boy leaned forward and indicated a square.

Dan eased the truck into the square and ground the vehicle to a halt.

"The truck was there," Paul said, pointing.

Dan eased the half-track forward a few metres, then climbed from the cab. He approached the area adjacent to a building where the truck had been parked, as evidenced by the churned sand, and the tracks leading away and out of the square ahead.

Kath and Ed joined him, followed by Paul.

"The truck was here," the boy said.

Dan swore. "What now? He could be miles away. We could always try to follow..."

He looked at Ed. It was the old man's call.

Ed shook his head. "What would we gain from going after them? I know I said I'd gladly shoot the bastards, back then... but, to be honest..."

Dan nodded. "I understand, Ed."

Kath said, "And how far will they get? They won't go back to Copenhagen, that's for sure. They wouldn't let them in. Do you know any more colonies within striking distance?"

Ed shook his head. "With luck they'll break down in the desert and starve to death." He smiled, bitterly. "It'd be nice to watch, though."

"If Hamed doesn't kill Hans first," Kath pointed out. "There was no love lost between those two."

Dan said, "Paul, you said there was a pumping station nearby. It'd be an idea to fill up with water before we left."

They returned to the truck and Paul directed them around the block to the building he called the pumping station. They climbed out and Kath fetched the empty canisters from the lounge.

For the next twenty minutes they filled the containers from a leaking bucket on the end of a long rope, which Paul dropped through the floor of the building; they took it in turns to haul the buckets up from the depths. It was back-breaking work, and the resulting water was evil smelling and brackish.

Kath took a sniff and recoiled. Paul said, "I always boiled it before we drank it."

"I'll run some tests on it in the morning," Ed said, "but if you drank it without dire consequences..."

They were returning to the truck, laden with brimming containers, when Ed paused and said to Paul, "You said Hans and the others took Lisa to a nearby building?"

Paul gestured across the boulevard. "They lit the fire in there."

"I'd like to see where..." Ed began.

Dan exchanged a look with Kath. Her return expression said, *Go with him.*

Ed moved across the street, a stark figure in the moonlight. Dan accompanied him. The old man paused before the window opening and stared into the shadows. Dan could just make out an empty room, the blur of scattered embers.

He felt tears sting his eyes as he recalled Lisa, so full of life and laughter, at her father's eightieth birthday party just a couple of months ago.

In silence, Ed took in the scene of his daughter's death, his expression carved from silver in the light of the moon.

Dan lay a hand on Ed's thin shoulder and murmured, "Let's get back to the truck, okay? It's time we were heading south."

They boarded the truck and drove back to the square. Dan scoured the sand as he headed east, fowling the churned sand made by Hans's truck. The tracks were discernible in the city streets between the buildings – parallel furrows leading into an unknowable future – but as the last of the buildings fell away, so the tracks disappeared, blown over by the constant wind that raked the open desert.

Dan halted the truck and consulted the map. "Hans was heading south-east when he left the city," he told the others. "Of course, that doesn't tell us a lot."

"His options are pretty limited," Ed said. "Turin, if it's still going. Where else?"

Kath said, "Where was it Hans said he'd come from? Some place in the south?"

Ed shrugged. "Any port in a storm. I pity the poor bastards down there."

The old man retired to his berth. Kath showed Paul where he'd be sleeping, on an old chesterfield in the lounge. She returned to the cab and sat beside Dan as he gunned the engine, turned the truck and set them on a south-west course.

She reached out and squeezed his hand.

Ahead, the moonlight lay like silver lamé across the undulating sands.

FIVE HOURS LATER, as dawn was lacerating the far horizon to his left, Dan eased the half-track from the desert and accelerated up a long slope which terminated, a couple of kilometres distant, in the remains of an ancient village sitting on a high hilltop.

It would be a good place to rest up for a couple of hours, have breakfast and talk, and maybe then, before they set off again, do a little exploring.

In the early days, on his sorties from the castle, he had come across long-abandoned villages and towns and experienced a curious ambivalence: something in him relished the opportunity to explore, the chance to find things he could utilise back at the colony, and at the same time to lose himself in an environment wholly different from that to which he'd become accustomed over the years. Yet he never moved among these relics of another time without sadness, without the knowledge that these houses, these rooms and objects, once represented the basics of existence for people, families and friends, long gone. Immersing himself in the past like this had only ever served to point up the precarious present, and the uncertain future.

He peered through the windscreen at the hilltop village. If he squinted, blurring his vision, he could make-believe the village was as it might have been a hundred years ago: a typical French rural hamlet waking up at the start of another day.

The half-track growled up the incline, passing derelict farm buildings and cottages. He eased the truck into the village and braked, gazing around at the buildings framing the cobbled square. They seemed remarkably intact, save for one or two which had lost roofs and chimney stacks – testament to the skill of their ancient builders. He eased the truck into the shade of the old town hall and cut the engine. The resulting silence was absolute.

He stretched, and climbed from the cab. The boy, Paul, was still asleep on the chesterfield in the lounge, curled in a protective ball and snoring gently. Dan moved down the short corridor to the sleeping berths. He looked in on Ed, tapping on the sliding door and receiving a quiet, "It's open."

He stepped into the tiny room. Ed was sitting up on his bunk; the red dress containing Lisa's bones was beside him on the bed.

Ed was reading a thick book, a pair of half-moon spectacles, repaired with tape and wire over the years, perched on the end of his nose.

"Anything interesting?" Dan asked.

"Kierkegaard," Ed said. "A good Dane."

Dan smiled. "Just the thing to cheer you up on a bright summer's morning. Anyway, breakfast in ten minutes. I'm brewing coffee."

"Coffee? What's the occasion?"

Dan shrugged. "Leaving Paris, heading south... the start of a new adventure." He backed from the room and opened the door across the corridor.

Kath stretched on their bunk, smiling up at him. "I heard you say the C-word, Dan."

He sat down beside her and ran a hand across the soft skin of her stomach above the band of her shorts. "Why not? It isn't every day we strike off into the unknown in search of the stuff of life."

"Speaking of which, I think I'm due my weekly shower."

He nodded. "Do that." The truck boasted a tiny shower cubicle and a water recycling system which he'd lashed together years ago.

Kath peered through the windscreen, and smiled. "Oh, a village. I thought we were in the desert."

"We were. Then I saw this place."

"Where are we?"

"About two hundred kilometres south of Paris."

"It's... it's beautiful, Dan." He detected the sadness in her eyes; she was looking out at the ruined village and attempting to subtract the damage.

"I mean, it must have been beautiful," she said quietly.

He leaned over and kissed her. "See you in five minutes."

He returned to the lounge and brewed the coffee,

or rather the beverage he liked to call coffee. Years ago, in the ruins of a warehouse in the outskirts of Copenhagen, he'd come across a catering-sized can of instant coffee – a near-miracle in an age when the ruins had been scoured, and scoured again, by survivors in search of foodstuffs.

His first cup of the scalding, aromatic liquid had been a truly blissful experience.

In order to make the coffee last, he'd thinned it with acorn shavings and powdered chicory he found in the storeroom: and it had still tasted ambrosial. He reckoned he had enough of the precious powder for another fifty cups.

The sound of boiling water woke Paul. He sat up quickly, his expression surprised as he looked around the lounge. Then he saw Dan and smiled.

"Sleep well?" Dan asked.

The boy nodded. "Very well. What's that?"

Dan pointed to the steaming pan. "Coffee."

Paul repeated the word. "I've heard of it, read about it in books. Elise... she said she'd kill for a cup."

Surprised, Dan said, "You can read?"

"Elise taught me."

Dan regarded the boy as he stirred the pan of coffee, chastising himself for his lazy assumptions. Outwardly, the boy looked like a savage, but the truth belied his appearance.

Kath entered the lounge, followed shortly by Ed. They sat around on the chesterfield and on cushions, and Dan poured out four big mugs of hot coffee and passed them around.

He watched the boy as he cupped the mug in both hands and took an experimental sip. He looked at first surprised, then pleased.

"What do you think?"

"It's... well, it's different. I've never tasted anything like it before."

Ed smiled. "It's an acquired taste, Paul. Ahh," he said as he took a swallow. "What would life be like without coffee? Do you know, sixty years ago I drank the real stuff, I mean made from real, Columbian ground beans, every day in an outdoor café in Montmarte."

Kath said, "And how does this compare?"

Ed smiled. "Do you know, I think it's a little better."

Dan fetched the map from the cab and spread it on the floor between them. "We're here," he said, "five hours south of Paris." He indicated the southeast coast of the country. "And this is where we're heading."

"How long will it take?" Kath asked.

He shrugged. "Taking in the detour to Mont St Catherine, around three, four days."

"And then, if we find water?" Paul asked.

"We'll make our way back to Copenhagen – whether we strike water or not. If we do, then we'll need to decide if we're going to relocate."

Paul nodded, gazing down at his coffee.

Dan said, "You'll be fine. The people back there are... civilised. Not like Hans and the others."

The boy smiled. "It's just that... I have memories of the Paris colony, just before the end." He shook his head. "I remember fights, terrible arguments. I didn't know what was happening at the time, but now... it must have been differences of opinion – what to do, how to do it. One time, there was a gun-fight. People died."

Kath said, "Did you live there with your parents?"

Paul's gaze flicked to her, and then away quickly. It was as if, Dan thought, he found Kath intimidating because she was a woman.

The boy said, "I don't remember my mother. She died when I was young. I lived in the colony with my father, until I was about eight or nine. One day he went out hunting – there were animals, back then." He fell silent, staring at the map before them, then shrugged. "He didn't come back. Someone told me he'd been hit by a falling building, but I don't know. He had his own ways of doing things, his own opinions. He had people who opposed him." He was silent for a while, then said, "I ran away, lived alone in the ruins for a long time. Then one day Elise found me, took me in..."

"She must have been a remarkable woman," Kath said.

He smiled. "I think she was."

"She taught Paul to read," Dan said.

"When she was younger," Paul said, "she was a lecturer at the Sorbonne."

Ed said, "But that closed... around sixty years ago, maybe more. How old was Elise?"

Paul shrugged. "She told me she was born in 2030."

Dan smiled to himself. "So she was over ninety. My God, the things she must have seen..."

Kath asked, gently, "When did she die, Paul?"

He looked at her, looked away. "Just yesterday," he said. "That's why I had to leave the city."

A silence greeted his words. At last Ed said, "I would like to have met her."

"Towards the end she was... her mind wandered. She had strange ideas. I like to remember her when she was younger, though she was always old to me."

"She must have loved you," Kath said.

He smiled. "She had a son when she was thirty. She told me he died in the plague of '65." He shrugged. "Yes, she loved me as if I were her son."

Dan finished his coffee. "I don't know about anyone else, but I'm going to have a look around outside, before it gets any hotter."

"I'll come with you," Paul said.

Ed remained in the truck, poring over his Kierkegaard, and Kath took the opportunity to shower.

It was hot in the truck, but even hotter outside – even in the shade. Dan cracked the hatch and felt a wave of hot air hit him. He reckoned it was around an hour after dawn, and in the low thirties. As the day progressed, so the temperature would climb to the point where, by mid-afternoon, it would be impossible to venture outside without adequate covering: unprotected skin would burn in seconds, and the air would be as breathable as steam.

A hot wind blew in from the west, drying his sweat and turning it to a fine, salty talc on his arms and face.

Keeping to the shade, they rounded the square

and approached what at one time might have been a farmhouse. Dan watched Paul as he moved; he had a light, almost bobbing gait, and he was constantly on the lookout, his head moving this way and that, like an animal vigilant for prey, or predators.

They entered the kitchen of the old building and gazed around.

Most buildings these days were shells, long emptied of everything of possible worth – whatever could be reused, recycled or burned was taken, leaving nothing; even floorboards were ripped up, and ceiling joists. In some places, Dan saw that even wallpaper had been stripped by people in order to get at the starch in the paste impregnated into the paper.

In contrast, mysteriously, this place was relatively pristine.

The floorboards were in place, even covered by an ancient, sun-bleached rug. A table stood beside the window, and a dresser against the far wall. Dan strode across to it and opened a door. It was bare, as he'd expected.

Paul said, "Look."

Dan joined him. Paul pointed to a child's picture book on the floor, and picked it up. He turned it over as if it were a priceless treasure, then opened it and began reading, hesitantly, "One day, Millie and her sister went to the market with their mother..." An accompanying picture showed a happy family scene of a mother and two little girls striding through town with shopping bags.

Dan moved away, some strange emotion filling his throat so that he found it hard to swallow. Tears stung his eyes. He didn't want Paul to see him like this. He moved to a flight of rickety stairs and climbed.

He entered a bedroom at the back of the building which looked out over the remains of the village and, in the distance and far below, the pervasive sweep of the desert, stretching from horizon to horizon – and Dan saw it then as something evil, the physical manifestation of everything that was choking the life and hope from the few human beings who remained on the face of the planet.

A long time ago, this scene would have been one of vineyards and sunflowers, shady plane trees and long lanes stretching through working countryside.

Paul was at his side. He gestured to the scene outside. "I wonder what happened?" he asked in a soft voice.

It was as if the boy had been privy to Dan's last thoughts.

He said, "Elise didn't tell you?"

The boy shook his head. "She only spoke about the past before... long before all this. She told me about the good times, and history, far back in history. And the books I read said nothing about the end."

Dan sighed. "Ed knows all about what happened, all the politics, the plagues, the wars... He'll tell you all about it, if you ask."

He turned and looked around the room. Two metal-frame beds stood against the far wall. For some skewed reason, Dan saw them as belonging to the girls in the picture book, and the idea, even metaphorically, struck him as almost unbearable.

Paul asked, "What nationality is Ed?"

"Danish."

The boy looked at him. "And you and Kath?"

Dan smiled and said. "Well, my parents were Belgian, for all that it matters these days. And Kath's folks were British. Why the interest?"

The boy was smiling. "It's just that... Elise gave me a book, a long time ago. About the nations of the world, the peoples... I was fascinated with it, with where people came from, their different types." He smiled. "It was like another world."

Dan nodded. "It *was* another world, Paul."

He moved from the room, descended the stairs and left the farmhouse, crossing the square in the full light of the rising sun.

Ed said he was up to taking the wheel for the next few hours, and Dan decided to get some sleep. He would leave the maintenance checks on the truck, the engine and the solar arrays, until the next time they stopped.

Paul took his new find to the chesterfield and began reading. As Ed started up the engine and rolled the half-track from the square, Dan left the lounge and lay on the bed.

Minutes later the sliding door rattled and Kath appeared, fresh from her shower. "Tired?" She smiled down at him.

He took her hand. "Not too tired," he said. "Come here."

He pulled her to him, reassuring himself with her solidity, her life, as the truck barrelled down the incline towards the desert.

* * *

DAN CAME AWAKE, refreshed, a long time later. He had been dreaming, and now his head swam with the fleeting residue of those dreams: images of two small girls going to market with their mother, and in his dream Kath was the mother, smiling and laughing as she led her daughters through the town.

Darkness was falling; he must have slept, uninterrupted, all day. Something had woken him, he realised seconds later – and then knew what it was. The truck had stopped. All was silent. In the half-light that seeped through the screen, he made out Kath lying beside him, wonderfully naked, her body dewed with sweat.

He turned onto his belly and peered through the screen. All he could make out was desert, and a sky shot through with fiery streaks.

"Mmm?" Kath was coming awake beside him, disturbed by his movement.

"We've stopped. Ed must've driven all day. Christ, he'll be tired." He felt a stab of guilt at not waking before now and relieving the old man.

The sliding door rattled open and Paul leaned through. "Dan! Ed said... Oh –" He stopped, staring, as he saw Kath. "I'm... I'm sorry. I didn't mean to..."

Kath drew a sheet to her chest. "Don't worry." She smiled at him. "What is it?"

"Ed's going to cook some food later – he said I can help him. But... he wants you to come and look."

Exchanging a glance with Kath, Dan said, "Tell him I'll be right along."

They dressed quickly and moved to the lounge, Ed was easing himself through the hatch from the cab, grimacing as he did so.

"What is it?" Kath asked.

"Take a look at this."

He moved to the door, opened it, and stood back with old-fashioned courtesy to allow Kath and Dan to pass through before him.

They climbed out, walked to the nose of the truck and stared ahead. Ed joined them, Paul at his side.

"We're in what was the Auvergne," Ed said. "That, I presume, was once upon a time the city of Bourges."

"Jesus Christ," Dan whispered to himself. "What happened?"

They were on a plateau which stood proud of the surrounding desert. Before them, extending for as far as they could see, was what looked like a frozen, glassy sea: a film of the ocean, Dan thought, frozen on a slight swell. He looked down at his feet and was aware of sand beneath his feet, and beneath it the hard, ungiving surface of glass. It stretched away, jade green, speckled here and there with shots of colour. Under the moonlight, it looked beautiful.

Ed was shaking his head. "I'd guess it was a nuclear strike, or multiple strikes. God knows when it happened, or who was responsible. But the entire plain is vitrified. There were signs back there, warning that the plain is a no go area. Radioactivity, I suspect."

Kath hugged herself, despite the heat. "Are we safe here?"

Ed said, "If we don't hang around."

Dan wondered if that might explain the reason the farmhouse back there had survived relatively unransacked. People must have kept well away from the area after the blast and the subsequent evacuation.

They climbed back aboard the half-track and Dan took the wheel, Kath beside him. Ed and Paul stood in the opening, staring ahead through the windscreen at the phantasmagorical landscape passing outside.

They made good progress over the glassy terrain. After the desert, this slick surface was conducive to speed. They charted a course around undulant swells, passing swirled hillocks and slurred rises; it reminded Dan of old, inexpertly blown glass bottles, uneven and thickened in places. It was a landscape that, in the light of the moon, appeared almost magical.

He wondered how many hundreds of thousands, maybe even millions, of people had died here.

He slowed. They were passing down a narrow defile between two gentle banks. The shape of the terrain was no more remarkable than any they had witnessed over the course of the last thirty minutes, but what was unique was what was buried within the glass, like flies in amber.

"No..." Kath said, looking away.

Appalled but at the same time fascinated, Dan slowed the truck to walking pace and peered out.

Embedded within the bank of glass to his right and left were a series of white stalks, scattered in a jumble like jack-straws: only when he saw, staring out at him, the orbs of skulls did he realise that the tableau consisted of thousands and thousands of skeletons, innocent citizens caught in the blast and stripped instantly of flesh, meat, internal organs...

Among the skeletons – in a surreal touch that seemed to emphasise and add poignancy to the carnage – were these people's possessions, which tragically seemed undamaged in comparison: tumbled cars and bicycles, television sets and tables, a filing cabinet and the frame of a child's buggy...

It was a fresco of death, Dan realised, that would last as long as the planet itself.

He wondered if, one day in the distant future, the dominant species on the planet – be they humans, if the human race survived, or perhaps even the evolved ancestors of ants – might tour this gruesome avenue as tourists once flocked to Pompeii, and shake their heads at the spectacle of human folly.

Paul murmured to himself, "*While the terrible stupidity grinds and crushes, and makes a smoking heap of a thousand men...*"

Ed said, "Rimbaud? Appropriate."

It was oddly salutary, and macabre, to behold the skeletal relics of the dead. Dan had rarely seen the remains of the long dead: across the land, only the works of humankind remained as a reminder of a fallen civilisation. The bones of the people themselves had mostly vanished, picked clean of meat and marrow by desperate survivors, and discarded.

Now only the present generation roamed the land, heirs to a world destroyed by the ignorant armies of their forebears.

He tried to shake such thoughts from his head and concentrate on driving. He accelerated, and soon they were racing back out across the open plain.

An hour later they passed from the vitrified land and sloughed through the desert, and Dan halted the truck.

They agreed they needed another coffee, and sat outside in the relative cool of the sand and drank hot mugs of the invigorating liquid.

In their wake, the raised glass plateau glowed a sickly green in the moonlight.

Paul, with the curiosity of the young, asked, "What happened, Ed?"

The old man clutched his mug, staring into the surrounding darkness. "You mean in general, not just here?"

The boy nodded, watching the old man.

Ed smiled, an almost ghoulish expression on a face so skeletal. "Stupidity happened, Paul. Greed happened. Humans happened. The same thing happened as is happening now. You saw it yourself just yesterday. One group of humans wanted more, and thought they knew the best way to go about getting more, and did so, and people suffered." He gestured a big hand across the expanse of darkness before him. "It's both very simple and very complex, so easy to understand and yet at the same time so difficult to comprehend. And, of course, it is impossible to ensure that it won't happen again."

A profound silence lengthened between them, as they sat drinking their coffee and thinking their thoughts. Dan opened his mouth, intending to temper Ed's pessimism with some platitude, but the old man was in essence correct.

At last Paul said, "But if we do find water, and bring the people from Copenhagen south, and maybe find other people with skills and expertise..."

"Then perhaps then there will be hope," said Kath quietly.

Dan said, "There is always hope, but what Ed's saying is that even if we manage to found a new colony, and it prospers, and if humankind prospers, then even then there will be self-inflicted injuries, injustices, terrible crimes."

"But also," Ed said, "there will be joy, and creation, and great works of art." He gestured towards Paul. "You quoted Rimbaud back there. If by some miracle we can build on what we've got, if we can make good the earth, then perhaps people will be quoting Rimbaud, and even contemporary scribes, in centuries to come."

The boy smiled and shook his head, and said, "It's all so confusing, and hard to understand. Just yesterday I was thinking only of myself."

"Were you?" Kath asked. "Weren't you thinking of Elise, also?"

"Well, yes..."

"Then there you are. You are just other people, multiplied. When you live in a community, you look out not only for yourself, but for others."

Dan reached out and took her hand.

Paul nodded. "I've a lot to learn," he said.

Ed said, "We all have, Paul. We all have."

They returned to the truck, and Dan took the

wheel with Kath at his side while Ed and the boy slept.

They drove in companionable silence for a long time.

If we can make good the earth, Dan thought; now there's the rub.

CHAPTER EIGHT

THE CEDAR TREE rose from the battlement garden, its lifeless trunk and branches stark against the sunset. This narrow stretch of land had been her father's pride and joy, the place where he'd come to be alone with his thoughts, to remember his wife, who was buried beside the tree.

The battlements were packed with mourners, and more stood in the courtyard below. Word of her father's death had spread rapidly through the community, and Samara was gratified by the sense of shock that gripped the place. People recognised that they owed much to the man who had founded the colony and ruled it, with the nominal aid of the council, for almost sixty years. Without him, they knew, the colony would have long ago succumbed to either anarchy or invasion.

Doctor Mortenson had come to her chambers shortly before the funeral ceremony. He'd made a short speech, stating that now was the time to look ahead, plan for the future, continue where her father had left off and gain the backing of the people with an announcement about her father's proposed expedition to Spain.

"He told you?" Samara had been surprised, perhaps because the doctor's words indicated that her father had informed him about his plans before he had said anything to her. The notion rankled, but she tried not to let it show.

"Your father ran through the facts with me, soliciting my opinion."

"Which was?"

"That the expedition was essential."

She smiled. "Excellent. That's what I think." She hesitated, then went on, "I've never been one for public speaking, and don't feel like making a declaration now... Mort, will you have a notice written out saying that I'll be taking a small expedition to Spain in search of provisions? You and the council will keep things running while I'm gone?"

"Of course, Samara."

She would do this for her father; it was his last grand project and she would see it through to its conclusion. She had told herself that her father's funeral would not be the end of an era, but the beginning of a new time of prosperity for the colony.

And then she had had word from Salif in the repair-shop: there was a problem with the main transporter's motor. They were working to get the vehicle running, but it might be a matter of days or even weeks, especially if more parts had to be made or scavenged.

Now she stared into the sandy pit which would soon receive her father's remains. It was a bleak scene, with the last of the sun on the horizon, and the crenellations silhouetted against the dying light, the dead tree lifting blackened branches into the air as if in petrified grief.

Six young men bore the body of her father on a timber frame across their shoulders; his remains were swaddled in white cloth, and they seemed diminished to Samara, nowhere near as bulky as they should have been. Her father's final illness might have whittled away flesh, she thought, but it had done nothing to dim his spirit.

She watched the men lay the body in the shallow pit. She stared at the tightly swaddled corpse, beset by memories good and bad; her father's love, his cruel censure, his long absences from her life when he claimed he was too busy attending to council matters, when she knew for a fact that he was seeing women who eased the burden of his grief at his wife's death as she, Samara, was unable to do.

Dr Mortenson stepped forward, backed by the grey, bowed figures of the council, and addressed the crowd.

Samara heard only brief fragments, her thoughts elsewhere. "...And one example of that foresight," said the doctor, "was his purchasing the castle, which many saw as an expensive folly. But he, in his wisdom, foresaw the straitened times ahead..."

Samara stared down at the upturned faces in the courtyard. All eyes, she saw, were not on the speaker but on her, and she felt the weight of their expectation like a burden.

"He governed for nigh on sixty years, steering the colony through troubled times. While society and the rule of law broke down outside, he maintained order and stability within. His tactics were at times deemed draconian, especially in the early years when disease and conflict ravaged the outside world and we had to turn away the sick and the injured... but the very fact that we are here today, the very fact that the colony is not only surviving but prospering, proves that his policies all along were correct..."

She tried not to smile at the doctor's upbeat pronouncement.

"...In essence," Doctor Mortenson was saying, "nothing has changed, the council still governs, overseen by his daughter Samara, who with her father's guidance these past few years has been taking on more and more official responsibility for the smooth running of the colony. That things will change – and change for the better – is inevitable, and soon the council will be making an announcement detailing plans that will affect each and every one of us..."

A murmur swept through the listening crowd, as the doctor finished, "... and now we lay the remains of Fabio Mastriani to earth, in the knowledge of a great life well spent, and an eternity of peaceful rest..."

The six young men took spades and eased the sand back in place over her father's body.

Samara closed her eyes as the doctor said, "And if you would care to share a minute's silent reflection on the life now ended..."

A silence settled over the gathering, broken only by the soughing of the wind through the battlements. Somewhere, a woman began to sob quietly; Samara restrained herself from opening her eyes to see who it was who grieved. She had no interest in the identity of her father's old lovers.

The minute's silence had not yet ended when Samara was aware of a insistent sound on the edge of her hearing, and then a commotion from beyond the gatehouse. She looked to her left, across the courtyard to the great double gates that barred access to the castle. The small hatch at the bottom of the gate swung open, and half a dozen armed guardsmen filed out, securing the hatch behind them.

The crowd was alerted now, and all eyes were on the gates. The silence ended, and a murmur of speculation sounded below.

A minute later the hatch in the gate opened suddenly and the guards filed through, shouting orders to others that the main gates should be opened.

Samara watched as, inch by inch, the mammoth timber gates were hauled open and the drawbridge lowered.

Beyond the portcullis sat a transporter, a battered half-track barnacled with glinting solar arrays. When the drawbridge was fully down and level, the driver revved its engine and the truck kicked into life and rattled across the timbers and into the courtyard.

Samara moved to the edge of the battlements and stared down. The crowd had remained in place, silent, watching the truck as if with expectation. The vehicle came to a sudden halt, and the driver killed the drone of the engine. Samara could see a shadowy, bulky figure behind the dust-encrusted windscreen.

It was some seconds before the figure moved itself, as if weary after a long journey.

The cab door cracked open, swung loose, and a thick pair of legs emerged, followed by the man himself, dropping from the cab and standing foursquare beside the truck.

One or two people in the crowd stepped forward and embraced the driver; slowly, the crowd broke up as people returned to their various duties.

Samara stared down, aware of the thudding in her chest.

The tall, broad, bald-headed figure stared up at the battlements, taking in the gathering there, and then seeing Samara. His big, sun-scorched face broke into a smile and he lifted a hand in a nonchalant salute.

Her first instinct was to hurry down to the courtyard and fling herself into this man's arms; her second instinct, to make her way calmly to him and slap him across his smug, fat face.

She looked across at Dr Mortenson, who was staring down at the new arrival with a non-committal expression. He, like her father, had not approved of her relationship with the German. She heard a muttered comment from one of the council, "So the unprodigal returns..."

She moved from the battlements, still unsure quite how to greet the returnee. She felt a little sick, light-headed, and at the same time undeniably lustful. It had been so long, and the recollection of their love-making a year ago was strong in her memory.

She emerged in the cloister beside the courtyard, and still her impulse was to hurry across to him. It would not do for the colonists to see her reaction... whatever that might be.

He saw her and smiled, then crossed the courtyard and approached her. He stopped two metres away. He looked bruised and battered, and his left bicep was wrapped in a bloody makeshift bandage. She could smell his body-odour from here, and even this reminded her of what had been. Suddenly, she wanted him.

"Hans... you're back."

"Yeah... Glad to see me?"

She ignored the question. "The north didn't fulfil its promises?"

"Copenhagen. They were clueless." He looked her up and down, his gaze lingering on her breasts.

She kept her voice even. "I begged you to stay, Hans."

He waved, as if to cast her words aside. "We talked long and hard. You know what I felt for you."

Yes, she thought, it was never love he had felt for her, just as she had never loved him: it was something much more basic and ungovernable, more honest and heartfelt – a raw animal lust that she felt overwhelming her now.

"I had to get away, Samara. Things here, your father's ban on technology –"

"I was overturning that, little by little."

"And... things were failing here. You know that. I asked you to come with me."

"And leave everything I knew? The castle? My father?" She stared at his muscled torso, his arrogant grin. "And anyway, if things were failing here, why the eagerness to come back?"

"They had no idea how to run the place... Clueless liberals. I had to get away."

"And you chose here. Any port in a storm."

He shrugged. "You might be right there."

And still the bastard wouldn't admit that maybe, perhaps, a slight consideration in his decision to return was that she was here.

She said, "Things have changed. We need to talk."

He looked surprised, and said, "You'll allow me to stay?"

She tried not to smile. For the moment, she was in control. She had him; she could use him in more than the base way dictated by her biology.

"Come," she said. She led the way up the winding stone stairs to the battlements and then along to the residential tower. They climbed to her chambers and she opened the door and stepped inside.

The last light of the setting sun was seeping through the long windows.

They faced each other. She could see the uncertainty in his face.

She said, "Do you still desire me?"

He grinned. "What do you think?"

He wondered if she should tell him now about the death of her father, of her plans for the future... But that, she realised, would be showing her hand too soon.

First, she had to make entirely sure of his subservience... and at the same time slake her own needs. She was under no illusions that Hans was a bastard, but there were bastards and there were bastards, and

Hans was a bastard whose pheromones sang to her.

"Follow me."

She led him to her bedroom and faced him, the expanse of her bed between them.

She said, "Remove your clothes..."

He wore only a bandoleer across his bulging chest, and a pair of threadbare shorts. He shrugged off the bandoleer and dropped his shorts, and she stared at him. His cock was monstrous and she felt weak at the knees.

He said, "Perhaps I should wash?"

She managed to say, "I want you as you are."

They clashed on the bed like wild animals.

WHAT THEY DID over the course of the next three hours, she knew, could in no way be called making love; it was more brutalised combat, an orgy of unrestrained sado-masochism. She bit and scratched his flesh, revelling in drawing blood and hearing his pain. He restrained her in wrestling holds and rubbed and licked her and only then, when she was on the verge of passing out in ecstasy, would he set about her with his sex.

It was a cathartic release, both to receive pain and ecstasy and to give it; it was wonderful to be able to use all her strength to hurt the bastard, hitting him again and again until he cried aloud for her to stop; and just as exhilarating to be on the receiving end, to be overpowered by his might, the pummelling of his iron-hard cock, until it was her turn to cry submission.

In the end, however, it was Hans who called a halt, lying back on the sweat-soaked sheets in exhaustion, his lips dripping blood, his cock worked raw.

She lay on her back and laughed aloud.

He shouted, as if in triumph, "It's great to be back!"

She looked at him. He was so easy to please, and the beauty of it was that she had more than pleased herself in the process.

She wondered what Mort and the council would think now, if they could se her like this, so soon after her father's funeral.

She said, "Things have changed, Hans."

He grinned. "Have they? Things seem exactly the same to me, girl."

"I mean here, at the castle. My father is dead."

He looked at her, transparently attempting to come up with the correct response. "I'm sorry."

"You lying bastard! You're not sorry at all. You hated my father."

"I hated his regime here, his policies, the way he went about ruling this place."

She stared at him. "All those things," she said. "But even more, you hated *him*."

He shrugged, as if what he had thought of her father hardly mattered.

She went on, wanting to dominate him not only sexually, but intellectually; she wanted him to know that she understood the workings of his simple mind. "You hated him because he held all the power here, and you resented that. You wanted the power, and he stood in your way."

"So I hated him. He was doing things wrong."

"And your way would have been better?"

"Of course."

She reached out a foot and turned over his slouched penis as if it were a dead animal. "And Copenhagen? They didn't like the way you went about things there, too?"

"Like I said, they were soft liberals –"

"You mean, they drew the line at eating their own dead?"

He stared at her. "You had no objections when I made the suggestion."

She smiled. "But then I'm no liberal, Hans. You know that."

The silenced stretched. Provocatively, she attempted to coax life into the corpse of his cock with her toes. It resisted reanimation. Hans frowned.

He said at last, "So... with your father gone..."

"Yes?"

"What happens now? Has the council taken control?"

"Nominally."

He frowned. She wondered whether or not he knew the meaning of the word. "So, have they?" he said.

"I've been running things for a while now. To all appearances, the council runs the day to day operations of the castle, but what I say, goes."

He tried not to let his increased interest show, but it was like a wild animal feigning uninterest in a haunch of bloody meat.

"What have you suggested?"

"Well, I took up your idea. We're eating corpses. We're cannibals." She regarded his smile. "I thought you might like that."

He shrugged. "It makes perfect sense."

She went on, "And I've slowly, behind my father's back, been introducing technology."

He nodded. "I'm impressed. Things have really changed round here."

"But not as much as they'll be changing pretty soon." She waited, smiling, then said, "I'm leaving here."

He blinked. "Leaving?"

"I'm taking a transporter and heading to Spain."

"Barcelona?" He sounded surprised. "But the colony there died out years ago."

"Not Barcelona. Bilbao."

He shook his head. "What's there?"

"Provisions. Supplies. Enough food and water to last a community like this, oh... decades."

He grunted a sceptical laugh. "You're bullshitting!"

"My grandfather worked for the European Space Agency. They built an underground base in northern Spain. Before they could launch the ship, there was a terrorist raid. They managed to lock the place up before they evacuated it, leaving food and water enough to equip a city. And before my father died, he gave me all the codes."

Hans stared at her. "You're serious, aren't you?"

"Deadly serious. This could mean the long-term survival of the colony." She regarded him. "So... I'm leaving here, but what about you?"

He grinned. "I'm up for it."

"Are you? But how would you earn your place on the mission?"

He grinned and looked down at his crotch.

She shook her head. "No deal, big boy. Not enough."

He said, "You need an engineer?"

She smiled. "Now you're talking."

She sat up and took his cock in her hands, attempting to massage it to attention. Her efforts failed and it flopped miserably. She cast it aside and jumped from the bed.

"Well, if you can't fuck me any more, I've got something to show you."

He looked down at his sweat-soaked body. "I really need a wash, Samara."

"Later. Get dressed and come with me."

She slipped into her shorts and moved from the room, watching him with amusement as he struggled into his shorts and hurried to catch up with her.

She led him from the tower, across the courtyard to the repair-shop.

For the next couple of hours, Hans examined the transporter's engine, with Salif and Giovanni in attendance. After that, he turned his attention to the couplings from the solar array, discussing his findings with the old man.

Samara sat on a work-bench, watching the way the sweat dribbled across Hans's bulky torso, the way Giovanni's smaller, boyish muscles rippled and flexed as he worked on a solar panel. The boy cast her covert glances from time to time, like a dog in heat.

She smiled at him, keeping him hoping.

"Well?" Samara asked Hans as he stood over the engine housing, wiping grease from his hands with an old rag.

"The engine looks fine enough to me, but there's something wrong with the link from the arrays. That's no problem. I'm going to take bits and pieces from the truck I came in. A bit of cannibalisation should do the trick."

She smiled. "It always does."

Hans slapped the flank of the transporter. "This is a bigger, better truck then mine, so it makes sense to get this up and running."

"How long you reckon before it's in working order?"

He pulled a face, considering. "A day. Two at the most." He smiled across at her. "That'll earn me a place?"

"I'll think about it... But you've got to get it running, first."

Grinning, he hoisted a tool-box from the bench and got to work.

Now that the expedition looked like coming off, she turned her thoughts to who should accompany her. She wanted people she trusted, who were bright enough to fulfil their allotted tasks – cooking and fighting off potential marauders – but not too bright so that they might question her command or vie for her leadership. Also, she didn't want women along, causing division among the men. She wanted the five or six males on the trip to be loyal to her and her only. So... Giovanni was the obvious choice:

he was unquestioningly loyal and not too blessed with brains. Ivan the Cossack, as strong as an ox and about as dim. She had three others in mind, mindless slabs of muscle who would protect her and themselves unfailingly and ask no questions. And Hans, of course: he craved power but was, she suspected, too stupid to use it; if she kept him on a tight leash, he would do whatever she wanted and be quite unaware of the fact that she was in total control.

She smiled to herself. Her father would be proud.

CHAPTER NINE

SHORTLY AFTER XIAN'S tenth birthday, the farm where her mother worked was raided by hungry citizens, the hydroponic chambers ransacked and some of the residential domes burnt down.

Xian and her mother escaped with their lives, but three other workers died in the fires and the fighting.

Later, when she looked back on her childhood, it was this event that marked the end of what had been until then an idyllic period of her life. After the fire, she saw the world as a different, more dangerous place.

Her mother found job after job in various research facilities and hydroponic stations, but for whatever reasons these periods of employment, up and down the length of the country, never seemed to last for long. They were always on the move, from one rented house to the next, and they never seemed to have money for anything but the basics of existence. Her mother explained lack of government funding meant the closure of the stations; also, the money she had received after Xian's father's death had not gone far, what with inflation and the devaluation of the euro.

Her mother was forty, but she looked a lot older.

Around this time, in the year after her tenth birthday, Xian took more interest in the news on TV. It seemed that there were wars and riots everywhere, in every country of the world. She could never switch on the television without seeing processions of tanks rolling through lifeless countryside, and refugees streaming in the other direction. And when it was not wars, it was floods.

At school she learned that the Maldive Islands were no more, and that vast swathes of Africa were uninhabitable. Millions of people worldwide were dying of starvation.

Her mother planted a pineapple plant in the garden of one of their rented houses, but a couple of months later she found a new, better job in Scotland and she and Xian moved yet again.

She often wondered whether the pineapple had ever borne fruit.

The clear night skies of the highlands, free from light-pollution, allowed Xian to study the stars with a pair of binoculars.

She still dreamed of exploring those distant points of light.

CHAPTER TEN

THEY WERE HALF a day into their journey west and the landscape had changed completely. The familiar desert terrain surrounded by bare grey mountains was no more: now all that could be seen in every direction was a limitless expanse of ochre desert. Samara felt out of her depth, vulnerable; she had left behind everything she had known since childhood, all the familiar comforts of home, and now nothing at all was familiar.

The physical feeling of vulnerability, the idea that at any second some unforeseen calamity might overcome them, was matched by a similar psychological fear. Back at the castle, with the weight of the council behind her, she had been sure of her place in the scheme of things: at the very top, thanks to her lineage. What she had suggested to the council had, in time, always been acted upon; she had had a quiet hold on power, the knowledge that she was respected, if not for the changes she had made, then for the fact that she was her father's daughter. In a closed society like that of the castle, lineage meant everything.

Out here, with her father dead and the day to day

rules of conduct much changed, she feared she was losing her grip on that power.

The very landscape through which they were travelling seemed to mock her uncertainty.

For the first few hours, she rode in the cab with Hans, staring out in amazement at the sun-blasted land. The lack of landmarks on which to fix the eye was disconcerting: distances out there took on exaggerated proportions. She was unable to tell whether the horizon was fifty kilometres away or just metres distant. It seemed at times that she might reach out and touch the undulating line where the land met the sky, and at others as if the horizon was a million kilometres away, and that they might travel forever without attaining it, or their goal. She experienced a kind of vertigo that turned her stomach and made her wonder – irrationally, she knew – at the wisdom of embarking on the trip.

She felt relief and the return of comparative normality when the sun sank eventually and set; the bloated red oblate on the horizon restored a sense of proportion to the world. It reminded her of all the times she had sat at her window seat, often with her father, and watched the sun setting. She recalled the times she had likened her father to the sun, and smiled to herself. Watching it now, she felt a little better.

Her equilibrium was short-lived, however.

Before the sun was fully down, Hans pointed. "Look."

She peered ahead. Strange, upright forms emerged from the sand; it was impossible to tell their size or how far away they were. As Hans steered towards them, Samara stared and tried to work out what the shapes were, or might have been. Dark against the sunset, they rose at random from the sand, perhaps a hundred or more spines that had no corollary with anything she had seen before.

She looked at Hans. "What are they?"

"They were trees," he said. "It was a forest."

As soon as he said the word, it was as if something in her brain flipped a switch and she was able to make out the dark spines for what they were, a forest of trees blasted of every branch and leaf and left only with their central, spear-like trunks. Minutes later the truck was amongst them, and Hans cut the engine.

"How about we stop here for an hour, use the wood for fuel and cook up a meal?"

He had phrased the idea as a question, deferring to her perhaps, but it was a suggestion counter to what she had set out earlier: that they would eat dried provisions on the move.

She considered her response. The idea of stopping, of breaking the monotonous journey and eating a hot meal, appealed to her; yet if she gave in to his suggestion, might she not be conspiring to undermine her very own authority?

She decided to compromise.

"We'll stop for half an hour and eat dried provisions, okay?"

He indicated the trees. "There might not be fuel like this to cook meals further along."

She stared him down. "Okay, so fell a tree or two and store the wood. There's a rack on the side we can use." She went on, "I don't want to spend a long time lighting fires and cooking food, Hans. I want to get to Spain as soon as possible."

He stared at her, his expression unreadable, and finally nodded. "Very well."

They jumped from the cab, into the hot air of early evening, and Samara stared about her at the blackened forest.

Ivan the cook doled out dried food rations and litre bottles of water. Hans unstrapped an axe from the side of the truck. He moved to the first trunk and, perhaps in a show of strength intended to impress the others, swung the axe with all his might. It bit into the dried wood with a sharp snap, and three blows later the tree toppled slowly and hit the sand. He chopped the trunk into four equal lengths, then arranged them in a square next to the truck.

The party, so furnished, sat down and ate.

Hans sat next to her. Since the very start of the expedition, he had made sure the others knew that he and Samara were together. At a brief meeting in the repair-shop, when she had outlined the trip ahead, he had stood next to her, at one point placing what had felt like a proprietary hand on her shoulder. He had shadowed her ever since, if not exactly snarling at the other males to keep their distance, then suggesting as much with his possessive body language. He was the alpha male of the tribe, and he wanted everyone to know it.

Samara felt like a possession, and she didn't like it. She was aware of the stares of the others; Giovanni couldn't keep his eyes from her breasts, and though Ivan was more subtle, he didn't miss an opportunity to ogle. The other three, a couple of Africans, Edo and Lomo, and Hungarian Josef, affected a casual manner she knew masked latent lust.

The irony was, she had selected a complement of all male travelling companions because she thought they would be easier to control: but now, being at the centre of attention like this, she felt vulnerable. She wished she'd asked along a couple of women to help take the burden of all the testosterone in the air.

The others were chatting amongst themselves while Samara ate, her thoughts miles away.

Hans nudged her. "Eh, Samara?"

She looked up testily. "What?"

"Giovanni has a question."

The boy bobbed his head. "Earlier, back at the castle, you said we were going in search of provisions. You said you'd heard about a stash somewhere." He shrugged. "I was just wondering…"

Ivan stared her. "We all want to know exactly where it is we're heading, Samara."

"I told you." She held Ivan's gaze. "Spain."

Hungarian Josef chewed on a scrap of dried bat and said, "Raiding a colony, yes?" He looked uneasy at the idea.

Hans laughed at this. "Do we look like a raiding party? A woman, a boy, and Ivan here – fattened from spoils of the kitchen?"

Ivan chewed, staring at Hans, his expression neutral. Samara, then, shared his sudden loathing of the loud German.

She said, "My father discovered European government papers. They showed stockpiles of provisions, hidden in underground bunkers near Bilbao."

Giovanni nodded, eager to show Samara that her answer satisfied him.

Ivan laughed, "Underground bunkers? And how are we supposed to break into them? Dig our way through solid concrete with spades?"

Hans leaned forward and said in a low, soft voice, "No, Ivan, we intend to drop fat bastards like you onto them from a great height."

One of the Africans sniggered.

Hans said, to everyone, "We have codes that'll open the vaults, and maps that show exactly where everything is."

He grinned around the group, as if having scored a point.

Samara let her anger simmer. She didn't like the way he casually answered the questions directed at her, or the way he'd appropriated authority with, "We have the codes..."

She said, "Correction, Hans. I have the codes. I have the maps." She looked around the group, settling her gaze on Hans. "Isn't that right, Hans?"

Something flashed in the German's eyes: barely suppressed anger. He forced himself to say, "You heard the lady, boys. She's the boss. We're along to provide the muscle, right?"

Worried, Giovanni shuttled a glance to Samara. Josef tried not to look amused at the contretemps. The Africans just stared at Hans, perhaps surprised at his capitulation.

Ivan said, under his breath, "And I know what muscle you're using, Hans."

Samara knew, then, that things were getting out of

control – and that she didn't have the slightest clue how to bring order back to the gathering.

Hostility charged the air.

Hans lay aside his water bottle with frightening deliberation and looked across at the Russian. "What was that, Ivan?"

Ivan stared at Hans, seemingly unafraid. "Just wondering what muscle you might be offering Samara, Ivan? I mean," he went on, "it can't be your brain."

Hans said, "Repeat that, if you dare."

Ivan shrugged. "I'll go one better and explain: just because you're dicking the bitch, doesn't put you in control here."

Hans moved, but Samara was faster. She didn't know what she was about to do until the move was under way and she had no option but to carry it through. She grabbed her rifle from where she'd propped it against the trunk, and took two strides across to Ivan. As he stared up at her, open-mouthed and disbelieving, she brought the butt of the weapon down into his fat face. Something cracked, and he fell off the log and sprawled in the sand, wiping blood from his mouth with the back of his hand.

Samara stood over him, panting. She turned and looked around the group, making sure she had their attention. Hans stared at her, a comical expression of surprise splashed across his sun-reddened face.

"The very next person who shows disrespect to me gets a bullet, right?"

Ivan blustered, frothing blood, "I just said –"

"Listen to me, Ivan. Like Hans said, I'm in charge here. Not Hans, just because I'm fucking him."

A silence rang around the gathering.

She went on, "Remember this, you're all here to do a job. I give the orders and you follow them. That includes you too, Hans." She stared around at the semi-circle of shocked faces. "Any objections?"

Silence met her enquiry.

"Excellent." She nodded, breathing hard and wondering for how long order might maintain. "Giovanni and Ivan, you're taking the next shift in the cab. Josef, collect whatever food and water's left over and stow it. You two," she went on, gesturing to the Africans, "lash the logs to the side of the truck. We're out of here in ten minutes."

While the others broke camp, Hans stood and stared at Samara as she ducked back into the transporter. She could feel his gaze on her back, and she wondered how he would react to having his supposed male authority undercut like that.

She moved through the transporter to the large room at the rear of the vehicle, where she and Hans would sleep. If, that was, she wanted to share the room with him tonight. She stood by the rectangular window overlooking the darkening desert. She expected Hans to be along at any second, and she was right. She did not expect the timorous knock on the door, however.

"Who is it?"

The door opened and Hans ducked in. He combined contrition and a swagger that didn't quite work. "Samara..." His tone was almost pleading. "What was all that about?"

She turned and stared at him, marvelling at his lack of insight.

She almost laughed. "I didn't think it needed explaining. You're all fighting for control like a bunch of boys. And I don't like the way you're using me in that fight."

He frowned, her argument lost on him.

"Hans, just remember who's leading this trip, okay? Don't try to take over. I don't want to make an enemy of you, but I'll cut you out if you try to usurp my authority, okay?"

He stared at her. With his big, red face, made seemingly even bigger by the fact that he was bald, he combined a look of hurt innocence and utter stupidity.

He shrugged. "We're edgy because we don't really know what the hell's happening, Samara. There were rumours going around the castle before we left – people saying we might be moving the colony to this place in Spain."

"Who said anything about that?" she asked.

"Rumour was your father told someone on the council about Spain, that it might be wise to move..." He looked across at her. "So... what is happening, Samara?"

"Like I said, we're going in search of provisions. There's no plan to move. We don't even know what we might find there, so how can we plan that far ahead?"

"Perhaps you should tell the others that?"

She looked at him, wondering whether this was a little mind game he was playing, another attempt at undermining her authority – or was she being paranoid?

She heard the multiple slamming of hatches, and seconds later the transporter kicked into life and set off. Swaying, she moved to the bed and lay down, head propped on her hand, watching him.

He gestured across the room, to the table beside the shower-stall. "Are those the papers your father left?"

She decided she'd move them before he helped himself to a closer look. She ignored the question, "Hans, come here."

His face lit up. "Samara..."

She sat up and traced a finger down his chest, whispering, "Be good, Hans, okay?"

THE SEX WAS much as it had been before, a contest of wills with the intent of inflicting as much pain and extracting as much pleasure as possible. She was sure Hans had no idea why he submitted to being tortured – other than the kinky thrill of being subjugated by a woman – and Samara tried not to look too deeply into the reasons why she enjoyed both inflicting pain and receiving it. She was sure it had something to do with the love-hate relationship she had had with her father, but she looked no further than that.

As ever, Hans emptied himself while Samara wanted more, and like the selfish man he was he flopped onto his back, exhausted, as if with his own ejaculation he had discharged his obligation to the act.

They lay in a sweat-sodden heap as the transporter carried them through the night. A small solar-powered light cast a dim glow across the bed, highlighting the sweat on their naked bodies.

Samara moved from the bed and stepped into the shower stall. Above the hiss of water, she heard

Hans's voice. She looked across to where he lay watching her.

"I said, is there room in there for two?"

"That depends, Hans, on what you want to do."

He joined her and they made love again, less violently this time for fear of shattering the glass stall. Afterwards she luxuriated in the jet of hot water.

He said, "Do they know about this shower?"

She laughed. "Of course not."

"The privileges of power," he said.

"I'm surprised you know such long words, Hans."

"Which?" he asked. "'Privilege' or 'power'?"

Perhaps she had underestimated his intelligence. For all that his thuggish exterior suggested a limited mental facility, perhaps she'd be wise not to underestimate him in that department.

They returned to the bed, but were soon sweating again in the heat of the night.

"You never really said why you came back to the castle."

He lay on his back, his big bald head facing the ceiling. "Like I said, I didn't like the way they were running things up there."

Which was another way of saying they weren't running things as he wanted them to run. "But why choose to come back to the castle?"

He thought about it. "Where else was there?"

"Paris? Wasn't there a community there?"

He rolled his eyes toward her, great staring yellowed orbs, disgusting when seen so closely. "We tried Paris," he said.

She propped herself up on an elbow and looked down at him. "'We'?"

"You know, Hamed, Achmed, Yip and the others..."

"The same crowd you took with you from the castle..." She snorted a laugh. "I always thought they didn't have minds of their own. Sheep, they'd follow you anywhere. Anyway, what happened to them?"

He shook his head. "Ambush in Paris. They were killed."

"All of them? But you managed to get away?"

He nodded. "Me and Hamed. He was badly injured, though."

She stared at him, heartbeat quickening. "What happened to him?"

He shrugged. "Died on the way down here. Nothing I could do."

She didn't like the part of herself that was reacting to the thoughts running through her mind. "You two were never that friendly, were you? Hamed was bright, and you didn't like that."

He remained staring at the ceiling.

"So... what did you do with the body?"

"Samara... why the questions?"

She sat up, smiling as she joked, "Hans, I didn't think you had it in you to admit shame! What did you do, fuck the corpse or eat it?"

She felt the pendulum of power swinging back towards her, and she pressed, "I didn't think you went for corpses... or men. But, I suppose, when you're desperate..."

"I didn't fuck him, so shut up. I didn't have a lot of food, and Hamed died soon after we left Paris...

What the fuck would you have done?"

She smiled and fingered sweat from his chest. She was intrigued by the contrasts in this man, the contradictions between the clueless boy and the depraved animal that sat side by side in the same skull. Perhaps that was what gave the sex such a frisson, the fact that she enjoyed subjugating the child in him and at the same time being dominated by the animal.

Just so long, she thought, as she didn't allow the beast in him to gain dominance outside the bedroom.

Lulled by the motion of the transporter, she slept.

She awoke once in the night to piss, and did it in the shower. Squatting in the stall, she gazed across the room. Hans was a monstrous shape on the bed, with a swollen dome of a head, a great bulging chest and protuberant belly, big feet and ugly, broken toes. By contrast, she pictured Giovanni's sleek muscled torso and lithe limbs...

The sound of an explosion tore into her thoughts. She stood up. She moved to the door, then remembered her shorts and found them beside the bed. She pulled them on, calling, "Hans, for chrissake..."

His snores filled the room. She called his name again and hurried down the corridor. She heard shouts from the main body of the vehicle, then realised she was paddling through water. She was passing the racks where the big ten litre water containers were stacked, and several of them were punctured, pulsing gallons of water onto the floor. Confused, she pushed herself forward.

When she reached the cramped lounge, what

met her eyes was a scene of chaos, which quickly resolved itself.

The transporter had drawn to a halt, and Giovanni hung in the entrance to the cab; evidently he had been driving, and like Samara had come to investigate the explosion. In the lounge itself, Josef sat in an old armchair pointing a rifle across the room at Ivan, who was pinned to the wall in fright.

The Africans were at the far end of the small lounge, curled against the wall.

Giovanni said, "He must have taken my rifle while I was driving... I swear, I didn't realise –"

"Shut up!" she snapped, staring from Ivan to Josef. "What the fuck's going on?"

Josef, his lean face snarling wolf-like at Ivan, kept the rifle trained at the fat Russian. "I found this fucker stealing rations."

Samara stared at the Russian. His chin was smeared with cold bat stew. She turned back to Josef. "So you thought you'd shoot the bastard?"

"I fired to miss the –"

She cut in, "You fired to miss, you cretin, but you hit the fucking water canisters."

Behind her, she heard someone grunting with the effort of lifting something. She glanced over her shoulder. Hans had stirred himself, at last, and was making himself useful, turning over the containers so that the holes piercing the plastic were now at the top. Samara wondered how much precious water they'd lost.

Josef looked terrified, "I didn't mean to..."

"You didn't think, did you? Christ! And you..."

She said, turning to the Russian.

Hans joined them, looking thunderous. "Three containers – almost drained. You realise what that means?" He turned to Josef. "Put that fucking rifle down before you do any more damage."

"I'm sorry. I..." He lay the gun aside. Hans snatched it up.

"Sorry won't get us back the fucking water!" he yelled at Josef.

"He..." Josef began, pointing to Ivan. "I caught him stealing rations!"

Hans turned his fiery face to Ivan, who looked ill. The Russian's eyes fell to the rifle in Hans's grip, terrified now.

Very quietly, Hans said, "We've lost over half our water rations. That means some of us will have to go short, very short. Now, who will that be? Who do you think was responsible for..." he turned and gestured to the flooded corridor, "for this?"

He looked around the group. "Well?"

Ivan said, "I didn't eat all my rations earlier. I was only –"

"That's a lie!" Josef said. "I cleared up what was left. Your plate was clean!"

Hans intervened. "Josef, you're a moron. You've cost us about thirty fucking litres of water. But you..." he said, facing Ivan, "you're even worse. Stealing rations. Our rations. You can't be fucking trusted." He stared at the Russian, who was dripping with sweat and silently pleading, massive eyes shuttling between Hans, Samara and the others.

Hans seemed to be considering something. Samara

realised, only later, that at this point she should have intervened, both to prevent what happened next and to tip the balance of power back in her favour. Instead, she did nothing, genuinely at a loss to know how she might resolve the situation.

Hans took advantage of her indecision. "Outside," he said to Ivan, motioning with the rifle.

The fat man raised his arms, whimpering a protest. He shuffled sidewise, comically, past Hans and tumbled through the hatch.

Samara stared after him. Dawn light was showing on the horizon to the east. Hans stepped from the transporter, followed by the Edo and Lomo, then Giovanni and Josef. They all moved timidly, their fear at Hans's rage counterbalanced by their ghoulish curiosity.

Ivan stood whimpering in the sand, hands still raised above his head. He managed, "Don't shoot... I promise. I'll make up for it. I'll go without food for three days, four! And water! No water for four days! I promise..."

"Shut up!"

Samara noticed Giovanni wince at the command.

Ivan shut up instantly.

Hans said, "Move over there." He gestured to the flank of the transporter.

Perhaps guessing that he wouldn't be shot so close to the vehicle, Ivan obeyed with fawning alacrity. He stood against the truck, his back pressed up against the metal, and stared at Hans, an uncertain half-smile on his lips.

"Now, climb up there."

Unsurely, Ivan glanced at where Hans was pointing:

a metal frame-work welded to the side of the truck.

Perhaps guessing Hans's intentions, Ivan began pleading, "You can't! No, please..." He flung a pleading glance towards Samara. "Please!" he stuttered.

Samara said, "Hans, that's enough –"

Ignoring her, Hans stepped forward and pressed the gun barrel into the soft roll of flesh at the Russian's neck. "I said climb!"

Ivan climbed onto the frame, standing on the lower rung and facing his tormentor.

Hans gestured to the Africans. "Tie his hands and feet!"

The pair jumped as if shot, and hurried to obey. A minute later the Russian was lashed tightly to the truck, his vast belly protruding.

He was crying now, tears rolling down his cheeks. Samara wanted to look away, to absent herself from the torture, but found it impossible to move. A grisly fascination kept her rooted to the spot.

Hans smiled and turned, pointedly, to stare at the rising sun. "Now, how long do you think a man might last under the full glare of the sun, eh?"

"No please! You can't do this! Please!" His roving gaze implored the others, who looked away one by one.

Samara wondered at the motivations of each of them: if they truly thought Ivan should suffer for his crime; if they were too much in awe of Hans's power to plead for leniency, or if they were, simply, sadistically interested in the suffering of someone they had never really liked.

She wondered at her own reaction, and thought perhaps she felt a mixture of all three.

"I reckon... oh, half a day, if that," Hans said casually. "Certainly no longer." He smiled up at the immobilised Russian. "A very painful way to go, I imagine."

Ivan wept. "Please! Please, not this. I'd rather die quickly –"

Samara closed her eyes, knowing what was about to happen. She heard Hans say, "Oh... is that so? Well, you all heard him."

She opened her eyes in time to see Hans stride casually over to Ivan and place the barrel of his rifle beneath the weeping man's chin.

He delayed a few seconds, prolonging Ivan's terror, then casually pulled the trigger.

The top of Ivan's head flew off as if it were a cap caught by the wind, and a second later a fine mist of blood and atomised brain rained down around them.

Samara gagged and turned away.

Hans swung his rifle and found Josef, who backed up against the steps of the transporter, terrified. "And now it's your turn."

"No!" Josef yelled. "I didn't mean to..."

At last Samara found her voice. "Hans, enough. Enough killing for one day, okay?" She was surprised at how calm she sounded, despite her fear.

Hans looked from Josef to her, thinking about it. He nodded finally. "You're right." He smiled at Josef. "You're one lucky son of a bitch, man. But one more slip up like that..."

Josef nodded, almost eagerly, and scurried back

into the transporter.

One of the Africans gestured to Ivan's corpse. "We cut him down now?"

"No," Hans snapped. "Leave the bastard there. We don't want him stinking up the truck."

"But..." Giovanni looked nonplussed.

Hans laughed. "Think about it, kid. How long do you think we can stomach fucking bat meat?"

Giovanni opened his mouth to say something, then looked across at Samara and smiled weakly.

"Okay," Hans said, "what are we doing out here?"

Samara made the mistake of glancing at Ivan's carcass, and wished she hadn't. Of the head, only the lower jaw remained, something horrific in the visibility of its full, arched set of teeth. A mess of blood and brains dribbled down its chin.

Hans climbed aboard and moved to the cab. Samara followed him, shaking. Hans slipped in behind the wheel and pulled out a map, his face impassive, and Samara wondered if he felt anything at all about having just taken a man's life.

"Well, you certainly scared the hell out of everyone out there, Hans. Very macho."

He stared at her. "It wasn't about being macho," he said. "Just about showing people what they can't get away with."

She smiled to herself. "Well, let that be the last of the killing, okay? We might need these people later on."

He was about to reply, then bit it back. He stabbed the map with a blunt forefinger. "So what the fuck do we do about water? Even on half rations, what we've got won't last more than a few days. Shit!" He hit the wheel with the hams of his fists, making the vehicle shake.

She took the map and traced their route to the coast. "We don't pass any big cities where there might have been colonies."

He was watching her finger as it followed the route she had drawn earlier. He stayed her hand with his big, clumsy paw and said, "What's that?"

He indicated a village marked as Mont St Catherine, a good hundred kilometres north of their planned route.

She looked at him. "It's nothing. A village."

He repeated the name, turning it over in his mouth. He smiled at her. "I know it. There was a colony there – might still be there, for all I know. A guy back in Copenhagen, he mentioned it a few times. He left the place years ago... but it's worth trying."

"And if there isn't a colony there any more?"

Hans started the engine and eased the transporter forward. "Let's think about that when we get there," he said. "But I have a gut feeling we'll find what we're looking for."

And pity any poor colonists still hanging on in Mont St Catherine, she thought.

She turned in her seat and stared at Hans as he drove.

Outside, the sun climbed into the white hot sky.

CHAPTER ELEVEN

PAUL WOKE AND stared around him at the shabby, crowded interior of the truck. It made the basement back in Paris seem roomy by comparison. Beside the chesterfield and a couple of ancient armchairs, he made out stacks of tools: spades, crowbars and a bulky toolbox full of things Dan needed to keep the truck and the solar arrays up and running. A chest where the weapons were stored sat next to what Kath had told him was a refrigerator, a box that kept food – such as they had, the little meat and fresh greens – cool and edible. Pictures were pasted to the walls and ceiling: posters of old masters – Van Gogh's Sunflowers and the Mona Lisa – as well as advertisements ripped from old magazines showing happy families smiling in the age of plenty.

He sat up and swayed from side to side as the truck sped south. He held on and smiled; it was still an odd sensation to be in a room that moved. He had doubted that he would be able to sleep, but last night he'd fallen asleep instantly, rocked by the lullaby motion of the half-track, and dreamed of Paris and Elise.

He missed aspects of his old life: the freedom to go out and roam at will; he missed the familiar lines of the city's ruined architecture, the sense of confinement and therefore safety conferred by the enclosing buildings. Here, even in the truck, he felt vulnerable. They were a tiny point of life travelling across vast, hostile wastes, often without a building or any other sign of human agency in sight.

The other source of his unease was the people he was travelling with.

He passed through periods of knowing he could trust Dan, Kath and Ed, and then suffering doubts. They were strange in so many ways, and although they had taken him in and given him a bed and food, their shared past together seemed to exclude him, as did the easy familiarity with which they lived their day to day lives. Simple things like the give and take of conversation, which seemed to flow so easily between them, he found hard to grasp, and also their habit of sharing everything with him. They seemed too good to be true, and occasionally he was struck by a suspicion that they might, for reasons of their own, be using him.

At other times he knew he was being ridiculous, that they were good people who would have helped anyone in his situation, and he resolved to make himself as useful as he possibly could.

The sun was up and the temperature in the lounge was rising steadily. He moved to the cab and leaned through. Dan was behind the wheel, his solid bulk filling the driving seat. He smiled as Paul appeared. "Sleep well?"

Paul climbed through and settled himself in the passenger seat. "Very well."

"We'll be stopping soon, to take a break and eat."

Paul smiled. "I could prepare a stew with the lizards."

Dan smiled across at him. "Your speciality, Paul?"

He nodded. "I've had a long time to get it right."

He stared through the windscreen. An unvarying scene met his gaze. They were travelling over featureless desert sands. After a while, the limitless horizon, the flowing undulations, became mesmeric.

The size of what lay out there, the lack of recognisable features, frightened him. He shivered.

Dan glanced at him. "What?"

Paul pointed through the windscreen. "Is all the world like this?"

Dan rocked his square head. "I suspect much of it is, yes. The sand's reaching almost as far as Copenhagen."

"But humans can't survive in this, can they?"

Dan hesitated, then said, "Not without water, no. With water, then we could live in the desert. Long ago, people willingly made the desert their home, living in tents and travelling on animals called camels."

Paul nodded. "I've read about them, seen pictures."

"It's amazing what conditions humans can adapt themselves to. Have you read about the Inuit people? They lived in the far north of the planet, in icy conditions."

"I've read about them yes, but..." He smiled. "Ice. Snow..." He shook his head. "Elise tried to explain it to me, but I just couldn't imagine such a place."

They sat in silence for a while. Paul stared out at the limitless sand, the hypnotic rise and fall of distant dunes. "Do you think you'll be able to find water? I mean, enough of it to..."

"To raise a successful colony?" Dan shrugged his beefy shoulders. He leaned forward on the steering wheel to ease his back. "Most of the small aquifers are drying up. What I'm hoping for is to find a really big underground reservoir. We have seeds back in Copenhagen, and some creatures can survive in desert conditions: lizards, beetles and insects. I've even seen a few rodents, gerbils or whatever. Anyway, if we strike it lucky in the Atlantic... then who knows?"

Paul considered this for a while, and then he asked, "Why did you let me join you?"

Dan looked at him. "Well, we couldn't very well leave you alone in Paris, could we? You're young, fit and healthy. You'd be an asset on the trip south. But mainly, the colony needs to grow. We need young people. Without people like you..." He smiled at Paul. "How would we continue into the future?"

Paul nodded, excited by what lay behind Dan's words. "In Copenhagen... there are young women?"

Dan laughed. He nodded. "A few. There were more, but... a while back we were hit by an outbreak of cholera. We lost a hundred men, women and children. It was a terrible time. Anyway, yes, there are young women – and they'll be fighting over a fit, good-looking young man like you when we get back."

Paul shook his head, a strange emotion brewing

within him: part disbelief that anything so wonderful might happen to him, that one day he might meet a woman... and part a conviction that what Dan had told him would happen.

He said, "Are all the women in Copenhagen as beautiful as Kath?"

Dan laughed. "She'll be flattered to hear that! Well, as they used to say, beauty is in the eye of the beholder. I think Kath is the most beautiful woman on the planet – but you'll have to make up your own mind when we get back there, won't you?"

Paul nodded, smiling to himself at the thought.

Dan slowed the truck and said to Paul, "Can you pass me the map?"

Paul pulled it from the recess beside him and passed it across to Dan, who unfolded it and spread it across the wheel.

He looked up and pointed a stubby finger ahead. "Look, ahead and to the right."

Paul peered through the windscreen. He could just make out, hazy and shimmering on the horizon, a grey blur rising from the desert.

"A range of mountains called the Monts du Cantal," Dan said. "We've got to cross them. There were roads, way back, and they should be relatively intact. There were even communities there, not so long ago. When Kath and me headed north, twenty years ago, we stopped off at one or two in the general area... It'll be interesting to see what happened to them." He folded the map and passed it back to Paul. "Anyway, we'll be there in an hour. We'll stop, try to find some shade and grab something to eat, hm?"

Kath appeared in the opening beside Paul. "That sounds like a great idea. How far are we from Mont St Catherine?"

"Another day," Dan said. "Maybe a little more. When we stop, Paul promised to make a stew."

Kath smiled at him. "Come through and we can prepare it now."

Paul followed Kath into the lounge, where she selected a big pan and set a chopping board on the floor. He sat next to her, cross-legged, very aware of her breasts beneath her shirt as she bent forward. He reddened and looked away.

For the next fifteen minutes he showed her how he prepared the lizards. He skinned six of the creatures, gutted them and unzipped their spines. He removed the offal and cut away the darker lower intestines. "The rest we can use," he told her, "along with the spine. Lizard meat is oily, so it cooks to begin with in its own juices."

He laid the filleted meat in the bottom of the pan, and Kath folded down a device from the wall. She turned a switch and said, "A cooker, powered by the solar arrays."

He placed the pan on a hotplate and watched the meat sizzle. "In a few minutes I'll add a little water and some herbs."

Kath passed him a few leaves of rosemary from the plant Paul had presented to her back at the cathedral.

"Years ago I could find mushrooms, the odd leaf to go into it." He paused. "Elise taught me how to cook."

He looked at the pan, then at Kath's smiling face, and realised that he'd probably shown her nothing more than she knew already.

"I have some spinach, and salt." She added both, then more water, and they watched the stew simmer for ten minutes.

The aroma was making him hungry.

Kath said, "It smells great. Thanks, Paul."

Earlier, watching Dan drive, it had occurred to him that it would help if he too could take a turn at the wheel. Now he looked across at Kath and said, "Do you think Dan will teach me how to drive the truck? I'd like to learn – take my turn."

"Of course he would. It isn't hard. The truck almost drives itself – but it's tiring."

"I don't mind. I'd feel like..." He shrugged. "You let me come along. I've got to give something back."

Kath smiled at him, her head to one side, and laid a soft hand on his arm. Her touch was electrifying. He blushed and looked away.

He said the first thing that came to mind, "How's Ed? The remains of... did I do the right thing?"

Kath nodded. "Of course. He had to know what happened to Lisa. Can you imagine how he'd feel, not knowing? Always suspecting the worse but not knowing for sure?"

He stared down at the simmering stew. Kath added more water. He said, "She – Lisa – the girl in the red dress... she was the first girl I'd seen for... ten years, more." He smiled at the thought. "I even dreamed of saving her from the bastards." He shook his head. "But by the time I found them..."

She touched his arm again. "You did what you could. And you did right collecting her remains..." She smiled at him. "Ed's a strong man, Paul. He lost his wife not long ago, some disease he couldn't cure. And now Lisa."

He looked at her, alerted by a catch in her voice. She was crying quietly, tears rolling down her cheeks. He sat, paralysed, wanting to reach out, comfort her, but afraid the gesture might be misconstrued. Instead he sat uncomfortably, staring at the pan.

Kath laughed. "Look at me! We've got to be strong, haven't we?" She knuckled the tears from her cheeks and beamed at him. "Now, how's the stew doing?"

Five minutes later the truck slowed, the pitch of the engine dropping to a low drone. The churning sound of the tracks on sand gave way to a loud, dinning rattle. Paul peered through the window set into the door. They were climbing from the desert, along a road into the folded foothills of the mountain range.

He moved to the cab and hung through the gap. Ahead were the mountains, bare and stark against the bright white glare of the morning sky. Denuded of vegetation and leached of soil by the constant winds, the mountains presented ugly slabs and twisted knuckles of pure stone, their lines unsoftened and unadorned by anything like grasses or trees.

"A pretty sight, hm?" Dan said.

Kath joined them. "I remember, just forty years ago, when I was a girl... there were trees and fields full of vines around here." She looked at Dan, worriedly. "What do you think happened to the colony?"

Paul glanced at Dan, whose expression was grim. "I don't hold out much hope."

The road ahead was cracked and buckled, but still navigable. Dan accelerated, and they drove higher into the foothills. Five minutes later he pulled into the side of the road, the truck shaded by an overhang of rock.

"That stew of yours smells wonderful, Paul, and I'm starving. Let's eat."

THEY SAT OUTSIDE, their backs against the rock, and ate the stew in silence.

Afterwards Ed commended Paul on the meal, "They always did say the best chefs were French. I'll recommend you back at the colony."

Paul smiled shyly at the old man.

Kath said, "Paul wants to learn how to drive the truck, Dan."

Dan nodded. "Great. Just as soon as we're through the other side of the mountains, I'll give you a lesson."

He fetched the map and spread it on the ground, indicating their position. "We're here. There was a colony close by - Servian, in the mountains about ten kays south of here. We should pass through it pretty soon... if it's still there." He indicated a road that wriggled through the mountains, then headed dead straight south. "And from there it's another day to Mont St Catherine."

Paul studied the map. Dan showed him the distant line of the coast, and the sea – marked a pale blue on the map – where he said there was a deep trench.

They returned to the truck and Paul sat beside Dan while the older man drove, wrestling the half-track around tight bends and perilous loops in the steadily climbing road. Now Paul knew why he'd suggested lessons only when they'd passed through the mountains. One wrong move here and they'd be pitched over the edge of the road and into ravines hundred of metres deep.

Paul watched Dan carefully, taking in how the older man turned the wheel, used the brakes and the other foot pedals, aware of Dan's blocky strength as he manhandled the half-track through the mountains.

As they passed cliff-faces and eased through cuttings, Paul examined the rocks for any signs of vegetation, patches of moss or lichen. Years ago, members of the old Paris colony had collected similar growths for use in stews and soups, before the sand invaded, the temperature increased and all vegetation in the city died out. If he could locate even scraps of vegetation here it would be a valuable addition to their diet.

But for all he looked, he saw nothing.

They rounded a long bed and entered a valley wedged into a steep cutting. He looked for any sign of habitation, the remains of the old colony Dan had mentioned. All he saw was the parched valley, grey and lifeless, and the enclosing slabs of the ash grey mountains.

"Won't be long before we come to Servian," Dan said. "At the far end of the valley, just before the pass that leads from the mountains."

Further along the valley he made out the ruins of farmhouses, some of which had a couple of walls still standing, others which were nothing more than footprints outlining the main houses and out-buildings. He imagined this might have been a fertile growing area at one time.

Perhaps a kilometre from the end of the valley and the cutting where Dan said the colony had existed, he slowed the truck and said something under his breath.

Paul glanced at him.

Dan was staring ahead, peering as if unable to believe his eyes.

Paul followed his gaze and saw, standing in the middle of the cracked track, the thin figure of a child, tiny in the wilderness.

"What the...?" he began.

Dan said, "So I'm not seeing things?"

The child was standing in the sunlight, perhaps a hundred metres from the truck. Dan idled the engine and approached slowly.

The child was a girl, perhaps five or six, though it was hard to tell: she was thin and malnourished, and might have been older. Naked, tousle-haired and covered in scabs, she presented a pathetic sight.

"Kath!" Dan called.

Seconds later she appeared between the seats. "What?" she began; then, "Oh... oh, my God."

Dan rolled the truck to within a few metres of the girl and cut the engine.

Kath said, "I'll go and..." She disappeared, and seconds later emerged from the truck, walking towards the girl, holding out a hand and murmuring something.

The girl just stared at her with big, dark eyes, her face expressionless. She made no protest as Kath bundled her up in her arms and carried her back to the truck.

Paul and Dan joined them in the lounge, where Ed was already examining the girl.

The child seemed stunned, alive but in a walking coma, her eyes staring. She had a pot belly from malnutrition, and prominent pelvic flanges and ribs. A dozen sores covered her body and limbs, some scabbed over and others more recent and bloody.

A putrid odour of faeces and bad breath rose from the kid. Her lips and face were smeared, Paul thought, with something that might have been dried blood.

Ed said, "I'll need a while to examine her thoroughly. First, Kath, can you give her a shower? Then I'll dress the wounds. I suggest we get her something to eat, but not much. Her stomach probably won't be able to take a full meal."

Kath knelt before the girl, clutching her tiny hand. "What's your name, darling?"

The girl just stared at her, mute.

"Where do you live?" Kath asked. "Can you show us where you live? Do you have a mummy and daddy?"

Dan murmured, "Either she doesn't understand or she's too petrified to answer. She'll be from Servian, whatever's left of it. I'll drive on until we reach it."

Kath led the girl across to the shower cubicle, and Paul and Dan returned to the cab.

"Well, at least we know the colony at Servian survived," Dan said as he started the engine. The half-track surged forward. "But going from the state of the kid, I don't hold out much hope that it's thriving."

They drove the length of the valley, which opened out into a second, smaller valley. Paul noticed, to his left, a series of crude buildings carved into the rock, one atop the other, following the slope of the incline; dark window-openings looked out over the valley. In one of these, he caught a glimpse of a shadowy figure.

Seconds later the first shot hit the half-track.

Paul heard the blast, and the almost instantaneous *ping* as it ricocheted off the truck's superstructure. A second shot pierced the roof of the cab and shattered the plastic gear-housing between Paul and Dan.

"Christ," Dan cried, revving the engine and racing off the road, heading for a projecting spur of rock perhaps a hundred metres ahead to their left. The half-track bucked. Paul heard another shot, heard a cry from the lounge. Kath.

He turned and looked through the gap. Kath was on her knees, hugging the girl as the truck bucked back and forth; she gestured to Paul that she was okay. Ed was clutching the window frame and peering through, attempting to see who was attacking.

Dan pulled the truck behind the rock and braked. He moved into the lounge. "Okay, so what should we do? Keep on going, or try to find out what kind of set-up they have here? If the kid has parents..."

Kath stroked the girl's hair. She did not look Dan in the eye as she said, "Why take the risk? They're hostile. I say we get away from here."

Ed said, "We need to find out what state the colony's in... if it is a colony. But we need to go in well-armed."

Dan touched Kath's shoulder. "We can't just run, taking the kid."

"But look at her," Kath protested.

"I'm sorry, Kath."

He opened the chest containing the weapons and pulled out a couple of rifles. Paul moved to his bag and withdrew his crossbow and a handful of bolts, excited by the turn of events.

Dan said to Kath, "Into the cab – as far away as possible from whoever..."

He hauled open the door. The firing had stopped. He jumped from the truck, followed by Ed. Paul gave chase, emerging into the burning sunlight. They ducked behind the intervening rock.

Paul said, "I saw where the firing came from. I reckon there was only one person. If I climb up there..." He indicated the incline directly above, "I can skirt round and come in from behind –"

"I don't want you risking your damned life," Dan said.

Which Paul chose to interpret as a qualified approval of his plan. Gripping his crossbow, he darted from behind the rock and scrambled up the hillside. He looked ahead. The stone-built houses were a hundred metres away, and as he climbed, he made the angle between himself and the shooter's window all the narrower. Within seconds it was impossible for the sniper to get a sight on him, and he breathed a little easier.

He slipped and scrabbled in the scree, sliding back one metre for every two he progressed as he made his way in a semi-circle towards the dwellings.

High up, he paused and looked down. He could make out the half-track, glinting in the sunlight, and the shapes of Ed and Dan pressed against the rock.

He looked in the other direction, from where the firing had hailed. The dwellings were built from the same grey shale as the mountain-side, the rooms within embedded into the incline.

He reached the side of the building where he judged the sniper was concealed, leaned against the stonework and considered his options. The sniper was no longer firing, which in one way was a disadvantage; if he were firing, then at least Paul would know exactly where he was positioned. Now he might be anywhere, might even have chosen to follow up his initial barrage with a reconnaissance to see if any shots had hit home.

Somehow, though, Paul doubted it.

His suspicion was confirmed seconds later when he heard another shot, so close it deafened him.

He crouched and peered around the corner. The gun barrel projected from the window-opening, aiming towards the rock concealing Dan and Ed.

Paul regained his breath, counted his heartbeats until the ringing in his ears had ceased, and after ten seconds darted forward and gripped the barrel of the gun. He yanked, hearing a cry of surprise from inside. The weapon came away from its owner, and Paul leapt up and through the window, brandishing the rifle like a club in one hand while training his crossbow on the sniper with the other.

He looked down at the man cowering against the far wall, and lowered his weapons.

He leaned from the window. "Dan! Ed! You can come out."

He turned back to the figure on the floor. The man was old, skeletal and pathetic. He looked up wildly, through matted, oily hair, with eyes that seemed on the verge of insanity. He was gibbering to himself and gesturing with raised palms for Paul to show mercy.

Paul knelt. "Why did you fire on us?"

The oldster scrabbled away until he fetched up in the corner of the room. He jabbered something incomprehensible, eyes wide and staring.

Paul looked around the room. It was bare, but for a crude palliasse in the far corner, stitched together from sacking and stuffed with ancient straw. There was no hint of food or water in the room; and, judging by the old man's condition, it looked as if he hadn't had any food or drink for weeks.

A timber door to Paul's left scraped open. Dan stepped inside, followed by Ed, who had to crouch to keep his bald head from hitting the rafters.

They stared down at the old man, hostile expressions fading to distaste and pity.

Dan knelt before the man and said, "We won't harm you, okay? You're safe with us. Are you alone here?"

The old man muttered his first word. "Alone?"

"Is there anyone else here? Men, women?"

The man opened his eyes even wider, backing up against the wall and shaking his head.

"The girl," Dan said. "A little girl. Does she live here?"

"Dead. Everyone's dead."

"What do you eat?" Ed asked. "And water? How do you get water?"

"Water's gone. Eat? Lizards..." The man shook his head. "No more lizards." He glanced from Ed to Dan and began sobbing.

Dan whispered, "I can't believe she lived with him. There must be others. Let's go back to the truck, see if we can get more sense from the girl."

Paul moved to the door, then paused. "What about him?"

Dan thought about it. "We can spare a little food and water."

Ed said, "Can we?"

Dan looked at the old doctor.

Ed gestured to the weapon in Paul's grip. "It'd be kinder if we used the rifle."

"Would you be willing to pull the trigger?" Dan asked

Ed hesitated. "Perhaps we should wait until we've seen if we can find water?"

Dan nodded. "Okay, let's do that."

Paul pushed through the door, taking the old man's rifle with him. Ed and Dan followed, sliding down the scree-covered incline to the road. They hurried back to the half-track.

Kath was in the lounge, dressing the girl's sores with some grey, home-made salve. Washed and cleaned, the kid appeared to have retreated a few steps from death's door, and she smelled a lot better.

Kath looked up. "Thank God you're safe. What happened?"

Dan told her what they'd found.

He sat cross-legged before the girl. "Will you take us to your mummy and daddy?"

Kath fetched a bottle of water and offered it to the girl. She snatched it and drank greedily, almost choking as water dribbled from her mouth and over her chest.

Kath took the girl's hand. "Your mummy and daddy? Can you take us to them?"

The girl lowered the bottle and looked at Kath with massive brown eyes.

At last she nodded. "Yes," she said in a voice so soft Paul could hardly make out the word.

Paul looked at Dan, who murmured, "If they're in a similar state to the poor bastard back there..."

They gave the girl a little stew, which she ate ravenously, gulping it down with snatched jerks of her head like a starving dog. Kath held her, stroking her hair and murmuring for her to take her time. She found an old tee-shirt and drew it over the girl's head. It hung on her like a misshapen, outsized dress.

Ten minutes later they were ready to leave the truck.

The girl, holding Kath's hand, led the way. Dan and Ed followed closely, rifles at the ready. Paul shadowed them, scanning ahead for the first signs of renewed hostility.

The girl led them back towards the valley, passing the house where the old madman lived. Paul looked up as they passed, but there was no sign of the man's wild face at the window.

They moved from the direct, furnace heat of the sun and into shadow. Grey slab mountains rose on both sides, the sky high above resembling a strip of white-hot steel.

The girl stopped suddenly and pointed up the incline to her left. Paul peered up into the shadow, expecting to see another basic, stone-built dwelling.

Instead he made out a narrow cutting or defile in the rock high above. He also saw a series of crudely chiselled steps leading from the road up to the cutting. He moved past Kath and the girl and led the way.

He called down, "Careful. The stones are loose."

Kath nodded up at him, picking up the girl and lodging her on her hip.

He came to the narrow fissure in the rock-face and slipped inside; the path continued, though at a gentler gradient. The corridor was in semi-darkness, and cool; the perfect place, he thought, to hide away from both the sun and any passing trouble-makers.

He walked on for what he guessed must have been half a kilometre, until the pathway opened out into a small, high valley. Here, he saw as he looked around, were perhaps a dozen beehive-shaped dwellings built into the enclosing mountain.

He turned and watched the others slip from the defile and enter the valley.

Dan whistled. "What a place to found a colony. Secluded, safe from marauders –"

"And evidently, judging from the state of the girl and the oldster, lacking the basics of food and water," Ed said, smiling at Dan.

The stocky man conceded the point with a grin. "Well, there is that. But they must have scraped a living for a while."

Paul looked around the narrow valley, denuded of vegetation. To his left, between a couple of beehive dwellings, he made out another fissure in the rock and wondered where it led.

The girl was running across the bare rock of the valley bottom, dragging Kath after her. Paul followed.

She approached a domed dwelling and stood at the door. Kath stopped and looked back at Dan. "I'm not sure I want to..." she began, grimacing. Dan nodded, and eased himself through the flapping wooden door. Paul followed.

Scant light slanted in through a couple of small, high windows, but the illumination was enough show them all they needed to see.

A body sat against the far wall, a man in his thirties, naked and emaciated. Something had been gnawing the flesh from his thigh.

Paul recalled the smeared blood around the girl's lips, and felt his gorge rise.

He pushed back outside, crossed the clearing and peered into the fissure between the rocks. Perhaps five metres ahead, he made out a timber frame erected above a hole in the rock. He slipped into the fissure and knelt at the edge of the sink hole. A length of rope hung from the frame and descended into the depths.

He saw a plastic bucket on the end of it.

He lowered it on the rope, hand over hand, down the hole. The rope was long – he guessed perhaps twenty metres – and minutes later a distant rattle indicated that the bucket had hit the bottom. He yanked the rope around a few times to ensure that the bucket hadn't become lodged on a ledge, and then, satisfying himself that it had indeed reached the bottom of the well, he began hauling the rope back up.

The bucket emerged minutes later, containing only an inch of wet grey sludge.

He sat on his haunches, staring into the blackness of the well and thinking of the man back there, and the hell of his final days.

He stood and retraced his steps back through the defile. The others looked up when he emerged into the scorching sunlight.

"There's a well back there. It's dry."

"Jesus," Dan said. "The poor bastards."

Ed indicated the other dwellings. "The place is full of corpses. They've been dead quite a while."

Kath had picked up the girl and was nursing her, rocking her back and forth, tears filming the woman's blue eyes.

She said, "We've got to take her with us, Dan."

He nodded. "Of course."

She pressed her lips to the girl's jet black hair, sobbing quietly to herself.

Dan looked at Ed. "What about the old guy?"

A silence hung between them. At last Ed said, "If we leave food, water, it'll last a few days... and what then? He's facing a long, painful death, just like..." He gestured back to the dwelling. "And anyway, it's food and water *we* need."

Kath said, "Maybe we should take him along..." She faltered.

Ed shook his head. "You haven't seen him. He's ill, and quite mad. He'd be no welcome addition to the colony. I'm sorry, but I'm just speaking the truth. As I said earlier," he said, looking at Dan, "the merciful option would be a bullet."

Dan said, "I'm not sure I could bring myself to..."

"I'll do it," Ed said.

Dan looked around the group. "Any objections?"

Paul shook his head. Biting her bottom lip, still weeping, Kath agreed too.

"Very well, then..." Dan said.

Ed smiled, grimly. "It won't be the first time," he said. "I've saved lives, once or twice. Occasionally I've been called on to take them, too."

They left the valley, walking in single file through the natural corridor until they came to the steep flight of steps. Dan helped Kath and the girl down to the road and they approached the half-track.

Before they reached it, Ed checked his rifle and slowly climbed the slope to the old man's dwelling. The others hurried on. Paul lingered, watching Ed pause before the rickety wooden door. He pushed it open and stepped into the building.

Paul heard the murmur of Ed talking to the old man, and seconds later a single, muffled gunshot.

* * *

ED INSISTED ON driving, and being alone in the cab, and they left the mountains and descended to the sand-covered plain. Paul sat in the lounge with Dan, Kath and the girl, watching the interplay between the woman and the child. Already Kath had won the girl's trust. Kath was singing nursery rhymes, illustrating the words with exaggerated gestures that made the girl smile.

Dan fixed an evening meal of meat and spinach.

Kath said, "Now you know everyone's name, so what's yours? Do you have a name, or are you Miss No-Name? Is that it, are you Miss No-Name?" She tickled the girl's prominent ribs, and the girl laughed.

The child reached up to Kath's ear with a cupped hand and whispered something. Kath listened, wide-eyed. "Well, Millie, I think that's a beautiful name, isn't it, Dan, Paul? This is Millie."

Paul dug down the side of the chesterfield and found the book he'd discovered in the farmhouse that morning. He turned to the first page and checked that the girl was indeed called Millie, and passed it, smiling, across to Kath, indicating the first paragraph.

Kath read it and beamed.

"Well, what a surprise! Look, Millie, this little girl in the story is called Millie, too."

Millie said something to Kath in a tiny voice.

Kath said, "Of course I'll read it. Up you get." She hoisted the child onto her knee and began reading.

Dan looked up from the cooking, watching Kath with a smile in his eyes.

Paul listened to Kath telling the story of how Millie's mother bought fruit and vegetables from the market, and he marvelled at a time when food was so plentiful.

An hour later the truck slowed and came to a halt. Ed's whittled-down face peered from the cab. "Is that food I smell back there?"

"Almost ready," Dan said.

Paul opened the hatch from the lounge and stepped into the desert. The sun was going down, huge and fiery beyond a line of dunes. He walked away from the truck and turned in a full circle, marvelling at the great open space, at how vast the sky seemed, a deep blue speckled with the intense points of a thousand stars; beyond them, the chiffon arm of the Milky Way spread in a long stream from east to west. He looked back at the half-track and the trailer, the vehicle tiny against the desert backdrop. The others were filing out, laden with bowls.

They sat beside the truck, fashioning seats in the sand, and ate. Millie snuggled beside Kath, spooning stew. Paul devoured the meal.

Kath said, "It was an omen, the book." She gazed at Millie with something like love in her eyes. "It was meant to be."

Paul glanced at Ed; he had opened his mouth to say something. Paul thought he was about to state that nothing was meant to be, that all events were accidental, but the old man's expression changed from mild annoyance as he gazed across at Kath and the girl: he smiled.

A little later, Ed said, "She reminds me very much of Lisa, when she was little."

Kath stroked Millie's long, dark hair. "And we'll love her just as much as we loved Lisa, won't we?"

Ed dropped his gaze to his bowl. "Well, I'll be glad I won't be around to see her reach twenty."

Dan looked up. "You, Ed? You'll live a hundred years –" he stopped. At twenty, Millie would remind Ed of his daughter...

Ed smiled sadly. "As long as I have all my faculties about me if I do..." He thought for a few seconds, then said, "Not like that poor bastard back there."

Paul thought of Elise, towards the end. He said, "Elise... she lost her reason in the last few months. She'd talk about things... things that were impossible."

Perhaps sensing that Paul wanted to talk, Dan asked, "What like?"

"Oh..." He thought back. "She claimed she'd seen people in the city just days earlier, heard crowds and people laughing. Wishful thinking, or maybe she was reliving the past. It was... painful, painful to watch her lose her mind, painful to hear about a time when crowds of people and cars and things were common." He shrugged. "I don't know whether to be grateful I never lived through that time."

Ed said, "Perhaps you should be. It was a terrible experience, the end of everything we knew and took for granted, the breakdown of order. To see human beings acting as they did, driven by the dictates of survival..." He stared down into his half-filled bowl.

Paul smiled. "And the stars," he said. He looked up at the million scintillating stars massed overhead. "Elise liked to stare up at the stars at night, hour after hour. She thought that people lived out there. Not aliens, I mean real people, human beings. She claimed that before the end, before the Breakdown, the governments of Europe joined together to send a starship out there." He thought back to the time Elise had told him this. "I think it gave her hope."

Ed finished the last of his stew and set the bowl in the sand. He lay back and linked his hands behind his head, staring up at the heavens. "Well, I've heard rumours, too. More than rumours. I know the European Space Agency was planning something; some people said it was a ship to the stars, a colony vessel loaded with thousands of the brightest and best in every field of the sciences."

Kath said, "I've heard people talk about it, but surely it was beyond our capabilities, even back then?"

"And surely we'd know about it if it actually launched?" Paul said.

Ed shrugged. "Who knows. The governments back then were ultra-secretive. They could see the writing on the wall – the breakdown of civilisation. Christ knows, they'd done enough to accelerate the process over the years, through their inaction and greed. It would be quite within the realms of possibility that they decided to act at the eleventh hour and put together a last ditch proposal – send a ship to the stars! What a thought!" He laughed, without humour. "But I suppose it was easier than doing something about saving the planet, curing the ecosphere..."

Paul looked up at the stars. The idea fired something within him, invested him with a sense of hope and excitement. To imagine the human race living beneath far stars, on planets exotic and alien...

He wondered if right now there were children out there looking up into the stars, attempting to locate the sun, and asking their parents why it was that they had departed planet Earth.

"It's a nice thought," Kath said, gazing up. "I hope they're happy up there."

"Do you know something," Ed said, "I don't think the human race was ever happy. It's not built into the psyche for us to be content. In evolutionary terms, contentment is a dead end. We always strived, wanting more – even back then, when we had everything, when you'd think the race would be satisfied with its lot. But we were dissatisfied and strove for more..." He smiled. "I suppose that was our downfall."

Paul said, "And now?"

"Now," Ed said, turning his stark death's head to regard him, "now we sit on the edge of extinction, wanting only the bare minimum for survival, and nothing, really, has changed."

Kath called across the small circle. "Ed Ostergaart! Oh, you are a misery!"

"Guilty as charged, Kath," Ed smiled. "Let's have the market story again."

Millie jumped up and down on Kath's knee. "Yes! The story!"

Paul looked around the group as Kath read, and he considered the events of the day, his first full day among a group of civilised human beings for... for a long, long time. He smiled to himself. Despite his earlier worries, despite his doubts, he liked and trusted these people, and he felt accepted.

He lay back and gazed up at the stars as Kath's voice told a story of other times.

CHAPTER TWELVE

SAMARA CURLED UP in the passenger seat and stared through the windscreen.

They were about an hour from Mont St Catherine, travelling across a wide, flat expanse of desert that hadn't varied for the last hundred kilometres. The temperature was in the low forties and the cab was like an oven. Hans was sweating, giving off a particularly unpleasant body odour, an adenoid-pinching acid reek as if all his badness was being distilled into a concentrated perfume. Samara was sure that she wasn't smelling all that sweet, either. Sweat slid down her body and pooled on the hot vinyl of the passenger seat. She had tried opening the side panel in the window, but the breeze that resulted was like a breath from Hell.

To make matters worse, she was thirsty. They were rationed, thanks to Josef's inaccuracy with the rifle, to half a litre of water a day, and Samara had perhaps a quarter of that left and it wasn't yet midday. She had already siphoned off the water in the shower tank and redistributed it among the group – not that it had gone far. Now her throat was parched and she had a raging headache. If they failed to find water at Mont St Catherine... she tried not to dwell on the prospect.

A little earlier she'd moved back through the transporter to take a piss and to look in on the others. Edo and Lomo had been huddled in the lounge, muttering quietly to each other; they'd stopped abruptly as she'd passed, and stared at her with suspicion. Josef had been holed up in his berth, no doubt content to keep as far away from Hans as possible. She had found Giovanni near the water racks, lashing together a strut damaged by the gunshot. He'd jumped when she'd appeared, and then looked relieved.

She had touched his shoulder as she passed. "Good work, Giovanni," she'd murmured.

He'd smiled and said, "Will we be okay, Samara...? I mean..." gesturing at the sloshing water containers.

She tried to reassure him. "We're stopping off at an old colony. We're pretty sure we'll find water there."

He nodded and continued his repair work. Samara was taken by the odd urge to touch him, then, stroke his chest – not so much as a prelude to intimacy but merely as an act of futile defiance towards Hans. She restrained herself, realising the irrationality of the gesture and not wanting to encourage the kid.

She had returned to the cab and the sweating Hans.

His words jerked her from her slumber a while later. "I've been thinking."

She had the urge to ask him what with. Instead she said, "About?"

He kept his gaze fixed ahead. "You said earlier, you didn't know if we'd be moving the colony."

She shrugged. "That's right, so?"

"But if we find provisions there, a source of water, then we'd be moving, right?"

She was tired, and didn't really want to share knowledge about possible future plans with him. "What about it?"

"What I want to now is, how? If there is food and water in Spain, and the underground bunker is safe... then how do you plan to move all the colony over there?"

She wondered how much he knew about the Bilbao base. Last night she'd moved most of her father's papers from the table beside the shower and stowed them among her clothing under the bed. She'd left a couple of folders there, to prevent Hans from looking for the rest – plans she hadn't managed to work out, and a sheaf of documents in some language she, and evidently her father, couldn't read. Now Samara wondered if he'd gone through them; she was sure she hadn't mentioned anything to him about an underground bunker.

She shrugged. "I haven't thought it through completely. I suppose we'd do it in stages. We have two transporters and one we could fix. We'd probably do it in relays."

He nodded, then said, "We'd need someone to oversee things at that end, in Spain, right?"

So that was it. He was angling to set himself up in Spain, in charge of the bunker while she ferried colonists and supplies back and forth.

She was cautious. "Probably. Why?"

He turned his bullet-shaped head and smiled at her. "I think I could keep things in order down there, Samara."

She curled in her seat, staring through the windscreen at the ceaseless desert, and said, "I'm sure you could, Hans."

He returned his attention to the desert, smiling to himself.

Ahead, a range of hills rose on the horizon, grey against the white-hot sky. Hans checked the compass. "I reckon that's the place."

"You think you can find the village?"

He slowed the transporter and looked at the map, his blunt fingers outlining the lie of the hills as if reading Braille. "According to this, the village is on the first rise of the hills from the south... Right there." He pointed straight ahead at a jagged prominence in the foothills.

Thirty minutes later they approached the first fold in the rucked foothills, and obligingly an ancient road emerged from the sand and swept up the incline. Hans accelerated and the vehicle rattled over the cobbles.

Samara stared ahead, up the hill to the distant collection of tumbledown houses, and tried to make out any signs of life.

Giovanni appeared between the seats. "Where are we?"

Samara smiled and indicated the map. "Mont St Catherine."

Hans looked over his shoulder, grinning like a gargoyle. "You thirsty, kid?"

Giovanni smiled unsurely. "Just a little." He licked his cracked lips, reflexively.

Hans laughed. "We'll find water. Believe me, I can smell the stuff from here."

Samara looked ahead. There was certainly no outward sign that a thriving colony was still established here. They were passing straggling outbuildings now, lone houses and a couple of farmhouses before the start of the village proper. All the buildings looked derelict, walls caved in and roof-timbers collapsed or used for fuel long ago.

The transporter rattled over the cobbles of the main street, climbing to the heart of the village at the top of the hill.

Hans killed the engine in the main square and a profound silence settled around them. Samara looked around at the old town hall, the squat, concrete post office and the older buildings that surrounded the square. The plaque outside the Gendarmerie hung from one screw, swinging gently in the hot wind.

Giovanni said, in almost a whisper, "It looks dead."

Samara cracked the cab door and jumped down, almost floored by the direct heat of the sun. It beat down on her like something physical. She thought she could feel her skin shrivelling under its cruel rays.

Quickly she hurried across to the margin of shade afforded by the town hall and looked back at the long, low shape of the transporter.

The first thing she saw, strapped like some misplaced figurehead – minus its head, of course – was Ivan's sun-bloated body on the side of the vehicle. Hans had bled the body, and emptied its guts: he'd claimed it would keep for a few days before turning.

The corpse was blistered black in places, and a swarm of flies vortexed around the shattered gourd of the skull. She looked away.

The others emerged from the transporter and stood with Samara in the shade and scanned the square.

She said, "Okay, the best thing to do is spread out and take a building each." She clutched her rifle, staring at Hans and Giovanni, who each carried a weapon. "And don't shoot if we do come across anyone, okay? We're here to trade... if there's anyone here to trade with." She nodded to a barn across the street. "I'll take that. Edo and Lomo, the church. Giovanni, you check the Gendarmerie, okay?"

Hans moved away before she could allocate him a building. He kicked open the door of the town hall and stepped cautiously inside, rifle raised in readiness.

Samara moved across the sun-drenched square, thankful to reach the sanctuary of the looming barn. She passed into the shadows and looked around as her eyes adjusted to the half-light.

She had a bad feeling about the village. She knew what she would find: poignant evidence of a dead colony; mementoes of everyday life extinguished by the creep of the surrounding desert and the slow drying up of the village's water supply.

She moved further into the barn. If the colony here was extinct, then it had died out very recently. There were signs of repair to the roof-tiles, and in an old animal stall to her right was a stack of empty water canisters, arranged as if they had been left here just yesterday. Also, a rack of well-kept tools against the far wall – hammers, saws and screw-drivers – had seen regular and recent use.

Her hopes began to rise.

She moved next door to the old post office and stepped inside.

The floors had been swept of sand, and recently, she guessed. She moved down a hall, bare floorboards creaking underfoot, and came to a large room. Two single beds stood against the far wall, both impeccably made, sheets folded back, pillows arranged upright. A pile of books stood on a bedside table. There was something touchingly prosaic about the scene. She found herself smiling.

She left the room and looked into the next one; again, two beds and possessions, threadbare clothes laid out on one bed, a bible on another.

Stairs led to upstairs rooms. Carefully, she took the first step and heard it creak. She climbed the rest of the way. If anyone was upstairs, they'd certainly know she was coming.

She found herself in a large room which was obviously the colony's storeroom, and now she had no doubt that the colony had not only managed to survive but was thriving. Containers full of water stood against the wall to her right, and biltongs of dried meat hung on twine stretched from one corner of the room to the other.

A table stood against the far wall, under the window, and it was set with four places...

She heard a sound from behind her, a creaking. She turned and crossed the room to a door, pulled it open, and stepped back in surprise. A figure in the cupboard raised a hand, and Samara responded instinctively, swinging her rifle up and letting off one shot which hit its target. The man's chest erupted, ejecting blood in an oddly symmetrical spray. Someone screamed – a woman in the cupboard beside the man – and Samara found herself firing again.

The shot hit the woman in the midriff. She looked momentarily shocked and folded without a sound, sitting lifeless in the cupboard, with the contents of her stomach disgorging slowly across her trousered lap.

Samara lowered the gun and stared at what she'd done. The corpses lay very still, their immobility contrasting starkly with the activity of seconds ago. One of the man's shoes had come off as he fell: it lay on its side, worn and battered, in the slick of his blood, and for some odd reason it struck Samara as unbearably sad.

She heard nothing but a loud silence, soon replaced by the deafening pounding of her heart.

She looked at the body of the man, searching for the weapon she was sure he had lifted.

Both man and woman were unarmed. "Samara!" Giovanni came pounding up the stairs.

"I'm here. I'm fine."

He entered the room and stared wide-eyed at the bodies.

She gestured at the corpses. "I thought... I thought they were armed."

Giovanni nodded, averting his gaze from the

blood. "Hans has found people in the town hall."

Samara led the way down the stairs. The Africans and Josef were in the square, watching Hans. He was emerging from the town hall, his rifle aimed at the backs of an old couple, a man and a woman. They looked terrified and held their arms in the air.

Hans saw her. "You okay? I heard shooting."

She nodded, oddly touched by the look of concern on his face. "I'm fine."

"We've hit lucky. They have water, supplies. And food. They're leading me right to them, isn't that right?"

The old man looked at Samara, his eyes pleading. His mouth opened, but he was too frightened to articulate a plea.

Hans laughed and prodded the old man in the back. "In there."

The couple shambled ahead of Hans. The old woman was crying. They entered the post office. A long silence ensued, and she wondered what Hans was doing in there.

She knew she should follow them into the building and help collect the water and dried meat, but she had no desire to see the bodies again. She turned to Josef, Edo and Lomo and indicated the building. "Upstairs. You'll find water and meat."

They crossed the square and entered the post office, Josef fidgety and obviously ill-at-ease at the thought of entering a building which also contained Hans and a firearm.

Giovanni smiled and said, "Hans said he could smell water, didn't he?"

Blood, more like, she thought. She nodded. "He has the luck of the damned, Giovanni," she said.

He looked across the square to the post office. "What do you think he's doing in there?"

"I –" she began.

The first gunshot interrupted her, followed seconds later by another. She looked at Giovanni, shocked. "Jesus..."

Hans strolled from the building a minute later, rifle slung casually over his shoulder. He crossed the square and joined her and Giovanni in the shade.

She stared at him. "You killed them..."

He grinned. "Bang, bang. What the hell did you think I was doing?"

Edo, Lomo, and Josef emerged from the post office weighed down with containers of water. They staggered across the square and stowed them on the transporter.

Hans indicated the hillside rising behind the church. "The old woman said there's a working well at the top of the hill, and containers in the barn," he said. "Josef. You go with Giovanni."

Giovanni took Josef to the barn to collect the empty containers, then led the way around the church and up the hill. The Africans returned to the post office.

Hans said, "I had a quick look upstairs, Samara. Good work."

Still dazed, she said, "They were in a cupboard, hiding. When I found them, I thought..." She shook her head. "I thought they were attacking me. I did it in self –"

"Hey, you don't have to justify anything, okay?"

Angered, she said, "I'm not justifying anything!"

"I'll leave the oldsters where they are. They're skin and bone, anyway."

Her stomach turned. "And the other couple?"

"They were younger, fitter," he said. "We'll take them with us, okay?"

His stare challenged her.

She nodded. "Okay."

He returned to the post office to supervise the removal of the provisions and the bodies. Samara climbed into the cab and sat in the passenger seat, and for the next hour just sat there and watched the loading of the transporter, trying not to recall the expression on the woman's face as she died.

Giovanni and Josef made numerous trips up the hill and back again, ferrying a couple of dozen five-litre containers. The vehicle shook as they hauled the water aboard and stowed it on the racks. She reckoned they had more water aboard now than they'd set off with from the castle.

She left the cab and moved to the storage area. She filled her bottle from one of the new containers, then tipped the crystal clear water down her throat.

Edo and Lomo emerged with the last of the dried meat piled high in plastic boxes. When they'd placed them in the transporter, Hans called them back to the post office and gestured upstairs.

A minute later they emerged with the first of the bodies, holding its arms and legs. They'd taken the woman first, and now Samara saw that she was younger than she'd first thought: no older than herself, perhaps in her mid-thirties. She looked away.

She felt the vehicle rocking on its suspension as the pair lashed the woman's body to the side, next to the corpse of the Russian. They returned to the post office and brought out the body of the man, and went through the same process of securing it to the transporter's flank.

"We'll drive on 'til sunset," Hans said, "then stop for food." He stared at Samara. "And this time we'll eat something cooked, okay?"

She looked around at the others. "Any volunteers for kitchen duty?" she asked bitterly. "We seem to have butchered our only chef."

Hans grunted a laugh. "Chef is on the menu." He pointed at Giovanni. "You're our new cook, okay?""

Giovanni mumbled something and turned away.

Hans made his way to the bedroom at the rear of the transporter. Giovanni volunteered to drive, and Josef joined him in the cab. Edo and Lomo retired to their berths. Samara stood by the water rack, slaking her thirst before joining Hans in her room.

He was lying on the bed, and he'd taken the papers from the table and was leafing through them. She quelled her initial annoyance; she'd left them there expressly, after all, so that he'd read them and not go hunting around for the rest.

The truck started up and trundled from the village.

She sat next to him on the bed. He'd removed his shorts and flung them across the room, a sop to the increasing heat of the day, and now he sprawled out, gross and naked. She watched him poring over the print-out: he followed the lines of text with a forefinger, and his lips moved, almost endearingly, as he read. Despite herself, despite her disquiet at how events had turned out in the village – her killing of the couple, and the way Hans had so casually assumed command – she felt her belly spasm at the sight of his nakedness.

She looked at the print-out. It was one of the Dutch reports her father had left untranslated. "Anything interesting?"

He grunted. "Not yet."

She lay on her back and closed her eyes. The motion of the truck rocked her to and fro. Just a couple of hours ago, she thought, the colony back there, such as it was, had been going about its business with little realisation of what was about to descend.

And then we come along and I blast two innocent people to death – and how do I feel about that?

Did she accept what she had done because she'd been influenced by Hans and his dog-eat-dog approach to life, or because something deep within her genuinely believed that she lived in a world where if you didn't kill, then you left yourself open to the mercy of others?

But, she reminded herself, they were innocent, unarmed...

Hans cast the papers aside and was staring at the ceiling, frowning.

She sat up. "What?"

"Oh..." He gestured casually at the print-out. "It's nothing, just stuff about crew, technicians."

She stared at him. She knew he was lying about something. "What have you found, Hans?"

"I told you, it's nothing!" She considered pressing the point, but thought better of it. There would be plenty of time to find out later.

He reached out, cupped her right breast and bit the nipple. She removed her shorts quickly and he took her knees and eased them apart. She lay back and opened her legs wide. He rolled onto his gut and kissed the inside of her thigh, moving closer with each touch of his cracked lips.

His blunt fingers parted her, and before burying his face he paused.

She peered down at him. "What?"

He looked up, grinning. "Back there... what you did. I'm proud of you, Samara."

He ducked his head and began kissing her.

She lay back and closed her eyes.

SHE MUST HAVE dozed off, because she came awake abruptly some time later and sat up. The transporter had stopped, and the silence was so profound it was almost alarming. Beside her, Hans slept like a babe. The description was apt, she thought: with his padded flesh and his bald head, he resembled a fat new-born.

She recalled what she had done back at the village. She was rocked by a sudden, frightening image: she wondered what it would be like to take her rifle, place it against Hans's temple, and blow his brains out.

She shut her eyes, banishing the thought.

A knock sounded timidly on the door. "Samara." It was Giovanni. "We'll be eating soon."

She stood up and pulled on her shorts. Hans stirred sluggishly, opened his eyes and smiled up at her, his face radiant with recollection of his last act before falling asleep. Samara looked down at him, marvelling at the single-mindedness of the male of the species.

She hurried from the room and stepped from the truck.

The others had already lit the fire, using the tree trunks they had found on the first day. She looked up at the flank of the truck and saw the remaining logs lashed there. The corpses, she was pleased to see, were on the other side of the truck.

Flames danced in the darkness, and shadowy figures sat around the fire. She was sorry she'd missed the reassuring sunset. Overhead, massed stars filled the night sky.

Something fat and spattering juices was roasting on a home-made spit above the flames.

Hans ducked from the transporter, rubbing his face to wakefulness and grunting in appreciation at the smell of meat. He slumped down in the sand next to her, finding her thigh with his thick fingers and squeezing, painfully. She wondered if the gesture was in clumsy acknowledgement of their shared intimacy, or in anticipation of the feast to come.

The cooking meat smelled wonderful, but she wondered how safe it might be after a day in this heat.

He looked at Hans. "You sure the meat's safe?"

Hans laughed. "I cut off the bad bits before I spitted the body, Samara."

Giovanni gingerly sliced slabs of dripping meat

from the carcass, his lips pursed. Samara could see his reluctance at having to take on Ivan's role as cook. He loaded plates and handed them round.

Hans tucked into his like a starving man. Samara stared down at the chunk of meat on her plate and wondered at her reluctance. She'd eaten human meat before – the huntress, just before leaving the castle – but somehow this was different. She had known Ivan and had watched his ignominious death, and in some odd way this seemed to taint what sat before her. She wondered if, when the time came, she would be able to stomach the meat of the man and woman she had slaughtered.

Hans grunted like a caveman and nudged her. He said something around a mouthful of meat, a grunt that might have been, "Good!"

She lifted the meat in her fingers, overcome by the aroma, and took a bite. The sinews gave between her teeth, releasing ambrosial juices. Only then did she realise how hungry she was.

She wolfed down the remaining slab and held out her plate for more when Giovanni rose to carve second helpings.

She ate until she was stuffed and could take no more. Even the water, liberated from the colony, tasted wonderful.

She lay back in a comfortable, solid hollow of sand, laced her fingers beneath her head and gazed up into the night sky. The moon was almost full, as bright as a lantern, wearing its perpetual expression of open-mouthed surprise.

She smiled to herself... then remembered something.

She stood up and hurried back to the transporter. "Samara?" Hans called after her.

"I'll be back in a second."

She made her way to the bedroom and rummaged under the bed for the bag she'd stuffed with her clothing. She found the bottle and pulled it out.

Her father had called it *brandy*, and said that he was saving it for a special occasion. That special occasion had never arrived, and there was no time like the present.

She needed alcohol, she thought as she carried it back to the fire. She needed the balm it would bring, the blurring effect it would have on her emotions; it might even, if she were lucky, allow her to forget shooting the couple in the village. Before she emerged with the bottle, she unscrewed the cap and took a long swallow. She gasped.

The spirit filled her mouth with flavour and fire, and she laughed aloud as it burned its way down her throat to her stomach.

She hurried from the transporter and displayed the bottle.

Hans stared at her with massive eyes in his vast red face, and Edo and Lomo exclaimed in their own language. She insisted that everyone tip the remains of their water in the sand – a profligate gesture in recognition of the libation about to take place – and poured the brandy into their bottles.

Laughing, they drank. Samara filled her mouth, swilled it around as she'd watched her father do all those years ago, and swallowed. She was already a little drunk when Hans cried out, "Stop! Stop... A toast! Isn't that what they say? A toast?" He stood and raised his bottle. "A toast, to Ivan. To the best meal Ivan the chef ever provided!"

Samara found herself laughing as she tipped back the bottle and drank. Her head was spinning. Josef stood, mimicking Hans's posture. "To the success of the mission."

Then it was Edo's turn. "May we find much food and happiness in Spain."

They drank and resumed eating; Giovanni presented Samara with something from the carcass, a long, deep pink lozenge. She bit into it and succulent blood squirted from her mouth and ran down her chin. Ivan's liver, she thought...

She drank some more, and suddenly a long time seemed to have elapsed, as the fire was burning down to its embers and the others were racing around the transporters, shouting in delight at something.

Someone touched her. It was Hans, lying beside her with a stupid expression on his big, fat face.

She looked at her bottle. It was almost empty. She tipped the rest into her mouth and frowned. She had brought the bottle out in order to drink and forget something... but she had forgotten what it was she had meant to forget.

"Samara..." He was leaning over her, stroking her face.

"Hans?" she laughed. He wanted to make love here, out in the open, under the moon and the stars.

She pulled him to her.

CHAPTER THIRTEEN

SAND BLITZED THE windscreen, reducing visibility to zero.

That was no real problem, as they had progressed so far by following the direction of the compass. It wasn't as if there were any roads to keep to, anyway. The problem was, the wind was so strong Dan feared it might tip the truck and leave it stranded on its back like some helpless beetle. So he reduced speed, kept a straight course and ploughed on through the sandstorm.

Ed had driven till midnight, when Kath had taken the wheel and driven until dawn. After a quick breakfast – Mont St Catherine was half a day away, and Dan was eager to reach the old colony – he'd climbed into the cab and set off, and minutes later the sandstorm had descended out of nowhere, wailing like a demented banshee and peppering the truck with a billion microscopic missiles. Another fear, quite apart from the more immediate threat of being flipped by the wind, was the threat of wear and tear on the solar arrays. The arrays were more precious these days than gold had ever been; they were a lifeline, an assurance of power, and without them the half-track and the drilling rig would be just so much scrap metal. There was a workshop back at the castle devoted to nothing else but cannibalising old machinery and utilising the components in the manufacture of new arrays. Dan himself had spent a good third of his time repairing panels that had failed to work.

He hoped the storm would blow itself out soon, but he had known them to last as long as a couple of days.

Paul sat in the cab beside him, watching him as he fought to keep a straight course. He took in Dan's every move, eagle-eyed and learning. It was no doubt how he had survived until now, by observing and teaching himself as many survival techniques as came his way. Paul had amazed them, earlier, by corroborating Ed's diagnosis of intestinal worms in Millie. Not only that, but when Ed had prescribed a course of medication available only back at the castle, Paul had suggested an alternative and had even produced a vial of pills – well past their use-by date, but according to Ed safe enough – from his shoulder bag.

He also knew by heart dozens of classics of French poetry, and recited lines to himself, voluntarily and *a propos* of nothing, when the urge took him.

The boy would be an asset to the colony.

The wind beat against the cab. Along with the noise, making every conversation a shouting match, came the compensation that the sandstorm cloaked the sun and reduced the midday temperature by some twenty degrees.

Paul said, "I think Millie's taken to Kath."

Dan nodded. "And I know Kath's smitten with Millie." He had watched them last night, and it was as if they had been together for the duration of the girl's short life to date.

That morning, during the brief change-over in the cab, with Millie sleeping in the lounge, Kath had whispered to him, "She's a miracle, Dan. It's as if she's been sent." There had been a light in her eyes that had not been there before; she was more content that Dan had seen her in years.

"You're a lucky man," Paul said now.

Dan glanced across at him. "You mean Kath?"

Paul nodded.

"I know. I've never stopped telling myself that. Kath's a special person. Back at the castle she had countless jobs... I don't know where to start. She can mend anything, mechanical, metal or wood. She can make meals out of nothing. And, more than anything, she understands people. When anyone had a problem back there, they went to Kath. She listened and understood and gave sound advice."

"How did you meet her?"

Dan smiled. "She was at the colony at Mont St Catherine when I turned up there thirty years ago. I fell head over heels straight away."

"And Kath?"

Dan laughed. He recalled the introverted, shy girl she had been then, in her mid-twenties, still protected by her mother and father, who had run the small colony; the last thing they wanted was to have their daughter fall for the first good-for-nothing waster who happened along.

"Well, let's say that it took a while for me to win her over." And her parents, too. He'd had to pledge himself to the colony, work like the devil and prove that he was no fly-by-night chancer out for himself.

Dan recalled his second day at the colony, having arrived footsore and starving from Barcelona. Someone had allotted him a job in the fields, and he'd worked alongside a quiet, slim, blonde girl – who had a habit of letting her fringe fall over her eyes – and who only later that day, after toiling for hours, had acknowledged his presence and told him that her name was Katherine Ellington, whose parents were English.

Memories of his time with Kath, their long, slow falling in love, were mixed inextricably with the slow but steady decline of the colony; with the deaths of Kath's parents and others, and the hard decision they had made, over a period of weeks, that for the sake of their own survival they had to move north. It had been a hard decision for Dan to make, and even harder for Kath, who knew no other life than that at Mont St Catherine.

The trek north, with three other couples, had been hard – they had encountered marauders, both in gangs and acting alone – but Dan liked to think that the hardships faced and overcome had worked to make stronger their commitment to each other.

Copenhagen had taken them in, and for twenty years they had lived with what had seemed like the very real hope that they could build a prosperous future for themselves and the growing colony.

And then had come the cholera outbreak.

Breaking into his thoughts, Paul asked, "How long have you known Ed?"

"For as long as we've been at the colony – twenty years. He was a founder of the colony, some forty years ago. He's seen a lot."

Paul nodded. "It shows."

Dan glanced across at him. "It's odd, but each succeeding generation after the Breakdown has had it a little easier than the one before. Not that it's easy for anyone – but people of Ed's generation… not that there are many still alive… they actually experienced things before the fall, when life was easy, food and water plentiful. Then the Breakdown came, the wars and plagues… imagine what people went through, back then? I was born ten years after things fell apart; I never knew anything else."

"And I," Paul said, "I've only really ever known life alone with Elise."

Dan looked at the boy. "So… don't be too hard on Ed, okay? He might come over as a hardened cynic, but he has every right and reason to be. What matters is what's underneath that shell – he's a good man. I'd trust him with my life, and you can't say that about many people."

The first indication Dan had that the storm was letting up was the sudden drop in the roaring that surrounded the cab, followed by a sudden increase in visibility. A minute later the glare of sunlight showed ahead, and they broke through the last veils of flying sand and emerged into the white-hot glare of the midday sun.

Dan laughed and slewed the cab around so that

he could look back through his side window to the storm they had left behind. It seemed to fill the horizon and extend into the sky for kilometres, a great anvil of fizzing particles driven by a raging wind.

Dan set the truck back on a south-west course and accelerated across the storm flattened desert.

Ten minutes later he stopped the truck and relinquished the driving seat. "Your turn," he said.

Paul was wide-eyed as he slid behind the wheel and examined the controls.

For the next hour he instructed Paul in driving the vehicle as they headed south. Paul took to the task with ease, even enjoyed what to Dan had become a labour of necessity. Another hand to take a stint at the wheel would be a welcome relief of everyone's workload.

While Paul drove, Dan picked up the radio receiver and attempted to get through to someone, anyone, out there.

Only scratchy silence met his efforts. He shook his head in frustration and banged the receiver back onto its housing.

Paul said, "Nothing?"

Dan grunted a laugh.

Paul looked at him, gripping the wheel with both hands like a professional. "What?"

"I don't know... Call me stupid, but I had a hope that the old colony at Mont St Catherine might still be up and running. I left a second set there when we left. About twenty people decide to tough it out... We kept in contact on the way up, but I think the second set wasn't up to it." He shrugged. "I hoped that someone might have repaired it, so as we got closer..."

"What do you think happened to the people you left behind?"

Dan shrugged. "I tried to persuade them to come with us. Six of them did, but all the others... I did my level best, but the colony was all they'd known. It was their home, their life." He shook his head. "You know what I think? The realist in me thinks they died out within five years of us leaving them."

And in a few hours, he thought, I'll probably find out for sure.

Paul was silent for a while, concentrating on his driving, then said, "How many colonies do you think are still out there?"

Dan said, "Good question. We know there's one in the south of France – that was where that bastard Hans came from. And years ago, Copenhagen was in contact with a colony in Dublin, Ireland, and that was painful..." He broke off, reliving the memory.

"What happened?"

"It was a big colony – a few hundred people, just south of Dublin. They were hit by typhoid, then decreasing food supplies, then towards the end they fought amongst themselves..." He had been on duty that night in the radio shack when he'd received a call from a distraught woman – Moira – pleading for help from anyone. He'd come to know her, over the months, which made the call all the more painful. Gunfire and the sound of flames had raged in the background, and then the signal had died.

Dan told Paul what had happened. "And that was the last we heard from Dublin."

"I wonder how many survivors there are, world-wide?"

Dan shrugged. "A few thousand, tops. The Americas were wiped out by nuclear strikes. There might have been survivors, but not for long. India and China... they went the same way. The Middle East..." Dan laughed without humour. "Well, those crazy bastards were the first to annihilate each other."

"That doesn't leave much..."

"Apparently Russia became a radioactive wasteland when the winds blew north out of China. Now Australia... if anyone knows how to survive the heat and desert conditions, it's the Aborigines."

Paul smiled. "Perhaps there is hope for the human race?"

Dan said, "But Australia was suffering water shortages long before the rest of us."

And the irony was, before the water shortages, before the drying up of the seas, the ice caps had melted and the oceans had swelled, rising to inundate the thousands of countries and island states desperately clinging to life at sea level. They had been the first to go, while the richer, developed nations had stood by wringing their metaphorical hands and granting limited aid – too little and too late – while utilising their monetary funds and material resources in an attempt to save themselves.

And later came the long years of inexorable drought.

Paul said, "Perhaps we're the very last people left alive on the planet?"

Dan grunted another grim laugh. "Well, wouldn't that be a thought?"

They lapsed into silence, staring out across the ochre desert. Here and there, the monotony was interrupted by the bizarre protrusion, through the sand, of objects familiar and yet transformed: at one point they followed a line of lamp-posts emerging a metre from the sand, which seemed to monitor their progress like so many concrete periscopes. Later, electric pylons strode across the landscape, half-buried giants with their skeletal arms akimbo, as if unimpressed that their creators had managed to survive the Breakdown without them.

They passed through a town and entered a stretch of limitless desert once again.

One hour later, Dan consulted his map and peered through the windscreen.

"We should be within sight of the hills about now," he told Paul.

Paul nodded and pointed ahead and to his right. "On the horizon, just there. I've been wondering for the past ten minutes what it was."

"Ten minutes? I can hardly make it out now. Perhaps I need glasses..." There were hundreds of pairs back in stores, gleaned over the years by scavenging parties. He'd check them out when he got back. I really am getting old, he thought.

The range of hills showed as a charcoal blur rising from the sand. It would be a while yet before he could make out the village, the line of houses that followed the crest of the foothill, and at its highest point the church tower. His last sight of the village, thirty years ago as they had been leaving, had impressed itself upon his memory: the struggling vineyard on the hillside already succumbing to the creep of the sands, the terracotta-tiled buildings tumbling into disrepair, one by one, as colonists despaired and headed north...

He wondered what they'd find there now. Apprehension knotted his stomach.

As the half-track approached the foothills, the village on the first fold resolved itself, floating above the scorched desert like a mirage. He made out the line of buildings, their dereliction not apparent at this distance, and the church tower, its upper half toppled. The vines had long gone, of course, replaced by ubiquitous sand, along with the fields where they had struggled to grow potatoes and greens. He wondered if the colony had ever managed to get the hydroponics station in the old town hall up and running, but he doubted it.

Dan pointed to the cobbled road that emerged from the desert at the foot of the hill, and Paul nodded and steered the truck towards it.

Five minutes later the tracks clattered over the cobbled main street, and Dan lay a hand on Paul's arm. "Stop here. I just want to look around..."

Paul stilled the engine, and a silence settled over the truck.

Kath joined them, found Dan's hand and smiled. The memories flooded back.

She looked at him and said, "Let's walk up the hill, okay? Just me and you."

Dan smiled. To Paul he said, "Take the truck to the top. We'll join you there. If you see anyone, say... tell them that Kath and Dan are on their way up."

Paul nodded. "I'll do that."

Kath returned to the lounge to tell Ed and Millie what they were doing, and Dan climbed from the cab. The first thing he noticed was the heat, the pressure of the sun clamping down on his exposed flesh like a hot compress. He grabbed a hat from the cab and felt immediate relief in its scant shade. Kath emerged from the truck wearing the same floppy sun hat she'd worn to do the gardening here, thirty years ago.

The truck rumbled to life and ground up the cobbled street.

He took her hand and led her across the street and into the shade. They walked, slowly, peering about them like tourists.

It was a disconcerting experience to be back once again in a place which had been so important in his life and which had played such a big part in his memories ever since. It was chiefly important because he had met Kath here, of course, but also because it had been his first experience of true democratic communal living. Before that he had lived in a colony in the hills above Barcelona, where his mother had brought him as an infant. He had known no other life, and so had lived by the strict laws imposed on the colonists by a self-appointed dictator known as El Pedro. Only when he had reached his late teens and fled north to Mont St Catherine, and discovered what it was like to live in a truly free, equitable society, had he fully realised the true inhumanity of the regime in Spain. Here, he realised, he'd discovered what it had meant to share, to work for the community, to learn from elders eager to pass down hard-won knowledge – instead of hoarding it greedily like the elders did in Barcelona – and to reap the benefits of communal hard work. In an age of barbarism, the colony at Mont St Catherine had been an oasis of humane communalism.

It was something he had tried to duplicate in Copenhagen, with mixed success.

He would have been happy to have spent the rest of his life here, with Kath, had it not been for the encroachment of the sand and the merciless heat.

Kath leaned against him, weeping. "So many memories," she murmured. "Every stone, every cobble... The shape of that building there... the lie of the hill. For thirty years this was the only home I knew. It was my universe."

He kissed her temple. He had lived here just ten years, and the place was impressed indelibly upon his consciousness; what must it be like for Kath, who had known nowhere else before they'd left?

She pointed across the street to a house with closed shutters, the green paint peeling in the glare of the sun. "When I was six, I went to school there for the first time. There were ten of us. Lessons were... magical. Old Mme. Dupont..." She smiled at the recollection. "And here – this was where Dutch Henry lived, a poet who wrote about events in the village and recited his poems every... was it Sunday night?"

He squeezed her hand. "I remember Henry," he said.

The problem with returning after so long, he thought, is that every memory is bittersweet: every recollection of happy times, of past joy, is tainted by the knowledge of what followed, of what happened to the people who had made this place so special, Mme. Dupont and Dutch Henry and Kath's parents and dozens of other good people... All of them, every one of them, dead now. Mme Dupont had passed away shortly after his arrival, Dutch Henry and Kath's parents a year before he left... But what about the others, the youngsters who had elected to remain behind? Was it too much to hope that they had managed to survive, even prosper?

He peered up the length of the main street. There was no sign of life, no movement, no indication that, years ago, the village had been home to a strong and vital community.

Kath voiced his thoughts, "Do you think...?"

He shook his head, unwilling to share with her his doubts. "I don't know."

"Dan, look here..." She tugged his hand, leading him across the cobbles to a gate in the wall. She pushed it open and they passed inside.

They stopped just within the gate and stood in the sunlight, gazing across the open rectangle at the grave markers in the sand.

"Oh, look, Dan, even here... the sand is even here!"

He held her as she cried, emotion rising within his chest.

They had paid their last respects to the graves of loved ones before leaving here twenty years ago. Then, the cemetery had been immaculate and ordered; a little grass had grown in real soil, and wooden markers – as well as a few headstones – had stood proud and upright.

Now sand had crept into the cemetery, undermining the crosses and the headstones that leaned at drunken angles. The place seemed robbed of sanctity, no more now than an extension of the desert outside, and it struck Dan as a terrible symbol: not only had the heat and the dust taken the living; now it had laid claim to the dead.

Kath moved among the markers, reading names softly to herself, setting the crosses and stones upright in the shifting sands.

She came to the graves of her parents, the founders of the colony, and Dan joined her. They looked down on two simple crosses, placed side by side – they had died within months of each other, her father first, quickly followed by her mother, both of them peacefully in their late seventies. Dutch Henry had carved into the wooden crosses their names and dates of birth and death.

"Henry was a good man," Kath said. "My parents adored him."

He moved to the back of the cemetery, peering at the crosses and markers and reading out the names. He found the graves of people who were his own age when he left the village, and was shocked to find that they had been dead for ten years.

"What?" Kath said.

He pointed to the grave.

"But... Poor Sabine. Only forty-one. And Peter. He

was an engineer. I thought he and Sabine would..."
She shook her head, tearful again.

Dan counted the crosses and the grave markers;
there were forty-one in all, ten of them dating from
after they had left the village. The population had
stood at fifteen souls on the day of their departure.
He wondered what had become of the handful of
colonists who had remained.

He held her to him and they left the cemetery,
Kath wiping tears from her cheeks. "I'm so silly... I
knew what it would be like. Oh," she took a deep
breath. "Let's get back to the others, Dan. I want to
hold Millie."

They climbed the hill.

THE HALF-TRACK STOOD on the cobbles outside the
church on the top of the hill, its modernity out of
place in such an ancient setting.

Paul emerged from the church to their left, Millie
clinging to his hand. When she saw Kath, she cried
her name and ran across to her. Kath knelt, and was
almost bowled over by the little girl's momentum as
Millie leapt into her arms.

Paul said, "No sign of life. The place is deserted."

Kath led Millie into the town hall, telling her the
story of when she and Dan had lived there...

Ed was already in the hall; Dan could see him
inspecting the remains of the hydroponics system.

Dan said, "We drew water from a well above the
church. If it's dried up..."

"Let's go and see."

He led Paul around the back of the church and up a steep incline of rock, emerging from welcome shadow into the pummelling torture of the open sun. Years ago the rock here had been covered in soil; thin and denatured, but soil nonetheless. Now the hillside comprised of fists and protuberant knuckles of granite and schist.

They climbed to the concrete-enclosed well-head, Dan panting hard.

The well had been excavated since his departure. It had been a mere hole in the hillside, through which they had dropped buckets on long ropes. Now, a good chunk of the hillside had been dug away, and peering past the ramparts of the concrete surround, Dan made out a series of timber, switchback steps leading down into the well's shadowy depths.

He looked up at Paul. "I'm going to take a closer look."

He climbed over the concrete lip and placed a foot on the first plank, testing its solidity. It took his weight, and cautiously he descended. After twenty rungs he came to a platform and paused, peering down; he could see that the well had been widened and deepened.

A bucket hung on a hook hammered into the rock wall; it was attached to a long coil of rope.

He looked up.

Paul's head showed against the glare of the sky, framed in the rectangular concrete surround. "See anything?"

"I'm going to drop the bucket and see what happens," he called back.

He took the bucket and fed the rope into the hole. It seemed to descend for an age. At last it stopped and the rope slackened – then there was the unmistakable sensation of the bucket sinking as it took on weight: there was water down there.

He hauled it back up, smiling to himself. Minutes later, his arms aching, he pulled the bucket onto the platform and stared into the shimmering disc of water.

He looked up at Paul and waved.

Taking the bucket in his right hand, he climbed.

Paul reached down and relieved him of the load while he jumped over the concrete lip.

The water looked fresh and crystal clear. Experimentally, Dan dipped in a hand and took a sip.

"Christ, Paul..."

The boy copied him, laughing as water dribbled from his mouth.

Dan said, "It's the best thing I've tasted since my last beer, and that was thirty-five years ago."

Paul looked down the hillside, past the church, to the main street and the half-track parked in the square.

"I wonder what happened to the villagers?"

Dan shrugged uneasily. "It's the hottest part of the afternoon. Perhaps they're holed up somewhere..."

The thought filled him with a desperate joy. "Let's go tell the others."

They were scrambling down the hillside when Paul said, "Dan. Stop."

Dan came to a slithering halt. "What is it?"

The boy was pointing across the incline, to something sitting on the rock. He crossed to it and knelt, then looked back at Dan, grinning.

Dan hurried over. "What...?"

Paul was picking up a lizard trap, complete with trapped animal. "I think we'll find the owner of this somewhere in the village, Dan." He extricated the lizard, dashed it expertly against a rock and threaded it through a loop in his shorts.

Dan hurried down the hill, unable to contain his excitement at what he had to tell Kath. He wondered who had survived, whether they would be friends from all those years ago, or strangers; whichever, it would be great to meet up and swap stories. He rounded the church and came to the square.

Ed was still in the town hall. He looked up when Dan entered. "Well," Dan said, "we found water, plenty of it and crystal clear."

Ed nodded. "And they've been successfully growing greens here." He indicated a shallow nutrient bed. "But there's something about the set up..."

"What?" Dan said, heart sinking.

"What do we do at the castle? Sow as we reap, so there's always a supply of greens coming on, right? But there's nothing here. Nothing at all. As if everything's been taken in one go –"

"So they had a lean time..."

Ed was shaking his head. He pointed across the room, to a scatter of apparatus, a watering system and a lighting panel, smashed across the floorboards.

"It looks to me as if there's been a struggle, and recently."

A second later, before Dan had time to assess the import of Ed's suggestion, Paul appeared in the doorway, panting. "Dan, Ed. You'd better come."

"What?" Dan said.

"Kath... she found..." He gestured behind him.

Feeling sick, Dan followed the boy from the town hall and across the square.

Kath was leaning against the wall of what, many years ago, had been the post office. In Dan's time here it had been used as rooms for couples.

Millie was clutching Kath's leg, wailing. Dan reached them. "Kath, what – ?"

She looked grief-stricken. She pointed into the building, then knelt and picked up Millie and hugged her to her chest.

Dan took a breath and stepped inside, followed by Paul and Ed. "I'll look upstairs," Paul said.

Dan and Ed stepped into the first room, overlooking the hillside and the desert below; it was empty. Dan felt his fear mounting as they moved into the second room. There, between two beds, he found the body of an old woman.

He knelt beside the body. The woman lay on her back on the floorboards, a bullet hole in the centre of her forehead.

It was perhaps ten seconds before he saw past the dead features, saw past the fact of the violent death, and recognised the face.

The woman was called Marie, and she and Kath had been good friends years ago. She must have been in her late fifties, but looked much older.

He fought to catch his breath. It was one thing to die a death prescribed by harsh nature, death by starvation in this age of privations, but to die violently at the hands of another...

"Who could have done this?" he said to Ed.

Ed replied quietly, "There's another one..." He pointed to behind the door, and Dan saw another body there – an old man he didn't recognise. The corpse huddled against the wall, as if attempting to escape, a messy excavation in the back of its skull.

Ed knelt and examined the corpse, then told Dan, "He's been dead about ten, twelve hours, I'd say. He can't have shot the woman and taken his own life..." He gestured around the room. "There's no gun."

Dan said, "We never kept weapons of any sort here; it was against our ethos. Kath's parents and the other elders of the colony... despite the dangers of marauders, they wouldn't countenance weapons."

Paul appeared in the doorway, ashen. "There's blood all over the upstairs rooms. There's been a slaughter here."

Dan looked at him. "No survivors?"

Paul said, "Lots of blood, but no sign of any bodies."

"It must be the work of outsiders," Dan said. "The villagers couldn't have done something like this."

Ed looked at him. "You sure about that?"

"I'm sure. It was outsiders. They killed the old man and woman and..."

Paul interrupted, "And the others, who were upstairs?"

Dan shook his head. "My guess is... whoever did this wounded the others and took them with them."

He sank onto one of the beds. "Ed, this was a working colony. They had water, meat from lizard traps... they even grew their own food. And then some bastards came along and..." He wept; he sat on the bed and the tears came. "It was such a... such a peaceful place, Ed. They didn't deserve this."

Ed stood slowly, bones creaking, and limped across to Dan. He sat down on the bed and put an arm around Dan's shoulders, holding him.

Ed said, "If this happened around twelve hours ago, whoever did this will be long gone by now. Which is just as well."

Dan looked up. "Then again, I'd like to confront the bastards who did this."

Ed smiled grimly. "I know how you feel."

Dan gathered himself. "I'll go see how Kath is. Excuse me." He left the room, stepped from the old post office and emerged into the sunlight.

Kath was sitting on the steps of the half-track, in the shade, holding Millie on her lap and murmuring something to the girl. She looked up as Dan crossed the square, but her attempt at a brave smile broke down and she wept again.

She carried Millie into the truck and emerged a minute later. Dan held her.

"Ed... Ed thinks..." she sobbed.

"I know, I know." He said, then went on, "I want to bury them in the cemetery, Kath. There's nothing else we can do. It just seems right."

She nodded.

Ed emerged from the building. "Paul's going to fill every container he can find with water from the well. I'll help him. We'll scour the place for provisions."

Dan told him of his intention to bury the bodies, and Ed nodded. "When we leave here," the old man said, "I suggest we keep the rifles at the ready. If we do come across anyone, we need to be prepared."

He and Paul crossed to the church and climbed the hill to the well. Dan said to Kath, "Stay in the truck. I'll fetch the bodies."

Without a word she returned to the vehicle. Dan heard her talking to Millie, simulating levity.

HE CARRIED MARIE'S body down the hillside in the full glare of the sun. The body was surprisingly light; her thin right arm swung loose, patting his thigh with every step as if in a posthumous gesture of gratitude.

He lay the body on the sand of the graveyard and returned up the hill for the second corpse. The old man was a little heavier, and stared at Dan with his glassy eyes all the way down the main street, this time as if in silent rebuke for Dan's effrontery in assuming he might put things right with the simple act of burial.

"I know," he said as he entered the cemetery and laid the body beside Marie's. "I know I'm doing this more for me and Kath, but..."

He looked around the cemetery and found a spade leaning against the wall. He dug two shallow pits side by side, working the fine sand with ease, then eased the bodies into the graves and covered them with sand.

Beside where the spade had stood was a pile of ready-made crosses and markers, and Dan smiled at the fatalism of whoever had spent their time making them.

He selected two markers and planted them at the heads of the graves, and left the cemetery. It meant something – to him at least – that he had been able to counter the violence of the couple's death with a gesture of humanity, futile though it might have been.

Kath was helping Ed load containers of water into the truck. Millie was asleep on the chesterfield, and they worked quietly. "I found twenty canisters in the barn," Kath said. "Paul caught more lizards."

Dan nodded. "At least we can put it all to use."

Paul returned with the last of the containers. They stowed them in the lounge, and then stood in the square and gazed west. The sun was going down, laying scarlet and saffron banners across the horizon.

"If only we'd arrived here a day earlier..." Kath began.

Ed said, "Then we might be lying dead, too."

"Let's go," Dan said.

Paul said, "I'll drive."

They climbed aboard the half-track. Ed handed out the rifles and sat next to Paul in the cab.

The truck grumbled into life, shattering the silence, and the tracks ground noisily across the cobbles as Paul drove from the village.

Dan and Kath retired to their berth, lay down and held each other.

CHAPTER FOURTEEN

WHEN SHE WAS twenty, Xian graduated from Edinburgh University with a first-class degree in biochemistry.

She was recruited by the government to work on a top-secret project based in Greenland, studying the efficacy of setting up and feeding a vast colony of up to a million people on that landmass. Even now, twenty years before what would be known as the Breakdown, governments in Europe were looking to relocate sections of population away from the increasingly intemperate areas of Southern Europe. The British government, in a scheme with Denmark and Italy, were pumping millions into developing self-sustaining colonies in the north.

Xian considered the irony of working where her father had spent so much time, and where he had met his end.

A week into the project, she met a young doctor fresh out from England, a specialist in oncology who introduced himself as Richard Stearton.

Xian could hardly control her delight. "Richard? Richard Stearton? You lived in the Chiswick towerpile in 2025?"

The young doctor peered at her, recognition dawning on his broad, fair features. "Xian? Xian Lu!"

"Richard! I've so much to tell you..."

They were inseparable after that, as they caught up with their mutually turbulent pasts, worked together on linked projects in the present, and often spent their free time speculating about the future.

Richard was still full of the boyish enthusiasm and optimism Xian recalled from their childhood. "I think we'll survive, Xian. Not only survive, but prosper. We haven't come all this way, made so many ground-breaking scientific discoveries, to let all that go to waste."

"Try telling that to the dictatorships across the world who want nothing more than to save their own skins –"

Richard waved this aside. "They're doomed. They'll destroy themselves. Granted, millions will die, billions. It's inevitable. The facts are that resources are diminishing every year and the socio-economic infrastructure is collapsing. But Europe, the North American Alliance... we'll survive. I mean, look at this project. There's real hope here..."

Xian looked at him sceptically and said, "Reality update, Richard. This project is doomed. The biosphere is shattered; the seas, despite the floods of the last decade, are drying up. I predict that in forty, fifty years there won't be a sizeable ocean on the planet."

"You Jeremiah!" he laughed.

She could only stare bleakly across the rocky

wastes of the headland beyond the dome. "You mark my words, Richard."

"No!" He was adamant. "There is hope!"

Then she kissed him for the very first – but not the last – time, and whispered, "Still building improbable towers, Richard Stearton."

Chapter Fifteen

Paul drove in silence, very aware of Ed's stone-like presence beside him. The old man leaned forward, gazing intently through the windscreen. He seemed to be in a world of his own, and Paul wondered if he were looking ahead to the time they might apprehend the killers of the old couple back there, and what justice he might mete out – some compensation, perhaps, for his inability to find and deal with his daughter's murderers.

They left the village in their wake and were passing through a desert landscape of dips and rises, the truck making slow progress up the sliding dunes. Paul wondered when Kath would decide they had put enough distance between themselves and the village, and call a halt for food. He was starving.

He thought back over the events of the past few days. They were as full of incident as the previous ten years had been empty of any drama. He had witnessed, or seen the results of, more killing than ever before in his life. He had hazy recollections of his childhood in the Paris colony, of fights between aggressive men and women, and even dim memories of gun-fights.

After that, during his time with Elise, he had led a sheltered existence, shielded from the horrors of the world outside, and the even greater horrors of the past, by Elise's maternal care. Poetry and fairy tales, he thought; it had not exactly been the ideal preparation for the grim reality of the world outside.

And by a stroke of fortune, which Elise would have claimed he deserved, he had fallen in with good people. It might easily have been so different.

He heard something behind him, and turned to see Millie standing in the gap between the seats, holding a head-rest and swaying.

Ed smiled at the child and lifted her through. She sat on his knee as Paul eased the truck over the crest of a dune: they slid down the other side, the tracks spinning noisily without purchase. The girl laughed.

Paul glanced at the compass to ensure they were still heading west, and accelerated across a level stretch of desert to a distant line of dunes, curved like the blade of a scimitar against the star-filled night.

"Where are we going, Ed?" Millie asked.

"We are going," Ed said, "to what was once upon a time the sea."

"The sea? Like water?"

"And lots of it. Miles and miles of it. More water than there was desert, blue and sparkling in the sunlight."

Millie thought about that. "Where did it go?"

Ed smiled. "It dried up, Millie. It dried up and vanished, and now there's only the empty sea beds where the oceans once were."

The girl fell silent, frowning.

Paul glanced across at Ed. He looked content with the girl on his lap, for the first time since Paul had met him. He said, "Did you ever see the sea, Ed?"

The old man laughed, without much humour. "Seen it, Paul. Sailed on it."

Paul shook his head. He understood the words, but the concept of sailing on the sea, of crossing an ocean in a vehicle, as they were crossing the sand in the truck, was unimaginable. "In a boat?"

"In all manner of boats. Where I lived, in a city called Oslo, in my childhood... There were regular ferries south to Denmark, across to Britain. I crossed the sea often when I was young, and later when I began work in Europe..."

"I've seen pictures," Paul said. "But what did it feel like?"

Ed thought back. "A bobbing, surging motion. You were constantly aware of travelling across a medium not solid, like the earth. It wasn't dissimilar to flying, in a way."

Paul stared at him. "You've flown?"

Ed nodded. "A few times," he said, "before the Breakdown ended all that."

Paul considered the wonders of the past. "Elise said that all the seas might not be dried up, that there still might be smaller bodies of water somewhere."

Ed shrugged. "It's impossible to tell. I'd like to think so, but I've never even heard rumours. Around fifty years ago, the seas started shrinking. Twenty years later they were gone."

Millie said, gazing up, "But why are we going to the sea if it's all dried up?"

Ed laughed. "Because we'll be drilling for water, making a big hole in the ground to try to find drinking water."

Paul said, "But what about the water back there? What's wrong with it?"

"Nothing wrong with it," Ed said, "just not enough of it. The aquifers under the land are fast drying up, or being exhausted. There's more chance of striking a subterranean reservoir out to sea, which will last hopefully decades... Or, at least, Dan thinks so."

Paul nodded and lapsed into silence. He didn't want to ask Ed the obvious question: what would they do if they failed to find water under the old sea bed?

He concentrated on easing the truck up the gradient of the next dune. The only way to do it, according to Dan, was head-on: if you took the face of the dune at an oblique angle, which Paul had thought would be the obvious way of tackling a sand hill, you put the truck in danger of rolling over. To confront the dune head-on was far safer, even if it took time and put more strain on the engine.

They inched their way up the sliding incline, progressing a few metres then sliding back ten more. Millie thought it highly amusing and bounced up and down on Ed's knee.

Dan appeared between the seats. "I'm fixing a meal. We'll get to the other side of the dune and stop. You okay there?"

Paul nodded, gripping the wheel, determined to get the truck to the crest before admitting defeat.

The tracks bit then, and the truck surged, and seconds later they arrived at the crown of the dune.

Paul smiled with a sense of achievement and brought the vehicle to a halt.

They sat on the top of the dune; a plain of sand stretched out below them, silver in the light of the stars and a burning white moon.

Dan said, "Christ, what's that?"

Paul wondered how he'd failed to see it. A small, fiery glow showed perhaps two kilometres away. His stomach clenched as he realised that it was a camp-fire. Beside it, he made out the long, low shape of a vehicle.

Dan disappeared, returning seconds later with a pair of solid, black binoculars. He peered through them, then passed the binoculars to Ed.

Paul glanced at Dan. He looked grim. "Do you think...?" Paul began.

Dan shook his head. "I don't know what to think."

Ed passed Paul the binoculars and he adjusted them to his eyes. All he saw at first was a dancing circle of dim desert; he steadied his hand, then saw the truck, encrusted with solar panels, and beside it the tiny shapes of shadowy figures. It was hard to tell how many there were; some were hidden by the glow of the fire, others were moving about.

He returned the binoculars to Dan.

"Do you think they've heard us?"

Dan raised the binoculars to his eyes again. "I don't think so... and I don't think they'll see us this far away. But I'm taking no chances." He thought about it. "Start up the truck and back us down the dune so we're out of sight, okay?"

Paul fired up the engine and eased the truck into

reverse. It backed off the crest, slid ten metres and lodged in the sand at an angle.

Dan nodded, "That'll do."

Kath joined them. "What's the problem?"

"Climb out and we'll show you."

Ed stayed in the truck with Millie, and Paul followed Dan and Kath into the hot desert night. They slogged up the dune, and at the crest Dan dropped to the sand, Kath beside him.

Paul peered over the crown of the dune and sighted the camp-fire.

Kath looked through the binoculars. She lowered them, her moon-lit face looking worried. "They can only be the people who..." She gestured back in the vague direction of Mont St Catherine. "What do you think?"

Dan nodded. "Hell of a coincidence if they're not."

Paul took the binoculars. The camp-fire was burning low, and most of the people had climbed aboard the truck. He made out a couple of figures: they seemed to be lying on the far side of the fire, foreshortened at this angle, and conjoined as if in intimacy.

They returned to the truck and Kath settled Millie in her berth while Dan doled out bowls of lizard stew. When Kath returned they sat in the lounge and ate. Paul stirred the meal with his fork, his hunger of earlier banished by apprehension. The others ate in silence for a while, before Ed said, "So... what do we do?"

Dan looked around the group. "I'm open to suggestions."

"If they're the people responsible for what happened back there..." Kath began.

Ed said, "And in my opinion that's highly likely."

"Then," she went on, "we know they're killers."

Dan said, "And if we assume they killed Marie and the old man, then we might also assume they have the others."

Ed lowered his spoon. "If they took them, that is."

"There was a hell of a lot of blood on the floor of the upstairs room," Kath pointed out, "but no bodies. They must have taken them."

A silence settled, broken when Dan said, "The question is, did they take them dead or alive?" He looked around the group. "If they're dead, then there's nothing we can do. If the colonists are injured, but still alive..." He shrugged.

"What?" Ed said. "We drive in there and try to get them back?" He sounded dubious.

"I don't know what we do," Dan said, gesturing in irritation. "That's why we're discussing this. What do you think?"

Paul said, "There's four of us. We're well armed."

Kath said, "We also have the grenades."

"There's no way of telling if the villagers are still alive. But if they are... then it'd be wrong not to..." He shrugged.

Kath nodded. "I'm with Paul on this. We knew the villagers. They're peaceful people. It isn't right to let marauders just..."

"Okay," Dan interrupted. "I agree. Ed?"

The old man nodded. "I'm with you all the way."

"So..." Dan said, "how do we go about this?"

"Two options," Ed said, "we go in now, using the surprise of darkness, and confront them. Or we wait till dawn and follow."

Dan said, "The longer we wait, the more I fear for the colonists... if they're still alive. We've nothing to gain by waiting till dawn and confronting them then."

Paul felt fear clench his belly.

Ed nodded. "I agree. We approach now, cautiously. Perhaps suggest a trade. Try to work out who they are."

"That's a good point," Kath said. "Who the hell are they?"

"They're obviously from some colony," Ed said. "Barcelona?"

Dan shook his head. "The colony there was failing when I left, and that was years ago. And they'd have to come over the Pyrenees, which is asking a lot even of a truck that size."

Kath said, "There's a colony near Aubenas, where that bastard Hans came from."

"But what would they be doing this far west?" Dan asked.

Ed grunted a laugh. "Perhaps we'll find that out soon enough."

"Okay," Dan said. "Are we all happy with this? I'll break out the rifles and grenades and we'll make our way down there, slowly."

He opened the metal chest and pulled out four rifles. He strapped a belt around his waist and affixed to it four bulbous grenades that looked like metal fruit.

Dan passed Paul a rifle and gave him a quick lesson in its use.

When Kath returned, they made their way to the cab and Dan slipped into the driving seat. Kath sat beside him, and Ed and Paul stood between the seats, peering through the windscreen into the dark desert night.

Dan fired the engine and eased the truck up the calving face of the dune, gaining a few metres and then backsliding as many. Five minutes later they emerged on the crest with a jolt. Dan idled the engine and they peered into the distance.

Paul searched for the tell-tale glow of the campfire, without luck.

"Christ," Dan said, raising the binoculars. "They've broken camp and set off," he reported. "I can just make out the truck on the horizon."

"So much for the element of surprise," Ed said.

"Let's go," Dan muttered, and eased the half-track down the dune in pursuit.

WHEN THEY REACHED the plain and Dan increased speed, Paul took the binoculars and found the truck. It was a tiny shape on the horizon, its solar panels glinting in the moonlight.

"It's fast," Dan reported. "It's all I can do to keep pace."

For the next hour the truck remained on the horizon, a faint irregularity under the star-filled night.

Kath said, "Ed, Paul... go and get some rest. I'll come and wake you if anything happens, okay?"

Reluctantly, but at the same time realising how tired he was, Paul moved to the lounge and curled on the chesterfield. He rocked with the motion of the truck, recalling the events of the day and, at first, unable to sleep. He tried to banish the image of the dead couple from his mind's eye, then imagined the terror of their final moments.

At some point he slipped into sleep, and he was dreaming about Elise, her smiling face swimming in his vision as she shook his shoulder to wake him up. He stirred, opened his eyes, and Elise's face segued into Kath's as she said, "Paul. It's dawn. Here's some food."

She proffered a bowl of cold stew and water.

"The other truck?"

"Still way ahead. It's fast."

He sat up. "I'll take over from Dan."

"Eat first, okay?"

He obeyed her, hungrily wolfing down the stew and slaking his thirst with a bottle of the fresh water from the village. He found the rifle where he'd lodged it against the chesterfield, stood unsteadily and swayed through to the cab.

Dan glanced at him. "No change. Wherever they're heading, they want to get there fast."

"I'll take over." Paul gestured to the wheel.

Dan slowed the truck and slid into the passenger seat as Paul took his place. He felt Dan's cold sweat on the back of the seat, and the wheel was slick with the same. He stared ahead, made out the dark shape of the truck against the skyline, and minimally adjusted their course.

Dan pulled the map onto his lap and frowned down at it.

"Where are we?" Paul asked.

Dan indicated a point in the south-west of the country. "About three, four hundred kays from the old coastline."

"Any idea where they might be heading?"

Dan pulled his bottom lip. "On the coast there was a town or city called Biarritz. There might be a colony there, for all I know, though I haven't heard of one."

"If they are part of a colony, and they are the people who killed the oldsters..." Paul hesitated. "I'm not sure I want to run into any more of them."

Dan nodded. "Me neither. I'd rather confront them before they reach the coast. But we're going full belt and getting no closer..."

The desert here was flat and featureless; not a hill marked the horizon in any direction. Overhead, the sky was a white-hot expanse, with the sun burning bright behind them. Paul caught a flash of it in the side mirror: a blinding, magnesium glare that left after-images swimming in his sight for minutes.

"You know something," he said, "until a few days ago I'd come across no one from the outside for" – he shook his head – "for ten, twelve years."

Dan smiled. "Bet you still wish you hadn't, eh?"

"Are most of the colonies out there... well, full of people like the bastards who caught me in Paris?" He gestured ahead. "Like this lot?"

Dan looked at him with his tired grey eyes for a time without replying, then said, "People are driven to do things to survive which would have been unacceptable in an earlier age."

Paul glanced at him. "Have you?"

Dan nodded. "Back in Paris," he said. "That was the first time I've ever killed anyone." He fell silent, lost in thought, then said, "That kind of thing... that dog-eat-dog mentality... it wouldn't have been acceptable at one time, when there were laws to follow and people to enforce those laws. Now... now we have bands of humans trying to survive as best they can, making their own laws as they go along. Take those people..." He nodded towards the distant vehicle. "They probably justified the killing of the colonists, told themselves that they had to do it to survive, and that they were in the right."

Paul said, "But they weren't, were they? They were wrong?"

Dan regarded him. "Only from our point of view," he said quietly. "When there are no laws in the land..."

"But everyone knows the difference between right and wrong."

Dan smiled. "Do they? I don't know about that. People can do terrible things and call them right, to justify it to themselves." He clapped Paul on the shoulder. "You need to talk to a philosopher about that, Paul. I'm just an ignorant engineer."

Paul smiled, liking Dan and wanting to tell him so, but unable to find the words.

Dan peered through the windscreen, then turned to Paul. "Is it me, or does it seem to be slowing?"

Paul squinted at the truck on the horizon – except

that it was on the horizon no longer. It had slowed and, as they approached, Paul saw that it was in the process of turning in a wide arc.

"It's seen us, Paul. It's coming to investigate."

Heart jumping into his throat, he applied the brakes and slowed the truck to a crawl.

Dan turned and called out, "Kath! Ed! Here."

Ed appeared, peering through the windscreen and smiling at what he saw.

"What?" Kath said, squeezing in beside him. Then, "Oh..."

They watched the truck's gradual approach.

Five minutes later it was a kilometre away, and crawling slowly towards them. Dan indicated the brake and Paul applied it. The truck jerked to a halt and the sudden silence rang around them. Paul heard his own breathing, loud in his ears.

The other truck moved to within a couple of hundred metres, and then likewise came to a standstill. The vehicles faced each other across the flat expanse of sand with mutual suspicion, looking like a stand-off between crabs unsure whether to mate or to fight.

"It's a big bastard," Dan breathed, a note of admiration in his tone.

Paul stared out at the vehicle. It was perhaps twice as big as their own, twenty metres long and encrusted with a silver shell of solar arrays. In the light of the sun, it dazzled like an explosion made solid.

"What do we do now?" he found himself whispering.

"Keep our weapons handy," Dan said. "Kath, where's Millie?"

"Still asleep in our room."

The other truck squatted in the sand, totally still.

"Now..." Ed said, "let's see who makes the first move."

They watched, waited, and the atmosphere in the cab was tense. It was as if they were all holding their breath, afraid of being overheard by the occupants of the facing vehicle.

"Look..." Paul said, pointing.

A hatch cracked in the flank of the other truck, eased out on hydraulics and swung open. Someone stepped out, followed by three other figures.

The first figure was slim and tall, and it was impossible to make out at this distance whether it was a man or a woman. Two others flanked the first, holding some kind of home-made shade over their leader's head. A fourth stood close by with a rifle at the ready.

Dan said, "Okay, so... Now, shall we go and parley?"

Kath said, "Trade?"

Dan nodded. "That's what I'll suggest. I'll say we need water. We have a couple of arrays I can afford to lose." He hesitated. "I'll try to find out if they know anything about what happened at the village... Not that they'll admit to murder."

Paul found himself saying, "I'm coming with you," and was gratified when Dan didn't argue.

Ed said, "We'll keep you covered."

Kath passed a couple of sun hats through the gap. Paul grabbed his rifle and opened the cab door.

The heat hit him in a rush, causing him to gasp. Dan climbed out after him and glanced at the thermometer on his wrist. "Jesus, it's in the mid-fifties out here."

Paul nodded. "Feels like it."

They stood by the truck, looking across the desert at the tableau of figures standing beside the other truck.

"Okay, let's take this easy, Paul. Weapons down, heads up. We stroll across, exchange pleasantries, try to work out who they are, what they want, where they've been and where they're heading."

They set off walking, moving slowly in the enervating heat. "I wonder if there's just the four of them."

"Doubt it," Dan replied. "It'd make sense to leave people in the truck, covering."

Paul nodded, and stared across at the waiting quartet. As they drew closer, he made out the tall figure beneath the silver awning.

"Christ, Dan, it's a woman."

His heart hammered, and it had nothing to do with the danger inherent in the stand-off. The woman was tall, olive-skinned and wore a pair of tight shorts. Long dark hair fell sheer around her face. Her breasts were prominent beneath a tee-shirt cut short to show the skin of her belly, tattooed with a coiling snake seemingly diving head-first into her navel.

They drew closer and Paul could only stare. The woman's face was severe, something hard about the eyes. She reminded him of one of the statuesque models he'd seen in the old magazines back in Paris.

Her gaze fixed on him, and he looked away.

She was flanked by an African and a tall, hatchet-faced man in his forties. To one side stood a small, lean, dark-haired youth, his gaze hostile. He held a rifle, directed towards Paul and Dan but pointing at the sand.

Paul looked back at the woman, trying not to stare.

In French, Dan said, "I'm Dan. This is Paul. We're from the Copenhagen colony."

The woman's neutral expression gave nothing away. "Samara. The Aubenas colony," she responded in a low, smoky voice. "You're a long way from home."

Paul glanced at the truck, attempting to discern other figures behind the windows.

"We're prospectors," Dan said.

She said, "Prospecting for...?"

Dan smiled. "The usual. Food, water... And you?"

She inclined her head. She never smiled, nor allowed her expression to slip from that of intent watchfulness, and yet Paul received the impression that something like amusement – or perhaps superiority, or contempt – played behind her eyes.

"The same."

"And you're heading?"

The woman – Samara – said, "The old city of Biarritz. It is a city we have yet to... investigate."

Dan hesitated, then said, "Did you come through a village called Mont St Catherine?"

The woman held his gaze and replied without hesitation. "We came south of there. Why?"

Dan said, just as convincingly, "We passed through a couple of days ago, traded supplies."

The woman regarded him steadily. Her henchmen didn't move so much as a muscle. She said, "That's very useful information. We might stop by on the way back."

Paul tried to detect a note of dissimulation in the woman's voice, but she sounded utterly convincing. He glanced at her shade-bearers; they, too, were giving nothing away.

"Is that why you are following us?" Samara asked. "You wish to trade?"

Dan nodded. "We have solar arrays..."

For the first time, the woman's expression changed. She smiled, and Paul thought it made her face light up with beauty. "We, too, have solar arrays..." She gestured with a long-fingered hand to her truck. "Probably more than we really need."

Dan smiled. "In that case... I wish you good hunting in the city."

She inclined her head. "And you are heading where?"

"We're making for the coast."

"Then our paths might cross again," Samara said. She gestured for her shade-bearers to move to the open hatch, and stepped inside without so much as a farewell. The gun-toting youth was the last to enter, walking backwards until he reached the hatch, and then ducking inside.

Dan nudged Paul and said, "Put your tongue away and let's get back to the truck."

They turned and hurried across the hot sand. "Did you see her, Dan? I mean..."

Dan smiled. "She was rather striking, wasn't she?"

They reached the truck and climbed into the lounge. Kath and Ed were ready with bottles of water. Paul drank greedily, and water had never tasted as good.

"Well?" Kath asked.

"She was one hell of a woman," Dan said.

"Yes," Kath said. "We could see that from here. But what did you find out?"

Dan shook his head. "Not much. They're from the Aubenas colony. The woman claimed ignorance about the village..." He reported their conversation, the woman's reluctance to divulge more information than absolutely necessary.

"Do you think they're responsible?" Ed asked.

Dan said what Paul was thinking, "Well, her henchmen looked mean enough..."

"What now?" Kath said.

Dan thought about it for a while. He looked at Ed. "What can we do? I don't like the idea of going in there with all guns blazing..."

"There's little we can do, Dan. We could strike out south, head on to the coast. Or we could trail them as far as Biarritz... See what happens there." He shrugged. "We're putting ourselves in danger if we do that – if, that is, they did murder the colonists."

Dan said, "I don't know what I expected... Or rather I did. I thought it'd be obvious if they were the killers, but..."

Kath said, "But you don't think a woman like that could commit such crimes?"

Dan turned to her. "That has nothing to do with it. I'm sure she could. And she wasn't alone, remember? She might be their leader; she could have ordered the killings and kept her hands clean."

"So..." Kath said. "What do we do now?"

Dan said, "I say we leave, head for the coast. Having seen them, I don't want to get mixed up in a fight." Even if they did have the villagers aboard their truck, he thought... He felt a surge of guilt at the idea of running away

Ed nodded. "That's fine by me."

Kath said, "Okay. Paul?"

He nodded. "Let's go," he said.

Ed volunteered to drive the next leg of the journey, and Paul sat with Dan and Kath in the lounge.

As the truck started up and moved off, he crouched by the side window and stared out. They passed the long, panel-barnacled truck, tree trunks lashed to its flank, and then accelerated away.

He thought of Samara, and was unable to wipe the image of her from his mind's eye.

Ten minutes later he glanced through the window again, back the way they had come. His belly flipped. He called, "They're following us."

Dan and Kath joined him and they stared out at the ominous, hulking shape of the vehicle in their wake.

CHAPTER SIXTEEN

SAMARA LEFT JOSEF at the wheel with instructions to keep the Copenhagen truck in view at all times, then made her way to the rear of the transporter.

She considered the meeting with the northerners, and recalled the beauty of the boy. It was rare these days to come upon examples of true physical beauty, with disease prevalent and the grind of day-to-day living taking its toll on individuals. But the tall, blonde boy had struck her as something special: lithe and muscled, he also possessed a fine-featured face, high cheek-bones and full, sculpted lips. It was a face combining sensuality and intelligence.

When she entered the room, Hans was waking up from a long, alcohol-induced sleep. He sat up, bleary eyed, and peered at her. "Why'd we stop back there?"

She stood above the bed and regarded him. Seeing him so soon after looking upon the boy, Hans struck her as repulsive, an odd combination of soft, lardy fat and hard, callused hands and feet.

"A while back you mentioned a guy from Copenhagen," she said. "You said he'd come from the village, Mont St Catherine, years ago. What was his name?"

He looked up at him, his fat face moulded in an expression of stupidity. "Dan. Dan Sagar. Why?"

Samara smiled to herself. "I thought so... We stopped because I saw another truck, following us."

"Another truck?" he repeated, as if having difficulty with the concept.

"They stopped and a couple of guys climbed out. I went out to see what they wanted."

"And?"

"And one of the guys introduced himself as Dan, from Copenhagen, and he asked me about Mont St Catherine. Said he'd been there a couple of days ago, but I could tell he was lying. He wanted to see how I reacted when he mentioned the name. I reckon they saw what we'd done, and wanted to check us out."

Hans blinked. "Dan Sagar? You're joking, right? What the hell are they doing down here?"

She smiled. "He said they were prospecting. They had a trailer, and if I wasn't mistaken it was loaded with what looked like a drilling rig."

Hans nodded. "That's how the Copenhagen lot get their water."

Samara nodded, considering her options. "We could use a drilling rig, Hans. And whatever else they have aboard the truck."

She was speaking his kind of language now, and his big face broke into a smile. "I could go over, take Edo and Lomo, and blow them away..."

She shook her head. "Just like that? Without working out how many of them there might be, what weapons they have? Whatever happened to the subtle approach?"

He rubbed his face with a big hand. "There's just three of them. That bastard Dan, an old doc called Ed, and Dan's woman."

She looked at him. "How do you know that?"

He stopped rubbing his jaw and looked up at her, considering something. "It was the bastard Dan who ambushed us in Paris."

She sat down on the bed and tapped Hans on the ankle, twice, with her forefinger. "Hans. I think there's something you haven't been telling me. I thought you were ambushed by people from the Paris commune?"

"I said that?"

"You implied that."

He looked dumb, his lips loose, and shook his head. "It was Dan Sagar. His mob killed the people I was with..."

"So... they followed you all the way from Copenhagen to Paris, and then ambushed you?" She shook her head. "Why?"

He shrugged. "We stole a truck, supplies... They were pretty sore about that. So they followed us and gunned us down in the street." He grinned. "I never thought I'd have the chance to get even."

She thought about it, then said, "I don't want you going over there, shooting people and wrecking the truck. And anyway, there's more of them than just the three. They had a youth with them, tall, blonde..."

Hans frowned, as if recollecting something. "The same guy we found in Paris." He smiled at the thought. "Pretty boy. Achmed wanted to dick him something bad."

Samara smiled. "I can understand the urge."

He looked up at her. "So... he's with them now? He must have joined them after the ambush. Hey, Samara, imagine the look on their faces when they see me again."

She nodded. "Yes, just imagine. They'll be delighted." She shook her head. "But like I said, I don't want you going over there and exhibiting your usual subtle personal skills. In fact, I want you to lie low, don't show your face, and let me do this my way."

He looked disgusted. "You said you wanted the rig? And I want to get even with Sagar. So what's the problem?"

"Think about it, Hans. Why do all the hard work of killing them, taking the rig and doing our own drilling, when they can do it for us? Sagar said they're making for the coast. My guess is they'll be drilling somewhere beyond the old coastline, looking for sunken reservoirs. So... we bide our time, follow them. And if they strike water, then I'll let you loose."

"And if they don't?"

She shrugged. "Then we take what we want and continue on to Spain."

He nodded. "Sounds good to me."

"In the meantime... I might even try to gain their confidence, win them over." She thought of the boy again.

Hans pointed a blunt finger at her. "But you said they thought it was us who killed the villagers?"

She shrugged. "They suspected, but of course I denied the charge."

Hans bellowed a coarse laugh.

"What?"

"They see the meat on the side of the truck, Samara, and they might work out what we did."

She experienced a surge of irritation at overlooking that slight point. "You know something, Hans? You're not as stupid as you look, sometimes. I'll get Giovanni and Josef to cover the bodies with a canvas when we stop."

Hans grunted and looked down at his crotch. She followed his gaze, and realised that was another gross thing about Hans. Impressive when upright, on the slack like this his cock resembled the man himself: soft and repulsive, but ready at any second to leap into violent action.

He reached out for her, but she pulled her arm away and stood up.

"Not now, Hans."

"Samara, come on..."

"I said, not now!" She hurried from the room and slammed the door after her.

She could hear him muttering curses as she moved down the corridor, and she felt empowered by the simple act of defiance.

She moved to the cab and tapped Josef on the shoulder. "I'll take over. Go and get some rest."

He slowed the truck to a crawl and slid from the seat. Samara took the driving seat, and then accelerated after the small shape of the Copenhagen truck far ahead.

For the next couple of hours she wondered how the

days ahead might play themselves out, and wondered if it might come to killing the Copenhagen people over the matter of the rig. They had ambushed Hans and the others, after all, so were not averse to a little killing themselves, even if they might justify it by claiming that Hans had stolen the truck and supplies.

She recalled shooting the couple in the village, the savage thrill that had gripped her in the aftermath, tempered by the civilised side of her that had offered up remorse as some kind of sop. She wondered if she were nothing more than an animal who would do anything to ensure her continued survival.

She kept the truck in sight; it was slower than their transporter, less powerful, and there was no danger of the truck getting away from them.

The sun slid from its noon position, burning white in the colourless sky, and fell towards the west. The heat in the cab was insufferable. She wondered, idly, what they might have done if they had failed to find water at Mont St Catherine. Would Hans have rationalised that they had too many mouths to fill, and done something about it by sacrificing Josef, Edo or Lomo? When she thought about Hans, she had to admit that there was something about the brute, unthinking bestiality of the man that was at once awe-inspiring and terrifying.

In a way, she pitied Dan and the other Copenhagen people for being the focus of Hans's desire for vengeance.

Just so long as he left the boy alone...

She heard movement behind her. "That Giovanni?" she called.

Lomo showed his face. "No, ma'am."

"Go and find Giovanni. Tell him to come here."

A minute later Giovanni appeared. "Samara?"

"Fetch me a bottle of water, and then come here and keep me company."

He reappeared a minute later with the water and slipped into the passenger seat. He passed her the bottle and she drank, making sure she spilled some over her chin, neck and chest.

When she glanced at Giovanni, he looked away quickly.

She said, "What did you make of the people from Copenhagen?"

He shrugged. "I think they think we killed the colonists back at the village."

She nodded. "They're dangerous. Remember Achmed, Yip and the others who left the castle with Hans? Well, the Copenhagen people gunned them down in Paris. Hans is still pretty sore about it."

Giovanni looked ahead at the racing dot of the truck on the horizon. "Why are we following them? Hans want to...?"

She shook her head, silencing him. "No, I want to... They have a drilling rig. They're prospecting for water."

"What are you planning?"

"I don't know, yet. But whatever happens, I want you to keep close to me, okay? You got your rifle?"

He smiled and patted the rifle at his side.

"Good." She smiled at him. She was glad she'd brought him along, knew she could rely on his trust in her, his faithfulness.

They drove on. The heat inside the cab increased. She could smell the boy's heady body odour, but that only made her think about the youth with the Copenhagen crowd. The sun was westering, and she reckoned darkness would fall in an hour or so. She wondered when the truck they were following would stop, if indeed it would.

She said, "What do you think of Hans, Giovanni?"

She sensed him stiffen beside her. He asked, tentatively, "In what way?"

She glanced across at him. "Do you trust him?"

He shrugged, uncomfortable.

She lay a hand on his muscled thigh. "A word of advice, Giovanni. Don't, okay? Don't trust Hans as far as you can spit." She patted his hot flesh. "I just thought you should know that, okay?"

Silently, he nodded.

The sun was beginning to colour the western horizon an hour later, when someone loomed behind them in the gap between the seats.

Hans grunted, "You're in my place."

Giovanni made to vacate it, quickly. Samara said, "Giovanni and I were just having a little chat, Hans." She stared at him.

Hans indicated with his thumb. "Out."

Samara almost told Giovani to stay where he was, but held her tongue. She didn't want to involve the boy in her power struggle, just yet.

Giovanni slid from the cab and squeezed through the gap. Hans dropped into the seat with another grunt, took Samara's bottle from where it lay on the dash, and tipped the contents over his head.

"I'm getting hungry, Samara. Let's stop soon, okay?"

She nodded. "Just as soon as the Copenhagen people decide to stop. We don't want to let them get away, do we?"

"What do you think?"

They drove on in silence. The sun hit the horizon, torching the skyline with red and orange flares. The leading truck showed against the sunset as a tiny black beetle. A little later, the truck slowed and came to a halt.

Samara hit the brake and eased the transporter to within two hundred metres of the Copenhagen truck, positioning it so that the bodies strapped to the side could not be seen.

Hans eased his bulk from the cab. "I'll set up a fire," he said. "You coming?"

"Give me a few minutes, okay? And Hans, make sure the bodies are covered. There's a canvas sheet in the storage unit."

"I'll get Josef and the kid to do it, okay?"

She turned to the windscreen and stared out at the Copenhagen truck, orange lights showing in the window panels. From time to time she saw shadowy figures passing back and forth inside. As she watched, the short, stocky guy – Dan – stepped from the truck and climbed a ladder welded to its flank. He carried a tool-box, and when he reached the top of the truck he knelt and lifted an inspection panel. Then he opened the tool-box and set to work, and Samara wondered if they'd stopped because of a breakdown.

Now her own transporter rocked as someone untied one of the bodies, in preparation for the evening meal, and covered the other one with the canvas.

Across the desert, more people emerged from the Copenhagen truck, a woman and a little girl, followed by a tall, thin oldster and the boy. They stopped and looked across at her truck, then pointedly turned away and busied themselves with preparing their own meal, sitting outside to take advantage of the cooling desert night.

Minutes later, someone knocked on the glass of the side window, startling her. Hans gestured with a gobbet of cooked meat, inviting her to eat. She considered declining, but thought it best to placate him.

She slipped from the cab and joined the others around the fire on the far side of the truck from the Copenhagen people. She sat beside Hans and allowed him to rest a greasy hand on her thigh.

A corpse, suspended above the flames on the improvised spit, crackled and spat, and the aroma of cooking meat filled the air. Giovanni sliced chunks from the carcass and passed the plates around.

The flesh was succulent, and fell into tender threads in her mouth.

She didn't look too closely at the body, hoping – for some irrational, fastidious reason – that it was the man they were eating, not the woman.

Hans squeezed her thigh. "No brandy?"

"We drank it all last night." She looked around the group. "And that was probably the last bottle for thousands of kilometres."

Hans ate his fill, then lay back in the sand, wriggling to create a comfortable hollow, and stared up at the stars. "Remember last night?" he asked.

She looked at him, at his fat face grinning lasciviously in the firelight.

He reached for her. "Later, when the others...?"

She traced the bulging line of his cheek with a finger. "Okay, Hans." She climbed to her feet.

"Samara?"

"I'm just going to check on the Copenhagen lot. I'll be back."

He settled back into his nest and closed his eyes.

SHE WALKED AROUND the nose of the transporter, paused and stared across the star-silvered sand at the distant truck.

There was only one figure seated beside the vehicle and, with a quick throb of excitement, she saw that it was the boy. He was leaning against one of the truck's front tyres, hands laced behind his head, gazing up at the stars. She stared at the roof of the half-track. There was no sign of the other man, Dan.

She set off across the warm, giving sands before she realised what she was doing.

The boy saw her when she was about ten metres away, and sat up as if startled.

She spread her hands out wide so that he could see she came unarmed. "Is it okay if I come and join you...? Paul, isn't it?

He nodded, his face, and no doubt his surprise, hidden in shadows.

She padded across the sand, feeling suddenly in control. She wondered how many women he'd met in his life, how many women he'd experienced?

She came within a couple of metres of the boy and smiled down at him. He was as beautiful as she recalled him: fine-boned, tanned and very blonde, he seemed even more attractive for his air of vulnerability. He was looking up at her as if she might fall on him and rip him limb from limb with her teeth.

She smiled. "You looked lonely out here. I thought I'd come and talk... Okay if I sit here?"

He nodded, watching her suspiciously.

She stepped closer and dropped sinuously to the sand, smiling at him as she did so. He looked, Samara thought, like a startled animal, and though he tried to keep his eyes on her face, he dropped his gaze from time to time to her breasts.

She indicated the truck. "You break down?"

The boy looked at her. His lips moved, but no sound issued. She wondered whether he'd whispered, or had lost his voice. He coughed, and started again. "Trouble with the link from the solar array. It's fixed now."

"Good." She wriggled a hollow in the sand and sat back, the posture emphasising her chest. "How long have you been travelling?"

"We left Paris a couple of days ago. The others came down from Copenhagen."

"You're from Paris?" She feigned delight. "I've heard so many stories about what the city was like before the Breakdown."

He shrugged. "So have I. There's nothing there now, apart from old buildings."

"No people?"

He shook his head. "No one. I was the last."

She stared at him. "You lived there all alone?"

"For the last ten years I lived with Elise."

Ludicrously, she felt a stab of jealousy. "Tell me about Elise, Paul," she said.

He shrugged again. "She was old, in her eighties. She was good to me."

And he'd lived with her for ten years...? Perhaps, she thought, I am the first beautiful woman he's ever seen. "Good to you, as in...?" she said, suggestively.

He clearly had no idea what it was she was suggesting. "She taught me things. Taught me how to read, hunt lizards, cook... set bones. Stuff like that."

She nodded towards the truck. "How did you meet these people, Paul?"

"They saved my life," he explained. "A mob came into the city. They had a girl with them, only she escaped. Well, for a while she did. The bastards caught her again. I followed them... saw what happened."

Samara felt a cold, hard weight settle in her stomach. "A girl?"

"A young girl, very pretty. She was... she was Ed's daughter. They'd taken her from the Copenhagen colony. Ed's our doctor." He gestured at the truck behind him.

"What did they do with the girl, Paul?"

From the look on his face, Samara thought perhaps she'd rather not know. At last he said, "They raped her, killed her, then cut her up... put her in a fire and then..." He shrugged.

She held up a hand. "I don't think I want to hear..."

The boy just stared at the sand, unmoving.

"Who were these people, Paul?"

He shrugged. "Five or six of them. Their leader was a guy called Hans."

Which wasn't, she reflected, that much of a revelation. She'd known Hans was an animal, worse than an animal...

"Why have you come this far south?" She was being paranoid: there was no way they could have known that Hans had fled Paris and come to the castle.

He looked at her. "Like Dan said, we're prospecting, looking for water."

She nodded, allowing her gaze to drop, pointedly, to his muscled chest and flat stomach. She doodled a pattern in the sand between them, then said, "Dan... he thinks we killed the colonists back at Mont St Catherine, doesn't he?"

His eyes widened. "How do you know about the killing?

She had a line prepared. "I wasn't exactly telling the truth when I told Sagar we came south of the village. In fact we stopped by and saw the... saw what'd happened." She shrugged. "When I saw your truck yesterday, I thought maybe you were the bastards who –"

"No!" he protested. "We found the bodies, the blood..."

She nodded. "Well, I didn't really think you were the kind of people to have done something like that... But we're living in desperate times, Paul. There are some evil bastards out there. You can't be too careful."

He nodded in acknowledgement.

For the first time, he asked a question of his own. "You said you came from Aubenas. What's it like, the castle, the land around the castle?"

She smiled, picked up a handful of sand and let it drain from her fist. It felt as if there were a little animal in there, wriggling. "All around it's like this: sand, sand and more sand. The castle is built into the side of a massif, just a big, bare brute of a cliff, with nothing living for miles around but bats. That's what we eat mainly, Paul. Bats. The castle itself..." She shrugged. "It's a fine place to live, safe, secure."

"What about water?"

"Always a problem, isn't it? We have wells, but every year we have to dig deeper and deeper."

"How many people live there?"

"Just over a hundred," she said. "We've got quite a little community back there. My father ran the place, before his death. I'll take over when we get back."

He nodded.

"What about you?" she asked. "You going back to Copenhagen with the others?"

"Dan said I can, said I'd fit in well there."

She looked along the length of the truck, to the bulky trailer. "That's a drilling rig, right?"

He nodded minimally.

"You drill for water?"

"Dan does. I haven't seen it working yet."

"You're heading out past the coast, drilling in one of the deeper trenches, hoping to strike it lucky?"

He shrugged. "I don't know. Dan doesn't talk about that."

She said, "Like I told Dan yesterday, we're heading for Biarritz, and as you're going to the coast... I reckon if we travel together, then there's less chance that the bastards who killed the villagers will think we're an easy target. Tell Dan that, won't you? Don't let him get jumpy that we're following, okay? We're just looking out for you."

He nodded. "I'll tell him that."

"Maybe tomorrow night, when we stop again... why don't you come over? I'll show you around the transporter."

He nodded. "I'd like that."

Primly, she held out a hand, and he took it. His grip was strong, and she had to resist the sudden urge to pull him towards her. She didn't want to frighten him away this early.

She held on, and only slowly released her grip.

"Till tomorrow then, Paul," she said. She stood, smiled down at him, and then made her way across to the transporter.

ONLY HANS AND Giovanni remained beside the dying fire. Hans was bullshitting about some scrap he'd got into at the Copenhagen colony, how he'd taken on three Danes and beat the living shit out of them... When he saw Samara, he winked across at Giovanni. "Bedtime story over for the day, boy. Time you were all tucked up."

Giovanni took the hint, nodded to Samara and moved back into the transporter.

She sat down in the sand a metre from Hans.

"Quite some big guy, aren't you, Hans?"

"They were piss-weak little runts," he grunted.

She said, "I don't mean the Danes, Hans. I'm talking about the girl you took from the Copenhagen colony, raped and killed and cooked in Paris... Very manly, Hans. Very macho."

He was picking shreds of meat from between his teeth, watching her. "You been talking to the pretty boy?" He shrugged. "She was a bitch. Deserved what she got."

"And I've heard that line before." She looked across at him, and her flesh crawled. She said, "Anyway, you'd better stay pretty well hidden, okay? I don't want them knowing Hans the rapist girl-eater is hitching a ride with me. I want to gain their trust, not frighten them off – or worse, have them attacking us to get at you, understood?"

He grinned. "What are you planning, Samara?"

She wanted to tell him to go fuck himself. Instead she said, "I don't know yet. I really don't know..." Which was, she realised, quite true.

She stood quickly.

"Hey," Hans objected, spitting gristle into the sand, "I thought you said..."

"That was then," she said, striding towards the hatch.

Giovanni emerged from the truck. "The other truck," he said. "They're setting off. I thought you'd want to know."

"Good work. Get the others to pack up out here, then trail the truck, okay?"

Giovanni nodded.

She hurried through the transporter and reached her room before Hans had time to catch her up. She closed the door quickly, then locked it.

She lay on the bed, expecting Hans to come pounding on the door, demanding she let him in. Five minutes later the transporter started up and rolled through the desert. There was still no appearance from Hans, and she felt a sudden, weary relief.

She closed her eyes and thought of the boy.

CHAPTER SEVENTEEN

XIAN'S MOTHER DIED in 2050.

For the past ten years she'd lived on a meagre government pension, in a tumbledown cottage on the outskirts of Ullapool. She grew her own vegetables and tried to be self-sufficient. Xian had visited her three or four times a year.

Xian was in London, working on a government aid project for the victims of the nuclear war between Nigeria and Algeria, when a call came through from her mother's doctor.

She and Richard drove up to the highlands without a break. Her mother was still alive, hanging on, by the time they arrived fourteen hours later.

The local doctor was keeping vigil beside her mother's bed, taking it in turns with a neighbour.

Melanoma had blackened her mother's skin, whittled the fat from her bones. Xian wept as she beheld the shrunken figure in the bed. She had tired of reminding her mother, every time she visited, to remember to use her sun block while gardening.

She whispered to the doctor, "She should be in hospital."

The old medic regarded her with solemn, rheumy eyes. "Try getting a bed in Inverness, Ms Lu. The local hospital in Ullapool's been closed ten years or more. It's all I can do to get the sedatives to make her life bearable."

On Xian's last visit, six months ago, her mother had seemed relatively fit and healthy. She had been diagnosed with melanoma, but said that the medics were keeping it in check. She confidently claimed that she'd live another ten, twenty years.

Xian shook her head. "If I'd known how bad it was... I could have paid for the drugs."

The old doctor snorted at this. "If supplies could have been found, you mean."

Her mother died a day later, Xian and Richard beside her bed, gripping her bony hands. She was buried in the thin soil of the local churchyard, the ceremony attended by a few old neighbours and the medic.

The view from the church, across the barren fields to the deserted town of Ullapool, had never seemed so bleak.

In the warm wind that gusted in from the sea, Xian gripped Richard to her and thanked her lucky stars that she had him.

Back at the cottage, she and Richard went through her mother's scant possessions, salvaging photos from her childhood, ornaments that she recalled from their London days. At sunset they stood at the edge of her mother's vegetable garden, staring across the sorry crop.

Richard knelt and let the sandy soil run through

his fingers. "Lifeless," he murmured, almost to himself. "No wonder she couldn't grow anything."

That same day, Brazil declared war on the North American Alliance. Xian and Richard huddled by the radio, listening to the faint broadcast in silence. The first nuclear strikes had obliterated Brasilia and New Orleans. Xian recalled Richard's optimism about the North American Alliance, but she refrained from reminding him now.

As they were packing up to head south, they received a summons from Whitehall: their presence was required at a top level meeting of European government officials and civil servants, at noon the following day.

They drove non-stop through the night, passing unlit villages and towns, at dawn speeding through the struggling vineyards of the Midlands, and arrived in the weary capital with an hour to spare.

At noon they found themselves in a sumptuous Whitehall boardroom, fronted by a phalanx of high-up European officials. Alongside Xian were scientists she recognised, and other eminent researchers she'd only heard about in passing.

The Home Secretary gave a short speech, prefacing his remarks with the warning that what he had to say was between themselves only.

"We are facing, ladies and gentlemen," he began lugubriously, "the breakdown of all we have held dear for centuries... We are facing famine in Europe; already, austerity measures in Germany have led to civil uprisings. The news from the NAA and Brazil is bleak..." He went on from there, painting a dark picture of the future of life on Earth, and finished, "But there is hope, ladies and gentlemen. May I introduce Dr Rutger Berkhoff, Director of Operations, from the European Space Agency."

Something kicked in Xian's stomach, some stirring of hope, some reawakening of childhood dreams.

Dr Berkhoff stood and nodded graciously to the assembled scientists, and went on to outline Project Phoenix: a mission, he said, to the stars, utilising technology that was still in its design stages.

"And you, ladies and gentlemen, I invite you all to be part of Project Phoenix, as colonists on this bold and daring venture..."

Xian felt dizzy, and was aware only of Richard seated beside her, squeezing her hand.

Xian and Richard were seconded to the European Air Force, and for the next three years trained exhaustively to ensure the success of Project Phoenix. When Richard applied to be elected to the Project's command structure, Xian, not to be outdone, applied also.

A week later they were both elected, and from that day forward Xian experienced hope.

CHAPTER EIGHTEEN

THE HALF-TRACK POWERED on through the night, heading for the coast. Ed was at the wheel, Millie sleeping in Kath and Dan's berth.

Paul lay on the chesterfield, nursing a bottle of water.

"So..." Kath said. "What do you think she wanted?"

She sat cross-legged against the far wall, Millie's book open in her lap. Dan sat in a battered armchair, drinking occasionally from his water. The hum of the engine filled the lounge, which rocked with a steady, somnolent back-and-forth motion.

Paul looked across at them. "I don't know. I've been trying to work it out." He shrugged. "She frightened me."

Kath said, "She threatened you?"

"No." He smiled. "She was very... pleasant. Too friendly, almost." He felt himself colouring. "I've never met anyone like her."

She had intimidated him by her very physical presence. Despite his fear, he had felt himself responding sexually to her. Her conversation, on the surface, had been open and friendly, but he was too inexperienced to work out if she had had ulterior motives. His head said that she obviously had – his heart that she was simply being friendly.

"She mentioned the village, what happened there."

Kath looked up from the picture book.

"What she told us earlier, Dan, about her travelling south of Mont St Catherine. She was lying. She told me that they entered the village, found the bodies... When they saw our truck, she thought we were responsible. She still does, I think."

Dan peered at him. "So you think they didn't kill the villagers?"

Paul shook his head, baffled. "I honestly don't know what to think. She seemed genuine, honest. A part of me trusts her..."

Kath smiled. "I wonder which part?" She waved. "I'm sorry, Paul. But she's some woman."

Paul said, "Her father ran the colony at Aubenas, before he died. She said that when she gets back, she'll be in charge."

Dan said, "Hans mentioned the old man who ran the place. Said he was rabidly anti-technological, one of the reasons Hans left."

Kath snorted. "Or they kicked him out. Maybe they're decent people, Dan? If the two colonies could combine..."

Dan frowned. "Maybe they've changed policy since the old man's death. Going by their use of the transporter, it seems likely. We'll see how things pan out, okay?"

Paul said, "She asked about the rig, if we were prospecting for water."

Dan looked at him. "What did you say?"

"I said we were looking for water, but I said nothing about drilling."

Dan shook his head in frustration. "That's the problem with hauling such a damned big rig around with us. It's pretty damned obvious what it is."

"Maybe that's why they're trailing us?" Kath said. "They want to get their hands on the rig."

Paul took a long swallow of water and considered his words. "I... I don't know, but I didn't get that impression. She said we should stick close to each other until we reach the coast – for protection against whoever killed the villagers."

Kath laughed. "Well, she's either genuine, or one hell of a liar."

"Let's just keep our wits about us, okay?" Dan said. "Armed at all times, on the look out. She might be genuine, and we have nothing to fear. But it's best not to take anything for granted."

"How long before we hit the coast?" Paul asked.

"Another day and half, if the terrain remains this flat," Dan said.

Paul lay back and considered what Samara had told him. "Perhaps I can find out more about her, see if she is telling the truth."

Kath asked, "And how would you do that?"

"She invited me back to her truck, said I could take a look around the next time we stopped."

Dan rubbed his face, perplexed. "Now why would she do that? Perhaps she wants more information from you. About us, our truck, the rig..."

Kath said, "Or perhaps she really is just the friendly type."

"So... should I go over, the next time we stop?"

"Do you want to?" Kath said.

He thought of Samara's smile, the way she held onto his hand as she said goodbye. He nodded. "I might be able to work out if she's genuine." He paused. "And whether or not they took the villagers."

Kath said, "I don't know. I mean, if they did kill the villagers, take the others... Now, why the hell would they do that, drag bleeding and dying people back to their truck? Well, it's pretty damned obvious to me. And if Samara's mob is responsible, then I'm not sure I'm happy about you going over there."

She looked across at Dan, as if for back up.

"If you go," Dan said, "then go armed, just in case, okay? We have a handgun in the chest."

Paul nodded. "I'll do that." He looked across at the grey-haired woman with the lined, caring face. "Don't worry, Kath. I can look after myself."

She smiled across at him. "I know you can. It's just that I'm concerned, okay?" She paused, and looked down at the open picture book in her lap. "I'm concerned for all of us. We've found you, and then Millie, and if we were to strike water out there..." She shook her head. "Maybe things are taking a turn for the good, and I don't want any stupid mistakes wrecking that."

Dan reached out and touched her cheek. "Things'll be fine, Kath. Trust me."

She smiled sadly. "I hope so. It just seems that there's so much that could go terribly wrong."

A little later Dan roused himself from his chair and

went to see how Ed was getting along up front, and Kath said she was tired and left the lounge. Alone, Paul crossed to the side window and peered out. If he pressed his face against the warm glass, he could just make out Samara's truck in the distance, trailing them.

He returned to the chesterfield, lay down and closed his eyes. He was tired, after the hectic events of the day, but that night sleep was a long time coming.

HE CAME AWAKE slowly. Someone was digging at his shoulder with persistent little jabs. He opened his eyes and smiled. Millie was peering at him, waif-like in one of Kath's old tee-shirts.

"Kath said to tell you it's after midday. You've missed breakfast, Paul. I ate it!"

From across the lounge, Kath laughed. "She's kidding."

Grinning, Millie produced a bowl from behind her back, full of spinach and what looked like lizard meat – leftovers from the night before.

"You were snoring all morning!" Millie told him.

Paul sat up, tipped a handful of water from his bottle into his hand and splashed his face. He felt a little more alive for doing so.

"We've been tip-toeing around you all day, sleepy-head," Kath said.

He spooned cold stew into his mouth. Millie watched him, hungrily, and he relented and shared the meal with her. Even cold, it was surprisingly appetising.

The truck rocked back and forth as if they were crossing broken concrete, the tracks rattling. "Where are we?"

"Passing through the outskirts of a small town. Take a look."

He passed Millie the rest of the stew and crossed the room. Crouching beside Kath, he peered through the window.

The sand had retreated, or had never encroached this far. They were on a slight elevation in relation to the town, and what was left of it stretched away into the distance. Not a single building remained standing, merely the neat, geometrical lines of demolished walls creating a vast pattern of square and rectangular footprints.

Way behind them, bucking over the remains of a broken road, Paul made out Samara's truck, keeping pace.

Kath said, "The town was called Bayonne, not far from Biarritz."

"What happened to it?"

Kath shrugged. "Just another casualty of the wars. We don't really know what happened in the years after the Breakdown. The recording of history was just another casualty."

They stared out at the ancient destruction until they descended and passed into the desert once again. The track's loud rattle ceased and the truck accelerated across a vast, flat bed of sand.

He joined Dan in the cab, and a couple of hours later took his turn at the wheel. The temperature climbed as the afternoon wore on. The cab was always the hottest part of the truck, thanks to the greenhouse effect of the windscreen and side windows. Ahead, shimmering high above the horizon, the sun was a blinding white disc, its light diffused across a platinum sky.

"When will we reach the coast?" he asked Dan a while later.

"With luck, daybreak tomorrow. I just hope we lose our shadow and they stop at Biarritz. When we get out onto the old seabed, I'd like to start drilling."

"I'll try to find out later from Samara."

Dan smiled. "I don't think she'd tell you if their intentions weren't honourable, Paul."

He shrugged. "I might be able to work out whether or not she's lying." Even as he said the words, he knew that the chance would be unlikely.

Dan said, "Well, if they do follow us past Biarritz and onto the seabed, we'll know what they want."

Paul glanced across at him. "What'll we do then?"

"It'll be a bit of a stand-off. We're well armed – rifles, grenades. We'll wait for them to come at us. It's all we can do, really."

A couple of hours later the sun sank over the horizon and, gradually, a star-prickled night replaced the glare of the day. A little later, Dan suggested they stop for a while, and Paul brought the truck to a halt.

In the ensuing silence, Paul jumped from the cab and walked around the truck. The others joined him, and they stood and gazed in the direction they had travelled. Minutes later, Samara's truck halted two hundred metres away, its solar panels glinting in the starlight.

Ed ferried out bowls of stew and bottles of water and they sat in the sand. Paul scooped a hollow, finding a cooler strata of sand beneath the top layer, and settled himself into it, then excavated a smaller hollow for Millie beside Kath.

He ate distractedly, staring across the desert at the other truck. He felt a sickening sense of apprehension at the thought of his imminent meeting with the woman.

Samara and her band had set up a camp-fire on the far side of their truck, and in the distance Paul heard loud laughter, a snatch of song.

Ed muttered to himself, "I wonder what they're cooking...?"

Dan said, "Paul might find out, later," and told Ed about Samara's invitation.

The old man smiled at Paul. "You take care, okay?"

Dan slipped into the truck and came back with a small revolver. He passed it to Paul. "Safety catch here. Snap it off, and it's ready to use." He smiled at Paul. "Just in case, okay?"

Paul slipped the weapon into the waist-band of his shorts, surprised at its cold solidity.

Fifteen minutes later, as Ed was collecting up the plates, Paul saw a hatch in the side of the other truck snap open.

He stared across the sand, heart racing, as Samara stepped from the truck and paused beside the door. Slowly, she lifted a hand in either greeting or summons.

Without a word, the others packed up and moved back into the truck. Kath gave him a smile that could not hide her concern, and Dan said in parting, "I'll be keeping watch. Any sign of trouble and get out of there pronto, okay?"

Paul nodded and, as Dan closed the hatch, he set off across the sand towards the woman.

SHE STEPPED ASIDE and gestured for him to enter.

He ducked inside and found himself in a room about twice the size of the lounge back in Dan's truck. Every available inch of space was taken up with racks bearing great containers of water and other, smaller open-topped boxes filled with food; dried meat in strips and chunks. A narrow corridor passed fore and aft.

Smiling, Samara stepped after him. "Welcome aboard, Paul. This way." She led him towards the rear of the truck, and he squeezed down the corridor after her. Her shorts, he noticed, had split across the full cheeks of her bottom, and ellipses of brown flesh showed through. Paul felt his throat go dry.

They passed a section of the truck where the leads and cables from the solar arrays on the roof snaked through the metal and were connected to banks of machinery, similar to those back in his own truck. The arrangement looked lashed together, bound in places by lengths of rope: he recalled what Dan had said about Samara's colony having until recently proscribed the use of technology.

Samara looked over her shoulder and smiled at him. "And this is my room, Paul." She opened a narrow door. "What do you think?"

She stepped aside, and he had to squeeze past her to enter a surprisingly spacious room. She turned and secured the door. "So that we're not disturbed," she explained.

She stood next to him, her fingers hot on the small of his back.

The room took up the width of the transporter. A big bed stood against the far wall, beside a long, low window covered by vertically slatted blinds. Paul made out the diffuse glow of the fire in the desert, and the sound of raised voices.

The room was covered in rugs, a mismatch of colours and patterns, and in the far corner... Paul looked at the shower stall.

Samara smiled. "It's my little luxury, Paul. And the water is recycled." She looked at him. "Don't tell me you've never had a shower?"

He shook his head. "Never."

"Then how...?"

He said, "Elise taught me how to use sand. She said it's what the Arabs did, centuries ago." He shrugged. "It works."

"I don't doubt it, Paul, but there's nothing as luxurious as a hot shower. Perhaps, later, you'd care to have one?"

He felt his face flush, red hot, and nodded wordlessly.

She padded across to the bed, turned and sat down, patting the place beside her in invitation. Swallowing, Paul joined her.

She sat back against the piled pillows and lifted her hands behind her head. Her breasts thrust themselves towards him. She smiled, and he looked away.

She said, "I've heard rumours that the Copenhagen colony is failing, Paul?"

He shrugged. "They were hit by disease a few months ago. Water's hard to find."

"I think we have it lucky at the castle. The place was built over a hundred years ago by a business tycoon hoping to ride the storm of the Breakdown."

"What happened to him?"

"According to my father, he died in one of the viral plague wars around sixty years ago. My father was in business with him, and he bought the castle shortly after the tycoon's death."

He looked at her. "You said that you'd be in charge of the colony."

She smiled. "Do you find that hard to believe, Paul?"

He shook his head. "No, of course not." Which was true: there was something hard and commanding about her, a steeliness of intent that gave her eyes a forbidding intensity and her words an air of authority.

She wanted something from him, he was sure, but of course the question was... what?

A peal of course laughter rose from outside, and Samara frowned. "Just ignore them, Paul."

"If they come in...?" he began. He had a sudden fear that the men, one or all of them, might not take too kindly to finding him sitting here with the woman.

He realised he was sweating. Rivulets trickled down his neck, over his chest. Samara had noticed, too. She reached out with a long finger and gently wiped the moisture from his abdomen.

"Are you hot, Paul, or nervous?"

It was all he could do to shake his head and say, "No..."

She laughed, and inserted her finger-tip between her lips, sucking on his perspiration. "No, what? You're not hot, or not nervous?"

"Not... not nervous," he stammered.

He wanted, at once, to be a million miles from here, and yet... shackled by his lust, he desired nothing more than to reach out and...

Suddenly, startling him, Samara leapt up onto her knees and leaned towards him. She whispered into his ear, "Have you ever made love to a woman, Paul?"

His heart hammered. He shook his head. He tried to say, "No," but no sound came out.

"Would you like to?"

He opened his mouth again.

She whispered. "You have nothing to worry about, Paul. I'll be gentle."

She traced a line with her finger from her chin down to her navel, then said, "Stand up."

He stood beside the bed, trembling.

She unbuttoned the front of his shorts and pulled them down his thighs. The revolver fell out and hit the floor. Samara looked at it, then smiled up at him and murmured something about big weapons.

She took his painful erection in her hand and he gasped with pleasure. She pulled him to the bed and he sprawled, gasping, on his back, staring up at her as she stood and removed her shorts.

He stared, his vision blurring.

She grabbed his hand and pressed it between her legs, gasping and rubbing his fingers into her. He almost wept, feeling the slick slippery moisture of her inner flesh.

Then she was on him, taking his erection and straddling him, laughing as she eased herself down around it. He watched his penis slide into her and closed his eyes as she enveloped him, tight and hot. She leaned forward, thrusting her tongue into his mouth and working herself slowly up and down his length. He reached out and grasped her buttocks as they rose and fell, riding him towards ecstasy.

Then she sat back on him, bouncing up and down with a frenzied abandon he found more shocking than the fact of her nakedness. A minute later something happened within her; she yelled, and suddenly his abdomen was drenched in liquid at first warm, and then cool.

Seconds later he too came in a gushing rush that seemed to last an age, and then he was gasping in shock and drawing breaths in great, heartfelt sobs.

She collapsed on top of him, her hair in his face as she held him tight.

"Paul, Paul..."

He wiped his hand across his tearful eyes, wishing this could last forever, but knowing of course that that was impossible.

They held each other, panting. He laughed, and she joined in as if they had conspired in something wonderful and shocking and unique.

He had known the thrill of a hunt, that time he had chased a dog through the ruins of Paris; and he had known the thrill of being chased. He had known sexual pleasure, too, of a diluted, second-hand kind, when masturbating to the glossy magazine pictures of naked women... But this was real, and a dozen conflicting emotions raged through him, the joy of it and the depravity, and the elation.

"Stay with me, Paul. Stay forever. Don't ever go. Make love to me every day forever. Christ, but we've hardly started! If you think that was ecstasy..."

She reached down to him, and to his amazement and delight he was rigid again, only this time she was taking him, astonishingly, in her mouth, and he lost himself in the base carnality of the act, led by her and willingly following, committing acts he had thought impossible, and others he'd never even imagined.

His life now, he realised, was divided neatly into two distinct phases: the life he had led before tonight, and the life he would lead from now on, full of the knowledge of the pleasures of the flesh, the gross rampant mindlessness of pure sensuality, which before now had been an unattainable dream.

In the calm after the whirlwind, she squatted on his belly and stared into his eyes, stroking his cheek.

"I don't know why this was so different," she said, as if to herself. "Maybe because you're an innocent. It's as if I'm experiencing it all over again, for the first time."

He closed his eyes, experiencing waves of pleasure in syncopation with the beat of his heart.

"Before, it was almost like hatred," she went on. "Sex was pain, the pleasure of taking pain and giving it." He had no idea what she was talking about; it ceased to matter. All that did matter was the glorious weight of her on him, the wetness of her sex against his belly.

"With him... he takes no delight in me, not me.

I'm just meat, no different. Of course I thought it meant something, other than just the pleasure of sex. I wanted it, craved it, but not like this, Paul. Not like I want you."

He reached up, stroked the fall of her jet black hair. He could find no words in reply that would mean anything at all. His mind was empty, dazed.

"Perhaps in fucking him I was fucking my father," she said. "The love and hate... I wanted to hurt him for all the times he'd neglected me. And I wanted to be punished because I couldn't love him enough to make him love me..."

She was weeping now, her tears falling straight from her cheeks onto his chest.

He reached up, thumbed her eyes, said the first thing that came into his head. "You're mad, Samara."

She blubbered a tearful laugh. "You might be right. Mad. I might be mad." She shook her head. "Maybe it's because you... you're the child I've never had, but wanted, and by loving it I can make everything alright, prove that it is possible to love a child... prove my father wrong."

He pulled her to him, kissed her cheeks, her forehead, her full, hard lips.

It came to him in a sudden revelation, and he said, "Come with me, Samara. Join us. Come with me to Copenhagen..." It seemed wildly possible – Dan and Kath would allow her aboard. She was strong and fit, could obviously lead people, and would be a credit to the colony.

"We'll soon be drilling for water. And then we'll go back to Copenhagen, together."

She stared at him and shook her head, not so much dismissing the notion as clearing her mind to give the idea room to flourish. "But... but it's all I know... The castle, the people, the way of life. But..." Clouded with doubt one second, her face became suddenly radiant. "But... no, listen to me. You come with me. Leave those people – you hardly know them, Paul. You've been with them what, a few days? Come with me..."

His mind swirled. The idea was a possibility. More than a possibility; it was attractive. He shook his head in confusion. "I..."

She stared at him, biting her bottom lip, considering something. "Come with me, Paul. Come to Bilbao."

"Bilbao?"

She gripped his hand. "That's where we're heading, Paul. My father knew where... Hell, look, I'll prove it to you. I'll show you."

He shook his head. "Prove what?"

She laughed, leapt off the bed and crouched beside it, and he marvelled at the sensuous question mark of her body as she searched under the bed for something.

She returned with a sheaf of papers and print-outs and dropped them on his belly.

He sat up. "What are they?"

The top folder was embossed with the golden, intertwined letters ESA, within a stylised rocket ship. He leafed through the papers; he made out diagrams, and lines and lines of technical jargon that meant nothing to him.

She pulled the papers from him and found a large, folding sheet. She spread it across his lap and pointed. "There, and there..."

The map showed a large diagram made up of squares and rectangles, connected by what looked like corridors. The squares she had indicated were marked "stores."

She looked at him. "You never heard of Project Phoenix?"

He shook his head, repeating the phrase.

"My grandfather worked for the European Space Agency. He was some kind of scientist. Project Phoenix was a plan to send a ship to the stars... this was around fifty, sixty years ago."

He said, "Ed said something about it. He said they might even have succeeded –"

But Samara was shaking her head. "They didn't. There was a terrorist raid. The ship was either destroyed or damaged, and the underground base sealed up and left. The idea was to come back and resume the mission, when things got better in Europe."

"And?"

She smiled, sadly. "Well, things never did get better. Things got worse. Wars, plagues. The Breakdown."

He looked down at the map spread across his lap, at the reams of technical reports and print-outs.

She said, "My father found these among his father's effects. He translated some of the reports. A lot was just..." She waved. "Scientific stuff. But there was an inventory of provisions, stores."

He began to see what she was driving at. "And you think they're still there?"

She looked at him, brown eyes glowing, "There's a good chance, Paul. The place was sealed in a rush, and they meant to go back there. And all the provisions – there was enough to keep all the technicians and scientists going for years and years. Don't you see what this means?"

"What makes you think you can enter this base?" he said. "You said it was underground?"

She laughed, reached out and stroked his cheek. "Paul, I have the codes right here." She patted the folders. "They'll get us through the main entrance, down all the levels."

She lifted the pile of documents from the bed and dropped it on the floor. She straddled him, taking his face in her hands and saying, "What can I do to persuade you to come with me, Paul?"

"But the others, your friends? They might –"

"I'm in charge here. What I say, goes. You'll be... fine."

She jumped off the bed and took his hand, dragging him upright.

He laughed. "What?"

She dragged him across the room to the shower stall and stepped inside, pulling him after her. She turned a dial, and instantly a cone of water jetted down over her. He stepped under, laughing at the drumming sensation of the water on his head, at the muffled sounds that reached him through his wet hair.

She laughed and said something.

"What?" he asked.

She placed wet lips against his ear and said, "Rub me with this."

She handed him a block of something, slick and perfumed. "What is it?"

"It's called soap. My father found a stock in the

ruins of a city years ago."

He smiled at his ignorance. "What does it do?"

"Rub me with it all over and see."

He massaged her breasts and belly with the soap, and it left behind a thick swathe of bubbles, a luxuriant scented lather. He swept it across her belly and down to her vagina and massaged; she collapsed against the side of the stall, moaning. She reached for him, took him in a forceful hand and eased him into her. She hung onto him and whispered into his ear, "Slowly, Paul..."

He took her weight, holding her bottom and pressing her against the glass as she rode him. Like this he carried her from the shower and across the room to the bed. They made love again, slowly, as instructed, and he marvelled at how different it was this time, how a wholly new set of sensations overwhelmed him. They lay on their sides, her back to him, and he thrust slowly from the rear, Samara reaching behind him, gripping his buttocks and dictating the rhythm of his strokes.

He came minutes later in an explosion of euphoria, and as they lay, packed tight in the aftermath, she murmured sleepily, "Stay, Paul. Come with me to Bilbao."

He would have to go back and tell the others, of course; and that would be hard. They had, after all, saved his life, then given him food and shelter – and more; companionship. They had trusted him enough to give him weapons, responsibility... It would be difficult to face Dan, Ed and Kath and tell them what he had decided.

An idea occurred to him. What was to stop them joining forces, Dan and Kath and the others accompanying Samara to Bilbao? Dan had the drilling rig, after all. It would be a mutually beneficial arrangement.

"Samara?"

She was silent, her breathing even.

He closed his eyes. He would ask her when she woke up. And if she said no? If she wanted the spoils of Bilbao all to herself, what then?

He drifted into sleep, smiling at the thought of a beautiful woman slumbering in his embrace.

HE WOKE UP suddenly a while later. He blinked, felt the naked form of Samara leaning heavily against him. He wondered how long had elapsed. It was totally dark outside, apart from the glow of the camp-fire.

Then he realised what had awoken him. Samara's companions outside were shouting and singing. He stroked her flank, marvelling at the soft curve of her torso, from breast to rising hip.

She was snoring, very gently.

Another gale of laughter erupted outside, and he swung himself from the bed and padded across the room to the window. He crouched, drew the vertical blinds aside and peered out.

He made out five figures: a pair of Africans, the youth he had seen yesterday armed with the gun, and the tall, gaunt man. Another, bulkier figure was seated on the far side of the glowing fire.

Above the fire was erected the spindly frame of

a spit, on which was skewered the long form of whatever they were roasting.

Paul stared, at first disbelieving the evidence of his eyes. The dark, whittled down shape on the spit was a human body, blackened and contorted, skull flung back, one arm trailing into the embers. As he watched, the figure behind the fire stood, reached out with a knife and began hacking off chunks of belly from the roasting corpse.

And only then did he see the shoe, lying in the sand before the fire. It was battered and worn, the companion to the shoe he'd seen in the upstairs room back at the village, becalmed in a sea of blood...

He saw what was happening, wanted to persuade himself that the body was not human. Samara would not align herself with people like this, surely, people who would... who would kill innocent villagers and drag them off as if they were nothing more than cattle.

But the body roasting above the fire was indisputably human, and Samara had told him herself that she was in charge of this band of killers.

The man doing the carving ripped a slice of meat from the corpse and flung it across to the youth, as if feeding a dog, then turned and hacked off a slab for himself. He raised it to his lips, bit greedily.

Paul reeled back, losing his balance and rolling across the floor in shock and fear.

He lay there, propped on one elbow, staring out at the shadowy figures laughing and joking around the camp-fire. He crawled back to the window and stared out, his heartbeat loud in his ears.

The gross, bald-headed man had ripped a haunch

of meat from the spit and was tearing into it with his teeth like a wild animal.

Hans...

Paul pushed himself from the window and stood up shakily. He saw the revolver on the floor beside the bed and snatched it up. His vision blurred with tears. He stood above the woman, lying on her back now, sleeping like a child, so vulnerable, so – he could not dispute the fact – so childishly innocent.

He aimed the weapon. He wanted to shoot her dead, for the truth she had kept from him, the lies she had told. He wanted revenge, and yet could not bring himself to exact it.

He saw the folder and print-outs on the floor. Fear clutched him. If Samara woke and found him doing this... He knelt very slowly and scooped up the folders, and then rose and made for the door. His shorts lay on the floor beside the bed; he feared returning and waking her.

He paused by the door, took one last look back at the peacefully sleeping woman, and was about to turn the lock when he saw another set of folders on a table by the wall, marked like the ones in his arms with the ESA symbol. He picked them up, lodged them under his arm with the others, then very slowly turned the latch on the door. The click it made sounded deafening – but Samara didn't stir. He opened the door, slipped through and squeezed his way along the narrow corridor.

He stopped as he was passing the area where the leads from the solar arrays met the banked equipment.

He set the bundle of papers down on a water container and turned back to the machinery. The confusion of wires and cables meant nothing to him. He had no idea where to start, no notion of what he might do to incapacitate the vehicle. All he knew, with a rising panic at the thought of Hans or one of the others entering the truck and finding him, was that it was essential to disable the transporter; either slow it down or render it inoperative.

Weeping now, in fear and in rage at Samara's betrayal, he began pulling at leads and cables, yanking wires from the banked machinery and tearing at switches and levers. He expected explosions to result from his vandalism, or at least flashes and sparks, but the machinery yielded to his efforts without the slightest complaint. Fearing discovery, he retrieved the folders and paused again. A dozen big water containers filled this section of the truck: he should slice them open, leave the bastards dry... But he had brought along the revolver in favour of his knife, and anyway it was imperative he get away before Samara woke and wondered at his absence.

He moved along the corridor until he reached the door, and in the half-light tried to find the handle.

He was still scrabbling when he heard a sound. Someone had opened the hatch on the far side of the truck. He heard the sudden increase in volume of the revelry outside, and peered between the racked water canisters: one of the Africans. If the bastard moved to his right and looked through the gap between the containers, then he'd see Paul. He plastered himself against the door, tying to slow his breathing as if he might be heard. The African was filling bottles from one of the canisters. Paul almost laughed with relief that he had not sabotaged their water.

The African moved from the racks and stepped out into the night.

Paul turned his attention to the door, found the handle and applied pressure with one hand. It opened, swinging suddenly outwards and spilling him from the truck. He managed to remain on his feet and run, too fearful of being seen to assume that he was safe just yet.

As he neared Dan's truck, he expected at any second to feel a bullet between his shoulder blades and tried not to think about Samara's reaction when she discovered him gone.

The truck door burst open and Dan appeared, holding his rifle, and Paul wanted to collapse into his arms. Instead he cried, "They killed the villagers, Dan! I saw the shoe! We need to get away."

"The shoe?" Dan said.

"They're eating people!" Paul breathlessly told him about the shoe he'd seen in the post office, and its companion beside the roasting corpse.

Dan took his arm and almost dragged him inside. He called to Kath, "Get in the cab. We're going!"

Kath took off, diving through the gap to the cab and starting the engine. Ed led Paul across the lounge and eased him into the chesterfield, the bundle of folders and print-outs spilling across the floor.

Dan and Ed knelt before him, all concern. "What happened?"

"We've got to get away!"

Even as he spoke the truck kicked, bucked and surged into life.

"But we can't hope to outrun their truck –" Dan began.

Paul waved. "I've sorted that. I wrecked their solar leads. It'll be a while before they're up and running again."

Ed held his shoulder. "Paul, what happened?"

He took a breath. He realised he was weeping, and the odd thing was that he felt no shame, no shame or embarrassment at all, in showing such emotion before the pair.

He said, "Hans... Hans is with them. They... on the other side of the truck, they had a fire. They had... a villager in the fire."

Ed stared at him, his face a bony, sculpted mask of disbelief. "Hans? You're sure?"

"It was Hans! I'd know the bastard's face anywhere. He was..." He shook his head, then finished, "It was Hans."

Dan said, "So he went back to Aubenas, joined the woman..." He looked up at Paul. "How did you get away?"

Paul swallowed. "Samara was sleeping. I... I looked out, saw the bastards, the fire... saw Hans."

Dan nodded, and Paul saw understanding in his expression, and compassion.

From the cab, Kath called, "Is someone going to tell me what's going on here?"

Dan moved to the cab, and as Paul watched him go he felt a rush of emotion, an overwhelming gratitude that he was back among these people. Had he really considered, even for one second, leaving them and joining Samara?

Dan returned from filling Kath in on the events of the evening. He passed Paul a bottle of water.

He drank, then indicated the folders. Ed picked up one of the print-outs. "It's in Dutch," he said.

"Make any sense of it?" Dan asked.

Ed nodded. "A little, given time."

Dan looked at Paul. "Now why on earth did you bring us all this paperwork?"

As the half-track roared through the desert night, Paul told Dan and Ed all he knew about Project Phoenix.

CHAPTER NINETEEN

SAMARA LAY IN that luxuriously soporific state between sleep and wakefulness. She considered the boy, and wondered if she had done enough to persuade him to remain with her. She thought she had, and smiled to herself. Of course, there remained the problem of Hans to sort out, but she was confident that she would be able to engineer events so that the German wouldn't even realise, at first, that he was being usurped.

She reached out, intent on easing Paul to her and indulging in his eager innocence once again.

Her hand encountered an area of empty bed. "Paul?"

She opened her eyes and sat up. He was no longer lying beside her. She looked across to the cubicle, wondering if he had been tempted by the luxury of another shower.

Her stomach flipped as she realised that he was no longer in the room.

But why the hell had he left without telling her? She had captivated him, she was sure; not only with the delights of the flesh, but also with the promise of Bilbao and life back at the castle...

Then she looked across the room and saw the blinds

that covered the far window, drawn back. Outside she could see Hans and the others sprawling around the embers of the fire, and rage possessed her.

Clearly Paul had woken, looked out and seen Hans and the cooking corpse. Of course the sight would have been enough to scare him witless and prompt his flight.

And he would know for sure, then, that she was part of this, complicit in the murders, the cannibalism...

She wanted to kill Hans, empty her rifle into the bastard's gross belly and watch him die, slowly.

She moved across the room to the opposite window, ducked and peered out. As she'd feared and suspected, there was no sign of the Copenhagen truck.

She pulled on her shorts and hurried from the room. She came to the outer door and kicked it open. It slammed against the side of the truck and stirred Hans and the others to sit up groggily and stare at her.

"We're moving!" she yelled. "They've set off. Come on, let's get going!

She kicked over the improvised spit in order to dislodge the charred remains of the corpse. "Hey!" Hans grumbled. "We haven't finished –"

"I said we're moving!" she ordered. "Get your stuff inside, now. Edo, Lomo, pack this stuff away. Giovanni, in the cab and get ready to drive as soon as I say."

The boy nodded and scrambled back into the transporter. Muttering to himself, Hans followed him inside. Samara watched the Africans drag the spit across the sand and into the truck. "Hurry it!" she shouted, fretting at the delay.

As soon as they had the spit stowed away, she slammed the door and called to Giovanni. "Okay, let's go!"

Hans sprawled on a couch in the lounge, raking overgrown fingernails across his belly. She leaned against the water racks, staring at him and wondering what she had ever found attractive about the monster. His cock, she thought, the terrible aggression which she and only she had the power to temper. Now the sight of him repulsed her.

The simple fact was that Hans had probably cost her the possibility of a relationship with the boy, and she vowed that he would pay for that.

He looked up at her. "What's the hurry, Samara?"

She shook her head. "The Copenhagen people, remember? The rig? The possibility of drilling for water? That's what trailing them was all about, or has that fact slipped your tiny brain?"

He shrugged. "Things'll be fine when we reach Spain," he reassured her blandly.

I really should get my rifle and blow the bastard away right now, she thought. Instead she turned and vented her anger on Giovanni. "What the hell are you doing in there? I said get going!"

A shame-faced Giovanni leaned from the cab. "It's dead, Samara. It won't start."

"What?" Hans struggled to his feet. He pulled Giovanni from the opening to the cab and squeezed through. Samara heard his curses as he attempted to start the vehicle, followed by thumps as he rained blows against the wheel and dashboard.

He appeared at the end of the corridor, red faced, and Giovanni leapt out of his way as he barrelled past. Samara stepped aside as Hans made his way to the midsection of the truck, then followed and watched him as he stared at the banked machinery and array leads.

He looked disbelievingly at the mess of broken cables, then turned to her. "Who the fucking hell did this?" he said.

Giovanni came to Samara's side, staring at the machinery. "What?"

"This!" Hans bellowed. Samara saw leads torn from couplings and hanging loose, and switches wrenched from control panels. Her stomach flipped with the sudden realisation of what had happened.

Hans moved among the snaking cables, assessing the damage and cursing to himself. He turned and stared at Giovanni. "You know anything about this?"

The boy shook his head, mute and petrified.

"Josef!" Hans bellowed, "Edo! Lomo! Here!"

Seconds later Edo and Lomo appeared in the corridor, followed by Josef. Hans was ominously calm, holding his rage in check as he looked from the Africans to Josef. They were wide eyed, silent, and Samara felt something of their fear.

"You," he said to the Hungarian. He indicated the damage. "What the fuck happened here?"

Josef shook his head, stammering a feeble denial. He shrugged, cast a pleading glance at Samara.

Hans gestured to the lounge. "The four of you, in there. Sit down. Move it!"

"Hans..." Samara said, as Giovanni, Josef and the Africans slipped along the corridor and sat on the couches in the lounge.

"Hans," she said again. "What matters is getting it fixed, okay? Not finding out who did it."

He glared at her. "I'll find the fucker who did this, then I'll fix it, okay?"

He moved to the rear of the transporter, returning seconds later with his rifle. Samara closed her eyes, feeling sick. "Hans..."

He pushed past her. "Shut the fuck up!"

He stood in the entrance to the lounge, rifle lodged on his hip. Samara moved behind him. She was trying to recall where she'd left her rifle. She knew she had to act fast... Was it outside, or back in her room? For the life of her she'd couldn't remember.

Hans was pointing the rifle into the lounge. "Okay. This is simple. You tell me who did this, and you live. One of you bastards knows something about it, okay?"

Josef raised his hands. "I swear, I don't know... I mean, why would any of us...?"

"I don't know," Hans said, directing the barrel of his rifle at Josef's head. "You tell me. What are you planning between you, hm? You don't like the way I'm running things here?"

"Hans..." Samara said, pleading.

Hans grinned horribly. "You," he said to Josef. "It was you who shot the fuck out of the containers... and now the fucking arrays... What's your fucking game?"

"I swear, I swear," Josef wept.

Hans stepped forward, placing the rifle against

Josef's forehead. The Africans backed up against the wall, staring in terror. Beside Josef, Giovanni closed his eyes and wept.

"Tell me!" Hans ranted. "Tell me why you did it or I'll blow your fucking head off!"

"It wasn't him!" Samara cried.

Hans pulled the trigger, the detonation deafening in the confines of the lounge.

Giovanni sobbed with sudden shock.

Samara opened her eyes. "It wasn't... him," she repeated softly, staring past Hans's bulk to where Josef sat, his headless torso surreally upright.

Giovanni sat frozen, eyes squeezed shut, a mess of blood and brain splashed across his face.

Hans turned to her and stared. "What?"

"I said... it wasn't Josef." She turned and made her way along the corridor to her room. There, she stood with her back to the door and stared around.

The ESA files were no longer on the floor by the bed, or on the table beside the window. She wanted to weep. She heard Hans enter the room behind her. He closed the door, very quietly.

"What did you say?" he asked in an ominously soft voice.

She took a breath and turned to face him. "Hans, it wasn't Josef, or any of the others."

His features were slow to respond. He looked puzzled, at last. "Then who?"

"The boy, from the other truck..." She gestured. "He came over. He wanted to talk."

He shook his head. "Talk?" he repeated, as if he'd heard the word for the very first time.

He glanced behind her, at something on the floor, and his sudden smile was the ugliest thing she had ever seen.

He remained silent, shifted his gaze from the floor to Samara, then said, "Talk?"

She looked over her shoulder and saw the boy's shorts on the floor beside the bed. Oddly, she felt like laughing then, a hysterical reaction to what she knew would follow.

He said, "You fucked him?"

She made a small gesture with her right hand.

"You fucked the pretty boy?"

He was still holding the rifle. She expected him to lift it and shoot her dead. She said quickly, "Hans, I had to get him on our side. Win him over. We need the rig. The water. Don't you see? The others... he said the others were suspicious of us. I said they had nothing to fear..."

"So you fucked him?"

She swallowed, feeling sick. "It meant nothing. Not like when we..." She heard the words, heard the pleading in her tone, and hated herself.

He shook his head. "It didn't work."

His words confused her. "What?"

"I said, bitch, it didn't work. Win him over? So why the fuck did he...?" and he gestured over his shoulder.

She shook her head. "I... I was asleep. He must have woken up. And saw you out there." She nodded towards the window. "He saw you, Hans, recognised you from Paris. Imagine his fear. So... on the way out, he..." She went on, "If he hadn't seen you..."

He stared at her. "So... you're saying it's my fault?

You let the pretty boy in, fuck him senseless to 'win him over,' then he sees me and gets the shits...?"

He moved, too quickly for her to avoid what happened next. He took a step forward, raised the rifle, and brought the butt crashing down towards her. She cried out and fell backwards, and the solid club of the rifle grazed the side of her head.

She sprawled across the bed. He loomed above her, staring down silently as if calculating what to do next. He came to a decision, turned and moved to the door.

There, he stopped and stared at the low table by the wall. He turned to her and said, "The Dutch papers?"

"I..." she began, fearful of reigniting his rage.

"Pretty boy took the papers, didn't he?"

She could only nod, and brace herself for his reaction.

He said, "At least now we'll know where to find the bastards..." He turned and made to leave the room.

She said, "Hans... what now?"

He paused. "Now I'll fix the damage and we'll hunt down your pretty boy and make him pay, okay?"

He kicked open the door and barged from the room, calling out to Lomo to fetch him the toolbox. "Giovanni! On the roof – transfer the couplings from the primary array."

Samara lay still for a minute, her head throbbing, a part of her surprised to be still alive. She sat up, fingering the ridge above her temple where the rifle had almost cracked her skull... Then she looked across the room and saw her own rifle, propped against the shower stall.

She jumped from the bed, grabbed the gun and made for the door. She would come up behind the bastard while he was repairing the leads, shoot him in the back.

She stopped her headlong flight, smiling at her stupidity.

Killing him now would afford her a great deal of satisfaction, but it would also increase their chances of being stranded out here. She concealed the rifle behind the door. She would bide her time, wait until the transporter was up and running, and take her chance when it came.

She moved along the corridor and watched Hans while he worked on the leads.

A COUPLE OF hours later, Hans said, "There... that might do it."

Samara didn't like the part she had to play now, but it was necessary in order to mollify him. "That was fast."

He shrugged. "We'll see."

Samara could see no difference between the lashed together collection of pipes and cables as they were now and as they had been earlier, before Paul's sabotage.

Hans turned to Giovanni. "In the cab. Start driving."

The boy nodded and scurried to the cab.

Hans sat cross-legged on the floor, sweat coursing down the fat of his face. "Water?" Samara asked.

He nodded.

She took his empty bottle and refilled it from one of the containers. He grabbed the bottle without a word and took long, chugging glugs, then held the half-empty bottle over his bald head, dousing himself and grinning like a child.

The transporter kicked, surged forward. Hans's boyish grin expanded in self-satisfaction.

Samara said, "Well done you."

"Well, thank fuck one of us knew how to fix the mess."

They sat in silence as the vehicle rocked through the desert.

She reached out, laid a hand on his thigh. If she could tempt him back to the bedroom...

He let her hand remain where it was.

She said, tentatively, "You would have done the same in my situation, Hans."

He looked at her. "Huh?"

"Imagine the boy had been a girl, and we wanted their rig. And she came over here and... and you got talking, and it was obvious the girl was interested in you." She looked at him. "What would you have done then, Hans?"

He grunted. "What do you think?"

"Right." She nodded. "Well... that's just what I did, Hans. I wanted him to trust us, right? We needed the rig..."

"You shouldn't have fucked pretty-boy, Samara."

She opened her mouth in mute indignation, but stopped her protests and looked away. She imagined inserting the barrel of her rifle into his mouth and pulling the trigger.

He said, "He's got the papers. If we don't get them back... how the fuck do we get into the bunker,

Samara?"

She stared at him. "So it's my fault, is it?"

"If pretty-boy hadn't come sniffing around over here and you hadn't..."

She said, "Everything was going fine, Hans, until he saw you. I should have left you back at the castle..." She regretted it the second she said the words.

He tensed, and his hand moved as if in preparation to strike her.

He had second thoughts, dashed her hand from his thigh and stood. "You know where the base is, once we get to Spain?"

She nodded. "It's marked on the map, in the cab."

He turned, barrelled off down the corridor and climbed into the cab beside Giovanni. Samara looked up and down the corridor. There was no sign of Edo and Lomo. They had sensibly retreated to their berths. She stood and made her way back to her room, averting her gaze as she passed the lounge where Josef's body still sat upright.

She left the door unlocked, picked up the rifle and lay on the bed. He would come to her, sooner or later, and as soon as he entered the room she would take aim and blast him to shreds. The thought gave her great satisfaction.

All she had to do was wait, she told herself, and hold her nerve when he finally entered the room. After that, one big problem would be out of the way. All that would remain, then, would be to find Paul and convince him that it was the psychopath Hans alone who had been responsible for the killings.

She was confident, once she had the boy to herself, that her powers of persuasion would be equal to the task.

She heard footsteps approaching along the corridor. She tensed, expecting the door to burst open and Hans to stride in, affording her an ample target.

The footsteps halted, and a second later a series of timid knocks sounded on the door. She laid aside the rifle and said, "Who is it?"

A whispered reply, "Giovanni."

She sat up. "Come in."

The door opened and the boy crept in, sheepishly. "Hans is driving."

She smiled. "Just as well. I wouldn't want him finding you in here."

He caught her expression of amusement and smiled. "I came to..." He stood by the door, looking down at the floor.

She patted the bed beside her. "Tell me."

He joined her and sat down on the bed unsurely. "He's... he's insane, Samara."

She breathed, "I know," oddly relieved to be sharing this opinion with someone.

He went on, "The other day, you told me not to trust him, to stand by you..." He avoided her eyes, as if broaching a great intimacy.

She said, "Go on."

"He took my rifle," he said. He smiled. "He obviously doesn't trust me with it. But" – he paused, his chest heaving with a sigh – "but if you loan me your rifle... I'll kill the bastard."

She wanted to reach out and touch the boy in

gratitude, but was afraid of giving him the wrong idea. She smiled. "He deserves to die, Giovanni, for what he's done."

He nodded. "I'll do it. Gladly."

She watched him. He was so young, too young to kill a man and have the memory of the deed with him for the rest of his life.

She said, "But I don't want you risking your own life –"

He said urgently, "There's no risk, Samara. I'll go to the cab, shoot him while he's at the wheel. He won't know a thing about it."

She shook her head. "I'll do it. But... but I want him to know what's happening."

He looked at her, his eyes narrow.

"I want revenge, Giovanni. For everything he's done, to other people and to me. I want him to know it was me who killed him."

He gestured. "How will you...?"

She thought about it. "Do you know which cable to disconnect to stop the transporter?"

He nodded. "No problem."

"Show me how to do it, Giovanni, then join him in the cab. I'll pull the plug, and when he comes down the corridor..." She reached out and took hold of the rifle.

He swallowed. "You sure you can go through with this?"

"Sure I'm sure. Come on."

She took the rifle and followed him down the corridor. At the banked, humming machinery they stopped, and Giovanni indicated a thick cable socketed into a port on the side of a silver console.

"Pull this and a minute later there'll be a power drain... It'll be obvious there's something wrong."

She nodded. "Okay... Okay, off you go."

He paused, then touched her arm. "Take care, okay?"

She nodded and watched him hurry down the corridor to the cab.

Now that the time had come to take action, she realised how nervous she was. She was shaking, her hands trembling. She checked that the rifle was indeed loaded and went through just what she'd do when Hans came barging along the corridor.

She reached out and yanked at the lead. It came free at the second attempt, and the hum changed tone on a long *diminuendo*.

She backed off down the corridor, entered her room and left the door open a crack, staring through the gap at the corridor.

A minute later – a minute which felt like an hour to her – the transporter came to a juddering halt.

The rifle felt clammy in her grasp. Her throat was dry and her breath came with difficulty. She seemed to be having palpitations, her heart fluttering in her chest. She smiled: it wasn't the thought of killing Hans that was causing these reactions, but the idea of what might happen to her if she failed.

She started as a figure came into view at the far end of the corridor. Hans looked like thunder as he barrelled down the passage, muttering something to himself.

Step out as he nears the machinery, she told herself, raise the gun, aim, make sure he's watching you as you pull the trigger, so that he knows very well who killed him... It would have been nice to have the time to tell him why, tell him how much she despised him... but that would be a luxury too far. Be satisfied with merely ending his life and having him know that it was you...

Step out...

She opened the door and stepped out.

Raise the rifle...

She brought the rifle up as he came alongside the banked machinery.

Make sure he's watching you as you pull the trigger...

He stared at her, his face a comical mask of utter incomprehension.

She pulled the trigger.

The shot blasted a jagged hole in the side of the transporter inches from his chest, and no sooner had Samara realised she'd missed than he dived, and she had no chance.

She felt his massive weight thump into her midriff and she was down, fighting for breath. He snatched something from her grip... the rifle... brought it down again and again on her head, her face, grunting with satisfaction with each blow. Then he was dragging her along the corridor to the lounge, his fist knotted in her hair. He yanked her into the lounge, cracking her ribs against the door-frame, and launched her into the seat beside Josef's corpse.

She sat, stunned with shock and pain, terrified at the thought of what was about to happen.

Hans moved back into the corridor. She heard shouting, but her mind was too numbed to make sense of the words. She tried to sit up, but her ribcage protested with a jolt like an electric shock.

Seconds later Edo and Lomo appeared, cowering, and obeyed Hans's orders to get into the lounge and sit down.

Hans called out again, louder this time, an insane howl that froze Samara's blood. Someone appeared at the door, someone much reduced from the brave youth he'd been just minutes before: he was abject now, fear haunting his eyes as he looked at Samara and gave a ghastly smile... She wanted to plead, "I'm sorry, don't blame me..." but knew that the time for explanations, for self-justification, was over.

Hans shoved Giovanni in the small of the back and he staggered into the room and slumped down on the couch next to her.

Hans filled the doorway, face red with rage, and this time didn't even waste time going through the ritual of trying to ascertain culpability...

He raised the rifle and aimed at Lomo and pulled the trigger, and Samara closed her eyes as a portion of the African's head exploded and showered her with blood and brain tissue. She sobbed. Another explosion, deafening, and Edo's pleading scream was ended.

Then silence. Samara opened her eyes. The scene that met her gaze was horror beyond description, with Hans towering over proceedings, the look on his face the definition of sadistic enjoyment.

Beside her, Giovanni was sobbing quietly.

"I'm sorry," she whispered.

Hans turned the gun towards the boy and said, "Open your eyes!"

Giovanni remained with his head on his chest, weeping.

"I said, open –"

Without warning the boy launched himself from the couch and almost reached Hans. The explosion shocked Samara. Giovanni's body bucked, a bloody hole in his chest, and he fell back onto the couch. Hans stepped forward, very deliberately inserted the barrel of the gun in Giovanni's gasping mouth, and pulled the trigger.

"No!" Samara sobbed, as bits of Giovanni's head dashed against her cheek.

Hans moved back to the doorway, panting hard and looking down with satisfaction on his slaughter. There was something beyond macabre about the deliberate way he had gone about blowing away his victims' heads, so that they sprawled on the couches in similar ghastly postures, robbed of both life and dignity.

Hans levelled the rifle at her and said, "This is it, Samara. The end. All your days led up to this... So what does it feel like? I'm about to do to you what you wanted to do to me."

"But you deserved it, you mad bastard!"

It was painful, very painful, to die like this, at his hands.

He laughed and hitched the rifle. Then he backed out of the room, slammed the door shut and locked it.

She sat in stunned silence, surrounded by blood and gore, covered in the stuff, Giovanni's arm a dead weight across her thighs.

She had no illusions that she was going to die; this was a temporary reprieve, devised perhaps so that he might kill her in a slower and more satisfying way.

The door opened and Hans entered with a coil of rope. He knelt and bound her ankles, then did the same to her wrists, and tied the rope to the legs of the couch. He knelt beside her and whispered in her ear, and his words sent a chill of dread through her mind. "You're more valuable to me alive than dead, Samara."

He stood and hurried from the lounge and locked the door behind him.

She wept, and made a token struggle against the ropes, but her efforts only served to increase their burning grip.

She lay back, feeling waves of pain wash over her, followed by nausea.

Then she began giggling uncontrollably at the thought of what someone might think if they were to look upon this scene. She looked around. It was like the waiting room of the dead. The shattered gourds of four skulls, each one sculpted by bullets into a different formation, cupped a pulverised stew of blood and brains.

The transporter started up and accelerated across the desert, rocking the four corpses in grisly and comical unison.

Samara raised her head and wept with laughter.

CHAPTER TWENTY

DAN BRAKED THE half-track on the lip of the escarpment and stared out.

Kath appeared in the gap between the seats and passed him a bottle of water. "My God, Dan..."

"Impressive?" he smiled.

They had reached, at last, the edge of the country where, decades ago, the ocean had lapped at the shore. The emptied ocean had been his destination for so long, the place where he would erect the rig and drill for water. Now that day would be put on hold, until after they had investigated the base at Bilbao.

The land shelved away gradually to the vast expanse of the old sea-bed, a limitless plain of crazed silt, split here and there with great fissures, like photographic negatives of lightning bolts. The plain was populated with a thousand ancient maritime craft, from small boats which looked at this distance like upturned shells, to the hulks of huge canted liners and tankers. The vista was absolutely still, and silent. The early morning sun burned down, sending the shadow of the half-track sprawling ahead of them.

"How far to Bilbao?" Kath asked.

"We'll be there well before sunset." He took a long drink of water and fired up the engine. "Hold on."

Standing behind him, Kath gripped the seat as he eased the truck over the crumbling lip of the escarpment. The half-track tipped suddenly, and slid forward, then the tracks bit and powered the vehicle down the incline to the sea-bed.

Minutes later they were travelling at speed over the flat plain. Kath held her nose. "Ugh! What's that?"

Dan laughed. "My guess... the composted flesh and bones of millions – trillions – of fish and assorted marine life."

The reek filled the cab, sharp and unpleasant. All around them Dan could see, now that they were on the actual sea bottom, the limitless debris of fish bones, some still intact, others long ago reduced to powder. The half-track kicked up a fine talcum drift, increasing the heady, fishy aroma.

Kath eased herself through the gap and sat in the passenger seat.

"How's Paul?" Dan asked.

"Sleeping." She hesitated. "God, Dan, I'm glad he's back. When I think about it... it could have all gone so wrong back there."

"He did well to get away." He smiled to himself, bitterly. "And to think... Hans still haunts us."

Kath shook her head. "I hope they can't fix the damage, Dan. I want them to die of thirst and hunger, very slowly. What they did to the villagers..."

Dan reached out and took her hand. "Don't dwell, Kath. There's nothing we can do."

She smiled at him. "Ed wants them to make the repairs, catch up with us. Then he wants revenge."

"I understand his desire. Don't you, after what Hans did to Lisa?"

He looked at her as she bit her bottom lip, considering, and it was a measure of the woman that she shook her head, finally. "I do, Dan, but... it'll be enough if they die in the desert. If Hans did survive and find us, and Ed killed him... that wouldn't make things any better. Revenge won't bring back Lisa."

Dan shrugged. "But it'll make Ed feel better."

She looked at him. "Dan," she said tolerantly, "The meting out of justice isn't about ameliorating the feelings of the aggrieved."

He looked at her. "That isn't what you said a few days ago..." He went on, "Look at it this way. If Hans did come after us, and Ed got his way, then Hans wouldn't be around to kill any more innocents."

"I know, I know. It's just..." She squeezed his hand. "I've had enough of killing, Dan. And now that I've found Millie..."

She fell silent. He looked up at her; she was crying, silently.

"Kath..."

"I'm sorry. It's strange. Life seems much more... valuable, precious, now that we have Millie. Do you understand?"

He smiled.

She gripped his hand again. "I don't mean to say that it wasn't precious when there was just me and you. I love you, Dan, you know that. But now I feel... complete."

He smiled across at her, and something welled in his chest. "You're the most wonderful woman in the world, Kath."

She laughed through her tears. "I don't have much competition in that department!"

They passed into the shadow of a mammoth, rusted tanker, its bow rising above them like a cliff-face. Kath pointed to something directly below the prow of the ship, and as they approached, Dan slowed the truck.

A pile of bones, metres high, rose from the sea-bed. Dan made out rib-cages, spines, the occasional whitened skull.

Kath murmured, "What do you think happened?"

Dan accelerated away. He shook his head. "Perhaps there was a colony on the ship, and as things got bad, food and water became scarce and people began dying..." he shrugged, "the dead were simply pitched over the side."

A while later Kath said, almost to herself, "So many stories."

He looked at her. "What?"

"I sometimes think we're living at the end of time, that we're the last. The past teemed with stories, some happy, some tragic... and after us there'll be no more stories."

"Well, we're not dead yet, Kath."

"I fear for Millie, Dan. I mean, what kind of life lies in wait for her?"

He smiled and said, "A damned better life now that she's with us."

"You know what I mean," she said.

"Kath... Look, if things turn out well in Bilbao, if we can access the bunkers, this underground complex... and then if we do strike water later –"

"That's a lot of *ifs*, Dan."

"I know, but we can only take them one at a time, and hope."

They drove on in silence for a while. The sun rose towards the zenith, and the heat increased within the confines of the cab.

"I wonder if there is any real hope, Dan. I mean, long-term hope."

He shrugged. He didn't like these questions; he lived for the day, looking to the short-term. Kath's long view of things gave him the shivers. He said, "You know what I think about that..."

"That we'll evolve, adapt." She smiled at him. "Become blind, limited intelligence, living far underground, without any understanding of our illustrious history?"

"Well... Maybe something like that." He smiled at her. "But not for a long time yet."

"It must have been wonderful to live a century or so ago, when the future seemed certain, when the continuation of civilisation was taken for granted."

"It was taken for granted," he said, "and perhaps that was part of the problem."

"Dan, I don't want us to merely survive, evolve into some blind, burrowing animal with no sense of history. Wouldn't it be nice to found a civilised colony, with resources, food and water, hope for the future... Hope for Millie."

He wanted to tell her that Bilbao was that hope,

but was afraid to lay too much stress on it in case it came to nothing.

They drove on and the sun rolled overhead and appeared high to their right, a fiery white hole in an aluminium sky. Dan had never before seen a landscape as flat and featureless as this. The plain that stretched ahead seemed to extend forever, white and dazzling under the merciless sun.

Perhaps an hour later, Ed appeared in the gap between the seats. He passed a sheet of paper to Kath. "I've sketched a map of where the facility is in relation to the old city," he told them. "It shouldn't be too hard to find."

Kath said, "How's the translation going?"

"Slowly, but I'm getting there."

"And?"

"There's everything in there from technical and scientific reports, right down to lists of supplies. Like Paul said, there was a city down there. And if the supplies are still there, and we can get at them..."

"Always assuming people haven't got there first," Kath said.

Ed nodded. "Most importantly, whoever translated from the Spanish to French included entry codes to the various levels."

"What about the Dutch print-outs?"

Ed hesitated. "It's a slow process."

Kath looked at him. "But you've found something?"

Ed shrugged, non-commitally. "I... I don't know. Dutch isn't my strong point, and I don't want to raise hopes."

Dan said, "Can't you even give us a hint?"

Ed pushed himself from the seats. "Not until I've gone through it again."

Kath smiled to herself. "No sign of the other truck?"

Ed stretched a smile across the skull of his face. "Paul's at the back, obsessively keeping watch. I... I don't know whether he wants the woman to turn up, or not."

Kath said, "Poor Paul."

"And then... he told me that when the woman was sleeping, he saw Hans and the rest around the camp-fire."

What an introduction to the joys of the flesh, Dan thought. Kath said, "I just hope he can get over it, Ed, that it doesn't damage him."

"He's strong," Ed said. "I think he'll be fine. Right, I'll get back to it..."

Kath said, "I'll take over, Dan. If you want to sleep?"

"Take the wheel, but I want to be up and around when we get to Spain."

He slowed the truck to a crawl and they exchanged seats. He sat back, stretching, and took a long drink of water.

He stared ahead, to the flat horizon, attempting to detect the rise that would signal their approach to the landmass that had been Spain. He felt equal measures excitement and trepidation as he considered the Bilbao base. So much, he realised, rested on what they discovered in the next few hours. It was hard not to invest too much hope in what they might find there, and despite his pragmatism he tried not to dwell on the consequences of finding the base emptied, destroyed, or inaccessible.

He leaned back in his seat and, lulled by the motion of the truck, slipped into sleep.

"DAN..." KATH'S GENTLE summons brought him awake.

He sat up, rubbing his face. "How long...?"

"A couple of hours. Look."

She pointed through the windscreen.

They were grumbling up a shallow incline. They had left the sea bed in their wake and were now passing through a sand-covered landscape.

"It's been like this for the past hour," Kath said. "There's the ruins of a city to the left, there."

"Bilbao..." he said.

The ruins were minimal, and buried in sand: a few old towerblocks rose ugly and stark, along with older, more aesthetically-pleasing buildings; some sported ornate carvings of horses and bulls, cavorting on raised frescoes above the rolling desert dunes. All bore the ravages of war: scorch marks of incendiary devices and the pocked craters of a million bullet holes.

Beyond the seafront, Dan made out blasted suburbs for as far as the eye could see, burnt-out shells of houses caught in some long ago conflict.

Kath glanced at the map. "We go through the city and head west. Around ten kilometres along the coast... We should find the base there."

Dan nodded, found his water and drank.

They reached the outskirts of the city and trundled west, towards the bright ball of the sun hanging a hand's breadth above the horizon. They passed a line of statues of men and women long dead even when they were carved; Dan wondered if there was anyone alive now who might have any idea who these once illustrious people were. The statues' features were eroded, obliterated, made faceless as if by some form of leprosy.

They passed the last of the human landmarks and entered an area of sandy waste again; to their right was a long drop to the fissured plain of the sea, to their left an expanse of rolling dunes that might stretch, Dan thought, all the way around the world to the extremes of the southern hemisphere.

Thirty minutes later he made out, ahead, a series of concrete stanchions emerging from the sand. Beyond what had once been a high chain-link fence, which now existed in tattered fragments like old lace, he saw a series of concrete buildings, now mere shells, with blank, dark windows and doors. The half-track clanked over a concrete approach road that emerged from the sand. A sun-faded sign, hanging at an angle from a concrete post, showed the entwined ESA symbol within the sleek outline of a starship.

"We're here," said a voice behind them.

"Paul," Dan said. "Rested?"

The boy gripped the back of the seats as the truck swayed. He nodded. Dan passed him a bottle of water. He drank, and looked ahead, his face expressionless.

Kath consulted the map Ed had sketched, and steered across a vast concrete apron towards the low, hulking shape of what looked like a concrete hangar.

Dan indicated the ground around them, and Kath nodded grimly. The apron was pitted with shell holes, as if at some point in the past the base had come under sustained attack. Kath steered around the craters and drew the half-track into the deep shadow of the hangar.

It wasn't a hangar, Dan saw, but the blocky shape of an underground entrance fronted by a great metal slab of a door. The metal was scored with the indentations of a hundred bullets, scorched black by incendiary devices. The concrete to the right of the door had crumbled to reveal rusted wire-work beneath.

Kath cut the engine and they sat in the ensuing silence, staring out at the imposing face of the entrance.

Dan opened the passenger door and climbed out. Sand crunched underfoot and a wave of heat rushed him. He walked across to the great metal entrance and halted, staring up at its violated surface.

Kath and Paul joined him, and Kath pointed. "There, Dan."

She walked over to a metal box bolted to the concrete frame of the door. She reached up and pulled a lever, and a hatch on the front of the box swung open.

She looked back at Dan and shook her head.

Whatever had been in the box – some kind of

entry system? – was now a fused mess of charred plastic and wire.

Dan moved away from the door in order to get a better view of the complex. So far as he could see, this was the only structure obtruding from the apron that could conceivably give access to the complex below-ground.

Kath called across to him. "How are we going to get inside, Dan?"

He shook his head. "Let's get back into the truck, get some water and talk it over."

He should have known that the complex would not open itself magically at their first attempt, but he still felt a sense of disappointment – and a premonition that this might be the first of many such setbacks – as he joined the others in the half-track.

CHAPTER TWENTY-ONE

MIRACULOUSLY, SAMARA MANAGED to sleep.

She was jolted awake some time later by the motion of the transporter, and she realised with amazement that she had not dreamed, had not even been visited by nightmares.

The nightmares were here, all around her.

The bodies had failed to stay upright. The remains of Lomo and Edo were on the floor at her feet; Josef's corpse had slid forward on the couch so that its back lay on the cushion and its legs were folded under it. Giovanni had fallen sideways and lay across Samara, blood and spinal fluid dripping from the shattered remains of his head and pooling warmly on the seat beneath her thigh.

She strained, and the corpse slipped to the floor with a heavy *thunk*. The ropes that bound her wrists and ankles bit into her flesh painfully.

At least, she thought, if she kept her gaze level she couldn't see the carnage, even though there was no getting away from the smell. The lounge was hot and airless, and high with the reek of blood and singed brains; worse, one or more of the bodies had voided itself, and the smell of shit made her gag.

She wept, and she couldn't keep her thoughts from straying towards what Hans might be planning. She considered what Paul had told her, about Hans and the girl in Paris. Perhaps that was to be her fate: he would rape her senseless, then dismember her limb from limb, cook and eat her.

But what had he said after tying her up? That she was more valuable to him alive than dead... What the hell had he meant by that?

The steady thrumming of the tracks on sand had ceased a while ago, to be replaced by the loud rattle of metal on concrete or stone. A vibration went through the vehicle, lending spurious animation to the bodies on the floor. Samara could not help but stare in fascination at the remains of Giovanni, who had plotted with her to kill Hans, just hours ago.

The transporter slowed, and she wondered if they had arrived at Bilbao.

She closed her eyes, overwhelmed by sudden panicky terror, and counted her heartbeats. She wondered how many she might have left. Hundreds, thousands...? How many heartbeats were there in an hour, she wondered? She would count them, attempt to work out...

The transported halted, and seconds later she heard footsteps approach along the corridor.

Hans pulled the door open and stared in at her. His ugly bare feet stood in the pooled blood. He was slick with sweat, his face expressionless.

Without a word he stepped over the bodies and untied the ropes that bound her feet to the couch.

"Stand up."

"What... what are you doing?"

"I said stand up!"

She stood with difficulty, her movement restricted with her hands tied behind her back. Hans refastened the rope around her ankles, leaving the binds slack this time so that she could shuffle her feet.

He took a hank of her hair and dragged her, screaming, from the lounge and dropped her in the corridor. He knelt before her, gripping her hair at the back of her head to make her stare into his face.

"You think pretty-boy still wants you?"

The question made no sense to her. She stared at him, at his fat, sweating face, the crooked teeth, the broken nose. She shook her head, despite his grip. "What?"

"Pretty-boy? You think he still wants you?"

She managed to gasp a laugh. "To kill, perhaps." She wondered what Paul might think of her, now, the leader of the cannibal horde that had murdered the villagers... She was probably correct in her assessment: he would sooner see her dead, she thought, than enter into any bargaining, which was what Hans was presumably planning.

He grinned at her. "To kill? To fuck?" He shrugged. "Both?"

"You," she managed past gritted teeth, "would know about that."

He back-handed her across the face, painfully.

He left her on the floor, gasping, and came back seconds later with a rifle. He dragged her to her feet and pressed the weapon against her belly, so that its warm barrel lodged painfully beneath her chin.

The he tied the rifle to her, winding rope around her torso, holding the weapon in place. Finally he attached the rope to the trigger – she couldn't move her head, with the gun barrel pressed painfully to her throat, so she was unable to see what he was doing – then stood back and admired his handiwork.

She leaned back against the wall, immobile, breathing hard.

He smiled at her. "If you try to run," he said, "if you move your hands at all... you'll be headless like the other fuckers in there."

She wanted to test his claim, then; she wanted to end her life, and in so doing scupper the bastard's plans.

But the simple fact was that she was too afraid of dying to move a muscle.

"Now... do exactly as I say. He picked up a second rifle and grabbed her upper arm. "Out of the truck!"

He walked her along the corridor towards the exit and kicked the door open. Sunlight exploded in her face, blinding her. She felt for the steps with her feet, found the first one, then the second, and stepped onto the hot concrete.

He gripped her arm with his left hand, holding the rifle in the other and directing it past her at...

She stared ahead.

It was the Copenhagen truck, and standing beside it were Paul, Dan, the woman and an old man. They were perhaps a hundred metres away and she could not make out, thankfully, the expressions on their faces.

She did not want their hatred, or their sympathy.

Hans yelled out, almost deafening her, "Put your weapons back in the truck and you can have the bitch."

She sobbed, despite herself. The hot barrel dug into the soft flesh of her throat, and Hans's vice-like grip on her upper arm was like a tourniquet applied for too long.

She stared across at the four. Paul was saying something to the others. At last they turned, and with exaggerated care they set their weapons inside the truck.

Hans called out again. "I want the papers, the print-outs. Bring them to me, and she's yours."

She didn't believe a word, of course. The only way Hans could get out of this situation with his life and the print-outs was if he killed the four of them and herself... He was stupid, but not too stupid to realise that simple fact. And he would have no compunction at all in taking more innocent lives.

She smiled to herself. Could she possibly call herself innocent, she wondered?

Again the quartet consulted among themselves. Eventually the old man left them, moved back into the truck and ducked inside.

She wanted to shout, "No! Don't give the bastard what he wants..." They were all going to die, anyway.

She said, "Hans, tell me... You can tell me, now. What did you find in the Dutch print-out?"

He laughed, unpleasantly, leaned close to her and whispered in her ear.

She felt her gorge rise. She shook her head, as best she could with the hot gun barrel at her throat. "I don't understand..."

So he told her, and she wept.

CHAPTER TWENTY-TWO

PAUL STOOD BETWEEN Dan and Kath as Ed moved around in the half-track behind them.

He stared across the intervening hundred metres at Hans and Samara. The bastard had bound a rifle to her torso, rigged so that, if she moved, the weapon would blow her head off. The other rifle, in Hans's right hand, was directed towards them.

Samara stood upright, almost proudly defiant despite her situation: she seemed to be gazing directly across at him.

Dan whispered, "Paul, don't do anything stupid, okay?"

"He'll kill her," Paul said in a strangled voice. "The man's a maniac –"

"I know very well what he is, and I know he'll have every intention of killing all of us just as soon as he gets what he wants."

Kath whispered, "So what do we do?"

"We do nothing," Dan said, "but wait."

Paul stared across at Samara, flooded by memories of his time with her, the intimacu they had shared. He felt tears leaking from his eyes, down his cheeks.

At least, now, he knew that Samara had not been wholly responsible for the deaths of the villagers. He told himself that she'd had to go along with Hans's demented plans, to save herself...

Ed was taking a long time in the truck, longer than it should take simply to gather the print-outs.

At last the old man emerged, and Kath took a quick, indrawn breath.

Ed said, "This is how I want it, Kath. Don't stop me."

He carried the sheaf of papers beneath one arm – and slung over his back was the red dress containing his daughter's bones.

Ed looked at Dan, and smiled. He said, "Dan, I've made copies of all the entry codes, okay – and I've translated the important parts of the Dutch print-outs. You'll find them in the lounge."

"Ed...?" Dan began.

"Level seven. Go down to level seven and you'll find our future..." Tears welled in the old man's eyes and, before they broke and fell down his cheeks, he said, "And when I drop the dress, my friends, hit the ground, okay?"

He turned. Paul watched him walk away. He wanted to tell Ed not to do it... but at the same time he knew that there was no other way that they might survive.

Ed walked slowly across the apron towards Hans and the woman, holding the print-outs before him like an offering.

He came to within three metres of the pair and halted. They exchanged words. Paul wanted more than anything to eavesdrop on what Ed had to say then; he'd had plenty of time to rehearse his words, but whether Hans would have the intelligence to understand them... well, that would always be a moot point. He certainly would not have the humanity to assimilate Ed's final words.

Hans said something, gesturing with his rifle. Ed stepped forward, held out the papers. Hans released his grip on the woman's upper arm, reached out and snatched the folders.

Everything, up to that point, had happened slowly. Then, as Paul watched, time seemed to accelerate: events played themselves out in a rushed blur.

Samara twisted violently, wrenching the rifle from its position beneath her chin. The gun went off, but missed her head, and, sobbing, she staggered across the apron towards Paul.

At the same time, Hans swung his rifle and aimed at her... and Ed unhitched his bundle from his back, swinging his daughter's red dress around in an arc – a sweep of colour Paul would think beautiful to his dying day – and dropped it at the feet of Hans.

Dan grabbed Kath and Paul and pushed them to the ground. They hit the concrete as a deafening concussion echoed off the metal plate door and left a ringing silence in its wake.

Paul scrambled to his feet and stared across the apron.

He made out a scatter of charred bones and body parts and a scrap of red dress, lifting and swirling in the breeze above the carnage like a twist of flame.

Then he saw Samara. She was on her belly,

crawling across the concrete towards him, an arm outstretched.

Paul ran to her, fell to his knees and dragged the woman into his arms.

She was bleeding from wounds to her torso and arms, and as he cradled her she smiled up at him.

"Paul..."

He wept, rational words beyond him. He wanted to tell her that he understood, that he didn't blame her for the death of the villagers, that he knew how she had been controlled by the maniac, Hans – but the only sound that came out was a low moan.

"Paul, I'm so sorry..." She winced in pain. "Things could have been..."

He gripped her. "Samara."

She attempted to smile. "Is... is he dead?"

He looked across the apron to where a mess of blood and charcoaled flesh, none of it recognisably human, marred the concrete.

He nodded. "Very."

She laughed, "Good! Paul," she hurried on, "Level seven –"

"Yes?"

"Level seven. Hans wanted to... he wanted to..." Her eyelids fluttered, and her words became a whisper. Paul lowered his ear to her lips as she finished the sentence.

Then, smiling, she coughed once and closed her eyes. He hugged her bloody, lifeless body to him, and wept.

* * *

LATER, PAUL AND Dan walked around the carnage strewn across the apron and approached the transporter cautiously, rifles at the ready. Paul pressed himself against the metal wall beside the door and listened. He heard nothing, no voices or movement. Dan nodded and stepped into the truck, looking up and down the corridor. Paul followed, cautiously. A door stood, blocking the passage, and something dark and red flowed into the corridor. Messy footprints marked the passage of bare feet.

Dan moved towards the open door and peered into the small room. He recoiled, closing his eyes and taking deep breaths. Paul eased past him and peered into the room.

He closed his eyes, shocked.

Dan said, "The world's a better place without him... I wish I'd realised what a monster he was a year ago."

They retraced their steps from the transporter and crossed the concrete towards their own vehicle. Dan stopped before the half-track, staring at the trailer and the skeletal frame of the rig assembly, and smiled to himself, as if suddenly realising something.

They entered the truck and Kath looked across at Dan, questioning. Millie sat on her lap, bleary-eyed from sleep.

Dan said, "The others are dead. Hans must have..."

They shared water, then food. Kath said, "I've checked the chest. Ed took a grenade."

Dan smiled. "I thought he was taking his time in here." He indicated Ed's notes on the chesterfield beside Kath. "Did Ed say anything more about level seven?"

"It's just the entry codes," she said, "and something about 'finding our future on level seven.'"

"Well," Dan said, "let's follow Ed's wishes and get ourselves down to level seven."

Paul said, "But the door..."

Dan smiled. "Don't worry. I know how we can get in there."

CHAPTER TWENTY-THREE

XIAN SAT NEXT to Richard in the battered limousine as it tore through abandoned towns and villages north of Madrid. They had managed to find seats aboard a military plane from Brize Norton to the Spanish capital, staring down on a parched England no longer green, and then the vast, industrial farms that consumed kilometre after kilometre of central France. Great stretches of the farms below them had been abandoned due to water shortages; here and there, amid the sere wastes of dead crops, did the occasional field show a vivid emerald, but these were few.

"You once said there was hope," she reminded Richard now.

He smiled at her. "There is, Xian. There's always hope."

She replied, quietly, "Yes, but not here on Earth."

He replied, staring through the window at the vegetation-denuded Pyrenées, "Hope for humanity."

For the decade leading up to 2060, Xian and Richard had divided their time between training for their roles in Project Phoenix and working for the government in its increasingly hopeless task of attempting to bring stability to the chaos that was overtaking Europe.

Food and water riots were a weekly occurrence. Military rule had been declared in countries across most of Europe. In other parts of the world the situation was even more desperate. Vast tracts of Africa had been laid waste in nuclear armageddon, following the lead of the NAA and Brazil; China and India had committed national suicide with mutually destructive nuclear strikes. All told, billions were dead. Across the world, terrorist groups, out for their own selfish ends, were pitched against those attempting to maintain some kind of semblance of order and authority.

Xian gripped her seat-belt as the car raced towards the coast.

The first explosion came as they were approaching the perimeter fence of the ESA base outside Bilbao. At first, Xian thought it was an aircraft, crash-landing. Their driver put her right. "What we've been fearing. Terrorists. Even though the authorities have been denying all rumours about Project Phoenix..."

Through the windscreen, Xian made out buildings ablaze across the vast apron of the ESA base.

They were met at the gates by a high-up Project official, who nodded briefly to her and Richard. "We're assembling the colonists as I speak – they're coming in from all over Europe."

"Then – ?" Richard began.

The man nodded. "Preliminary tests on the drive have been successful. A week from now, the *Phoenix* should rise from the ashes."

Xian felt a mixture of excitement and dread. For ten years she had worked towards this goal, and now that it was upon her she found the fact impossible to take in.

The limousine careered across the tarmac. Seconds later a deafening explosion detonated a matter of metres away. The car slewed, slowed and came to a gradual halt.

With horror Xian took in the fact that the driver was slumped over the wheel, the windscreen shattered and shrapnel embedded in his skull.

The official yelled, "Out! Run for the bunker!"

Richard was pulling her from the car, dragging her at breakneck speed across the tarmac to the low shape of the bunker a hundred metres ahead. The apron was in chaos, with army personnel and trucks careening back and forth, dodging each other and the explosions which bloomed deafeningly in the twilight.

To die so close to safety, Xian found herself thinking as she ran. She wondered if this was where it would end for her, in the year 2060.

Christ, but she wasn't yet forty. Too young to die... She ran.

CHAPTER TWENTY-FOUR

FOR THE NEXT hour, as the sun set, Paul helped Dan erect the rig so that the massive drill angled towards the eroded concrete to the right of the metal door. The work was hard, under the pounding glare of the sun, and Paul had to concentrate to follow Dan's instructions. The process helped take his mind off what had happened earlier. Samara's body still lay where she had died, and Paul could not bring himself to stare across the apron towards it.

Now they stood back, Dan casting a critical eye over the assembly. "Well... I've drilled through harder stuff than this in the past. Here goes."

They donned protective face masks and ducked behind the wire cage. Dan activated the starter motor, and a high whine filled the air.

The drill-bit hit the concrete with the sound of a faulty jet engine, and within seconds the area around the rig was thick with a cloud of fine white powder. The assembly shook, vibrating their bones, and Dan shouted, "So far, so good!"

The whine changed tone, dropping an octave, and Dan called out, "It's through."

He stopped the motor and stepped out. Paul joined him as the dust settled. The drill was buried in the concrete beside the door. Dan examined the damage and reported, "I reckon the wall's around four feet thick. We'll make another incision here, then try to blast through."

They retracted the drill and repositioned it, then took their places in the cage and restarted the motor. This time Paul covered his ears as the drill hit the wall and whined. Minutes later, Dan gave the thumbs up, and Paul uncovered his ears.

Dan retracted the drill and Paul peered into the neat hole bored through the concrete. All he could see was darkness.

"What now?"

"Grenades," Dan said. "Crude, but effective."

They packed up the rig, fixed it to the tow bar on the truck, then climbed aboard and drove around the side of the bunker. Dan took two grenades from the weapons' chest and a roll of twine.

They returned to the bunker door, and Paul watched as Dan tied two lengths of twine to the pins of the grenades and inserted the first one into the top-most hole, wedging it in place with a shard of loosened concrete. He held the second grenade in his palm and stared at it.

"Christ," he said.

Paul looked at him. "What?"

"It's just struck me... These are old, Paul. I've had them fail in the past..." He looked up at Paul. "What if Ed had selected a dud?"

Paul shook his head. "Chances are, we'd all be dead."

Dan smiled. "Well, I'll take what happened as meaning luck's on our side."

He inserted the second grenade into the remaining hole, packed it with a wedge of concrete, then unwound the double lengths of twine away from the door and around the corner.

They ducked down and Dan said, "Cover your ears."

Paul did as instructed, and Dan pulled the cords and covered his own ears. A double explosion sounded, muffled through his palms, and a cloud of dust and debris billowed into the air.

They waited a moment, and Paul followed Dan around the corner, eager to witness the results of their labour.

Dan stepped over a mound of concrete and pulled away loose rubble and debris. He knelt and peered through. Paul squatted beside him, grinning as he stared through the ragged gap.

A narrow fissure, perhaps a metre wide, disappeared into the darkness.

Dan grinned at him. "Let's go get Kath and Millie."

Back at the truck, they packed food and water supplies into a backpack and Dan dug out a couple of candle-lamps, crude affairs fabricated from old glass jars and metal tins, with twine handles. Fat candles, scavenged over the years and used and re-used, would provide minimal lighting as they made their way down the levels.

Kath clutched Ed's notes and the print-outs in one hand, Millie in the other.

They left the truck and made their way to the

blasted entrance. The sun was down now, and Kath lit the candles and distributed the lamps. Dan went first, crouching into the gap and edging forward, clearing more debris as he went.

Kath and Millie followed, the girl hardly having to bow her head to enter. Paul followed on all fours.

The gap narrowed when he was part way through, and he was forced to turn sideways and scrape past the jagged obstruction. Dust and the stench of explosives filled his nose, and concrete bit into his ribs. He held his breath and worked himself through, and a minute later he tumbled free. He stood and joined the others as they lifted their lamps and peered around.

They were in a low, wide chamber, its unpainted walls pocked with evidence of a fire-fight. Here and there, on the walls and on the concrete floor, deeper pits testified to the use of grenades and mortars during the terrorist raid.

Dan led the way forward. Paul followed Kath and Millie, staring about him as he went. They came to the facing wall and Kath consulted the map. She indicated a series of lines, meaningless to Paul. "I think we're here. According to this, there's a couple of lift shafts to the left... and beyond them an emergency stairwell."

They moved left, their shadows dancing like giants against the wall. A minute later they came to a recess, inset with a polished steel plate. Kath reached out and pressed a stylised arrow set in plastic beside the door.

"Sorry. I didn't think for a second..."

Paul said, "What is it?"

Kath smiled in the candlelight. "An elevator. It was too much to hope it'd still be working."

"We'll try the stairwell," Dan said, and led the way.

As he followed, Paul wondered if this disappointment would set the trend for the rest of their descent: for all that they had the codes, they would be useless if the mechanisms governed by them weren't working.

They arrived at the stairwell and Kath pushed open the swing-door. Concrete stairs descended into the darkness.

Paul followed the others slowly. He had always avoided stairs where possible back in Paris, wary of their propensity to collapse. They descended for what seemed like an hour, turning on small landings at regular intervals before embarking on another flight. He found the repetitive stepping down motion oddly tiring, requiring the use of a set of muscles not often used. He was not the only one: Millie complained that her feet were hurting, and Kath hitched her up onto her hip.

At one point Dan halted, held his lamp up to the wall, and said, "Look..."

He indicated a series of bullet holes gouged into the concrete. "So the terrorists made it this far."

They resumed their descent, passing further evidence of the attack: more bullet holes and blackened areas of wall and floor.

Ten minutes later, Dan stopped and pointed. "There's a door."

They gathered at the foot of the steps and consulted the map in the flickering candle-light. "This should be level one," Kath said. "There's another six below this one. Each one is a little larger than the one above. The lowest level must be vast."

Dan pointed to the map, and Paul peered at the confusing lines. The levels seemed to be arranged in a series of circular galleries, surrounding a vast, empty well. He tapped the central vacuum. "But what's this?"

"If my guess is correct," Dan said, "this is where the starship would have been erected."

Paul shook his head. "But I thought rockets were launched above ground?"

"According to Ed, this one would have been different. It would have used radical technology. I don't pretend to understand it, but the ship wouldn't so much as blast off as phase into some kind of..." he hesitated, "sub-space?"

Paul laughed, and Kath joined him. "You've lost me," he admitted.

"Well," Kath said, "shall we continue?"

She indicated the door, and Dan invited her to lead the way.

She stepped forward and pushed at the door, which remained stubbornly shut. Dan raised his lamp to a panel beside the door and said, "Do you have the codes there, Kath?"

She consulted Ed's hand-written notes. "Here's the level one access code, Dan." She called out six numbers and Dan tapped them into the panel.

Kath pushed the door. Paul realised he was holding his breath. This time the door swung open, and Kath stepped through.

A second later Paul was blinded by a sudden pulse of white. He covered his eyes and stepped back. Ahead of him, Millie began crying. The door swung shut, pitching him and Dan into the relative twilight provided by his candle.

Sudden panic clutched him. A silent explosion... Had the chamber been rigged with some form of defensive technology...?

Beside him, Dan frantically entered the code again, then reached out and pushed open the door. Paul followed him through, squinting against the glare.

Dan moved to Kath's side, and they stood and stared up in silent wonder at what was revealed. Paul's eyes adjusted to the light, and he smiled. Not an explosion, as such, he thought. He looked up at the strip-lights in the high ceiling, illuminating the chamber.

They were standing on a gallery that swept away on either side to encompass the central well, and while the architecture of the gallery was impressive enough, it was what occupied the well that took his breath away.

He had seen huge buildings in Paris – constructions like the ancient cathedral and the metal tower – but nothing compared to this, and he felt a sudden, overwhelming sense of sadness.

The starship rose from the depths like a monument to what once had been achievable, and at the same time to what had been lost.

It shimmered electric blue in the light, and Paul's senses reeled as he realised that what appeared before him was merely a small cross-section of the entire craft, a great curving sweep of blue metal marked with ESA decals and entry hatches and a hundred other mysterious numerical markings.

Paul stepped forward to the great sweep of the gallery rail that matched the circumference of the ship, and he stared up. The craft swelled to a blunt dome. He pointed. "Look."

The others joined him and stared up.

A jagged hole marred the perfection of the blunt nose-cone, revealing a mess of blasted machinery within, blackened cables and twisted internal spars. Bullet holes pitted the ship's skin.

Kath said in a small voice. "I don't understand... Who could have done this?"

Dan smiled, bitterly. "Those who would have been left behind, who resented the people selected to leave the dying world."

Kath shook her head. "But why didn't they...? I mean, they could have repaired the damage, continued..."

"That was the plan, according to Ed," Dan said. "They sealed the place up, meaning to come back... But it never happened. War intervened, famines and plagues. Governments fell and our ability to..." He gestured up at the injured behemoth. "The opportunity to save the race and start again passed us by."

Paul looked down, and gasped. If the view so far had taken his breath away, it was nothing to what he saw as he gazed down into the pit: the sides of the ship sloped away, passing gallery after gallery, and disappeared into dimness.

"It's like a great bell," he said to himself.

Dan was beside him. "It's dark down there, on the other levels."

"At least we have power and light here," Paul said.

Kath said, "I have an idea. Stay here and don't move. I'm going back to the stairwell." She took Millie's hand and walked the girl back to the door. They pushed through.

Ten seconds later, the strip lighting that illuminated the gallery flicked off and pitched Paul and Dan into darkness.

Paul heard the door swish open, and a second later the level was flooded with dazzling light. Kath and Millie joined them. "So now we know. It's movement sensitive; something I've only ever read about."

"Perhaps the elevators will be working here..." Dan said.

Kath crouched and flipped through the print-outs. "This level is where the factories were based," she said. "Level two, the dormitory and living areas. Shall we take a look?"

"Let's do that," Dan said. "What about level seven?"

Kath riffled through the papers until she came to the map of level seven, and smiled up at Dan. "The area is marked, but there's no accompanying description."

"Mysterious," Dan said. "I wish Ed had told us what he'd translated."

Kath smiled. "We'll find out soon enough." She tapped the level one diagram. "The lift-shaft is over there."

They rounded the curving gallery and approached the recessed lift door. This time when Kath touched the decal beside the recess, it glowed red and seconds later the door slid open.

Paul stared in wonder at the thick, sliding door, and followed the others inside.

The door swished shut. A panel of lighted numerals indicated the seven levels. Kath hesitated, then reached out a finger and pressed the numeral 2. "Here goes..."

Paul almost shouted out as the floor fell away beneath him. His stomach lurched and he reached out to grip a rail.

Seconds later the elevator bobbed to a queasy halt. Kath hit another decal and waited. Something flashed on the panel before her, and Paul read: Enter entry code.

Kath consulted the codes Ed had transcribed. She punched six numbers into the panel. A second later the door opened with a brief hiss.

They stepped out onto a curving gallery identical to the one above; the only difference, Paul noticed, was that the view before them was of the next, broader section of the starship. He looked up. Level one was in darkness again.

Kath consulted the map. "The rooms are laid out in a radial pattern, accessed by corridors like spokes." She pointed to a door situated in the wall ten metres from the elevator recess. "Shall we take a look?"

They crossed to the door and she entered the access code. The door opened.

A plush, carpeted corridor stretched ahead for a hundred metres, lighting up as they entered. Paul was reminded of the brochures for five star hotels he'd unearthed in the ruins of Paris. He moved to the first door on the left and opened it, revealing an immaculately furnished bedroom: a double bed, chairs and table, a bathroom off. He moved across to the bed, sat down and bounced. A jug stood on a bedside table, next to a glass. Experimentally, he lifted the jug – it contained something – and poured. He lifted the glass to his nose. The water smelled brackish, and he decided not to risk a mouthful. He stared around the room. Pictures of another, better Earth hung on the walls, and magazines were stacked on a small table across the room. It was as if the occupant had stepped out for a time, would be back at any second.

He returned to the corridor and found the others investigating identical rooms.

Kath looked at the map. "Dan, there are twenty radial corridors on this level. That's..."

Dan said, "That's a lot of bedrooms, Kath."

"We could relocate here," she said, sounding amazed. "It's impregnable. If the stores are still intact..."

"Should we go and check them out?" Paul suggested.

They returned to the gallery and entered the elevator. The door swished shut and Paul held on as Kath pressed the decal for level three. They plummeted, his stomach flipping. When the elevator bobbed to a halt, Kath entered the access code and the doors parted.

Paul followed the others from the elevator, aware of his apprehension. If the stores proved to be non-existent, corrupted or raided... then what good would the underground complex be, impregnable or not?

Kath led the way to a doorway identical to the one on the level above. She entered the code and the door opened. Another hundred metre corridor was revealed, but this one lacking the sumptuous carpet and fittings of the one above: the corridor was bare, functional. Like the one above, though, doors led off to left and right.

Dan approached the first and pushed it open.

Paul pressed behind him, eager to see what the room contained. Metal racks lined the walls, stacked with what looked like bedding, blankets and sheets.

Paul hurried on to the next room. Likewise, this one was full of bedding, folded linen and thick, padded things the like of which Paul had never seen before.

"Here!" Kath called out, and he rushed back into the corridor. Kath appeared at a door five along. They joined her, and stared at the racked contents of this room.

"What are they? Paul asked.

Coloured boxes filled the shelves. Kath pulled one down and read the words printed on the back. "Christ," she breathed, smiling at Dan. "Detergent. Cleaning substances, Paul." She looked around. "Soaps, washing powder..."

Soap, he thought, the memory painful.

Kath looked at the map. "Each quadrant represents a corridor," she said, "and they're shaded different colours... My guess is that the next one will contain... I don't know, but something different to what we have here."

Paul felt dizzy. He imagined a hundred rooms filled with foodstuffs... But surely it was too good to be true?

They left the radial corridor and Kath hurried them towards the next door and entered the code.

The first room was stocked with what looked like machine parts, tiny electrical components in open plastic trays, each labelled with a description Paul didn't understand.

They moved onto the next radial corridor and Kath tapped out the code. This time Paul hurried along the corridor and picked a door at random. Brown cardboard boxes filled the room from floor to ceiling. He hauled one down, ripped open the lid. A dozen circular, silver discs stared up at him, and his heart skipped a beat. He'd seen the like before, when he'd fallen into that buried room in Paris.

He pulled out a can and stared at the label, and involuntary tears sprang to his eyes: a picture of some foodstuff, small, round and green objects. The writing said: Peas. And this time he would not require his knife to open the can: some kind of ring device suggested he could simply rip off the lid... He tried, and an amazing aroma hit him. He stared at the green things... peas... and scooped up a handful and crammed them into his mouth. He leaned against the wall, laughing through the mush, savouring the indescribable rush of taste that flooded his mouth.

He staggered out to the corridor. Millie was wandering towards him, beaming at him and eating something in a silver wrapper, followed by Kath and Dan, both chewing. He passed Dan the can of peas and in return accepted the silver packet of... He examined a small square of something pink and pungent, and slipped it into his mouth. It was incredibly sweet and sticky and hard to chew, but he persevered.

"And look," Dan said, producing a foil packet. "Coffee. Real Columbian coffee beans. If only Ed could see this..."

They sat on the floor, against the wall, and shared their finds.

"Peas," Kath said, "some kind of chewy sweets, biscuits..."

Dan passed him a biscuit, a pale square block with some kind of soft filling. He ate hungrily, the biscuit soft in his mouth, sweet. He wanted another.

Kath doled out the water. "When do we start moving the colony down here, Dan?" she laughed.

Dan bobbed his head in conjunction with a huge gulp of food and said, "If we hit water close by..." He shook his head, unable to restrain a smile at the thought.

Paul said, "All this... and whatever it was Ed read about on level seven."

They looked at him. "Our salvation," Dan said. "Christ, what can it be?"

"I can't wait any longer," Kath said, standing.

Millie said, "I want to stay here!"

Dan laughed and passed her a biscuit. Kath swung the girl onto her hip and they hurried from the corridor.

They made their way to the elevator and Kath pressed the decal for level seven.

THIS TIME THE descent seemed to take an age. Paul closed his eyes, looking back and thinking of the person he was just days ago, scrabbling for survival in the ruins of Paris. He thought of Elise, and wished she was with him now. She would be happy that he had made it here, he thought, with these good people...

The lift halted and Kath entered the code. The doors swished open.

Before them, the lower section of the starship filled the circular well, bulbous fuel tanks and flaring fins. Dan pointed up to the letters painted across its curving flank: *Phoenix*.

Paul looked around, searching for the doors to the radial corridors but seeing none. Kath examined the map and tapped the place diametrically opposite the elevator exit.

"There's only one chamber down here," she said. "So whatever's in there... there can't be many of them."

They walked around the curving gallery, staring up at the electric blue swelling of the *Phoenix*, and came at last to the double doors set into the wall. They were, Paul noticed, directly opposite a great hatch, sealed now, in the base of the starship. Dan saw it too. He indicated the double doors. "Which suggests that whatever's in there was positioned for easy admission to the ship."

"Let's find out," Kath said, and approached the double doors.

She took a breath and, smiling at Dan and Paul, tapped in the code.

Paul held his breath. This time, the doors seemed to take an extra few seconds before consenting to open.

Paul opened his mouth and stared. They stood on the threshold of a great chamber bathed in a radiant, sourceless light. Down the centre of the long room, a bank of machinery – computers? – ran into the distance for as far as the eye could see, and on either side of the consoles, lining the walls five high, were a series of silver, glass-fronted tanks.

Wordless, Paul approached the glass tanks and stared. Slowly, reverently, he raised a hand and placed it against the glass. It was cold to the touch. He looked along the length of the tanks, estimated that they numbered in their hundreds, even thousands.

Activated by his presence, a strip screen along the foot of the tank flashed on, and he read the caption: Alvarez F. D., bio-molecular engineer, code f7HG-176.

His heart hammered in his chest. He leaned towards the glass and peered inside.

He made out a figure, lying within.

Shaking, it was all he could do to move on to the next tank. The screen activated. He read: Chang X. P., geneticist, code f8HH-784.

He stood back, rocked. Tears stinging his eyes, he recalled Samara's last words to him.

He turned, wondering if the others had made the discovery. Evidently, they had. Dan and Kath were holding each other, weeping. Millie, unmoved by what they had found here, was sitting cross-legged on the floor, munching her way through a packet of biscuits.

Kath looked up tearfully and gestured for Paul to join them. He crossed the chamber and they embraced, while Dan moved down the row of tanks, counting as he went.

He returned. He looked shaken, bewildered. "There are almost five thousand," he said, "specialists in every field you can imagine."

They sat down, and Kath read through Ed's notes.

Paul said, "Samara said... she told me that Hans had read the papers. He knew about the sleepers." He shook his head, recalling her very last words. "And he saw them as nothing more than a supply of meat."

Kath reached out and took his hand.

A while later she said, "Ed wrote, 'Once you've reached level seven, access the terminal core with this code: Px-905-37a.'"

Dan said, "The terminal core?"

Kath smiled and indicated the banked computers in the centre of the chamber. A proximity-activated screen read: *Terminal Core*.

They stood and approached the screen.

Kath reached out to the touchpad and entered the code.

Instantly, words filled the screen. Paul read, "Emergency Resurrection: enter personal identity code of subject resurrectee to commence reanimation procedure..."

Kath was weeping. "Christ... Who? I mean, to awaken someone to... to this world."

"Kath," Dan said, gently. "We have to do it. As Ed said, it's our salvation. With these people... with the help of their specialisms..."

She smiled through her tears. "I know. I know... It's just, they must be dreaming wonderful dreams of other worlds right now..."

Paul gestured at the tanks. "But who?"

Dan moved to the very first tank, nearest to the entrance. "How about the Captain?" he said. "Here's the code."

Kath nodded. Dan joined them before the screen and Paul watched as Kath tentatively reached out and entered the code.

The screen flashed, blanked, and the words appeared: "Subject f9-405-854, Reanimation Procedure commenced. Estimated time until consciousness: one hour and five minutes."

Across the chamber, the glass front of the tank eased open to reveal the small figure of a recumbent woman within.

Slowly, reverently, Paul, Dan and Kath approached the tank.

CHAPTER TWENTY-FIVE

XIAN ASSESSED THE damage to the *Phoenix* from the gallery closest to the starship's nose cone. The hull had been breached, a great hole punched through the membrane, displaying its innards of sheared fibre-optic cables and burnt-out com-systems. She would have to revive the specialists in order to get a better overview of the damage, and how long it might take to repair. As for the hull, she judged that the damage was not as drastic as it appeared. There was no reason why the ship could not phase out with the hole *in situ*, just so long as the interior bulkhead beyond was made air-tight. Engineers would be able to give their expert assessment in time.

She moved around the gallery rail, staring at the sleek magnificence of the ship. She felt bone-weary and cold, despite the heat in the bunker. Two hours out of cold sleep, and she was just beginning to feel as if she might not die. The first hour had been a hell of internal pain, muscular spasms and stabbing migraines. She felt a lot better now; as if she were merely suffering a bad dose of influenza.

She turned and smiled at the people who had

resurrected her.

And that had been one hell of a shock.

She had expected to be brought around by the ship's medic, many light years from Earth... But she had known, just as soon as her blurred vision focused, that something was not right.

She had seen three strange figures staring in at her with something like awe and apprehension.

Two of them were short and stocky; the third, perhaps in his twenties, was taller. All were burned a deep, copper brown by the sun, their faces lined; even the youth had a face engraved with crow's feet from squinting against dazzling light. Their bodies were covered in sores, and they wore the last shreds of clothing like the defiant survivors of a shipwreck. And yet, Xian thought, they appeared a proud trio. She wondered at the story of their lives, the horrors they had lived through.

They had told her, when she asked, that the year was 2120... She had been in suspended animation for a little over sixty years, and in that time the oceans had dried up, the vegetation had died... and yet, humankind still clung tenaciously to life; against all the odds, against all privations, against the dying of planet Earth, they survived.

She had looked upon the three with wonder and then saw, beyond them, the small figure of a little girl sitting on the floor ravenously devouring a packet of old biscuits, and she wept.

Over the past two hours, she had come to know these survivors a little better. They were like children in their eagerness to know two things: if the starship might one day fly, and if, with the help of the specialists still sleeping, they might save the dying planet.

Now, in the shadow of the *Phoenix*, she turned to them and they said in English, "Well?"

She smiled at the woman, Kath, who had posed the question. She was gripping her husband's hand, and the gesture reminded Xian suddenly of Richard.

She said, "I see no reason why, in time, the ship might not be made serviceable again. As for the planet..."

They rose in an elevator towards the surface, Xian trying not to react to the smell of these people, the overpowering reek of old sweat made almost unbearable in the confines of the elevator.

They came to level one and proceeded the rest of the way via a staircase, Xian apprehensive at what she might find beyond the bunker.

They emerged into a dark chamber, and Dan lit a crude lamp and led the way across to the entrance. "We had to drill and blast through," he said in his oddly accented English, gesturing to a gaping hole in the concrete beside the metal door.

Kath gestured for her to go first, and she squeezed through on her hands and knees. She emerged, seconds later, gasping, into a world bathed in the light of the rising sun.

She climbed to her feet, walked away from the bunker and stared around her in awe.

The others joined her.

"Sweet Jesus Christ," she murmured.

She began walking and came at last to the lip of the apron, which fell away in a steep escarpment.

Sixty years ago, there had been a sea out there. Now a white desert, dotted with ships and boats, stretched on for as far as the eye could see. The sun, huge and ruddy, was leering over the horizon, and already Xian could feel its shrivelling heat on her unprotected face.

Inland, beyond the base, where sixty years ago green hills had rolled, dotted with orange trees and vineyards, a desert stretched now, lifeless and inhospitable.

The others were beside her.

"Welcome to our world," Kath said.

She tried to speak, but words would not come. Tears rolled down her cheeks; amazingly, she felt them dry up in seconds, tightening her skin.

Kath came to her side and hugged her.

"Everything..." Xian managed, "everything I know... civilisation, cities, the people, all gone."

Oddly, she thought of her mother's grave in a churchyard in Scotland.

"Almost all gone," Dan murmured.

She looked at the four survivors and felt a sudden welling of affection for these people. "How many did you say?"

The boy, Paul, shrugged. "What? A hundred and fifty in Copenhagen, around a hundred in Aubenas, according to... according to Samara."

Dan said, "There might be other colonies, but..." he shook his head. "We haven't heard from them in years."

"So humanity numbers in its hundreds now," Xian said, "maybe, if we're lucky, in its thousands."

They stared at her. She wondered what they were thinking, what they thought of her. Their expressions were as if they were staring at an angel fallen from Heaven.

"All is not despair," Dan said. "There is hope."

She smiled. She wanted to cry. "That..." she began. "Those words remind me of someone. Richard..." she murmured to herself.

She looked into the dazzling face of the rising sun. "Come on, let's get back inside. We have a lot of work to do."

She turned her back on the sun and led the way back to the bunker, the survivors in her wake.

EPILOGUE

PAUL WATCHED AS Dan and Kath loaded the last of the provisions aboard the transporters: water and a variety of food from the store rooms far below ground. They would be returning to Copenhagen with not only the remarkable news of Project Phoenix, but a horde of luxuries to show for their gruelling endeavours.

Millie was chomping on an energy bar, running around Kath's legs and singing at the top of her voice.

Last night, at sunset, Paul had helped Dan remove the headless corpses from the second transporter. It had been a messy procedure, and he'd felt his gorge rise as they ferried the grisly remains from the truck and buried them in the sand of the escarpment.

Dan and Kath had helped Paul bury Samara, away from the other bodies.

Then they had paused in their work and gazed across the apron at the scattered remains of Ed and the psychopath Hans. Two days of searing sunlight had welded the blood, bones and internal organs to the tarmac. Paul, for one, had not cherished the prospect of disposing of the mess.

Xian had come up with the answer, disappearing back into the bunker and returning fifteen minutes later with a jerrycan of fuel. Paul had doused the shattered remains with the petrol, and Dan had applied the flame. Then, as the sun set, they stood around the blazing inferno and Dan had given Xian a truncated version of the drama enacted here two days ago.

For that long, Xian had been busy resurrecting her compatriots from cold sleep, starting with her lover, Richard Stearton.

Paul had watched the process in amazement, as much awed by the technology as amazed by the people who emerged: they seemed giants, tall, strapping men and women, physically perfect despite complaining of the after-effects of being in suspended animation for sixty years.

He'd been unable to take his eyes from the diminutive figure of Captain Xian Lu, an English woman of Taiwanese descent, she'd told him; her flawless, porcelain face a study in perfection, her tiny body lithe and graceful. Richard, by contrast, was huge and muscular, a Nordic god with a booming laugh and a constant smile. He seemed as in awe of Paul, Dan and Kath, and their stories of survival, as they were of him.

Yesterday, the survivors – as Xian was wont to call them – had undergone thorough medical check-ups by Richard and another medic. They'd pronounced the four in remarkably robust condition considering the privations of their enforced lifestyles. The doctors prescribed balms for the running flesh sores which all four suffered, a course of antibiotics, and a dose of vitamins – all available from the store-rooms. Already Paul persuaded himself that he was feeling much fitter and more alert.

Now Dan emerged from the half-track and crossed to where Paul, Xian and Richard were standing. He peered at the eastern horizon, where the sun was just showing itself.

"Well, that's just about it. If we aren't ready now, we never will be."

Kath said, "The journey back should be a lot easier than it was coming here."

Dan and Kath embraced Xian and Richard, then stood before Paul. He hugged Kath, and she murmured, "See you soon. We'll miss you."

"Take care, Kath," he returned.

Dan shook his hand, then pulled him into a strong embrace. To Xian and Richard he said, "Make sure he behaves himself, and work him hard."

Xian smiled. "We'll do that, Dan."

There were trucks and transporters in the bunker, Xian had informed them; if Dan left the drilling rig, she would detail specialists to drill for water while they were away.

Paul felt sadness in his heart, and part of him wished he was making the journey with them. But, as Dan had pointed out, it made sense if he remained here: he would not be consuming provisions on the journey, and there would be more room for someone from Copenhagen on the way back.

"We'll be back in... what? A couple of weeks, maybe less." Kath laughed. "Wait till Klausen and the rest see us!"

Then the slow process of moving the Copenhagen colony down to Bilbao would begin, using the village of Mont St Catherine as a stop-off point.

Xian said, "By the time you get back, we should have a better idea of the way forward. We'll have more specialists resurrected, and the results of their studies might be emerging."

Paul thought about the future: was there hope for planet Earth, or would the experts be able to repair the *Phoenix* and elect to attempt to reach the stars?

Whichever, he felt energised by optimism and excitement.

Dan climbed into the cab of the half-track and waved down at them. Kath helped Millie into the second transporter. Paul stood on tip-toe and kissed the little girl through the open side window. "See you soon, Millie."

The vehicles started up and ground slowly across the sand towards the escarpment. Paul walked after them, watching the first truck dip over the crumbling edge of the sand, followed by the second. He stood on the lip of the ridge and stared out across the empty sea as the trucks gained speed and beetled away into the distance.

He raised his hand in farewell, and wished them a safe journey.

He turned. Across the apron, Xian and Richard were standing in the shadow of the bunker with their arms around each other, watching him.

Smiling, Paul turned and made his way towards them, the rising sun hot on his back.

ABOUT THE AUTHOR

Eric Brown's first short story was published in *Interzone* in 1987, and he sold his first novel, *Meridian Days*, in 1992. He has won the British Science Fiction Award twice for his short stories and has published thirty-five books: SF novels, collections, books for teenagers and younger children, and he writes a monthly SF review column for *The Guardian*. His latest books include the novel *Engineman*, for Solaris Books. He is married to the writer and mediaevalist Finn Sinclair and they have a daughter, Freya.

His website can be found at: www.ericbrown.co.uk

ENGINEMAN

"Eric Brown is the name to watch in SF."
Peter F. Hamilton

ERIC BROWN

UK ISBN: 978 1 907519 42 0 • US ISBN: 978 1 907519 43 7 • £7.99/$7.99

Once, Enginemen pushed bigships through the nada-continuum; but faster than light isn't fast enough anymore, now that the Keilor-Vincicoff Organisation's interfaces bring distant planets a single step away. When a man with half a face offers ex-Engineman Ralph Mirren the chance to escape his ruined life and push a ship to an unknown destination, he jumps at the chance. But he is unprepared when he discovers the secret behind the continuum, and the mystery awaiting him on the distant world...